# TEXT ME NEVER

## BURN AFTER TEXTING SERIES

### CEDAR JAMES

Published by North & Anchor Co., Houston, TX

Cataloging-in-Publication data is on file with the Library of Congress.

ISBN: 979-8-9987306-0-3

❀ Formatted with Vellum

*For my love, Ben.*
*My husband, my heart, my muse.*
*You are the wit behind every clever line,*
*the fire behind every look,*
*and the quiet strength woven into Nolan's soul.*

*Thank you for being the kind of man who inspires —*
*loyal, layered, infuriatingly stubborn,*
*and endlessly worth loving book boyfriends.*

*This story wouldn't exist without you.*
*You are, and always will be, my favorite plot twist.*

# NOTE FROM THE AUTHOR

While *Text Me Never* is primarily a witty enemies-to-lovers romance packed with banter, rivalry, and slow-burn tension, it does contain brief references to:

- Infidelity
- Parental grief/loss
- Emotional betrayal
- Mild workplace harassment themes

If these topics are difficult for you, please proceed with care. I understand that every reader's experience is different. Take what you need, skip what you must, and know that at its heart, this is a story about healing, hope, and love that chooses you, flaws, cracks, and all.

Take care of yourself while reading.

-Cedar

# PROLOGUE

## RORIE

THE ROOM DRIPS WITH POWER. And I'm doing my best not to drown in it.

Six executives. Zero tells.

Silence envelops the room, unbearable in its intensity as light slants through the tall windows of Stanfield Investments, streaking the glass with the colors of an almost-sunset.

Outside, the first rainstorm of the spring season drizzles in a steady curtain, smearing the skyline into a ghost of itself. The world beyond looks distant. Muted. Like it knows better than to intrude.

My stomach knots tighter as I scan their expressions.

Nothing but shadows and silence. Boardroom gargoyles, carved in stone and ego, backlit by the Manhattan skyline.

If this pitch is a trial, I'm on the stand and losing the jury.

Still, I smile.

Straighten my spine.

Lift my chin.

I didn't come here to coast.

I came to conquer.

I clear my throat.

One breath. One shot.

Here we go.

"And with this engaging campaign," I say, my voice faltering slightly.

Their eyes dart between me and the tablets before them with a disconcerting detachment making the room even more confining.

"...you'll create a unique experience and go beyond traditional marketing. It's... it's about engaging all the senses. Making your audience feel as though they're already living the dream."

*Oh, God, I said engaging twice.*

Beneath the blazer and bullet points, I'm bleeding out. My chest tightens. It's a familiar pressure. Failure knocking on the back of my mind, reminding me it's not done with me yet.

The clock on the wall rotates steadily, each tick a thunderous reminder of the seconds slipping away, counting down to the moment I either salvage some dignity with this pitch or watch it disintegrate along with the fading daylight.

Mr. Gaines, senior partner and key decision maker, leans forward, his wide shoulders dominating the space as he rests his elbows on the table. Silver slicked back hair gleams beneath the overhead lights.

"Ms. Adams." His voice is courteous but carries an undercurrent pointed enough to puncture tempered steel. "I'm struggling to understand how this proposal differentiates from the dozens of others we've received. Virtual reality? Cliché. Sensory integration? It's... tired."

"Tired," I repeat. The word scrapes down my throat, jagged and cruel, ripping through the walls on the way out. I swallow hard, pushing past the ache. "With all due respect, Mr. Gaines, this approach isn't just about VR. It's about creating an emotional connection—"

"It's a nice idea," a woman with a perfectly styled updo and an equally perfect frown interrupts, her tone clipped.

*Nice?*

"But..." she draws the word out, "you're overcomplicating a strategy that should be simple. We want bold, yes, but we also want streamlined. Efficient."

Heat crawls up my neck. The pitch I honed to perfection is coming undone in real time. "I—I understand. Perhaps if I could clarify—"

"No need," Gaines cuts me off. "We appreciate your effort, but we've seen enough."

The finality in his tone sets me on edge. *He's dismissing me?*

"But I—"

Gaines holds up a hand, halting me. "Please give my regards to Laurel."

The mention of Laurel's name punches straight through my gut. She'll be disappointed. Possibly furious. I've already tested her patience more than once, and I'm hanging by the thinnest thread of a promise she made to a ghost.

But part of me—the *I dare you to survive me part*—believes this isn't over yet. That there's still a sliver of space to prove I'm worth the gamble here.

"Have a wonderful day," he says.

Well, that answers that.

Pressing my lips together, I nod once in forced politeness. While gathering my notes with trembling hands, my mind flutters back to a time when my name held weight. When I was the one ruling over the room. Not being dismissed as just another name on a list, instead of the woman who was once the future of this industry.

Once everything is packed, I pause, keeping my phone in hand instead of burying it. "Thank you for your time," I manage, voice steady even as a lump pushes up in my throat.

I'm almost out the door when it swings open, and in walks the notorious Nolan Rhodes, Chief Creative Executive for one of the most ruthless firms in the game–Big Stream Marketing.

The air shifts subtly with his arrival. I'd expect nothing less. Nolan Rhodes doesn't just show up to the meeting, he declares war and wins.

And here I am, shaking from a rejection I didn't see coming.

My pulse stutters when I see he's moving in my direction with quiet confidence, commanding the space. Everything about him exudes power and control, wrapped in a package so stunning it's unfair. As though he was meticulously designed to make everyone else seem average.

His dark hair is styled with precision, yet unruly enough to tempt my fingers into ruining it. He's tall, with a lean, muscular strength that speaks for itself. The tailored suit jacket hugs his frame, emphasizing broad shoulders and a trim waist in a way that's almost criminal.

His honey gaze falls on me, making me feel even smaller. It's infuriating. And kind of… annoyingly attractive.

"Excuse me." I attempt to sidestep him, but in my haste, my phone slips from my grip and crashes to the floor with an abrupt *crack*.

"Shit," I mutter, crouching down.

He reaches it first, fingers brushing mine as he picks it up. The screen now sports fresh, jagged cracks running diagonally across it.

Straightening, he studies the fractured glass, then looks up and says, "Crack's mean change. They let the light bleed in." And hands it back to me.

I blink, caught off guard by the weird poetry of it.

"Thanks," I say, too flustered to come up with anything smarter.

But his line sticks, threading itself into the moment as one I'll remember later.

His gaze meets mine again. Flecks of gold shimmer inside amber, so intensely, it's like he's seeing more than I want him to.

I step to the left. So does he.

To the right. Blocked again.

A frustrated huff escapes me. We keep shuffling awkwardly until I stop and look up at him fully.

Carved features, a tiny dimple teasing the corner of his cheek, somehow making his god-tier face even more ridiculous.

"After you," he says, his voice silk-wrapped and smug.

Then he smirks.

And it's not just a grin—it's an event. A perfect curve of amusement and self-assurance. If I didn't have a boyfriend, I'd be drafting our wedding hashtag right now. Not that Nolan Rhodes would ever look twice at me. He probably dates heiresses and mysterious women who wear dark lipstick and never cry in elevators. Like I'm about to.

My phone vibrates.

I ignore it.

"Ms. Adams..." Gaines gestures toward the door with a tight expression that screams: *You've outstayed your welcome.*

I nod again, force a smile, and walk away, spine stiff and ego bruised.

The elevator is my salvation. I jab the button, letting the curses fly.

As the doors shut, I exhale, shakily. My mom's voice echoes in my head: *Adams women don't crumble, baby. We rise.*

The phone buzzes again.

Fishing it out of my bag, I glance at the screen before pressing it to my ear. "Aunt Jane?"

Her breathing is too quiet, too shaky.

"Rorie..." she starts, her voice barely a whisper. "Honey, it's your dad. There's been an accident..."

Everything stops.

The elevator. The city. My breath.

The walls of my world close in.

The cracked screen in my hand is a mirror of everything splitting beneath the surface.

Shattered.

Irreparable.

*Changed.*

# CHAPTER 1
# THE KEY MOMENT

## NOLAN

I'VE GOT five unread texts, a blinking GroupThink notification, and an account manager hovering by my door pretending not to wait for me.

Welcome to Tuesday.

I snatch my phone off my desk and text Rishi.

> If you say "synergize" at the Vanguard pitch, I'll walk into traffic.

> Can I at least leverage that walk into a brand opportunity?

I don't respond. Instead, I push away from my desk with a quiet chuckle, adjust my tie, and head out of my office. I nod at the account manager on the way out. Timothy is his name. Or Todd. Something with a T. He trails behind, trying to keep up with my long strides.

Before I pass through the glass doors of the conference room, my phone buzzes with a message from Chloe.

> Probably won't be home until late. Meetings are running past dinner then I'm grabbing a drink w/ a friend. Call you after. <3

I stare at the message a beat longer than necessary. The <3 feels... off. Not wrong. Just—obligatory.

I'm being paranoid. Chloe's been under pressure. She's buried in pre-trial motions and caffeine. Her latest case has been her Everest.

Still, she's been "grabbing drinks with friends" more and more lately, ducking out, showing up late, leaving barely any time for us. A slow drift I've been ignoring.

> No worries, babe. Talk then.

I pocket the phone and head into the meeting. Inside, the air is tense. Not unusual, but different somehow.

Thatcher, my CEO, is seated, fingers steepled under his chin, watching his nephew present.

Nepotism in action.

Jackson's voice is puffed up with small dick energy, and he sounds like a man who's never satisfied anyone but himself. I've seen Power-Points with more charisma and less entitlement.

He's going on about trimming overhead as though he invented the concept of spreadsheets.

It's no surprise the way Jackson speaks makes my skin crawl. It's the way he says *"operational efficiency"* like he plucked it off a word-of-the-day calendar and decided to make it his personality.

Or maybe I'm just bitter over the fact that he's a Wall Street reject with a finance degree he's never used, currently living in his parents' Upper East Side brownstone, playing corporate dress-up in the job his uncle handed him–neatly gift-wrapped and unearned–like a participation trophy for showing up with the right last name.

Meanwhile, I—and most of the people who make Big Stream the best—have bled for the wins he takes credit for. Blood, sweat, and too many weekends sacrificed to pitch decks and impossible deadlines... all while he waltzes in with his pre-approved business buzzwords and thinks that counts as leadership.

"We've been offering strategic flexibility..."

Right.

As I was saying—pre-approved buzzwords.

"Clients want quick wins. We meet them where they are—on time-line, on expectations, even budget. Sometimes under. That kind of responsiveness drives growth." Jackson taps the screen like he's delivered a masterstroke.

I almost applaud. Look at him, quoting case studies like scripture. Reading *and* pretending to lead? Banner day for Jackson.

But I know what he's doing.

Strategic flexibility sounds noble. Adaptive. Makes us appear agile, not desperate. But what he's offering isn't strategy—it's surrender in a tailored suit.

Jackson is selling short-term appeasement, undercutting pricing to secure the win, calling it value, and hoping no one notices what we've lost in the process.

That might work if we were some scrappy startup clawing for attention.

But we're not.

We're Big Stream.

We don't bend. We don't chase. And we sure as hell don't devalue the brand in order to inflate the scoreboard.

Thatcher nods along, approvingly.

*What the fuck? Is he actually listening to this dumbass?*

It's not enough for me to challenge, not here, not in front of a room full of analysts and other business professionals.

But it's close.

Close enough to raise the hair on the back of my neck.

I can't decide what unsettles me more, Jackson delivering *"operational efficiency"* in a deceptive package, or Thatcher letting it slide when he should be shutting this shit down.

Instead, he's nodding. *Nodding.*

Mental note made. Check into that shit.

"Let's flag this for follow-up." I keep my tone neutral. "We need to make sure client expectations match long-term margin goals."

After an excruciatingly painful hour goes by, the meeting concludes. I duck back into my office to breathe. And also pour myself two fingers.

Rishi walks in, juggling his phone and a protein bar in one hand, a folder in the other.

"Bagged another one, boss." He tosses the folder onto my desk with a cocky grin. The Vanguard logo on the front says enough. "Locked them in by the second round, and the CEO shook my hand before I even wrapped the pitch."

Satisfied, I nod. "Solid work, Rishi. Really solid."

He shoves the bar into his mouth, and immediately regrets it. "God, these taste like stale almonds and ass."

"You bought a box of them."

"Mistakes were made." He tosses the bar into the nearest trash bin.

"Who else was there?"

"The Laurel Group," Rishi answers. "And their point was definitely a killer. *Almost* made us sweat."

"That's saying something."

"Fucking gorgeous too," he adds.

I glance up from the folder, arch a brow. "You gonna ask her out or just admire her LinkedIn profile in the dark?"

"I don't dip into the competition."

"That's hilarious, considering you *absolutely* dip into the competition."

He snorts. "What can I say? I like high stakes and poor judgment."

I tap the file. Another win. Another payday. This is the life I built— the hours, the hustle, the never-stop grind. Control. Respect. Power.

Yet somehow, it still isn't enough.

Rishi leans against the corner of my desk, eyeing me. "So. Chloe. Big night?"

I raise a brow. "Why do you sound like a dating show host?"

"Because you've been insufferably cryptic for three weeks and I deserve updates."

A hint of amusement curls on my lips. "You'll know tomorrow. Assuming she says yes."

Rishi whistles. "Damn. You're actually doing it."

"Don't make it a thing."

"It is a thing, man. You put together a freaking video montage."

"It's not a montage—it's a narrative arc."

"Jesus." He grins. "You proposal-pitched your girlfriend."

"It's not a proposal. It's a *key moment*. A next-step thing."

"A next-step key in a decorative velvet box, with your initials engraved in it, champagne, and that playlist you forced me to help make."

"You're remarkably judgmental for someone who once bought his girlfriend a commemorative brick at a science museum."

"She was into physics! It was meaningful." He stands.

"Hey, you leaving for the night?" I ask, gathering my things.

"Yeah, I'll walk with you."

At the wall of elevators, I push the down button.

"You nervous?" Rishi asks.

I shrug, but my chest is tight. "A little."

"She'd be crazy to say no. You're the full package—smart, hot, tall, gainfully employed."

"Don't forget emotionally repressed and a tad smug."

The elevator dings.

"Obviously. That's your edge."

The doors open and Jackson steps out.

Speaking of smug.

"Yo, Rhodes," he calls, casually tucking his phone into his navy pinstripe suit jacket. "Ditching early?"

"Client happy hour," I lie, stepping inside the elevator. Rishi follows. "Kenyon Group." I push the button to the lobby. "You?"

"Meeting a friend." His tone is smooth, his smile relaxed. There's a weird beat of silence between us.

"Okay, well, have fun," I say evenly.

"Definitely."

The elevator closes.

Rishi slides his hands in his pockets. "That guy make your skin crawl, like he does mine?"

I don't answer. But I smile, despite my gut churning. I tell myself it's nerves.

Outside, I wait for my driver, Alan, to pull around while Rishi hails a cab. "Good luck tonight, man. I'm happy for you."

I nod feebly. "Thanks, see you tomorrow."

The city scurries around me, alive with a restless energy only New York can conjure. The sun's starting to dip behind the buildings, bleeding gold over glass and steel.

And the air feels full of possibility.

The quaint little florist on Fifth smells like a bottled summer when I walk inside.

"Looking for anything specific?" the florist asks.

"I need timeless. Elegant. Understated, but still says everything."

She smiles. "Got it."

I pay for the flowers and head to the market. Garlic, lemons, asparagus, cream for the potatoes Chloe pretends to hate. Her favorite wine is already chilling in her fridge. I even stashed a couple of steaks from Muncan's behind the wine for my domestic surprise attack.

And if anyone would clock a surprise down to the last detail, it's Chloe.

She's meticulous—Type A down to her marrow. The woman's closet is color-coded, itemized, and tracked in a spreadsheet and she sets reminders to flip the mattress every six months.

Which isn't me.

But somehow, for the past year, it's worked.

Funny how fast I fell for such a brilliant, unshakable woman with perfect posture and napkins folded into military-grade triangles.

And I want all of it. All of her.

The idea to ask Chloe to move in with me sparked a few weeks ago. She was curled on my couch, half-asleep, some artsy film playing in the background.

And I knew…this is it.

The next step.

I want her here, in my space. I want it to be *our* space.

So, I did what I do best: made a sales pitch.

The "Key Moment" video is one part nostalgia, two parts future. It starts with glowing letters—*Home, Where Our Story Begins.*

Then it moves through snapshots of us—vacations, birthdays, stolen moments. Her laugh. My grin. Our rhythm.

The final frame is a video of me, holding up a key. "Will you move in with me, Chloe? No pressure, but you already have the best parking spot. What do you say?"

Cheesy? Absolutely. But that's me.

It's scheduled to ping her phone in exactly twenty minutes.

By the time I reach her building, my arms are full—flowers in one hand, groceries in the other.

I ride the elevator with a flutter of nerves. This is it. The kind of moment people write about. The kind of love people want. She's going to say yes. The certainty sits in my pocket.

Stopping outside her door, I inhale, straighten, unlock it—

And pause.

Her designer handbag sits on the table. Slightly open. Unzipped.

Weird.

Her keys are tossed carelessly beside it.

Weirder.

Taking a step inside, the cherry blossom candle she loves is still burning. The scent hangs heavy in the air. Sweet. Cloying.

Something's wrong.

Deeply, terribly wrong.

One) Chloe would never leave a lit candle unattended.

Two) Everything in her world has a place, a purpose. Nothing is ever out of order.

And things are definitely never left *slightly open. Or unzipped.*

My heart thuds harder than it should. The nervous flutter in my chest spikes into a prickling unease.

At first glance, everything appears perfect. The throw blanket draped neatly over the stark white couch. The coffee table books are stacked with surgeon-level precision. It all screams Chloe, practiced, staged.

Then my gaze snags on the armchair.

A suit jacket. Navy pinstripe. Tossed over the back.

Next to it, a pair of leather shoes.

My stomach knots. I scan the room again.

A bottle of wine on the counter. Her favorite. The one I stored in her fridge. Two glasses. One with a crimson lipstick stain. And the other...

The flutter in my chest nosedives into my stomach, turns to stone. It sinks further, cold and crushing. Confusion collides with denial. Fear tangles with fury.

The jacket. The shoes. The wine.

The groceries slip from my arms. The flowers tumble out next. I move down the hall where sounds bleed from the bedroom in a rhythmic, intimate, and unmistakable echo.

My head spins, desperate for an explanation, or a lie I can cling to, but one truth barrels through the noise—

I know exactly what I heard.

My hand lands on the doorknob. Ice-cold. It creeps up my arm as I brace for the moment that ends everything.

I push the door open.

My world detonates.

Naked. Straddling…is that…

Jackson Butler?

My boss's nephew?

*Fucking hell.*

The woman I've been building a life with for the past twelve months is ripping it apart one moan and thrust at a time.

Her auburn hair tumbles over her bare skin as she grinds on top, her gasps drifting throughout the room.

The betrayal is instant. Atomic. My blood ignites, rage blazing under my skin. My fists tremble, jaw locked so tight my teeth ache. Every instinct demands I break something. Him, preferably.

He looks up. Casual as hell. "What's up, man?"

My head tilts. Did he just—?

"Nolan," Chloe stammers, grabbing for the sheet. Jackson doesn't even bother. His dick is at full attention as he smirks that smug, punchable smirk.

I gape at her, pleading without words, begging for an explanation. Something. *Anything.*

"I thought you were out with the Kenyon Group," Jackson says.

Bitter laughter escapes me. I ignore him. My eyes lock on Chloe. "And I thought you were finishing a deposition. And having a drink with a friend."

"I—I did," she stammers. "This isn't what it looks like."

My voice is low, level. "Then what is it?"

My eyes bounce between Chloe and Jackson. That *fucking* smirk.

My hands shake. One wrong move, and I'll crush him.

"See, from where I'm standing," I grit out, "it looks like you're cheating on me. Tell me I'm wrong."

Chloe clutches the sheet, her eyes flicking back and forth, panicked. "I didn't mean for you to find out this way," she whispers.

I blink. "Oh? How were you hoping I'd find out? A fucking group text?"

"I—we—"

"We?" I hiss.

Jackson leans back, totally unfazed. "No hard feelings, man. Chloe and I are in love. Right, babe?"

She gives him a weak smile. The stone in my stomach flips.

I zero in on her. "Is that true?"

A pause. "Yes. Nolan—I'm sorry—"

I shake my head. No way this is fucking happening. "In love?"

She nods. And that's it. Everything snaps.

I lunge. Chloe screams.

But I stop myself with my arm cocked back, fist shaking with rage that could break orbital bones. Jackson's right below me. I'm one second from gifting him a face only a surgical team could salvage.

My jaw locks. Breath rips its way out of my lungs. And then I look at her—the woman who was supposed to be mine.

And everything in me fractures.

"I thought you loved me."

Chloe opens her mouth, but before she can answer, her phone buzzes, the sound cutting through the air like a gunshot.

She snatches it from the nightstand, her face twisting when she swipes at the screen.

The music starts.

*Welcome Home.*

My Key Moment.

*Fuck.*

The slideshow. The grand gesture. Our story.

Eyes wide, mouth slack, she watches in silence.

Jackson glances at the screen and covers a chuckle with his fist. "Oh shit, man."

The air goes thick, and suffocating. My throat constricts. I want to grab the phone. Smash it. Make it disappear.

But I don't.

Rooted to the ground, I stand there watching Chloe, feeling every stab of pain her knife is giving me.

When it ends, she whispers, "Wow. That was...beautiful."

The words are a thousand jagged pieces of glass slicing through me.

I turn and leave.

She calls my name. I don't stop. Can't.

Jackson mutters under his breath but I'm already gone.

In the hallway, I delete her number—even though I know it by heart. I'm going to spiral tonight. That's inevitable. But at least this way, I won't be tempted to send some pathetic 2 a.m. message I'll regret by sunrise.

Once I'm in the elevator, I hurl my phone at the wall, because why the fuck not? Betrayal, heartbreak, almost assault, and now property damage.

Of course the screen is now cracked.

Still not enough.

I consider ripping out the panels on the walls. But think better of it when the doors ding open.

The lobby is quiet. My footsteps echo as I push through the exit.

The night air slaps my face ad reality finally catches up. My hands twitch. My chest aches. I shove my fists in my pockets to keep from shaking.

And I keep walking. One step. Then another.

Because if I stop, I'll fall apart.

# CHAPTER 2
# HAIRNETS AND HIGH STAKES

## RORIE

LAUGHTER RIPPLES THROUGH THE BREEZE, braided with conversation and the thrum of bass from overhead speakers.

String lights twinkle with a soft glow across the rooftop terrace, catching on the polished rims of cocktail glasses and the edges of mirrored tabletops. The city sprawls beyond the railing, a restless, glittering beast of breathing heat, buzzing light, and the occasional wail of distant sirens. Its towering buildings pulse with summer's energy, as if the skyline itself is raising a toast to the season.

I'm perched at a high-top table, one ankle hooked behind the chair leg, posture loose in a way that looks breezy but is tightly managed.

My jacket is draped over the back of my chair. Even though I've loosened my bun, and ditched the button-down for the tank underneath, my lipstick is fresh.

On the outside, I look composed, but every inch of me is frayed beneath the surface. Still, I slap on my best mask and nod along.

Jeremy's mid-story, laughing so hard he nearly spills his drink, mimicking the world's worst date from his hook up app, Romance Roulette. He's got messy hair, black-rimmed glasses, and a smirk sharp enough to draw blood.

He's one half of my ride or die work besties and the one who travels with dry shampoo, a portable phone charger, and enough audacity to tell off your toxic ex *and* fix your eyeliner in the same breath.

"So then I said, 'Sir, if your idea of foreplay involves a Groupon and two-for-one mozzarella sticks, I'm calling an Uber.'"

Maya, the other half, props her chin in her hand, elbow braced on the table. She idly taps her nails against the surface, each click a punctuation of calm competence while listening.

Then her gaze slides to me. She catches the far-off look I'm wearing and nudges me with her knee under the table. "Stop thinking about Vanguard."

"Easier said than done."

"I heard it was brutal," Jeremy adds, his tone softening just enough to sting.

"*Brutal* doesn't even begin to cover it." I take a sip of my martini. The chilled vodka slides down my throat, briny with a tang of olives and a whisper of citrus, but it might as well be water for all the good it does.

"Who said it was brutal?" Maya asks.

"Laurel," Jeremy replies hesitantly.

I exhale, my grip tightening around the stem of my glass. Laurel is my boss and mentor. And she's way too gracious. She once shared dreams with my mother back in a dorm room with cheap wine and endless ambition. Laurel rose through the ranks, and my mom wrote stories that changed people. Until she traded deadlines for bedtime stories.

Now Laurel writes my checks. And sometimes, I wonder if she's only doing to it to keep a promise to the friend she buried rather than investing in that friend's daughter and her potential.

That's what cuts the deepest.

"I needed that win. Vanguard was supposed to be the rebound. My redemption. The clean slate." I fall back against the seat, cross my arms. "Instead, it was just another door slammed in my face. It's been months since I landed a client that mattered. The little ones keep the lights on. But no headlines. No momentum."

Maya's voice cuts in. "So... who landed Vanguard?"

I uncross my arms, swirl my drink. "Big Stream."

"Shut up." She straightens. "Again?"

"Yep."

"I don't get it. How do they keep edging you out?"

"Because apparently," I deadpan, "they give amazing head in pitch meetings."

Maya raises an eyebrow. "Better than you?"

Jeremy nearly snorts rosé out his nose. "Honestly? If true, then I respect the hustle."

"Wow. You're both fired from friendship. I don't get on my knees for a contract."

Jeremy holds up a hand. "That's fair. But I don't think competitive dick sucking is why they're winning."

My brows knit together. "What do you mean?"

He shrugs. "I heard a little something from someone at Vanguard."

I pause, glass halfway to my lips. "What kind of something?"

"They undercut your rates." Jeremy waits a few seconds before delivering the next blow. "By thirty percent."

I gape at him. "They *what*?"

"Took a loss to win," he says, grim. "Locked the deal. Made sure you never had a shot."

Maya's expression ices over. "That's shady as *fuck*."

It clicks.

I thought I was losing because I wasn't good enough. Brilliant enough. Creative enough. Or ruthless enough. But it was never about talent.

It was about leverage.

Power.

Control.

Greed.

Corporate *fuckery* in its finest form.

"That's not just winning," Maya mutters. "That's clearing the goddamn board."

"*Those fucksticks!*" I hiss, slamming back the rest of my martini. "I'd flip this table if I wasn't emotionally fragile and wearing four-inch heels."

Jeremy claps once, delighted. "There she is. Rage looks *so* good on you."

"Agreed," Maya says, already snatching three shots off a passing tray. She plants them in the center of the table then lifts hers high. "Let's toast to Rageful Rorie."

Jeremy and I grab the other two shots.

Maya says, "May their coffee always be lukewarm and their Wi-Fi unstable."

We clink.

We drink.

Jeremy's eyes glitter. "Okay. Cards on the table. What are you gonna do about it?"

I laugh once—low, bitter, honest. And then I fire back, "I don't know—what *can* I do? Big Stream is the monster with the big swinging dick in this industry. We're the ones getting railed from behind with no warm up, because that's the cost of a seat at the damn table."

"That mental image gave me whiplash and a semi." Jeremy shifts in his seat. "Now I'm horny and probably going to hook up with either Groupon Guy or the bartender."

Maya doesn't miss a beat. "Go with the bartender. Groupon Guy called his podcast 'redefining masculinity through kettlebells and crypto.'"

Jeremy makes a face. "Right. Bartender it is." He wiggles a little. "Anyway. I have a surprise that might make you feel better."

I arch a brow. "This better not involve tequila and hairnets again."

"Oh, it *absolutely* does."

"No! Did we not learn our lesson after the churro stand incident?"

"Worth it. That launch event was epic. Plus, I got a Yelp shoutout."

And because I can't help myself—because *this is Jeremy*—I say:

"We got banned from the entire food truck district. Laurel is still holding a grudge about that one."

"Well, *technically*, I wasn't on the clock when I climbed onto the counter and tried to demonstrate the 'sensual art' of churro dough extrusion."

Maya groans. "You yelled *'watch this, it's going to change your life'* and then dumped an entire vat of cinnamon sugar down your pants."

"And yet," Jeremy says proudly, "I still served fifty of their customers and got a five-star review for 'passion and flair.'"

"From your *mom*," I mutter.

"She stands by it."

Maya and I laugh because how can you not?

"Anyhoo." Jeremy slides his phone across the table, the screen glowing with an invitation. I read it.

"Okay, maybe not the hairnets this time," he adds," but definitely the tequila." His grin wide. Too wide. That's *never* good.

# CROSSFIRE
## HOSTED BY ASHER CROSS

One57
157 West 57th Street, NYC
June 6th

RSVP TO SHELBY DAVIDSON 555-456-7890

"*The* Asher Cross?" Maya asks.

"And we're VIP, baby," Jeremy says, visually vibrating with glee.

"How?" I say, skeptical. *Very* skeptical.

Jeremy straightens his posture. "I may have... loosely dated his second assistant's ex-roommate's cousin. Briefly. For like... three weeks. Maybe two."

Maya squints. "Is this the one with the ferret?"

"No, that was the magician. This one had a food truck and commitment issues. Anyway, point is—I'm connected."

"You're *adjacent* to connected," I say, swiping a stray hair from my face. "There's a difference."

"Semantics." He waves me off. "The point is, we're in."

Maya sets her drink down, eyes narrowed. "Okay but like—*in in?*"

Jeremy nods solemnly. "Look, word is, Cross is looking to expand his brand beyond the clothing line and the hair serum that made him a household name with the 'hot dad' demographic. Think luxury lifestyle. Think private island resort. Think... legacy-level branding."

The Crossfire invitation is still glowing on Jeremy's phone screen when I glance back at it.

"Play it right," Jeremy says, "and this could be your main-stage moment, Ro. Use this gift of an opportunity to get in front of Cross and work your magic."

I blink. Yeah, I've lost a few lately—Vanguard, my momentum, even a little faith in myself.

This could be the shift though. The moment it all turns.

I don't know if I'm ready. But I know I want it. And if Asher Cross is really shopping for agencies, then I'm not just going.

I'm going all in.

And this time I'm not walking out empty-handed.

# CHAPTER 3
# 30% ALCOHOL, 70% RAGE

## NOLAN

THREE HOURS LATER, I'm slouched over the bar at Jack's—a hole-in-the-wall dive that reeks of cigarette smoke and stale beer. The lighting's dim and jaundiced, the world around me blurred like the brand new memories I'm now trying to erase.

The bar's sticky under my forearms, scarred with initials and God knows what. I stare into the amber depths of my glass as though it might give me answers. But after three of them, I still have none.

My gaze drags to my phone, cracked and scraped from its violent introduction to the elevator wall. It lies facedown now, silent and useless—like me.

Rishi slides onto the stool beside me, throws a finger in the air to flag the bartender. I texted him about an hour ago, told him about the whole mess.

"Thanks for coming," I rasp.

"Wouldn't miss it."

That's Rishi in a nutshell, loyal to the bone and weirdly intuitive about my stress levels. He's been showing up since the beginning.

First week on the job, I blew a key slide in front of Thatcher. He covered for me like it was nothing, then bought me a beer like I'd earned it. He's talked me out of three rage-fueled email drafts, one questionable haircut, and a doomed office romance—well, he *tried* on that last one.

Rishi's the guy who drags me out when I need a drink and drags me back when I need reality. The one who sees what I don't say. Who pushes when I need it. Who shuts up and sits beside me when I need that more.

We've weathered firings, mergers, heartbreaks, and too many client dinners where the egos were massive and the appetizers microscopic.

He's not just my teammate.

He's my tether.

Rishi looks me over. "Jesus, did you get hit by a truck full of misery and regret?"

"Close," I mutter. "It was a Benz. Driven by my girlfriend. Into Jackson's lap."

Rishi winces. "Too soon for jokes?"

"I hope they both choke on his trust fund."

"That's more like it," he says, nodding approvingly. "I was worried you'd be in full 'Nick from *New Girl*' mode, writing sad poetry and humming Adele into your bourbon."

I scoff and take a long sip. "Already did that. Moved on to rage."

"Good." His hand slaps my back. "Rage we can work with."

The bartender delivers Rishi's beer, he snatches it up and takes a sip.

"She didn't even try to explain. Just…sat there."

"She's not worth the aneurysm," Rishi says. "She's a coward. And he's a parasite. What's your play now?"

"I don't know. Burn their lives to the ground?"

"Healthy."

I laugh, but it's hollow. "I gave her everything. Every unguarded piece of me. And she torched it."

"You're better off," Rishi replies, still trying his best to uplift me. "Seriously. Chloe always looked like she practiced crying in the mirror. And Jackson? He's just gross."

"How did I miss it? I'm a strategist. I *see* people."

"Yeah, well, strategists make shit poker players. You loved her. That was the tell."

My jaw clenches. "She made me believe I mattered. That I was… safe. And the whole time she was screwing Jackson."

Rishi's gaze sharpens. "No. She was screwing her own future. You? You're going to be fine. You're Nolan fucking Rhodes. You get back up."

"Easier said than done, my friend." I down the rest of my drink and toss a hundred on the bar. "Let's get out of here before I put my fist through the jukebox."

"Now *that's* the energy I came for," Rishi says, standing.

We step out into the night, the city slapping me in the face with its clean summer air and neon charm.

"Where are we off to?" Rishi asks, keeping pace beside me. He's got that casual swagger, the kind that says: *I could be at the office winning an account right now, but instead I'm making sure you don't spiral into a country song.*

"I don't know."

Rishi cracks his neck. "Wanna go to my place and get blackout drunk? Or do we go full *Fight Club* and find a bar with peanuts and bloodstains?"

"Pretty sure that was the bar we just left."

He grins. "Okay, plan B: strip club. Breakups were practically invented to fund those places."

I give him a look. "I'm not that guy."

"Every guy's that guy for about thirty-six hours after something like this. There's healing in glitter and shame, my dude."

I shake my head, but I hesitate, and Rishi notices.

"Ah, there it is. You *are* tempted."

"Only because it's been a while," I confess.

He blows out a breath. "Understood. Still, credit for the restraint. That's personal growth."

"Yeah, well, personal growth can kiss my ass."

"There's a whole subgenre of guys who try to heal with green juice and yoga. You don't strike me as one of them."

"I caught my girlfriend screwing the CEO's nephew. I saw his dick. I want bread and vengeance."

"Atta boy." He laughs. "I've got the perfect place. Come on." Rishi jerks his chin toward the corner.

We end up at a twenty-four-hour pizza window sandwiched

between a tattoo parlor and a place that sells knockoff sneakers out of the back.

Rishi orders two slices. "Grease and carbs. Step one in heartbreak triage."

I lean against the wall while we wait, the scent of hot dough and body odor coats the air.

Taking our pizza to the curb like the classy professionals we are, we sit on the edge of a planter filled with what may or may not be a dying shrub.

"You know what the worst part is?" I ask around a bite.

"That she picked Jackson?"

"That she picked *him,* and I still want her."

Rishi doesn't flinch. He nods and wipes sauce off his thumb.

"Yeah, well. Hearts are stupid. Brains know better, but hearts? They're like toddlers with access to fireworks."

I laugh, despite myself.

Rishi eyes me as we toss our empty pizza plates into a can. "You don't wanna go home."

He says it like a fact, not a question.

I exhale through my nose. "It's too quiet. It'll feel like the furniture's judging me."

"Bro Code, Section Nine: No man gets left to sulk in a silent apartment post-breakup. Let's go."

"Go where?"

He's already walking. "Everywhere."

What follows is less a plan and more a fever dream of tomfoolery:

**8:43 PM** – we hit the Korean grocery on 38th and buy two random bottles of imported soju, a jar of pickled quail eggs, and a single peach.

"For luck," Rishi says, tossing it to me.

**9:11 PM** – we're at Bryant Park, daring each other to jump the fountain. We don't—but we *almost* do. Two tourists ask if we're TikTokers. Rishi says yes.

**9:58 PM** – we find a random stoop, sit on it like old men, and pass the soju back and forth.

"I thought she was it," I say, continuing my woe is me rant.

"You were all in."

"I was ready to build a life with her."

"You were only halfway through the blueprints."

"I made a digital presentation."

Rishi winces. "With music."

"I know where Jackson parks his Audi."

He lifts a brow. "You don't say."

**10:32 PM** – we're standing in front of said Audi. It's gleaming under the garage lights, pretentious as hell. Like its owner.

"I might want to commit a misdemeanor," I mutter.

"I'm not saying we key it," Rishi says. "But if someone *were* to draw a very accurate micropenis on the hood... I wouldn't stop them."

Rishi pulls a travel-sized tube of sunscreen from his jacket pocket.

I hesitate. "Why do you have sunscreen on you?"

Rishi shrugs. "You never know when emotional vengeance and UV protection will collide. It's SPF 30. Messy, but non-permanent. Like your last relationship."

Ten minutes later, Jackson's car is sporting the worst rendition of manhood imaginable in bright white cream.

Security yells in the distance.

We run.

**11:30 PM** – we're posted up at the edge of a rooftop bar in Hell's Kitchen, sweating out adrenaline and sunscreen crime, city lights bleeding around us.

I swirl the last inch of my drink, throat raw from too much soju and not enough answers. Rishi leans against the railing, scanning the crowd.

He nudges me. "Feel better?"

"Not even close."

"But slightly less homicidal?"

I consider. "Yeah. Slightly."

He claps me on the back. "That's progress."

I grunt.

"Yo," he says, tipping his chin. "Is that...?"

I follow his gaze.

White tank. Pointy heels. Black hair draped over one slim shoulder. She's laughing with two friends—one, a woman with a slick, straight blonde bob, and the other, a guy I don't know, but I hate his shirt.

The tank she's wearing is doing unspeakably excellent things for her boobs. Even the bartender's pretending not to look.

"That chick was at Vanguard today. From the Laurel Group. What was her name?" He thinks it over, then snaps his fingers. "Rorie Adams."

The name clicks. The posture. The laugh. That spark in her eyes I saw at Stanfield some months ago is now full of fire as she sits there in heels and confidence.

"What are the odds?" Rishi asks.

"Shit," I say under my breath. "I've seen her before."

"What?" Rishi asks, tracking my face. "You know her?"

"No," I say slowly. "But... yeah. I mean, I ran into her once."

He cocks a brow. "Literally, or figuratively?"

"The latter. A few months ago," I say. "She was leaving Stanfield as I was walking in. Dropped her phone. It cracked. I picked it up."

Rishi nods. "Smooth."

"It wasn't like that. She looked... defeated. Hollow. I don't know why, but I told her that cracks mean change."

Rishi stares at me. "Dude."

"I wasn't flirting. But for the half a second we stood face-to-face, I felt whatever she was carrying with her that day. It was pretty heavy."

"You sure it's her?"

I nod, eyes on that beaming white smile. "Yeah, it's definitely her. But I haven't seen her since. She was an up an coming force to be reckoned with, but then she dropped off the face of the earth."

"Go say hi."

I watch her throw her head back at something the guy says. She turns. She sees me. And then it's a flash. A flicker. Recognition crackling across the rooftop like lightning.

Reality and the weight of the day slam into me, crushing any ounce of confidence I might've still had.

I shake my head. "Yeah, no."

"Why not?"

"Because I'm a wreck. Not to mention, she's probably still pissed you smoked her at Vanguard today."

"Nah, it's business," he says. "She's an adult."

"No."

After a beat, she turns back to her friends, laughs again. But it's different this time. Forced.

I stare at them. She's trying not to look. But she's failing.

"Not tonight." I exhale, set my glass down.

# CHAPTER 4
# STARE HARDER, I DARE YOU

## RORIE

MAYA LEANS OVER. "WHO. IS. THAT?"

"Rishi Patel from Big Stream," I bite out. "He's the fuckstick who pitched against me at Vanguard today. Or—sorry—*strategically undercut* our value, dragged it into a flaming dumpster, and somehow got a standing ovation for it."

Jeremy leans over, squinting in the direction I'm burning holes through. "The tall one with the untouchable bone structure, feral heartbreak eyes, and smolder levels set to brood?"

I don't answer. My gaze shifts a fraction to the left, lands on the man standing next to him.

Broad shoulders.

Carefully-rolled sleeves.

A glass of amber liquid in his hand.

The smile he gives Rishi is tight. Uncomfortable. And when he glances up, our eyes lock.

Everything inside me goes very, very still. I know that face. That dimple. Those eyes.

My heart kicks against my ribs.

Oh, God.

It's him.

"No," I say. "That's Nolan Rhodes. The fuckstick's boss."

Jeremy whistles low. "Well. If that's corporate evil, sign me up for corruption. He looks like a bad idea written in cursive. I'd let him emotionally devastate me and then thank him for the experience."

"You need therapy," Maya chuckles.

"I need five minutes and a closed door," Jeremy says. "Preferably with *him*."

"Stop fanning yourself," I scold Jeremy. "They're the enemy. Remember?"

I glance back at Nolan. Same calculated intensity as the last time I saw him. He's leaning over a high-top table. Expression unreadable.

My mind tumbles back to the day at Stanfield. Dropped phone. The flash of contact when our hands brushed. That tiny pause—the one I told myself meant nothing. Weird poetic line.

*Crack's mean change. They let the light bleed in.*

Except in my case. It was darkness.

"Okay, well you didn't tell me the enemy was so delicious. Mmm… mmm…mmm. I want to lick him up…and down."

Maya sips her drink. "They're heading this way."

"No, the *fuckstick* is heading this way," Jeremy corrects. "Oh god, the hot, broody one is doing that thing. The tall guy hover."

"He's probably calculating the ROI of ruining my night," I say flatly.

Maya purses her lips. "Or staring at you like he wants to fill your—"

"I swear to god, if you finish that sentence," I cut in.

"What?" She smiles. "It's obvious he's checking you out."

"Brace yourself," Jeremy whispers. "The Smug One approaches."

A few seconds later, Rishi hits our table with the confidence of a man who definitely didn't lose an account today. Must be nice.

"Ladies," he says, eyes twinkling. "Gentleman." With narrowed eyes, points at me. "Rorie Adams, right?"

"Yeah."

Rishi's all swagger and good lighting. He waves to the bartender. "Another round," he calls out.

And sidling up next to him—

The hot, broody one.

"Thought I'd come over and say hi," Rishi begins, flashing a grin as he drapes one arm over the back of an empty barstool. "That Vanguard pitch was tight. You made us sweat."

My smile is all bite. "Oh, you must run hot, Rishi. Didn't see a drop of sweat when you slid in with a proposal that felt... familiar. I swear I'd seen someone else pitch it recently. Taylor and Blythe maybe. Or was it Halston, Inc."

I'm lying. Rishi's pitch was very much original. I just want to be a bitch. Although I wouldn't put pitch theft past these Big Stream boys.

Jeremy sips his drink audibly while Maya's eyes bounce between us, that third drink is taking effect.

"Whoa," Rishi raises his hands in mock surrender, "that was all original." He taps his temple a few times, still grinning. "Straight from here."

"Right." I roll my eyes. "So, it's pretty bold of you two to show up in my line of sight after today."

Nolan almost smiles. Almost.

"Came over to compliment a worthy opponent and order drinks with embarrassing names." He turns back to the bartender. "Make it four Flirtinis and one Dirty Misunderstanding."

"I feel seen," Jeremy says.

Rishi winks. "You should."

Meanwhile, Nolan still hasn't spoken. He stands there quiet, awkward, observing like he's filing away every micro-expression for later use. It's weird. And unsettling. His eyes keep drifting to me, but I refuse to look away.

Let him blink first.

Rishi follows my gaze, then sighs. "And this is Nolan Rhodes. Our agency's closer. Human spreadsheet. Professional smolderer. And Chief Creative Officer."

Nolan shifts, like he's about to say something more—then doesn't. Instead, he slides his hands into his pockets and just stands there, silent. Stiff. Weirder than before, somehow.

How is this guy their highest exec? Rishi carries on better conversations. At least he cracks jokes, charms the table, keeps everyone's attention. Everyone except Nolan.

Who's still not talking.

Still not smiling.

Just staring.

At me.

*Hard.*

It's making me twitchy.

Heat simmers low in my chest. One part annoyance, two parts left-over disappointment from my loss today. And they're all wrapped up in vodka.

Which has fully kicked in. I *don't* want them here. They could've stayed on the other side of the bar with their victory poses and over-achiever jawlines.

But no.

They *slithered* over, all faux humility and quiet arrogance, and I've had just the right amount to drink to let my bitch flag fly.

Nolan Rhodes is still eyeing me like he's trying to solve for X.

So, I say, "Stare any harder and I'm invoicing you."

Nolan blinks, finally snapping out of whatever analytical fugue he was lost in.

"Jesus, I've met statues with more game."

"Are you always this prickly?"

Well, well, proof of life.

"Oh good—it speaks." I arch a brow. "I was starting to think your jaw was decorative."

He grunts.

"To answer your question, only when provoked," I say sweetly, picking up my drink just as the bartender drops off our technicolor disasters.

"She's actually being polite," Jeremy chimes in. "Usually there's more swearing."

Out of nowhere, Nolan decides to get snarky. "Well, sorry to crash your post-loss pout parade."

He tilts his head a little, like he's trying to figure out what part of me bites and what part breaks.

*Fuck around and find out, Rhodes.*

"I had to buy my guy a drink after he cleaned up at Vanguard," he adds, lifting his glass. A toast. To salt in wounds.

And I see red.

"Oh, so you're a funny guy?"

He takes another sip of his drink, eyeing me from the rim of his glass.

"You know, there for a second, I mistook you for someone who actually does the work, instead of hiding behind account managers, like Rishi here, who cut budgets and take insider tips to win accounts."

That wipes the smile right off his handsome smug face.

Rishi steps in. "I didn't—"

"You think we cheated in order to beat you?" Nolan cuts him off.

"I think you needed a coupon and a mole. But sure, spin the narrative."

Nolan's gaze flits to Rishi briefly before returning to me, cold and unbothered. "Well, I certainly didn't expect to run into someone who speaks in weaponized subtext tonight. What a treat."

In the background, gazes volley.

"And I didn't expect to run into someone who flirts like it's a hostile negotiation," I shoot back.

"Oh, I'm definitely *not* flirting."

I arch a brow, sharp as glass. "Sure you aren't. Must've been someone else mentally guessing my bra size from across the bar."

His jaw ticks.

"No come back?" I smile. Deadly. "Next time, try starting with hello instead of a slow striptease."

Maya eventually leans in, pretending to whisper but failing spectacularly. "Should we leave you two alone or should we set up a boxing ring?"

Jeremy drags her back. "Nah. This is the foreplay portion of the night. Let it play out."

When did toe-to-toe rooftop banter with the enemy become my kink?Is that something I should unpack in therapy? Because Nolan smirks—and that smirk short-circuits my brain, sends a pulse straight between my legs, like my vagina's a damn smoke detector and he's hellbent on setting off the alarm.

"Don't flatter yourself," Nolan says.

I narrow my eyes at him. "You always this arrogant?"

"Yes," him and Rishi say in unison.

"Well, at least you're self-aware. That's one trait we can build a personality around."

"I hate how hot this is," Maya whispers.

"*This…*" Rishi lifts his glass, grinning. "This is exactly what he needed. A good old-fashioned head-to-head to knock the heartbreak right out of him."

The words hit Nolan deep, and I snatch them up instantly.

"Heartbreak, huh?" I'm all faux sympathy. "Is that why you've been brooding like an abandoned groom at the altar? Definitely explains the sad eyes. Guess she picked someone who *does* close deals."

Nolan stiffens. His jaw tightens. No words. Then he sets his drink down and walks away.

Jeremy's head swivels to me. "Well. That escalated sexily."

I stare at the space where he was. No retort. No final jab. Just silence.

I should feel victorious. On some level, I do. But the burn of triumph fades fast when Nolan turns the corner toward the elevators. What's left behind feels sickening. Like I missed the mark, and hit something softer instead—something raw.

Because the look in his eyes before he turned away wasn't ego. It was loss. And I know that look. I've *worn* that look.

It's hollowed me out when I stood in an empty hospital room. It crept in when people stopped calling, when the world kept spinning, and I didn't know how to keep up.

I wouldn't wish that on any human, no matter how much I hated them.

My jab was reckless, and unthinking. I threw a punch, and I hit bone. And now Nolan *"The Rate-Cutting Rat Bastard"* is gone, walking away in a pair of polished Oxfords with my claw marks still in his pride and a deeper emotion I didn't mean to touch.

# CHAPTER 5
# THERE IT GOES
## NOLAN

I LEAVE the rooftop without a word.

The city howls past me, but none of it touches the static whipping around inside my chest.

Rishi trails behind me, quiet.

At the curb, I throw up a hand for a cab. One screeches over. Rishi gets in after me, slamming the door, bracing for turbulence.

The vinyl seat sticks to the back of my neck. The cab smells faintly of sweat and weed. My molars ache from how tightly I'm grinding them.

She hit me where it hurts.

The worst part?

I liked it—right up until I didn't.

Rorie Adams, with her kill-shot eyes and venom-tipped voice. She met me, jab for jab, glare for glare.

For a few minutes, she became the punching bag I needed. And I must've been hers, too. But then she landed the hit of the fucking century. The one that split me open. If I hadn't walked away, I would've bled out right there. Right in front of her. In front of everyone.

I can't have that. So, I left.

Rishi breaks the silence with a sigh. "You gonna talk about it?"

"Nope."

"You sure? Cause your face looks like someone just told you football was canceled forever."

I stare out the window. The streetlights stretch across the glass like scars. "You gave her the kill shot."

"Shit, I'm sorry, man," he says. "I wasn't thinking. It was the first time you've looked alive all night and it just slipped out."

I don't respond. I'm still replaying her words. That stare. The moment she *saw* me—and all my hurt, and my pain, and she twisted the knife anyway.

Rishi was right. She's a real killer.

"Look," he says carefully. "She got under your skin."

"I'm fine. She's arrogant."

"So are you."

I roll my neck, trying to ease the tension there. "She was mad about Vanguard. I was her chosen target. It's all good."

Rishi chuckles. "Maybe. Or maybe you were the only one who could take the hit and dish it right back."

I say nothing. Because yeah, she pissed me off. But she also challenged me. Lit a fuse I didn't know was still wired. I haven't felt that in a long time.

I didn't just enjoy it.

I *wanted* it.

Every glare. Every bite of her words.

For a second, she made me forget Chloe. Made me forget everything except how badly I wanted to win that argument.

"That last jab though," Rishi mutters. "Damn. You flinched."

I let my head fall back against the seat. "She came for my pride."

"She came for your *ego*," Rishi corrects. "Your pride loved it. She hit you right in the balls, man."

I shake my head, biting down on the anger bubbling up inside.

"You were flirting," he says,

"I was not."

He gives me a look. "She basically slapped you and kissed you in the same breath. And you said, yes, please, again."

I roll my eyes.

"She got in deep, and fast," he says. "You wanted it. And sorry, dude, but it was written all over your face. You wanted her. That's why you didn't speak for fucking ever. She made you nervous."

I don't respond.

I'm still thinking about the way her voice dipped when she delivered that final line. How her eyes didn't blink. How the air between us shifted from sparring to something else entirely.

I want to believe it was just heat. Just chemistry. Just two rivals biting at each other's throats.

But it wasn't.

It was personal.

And I wasn't prepared for that.

The cab pulls up to my building. The lights from the lobby glow. I reach for the handle.

"Want me to come up?" Rishi asks.

"No. I'm good."

"Text me if you need to bury a body."

"Yours or Jackson's?" I smirk.

"Ha, ha. I said I'm sorry, get over it."

"Night, man."

The cab drives away, tires hissing over asphalt. I'm left standing in the kind of quiet that doesn't soothe—it strangles.

The walk from the curb to my building is a crawl through cement. My shoes scuff against the concrete. The night air stings and the city is pretending it didn't just watch my life fall apart.

I let myself into the lobby, each footstep echoing off polished tile. The elevator dings too cheerfully. My reflection in the brushed steel doors is of some tired, worn out shell of a human. I don't recognize this barely stitched together version of me.

Inside my apartment, the stillness is worse. The loft is cold. Open. Sterile. A showroom staged to look like a life.

I toss my keys into the bowl by the door. Pour a drink. Bourbon. Neat. It scorches the back of my throat, but not in a good way.

The record player groans to life. *Killswitch Engage*. The guitar hits, followed by a guttural scream, the vocals punching to the chest, loud and violent.

I collapse onto the couch and close my eyes.

All I see is Chloe. Her tangled hair. Her bare back. Jackson's face twisted in that smug grin.

Them, together.

My stomach flips. I grip the throw pillow and hug it tight, but it smells like her shampoo.

Now I want to burn everything she ever touched.

My phone buzzes. I check it. ESPN.

Of course it's not her.

I scroll anyway. Not because I expect a message, but because some broken part of me wants one. Is that so wrong?

I toss my phone to the coffee table. It hits with a dull *crack*. The shattered screen reflects back at me. Then it buzzes again.

I snatch it up. Jackson?

> Let's be adults, Nolan. I respect your work.
> This was...unfortunate timing. That's all.

*Unfortunate timing?*

My pulse thunders. Here is, minimizing it. Rewriting it.

He wants me to let it slide. To make it easy at Big Stream. Because if I don't, his spot in Thatcher's world gets shaky. And he knows it.

Jackson wants grace. But all I've got are bullets.

> You don't respect shit.

> Take your unfortunate timing and shove it up
> your Nepo Baby ass.

Three dots blink. Pause. Blink again.

Then—

The audacity. The passive-aggressive corporate sociopathy of a fucking emoji. It's the equivalence of a shrug.

I almost launch my phone across the room.

Again.

Instead, I squeeze it until my hand goes numb. This is war.

Also...FUCK YOU!

Then I turn my rage to Chloe. Because fuck her too.

Her number isn't in my phone anymore. Doesn't need to be. It's seared into me just like everything else I wish I could forget.

My thumbs move on instinct. Fueled by bourbon and fury. The message is brutal. Blunt. No poetry. Just shrapnel.

I hover over send. My reflection in the screen looks warped.

What am I doing? This isn't me. I'm not this guy. The one who rage texts the people who fucked him over. I'm the guy who walks away because the fight just isn't worth it.

But then I see her again, bare skin, Jackson's hands, that smirk.

Screw it.

I hit send.

# CHAPTER 6
# UNKNOWN NUMBER

## RORIE

THERE'S nothing like coming home with sore feet, smeared lipstick, and absolutely no idea where your left earring is. Ugh!

The door clicks shut behind me with a soft thud, and I kick off my heels with a groan. Cool relief floods up from the plush rug as it meets the soles of my aching feet.

My apartment greets me like an old friend—cozy, chaotic in a way only I can decipher.

Unopened mail leans over the edge of the kitchen counter. A jacket I meant to hang up days ago lounges across a dining chair, possibly claiming permanent residence. It smells faintly of candle wax and lavender cleaner, but there's a whiff of a less charming scent—probably the leftovers I forgot to throw out.

Still, it's home. Cluttered, imperfect, but safe. And all mine.

I shed my dress, swap it for an oversized tee, and collapse onto the couch. The cushions sigh beneath me, worn and familiar. My fingers graze the spine of the small town romance I've been half-ignoring for weeks. I flip to the bookmarked page, but the words blur, too sweet, and too tidy for my frayed mood.

Should've picked up that dark romance. The why choose with pages and pages of smut. Definitely a better fit for my current mood.

With a dramatic sigh, I toss the book aside and pad barefoot into the kitchen. Ice cubes clatter into a glass. The vodka tonic bites cold and clean, cutting through the ambient drone of appliances and the quiet shuffle of the city outside my window.

I take a sip. Let the cold burn distract me.

*What the fuck was that with Nolan Rhodes tonight?*

One minute he's looming at a rooftop bar like a fallen angel in rolled sleeves, and the next he's tossing verbal grenades left and right. And I let it happen. Worse, I enjoyed it. For a full thirty seconds, I forgot to hate him. I forgot his firm beat me. Again.

I take a longer sip, trying to wash the thought down with vodka and denial.

*I mean, really. What* was *that?*

His stare felt like he was dissecting me, sorting reactions for some internal dossier.

For a bit, I let him win the stare-down. Barely. But still.

Infuriating.

And, unfortunately, hot.

Not that I noticed.

Okay, I noticed.

But only in the anthropological sense—like observing a wolf in business casual. A deadly predator with feral patience. Probably smells expensive too.

I top off my drink, grab my dad's gold compass from where I keep it on the counter, and slip it into my pocket on instinct.

The balcony door groans as I push it open. The city greets me with humid air tinged with exhaust, and remnants of whatever someone grilled earlier in the day.

Leaning against the iron railing, glass in hand, I listen as Astoria hums below—footsteps on pavement, a burst of laughter, the low roar of the N train sliding through shadows.

Above, the sky offers nothing. No stars, just haze. Still, I search for constellations I know I won't find. A habit leftover from nights spent on the hood of my dad's Jeep, listening to him trace the stars with quiet certainty.

*"If you ever get lost, Rorie," he once said, pressing a compass into my palm, "look for the North Star. You need a North and an Anchor."*

I remember the needle trembling, then settling. Him smiling like he was handing me a secret map to the universe.

A guide. And a tether. Something to follow. Something to hold onto.

Only, I don't know which I'm missing.

Maybe both.

My mom was my North. Big dreams, bigger beliefs. She saw me completely, even when I didn't.

My dad was my anchor. Steady. A soft voice in the darkness.

Now, they're both gone–taken months apart. It's poetic in its own way, knowing they're up there together. That they couldn't bear to be apart in this world.

But losing my mom was like losing gravity. Then my dad followed way too soon after, and the ground beneath me vanished.

I've been chasing stability ever since.

I press the compass into my palm. It's solid. Familiar. Still pointing.

But I'm adrift.

Ever since I lost them, my career has collapsed. The grief has swallowed my focus, shattered my confidence, and left me in a world that keeps moving without them.

If they could see me now, Would they be disappointed?

I feel like they would. Only because they raised me to press on through the storms of life. And I'm not. I'm stuck.

My eyes scan over the stars one last time but the couch beckons. I head back inside and sink into it, digging out the remote from between the cushions. I scroll until I land on my brainless, trashy reality TV the *Bachelor Barn*.

Somewhere between an on-screen tantrum and an overcooked proposal, I grow bored and reach for my phone. No messages. Just me.

Instagram tempts me. And of course, there he is.

Quinn. Grinning with a drink, surrounded by guys who wear matching polos and call it culture. Caption: Work hard, tequila harder. #BossLife #VibesOnly.

"Vibes only?" I mutter. "You wear loafers without socks."

He looks happy. *Unburdened.* My grief was a detour he didn't have time for.

Meanwhile, I'm here, half-drunk, smeared lipstick, mascara smudged, grief curled around my ankles like a slithering snake.

Every serious relationship I've had taught me the same lesson: love is temporary. People leave.

It's safer to expect nothing. At least that way, you see it coming.

A message dings my phone.

Curious, I open it. And immediately wish I hadn't.

> Jackson?! His dirty dick is a perfect match for that rank ass pussy of yours, Chloe. Enjoy!

*Whoa.*

I blink. Then read it again.

It's unhinged. Horrifying. And... kind of fascinating.

Who sends this?

More importantly, who receives this?

I should ignore it. Go to bed.

Mischief flares in my chest. It's been a long day. And honestly, I could use the distraction.

My fingers fly across the keyboard. The words practically write themselves.

> Wow. That's... poetic.

An immediate response.

> Fuck. You. Chloe!

Typing bubbles appear. Disappear.

> Shit. Wrong number.

I snort.

> Yep.

> Who the hell is this?

Who do you want me to be? Chloe?

Anyone but Chloe.

Clearly.

And just like that, I'm texting a stranger. Which was not on my vision board for today. Yet, here I am.

You text like a stand-up comic testing material.

You text like you're auditioning for the lead in Sad Boy: The Musical.

I'm not sad. Or musical.

Says the guy rage-texting about genital hygiene.

Moment of weakness.

A moment? Is that what we're going to call it?

Just trying to paint a picture.

Mission accomplished.

Why are you responding then?

Entertainment value. And you have decent punctuation.

I could be catfishing you right now.

Please. Even if you're a middle-aged man named Carl who collects porcelain dolls, I'll take my chances.

Jokes on you. Carl's doll collection is world-renowned.

Can Carl spell world-renowned?

Probably not.

I don't know why I'm still texting. Maybe because so far, it's fun. Or because the silence tonight is too heavy.

So, tell me about you.

I'm guessing this is your smooth segue into: are you male or female?

Busted.

Soooo...

Does it matter?

Not really. Just curious.

Fair.

Female?

Correct.

And now let me guess... you're going to jack off later while rereading our entire thread?

Only if you promise to narrate it like an audiobook.

I'm not opposed. But I also am.

To answer your question, I'm selectively social, emotionally elusive, and still baffled by fitted sheets. Basically, I'm a human starter pack of red flags—but I do recycle.

Recycling's hot.

Also, fitted sheets are a trap. Sent from Satan.

Got any skeletons in your closet I should know about before continuing this absurdly odd conversation?

Only if you count the shoes I refuse to throw out. You?

Oh, I've got skeletons. But they're color-coded and alphabetized.

Psychotic. And yet, still not impressive.

Sarcasm and trauma aren't enough?

For friendship? Maybe. For entertainment? The jury's out.

But, go on, try to impress me.

Okay. I can cook, fix anything with duct tape, and once won a bar trivia night by naming all the Spice Girls' middle names.

Who are the Spice Girls?

Please tell me you're joking.

A little. Proceed.

Baby Spice...Melanie Jayne.

Googling as we speak.

Wow. Zero trust.

You're a stranger. I trust nothing.

Fine. Google away. But I'm right.

> If you're wrong, you owe me.

And if I'm right?

> Then I owe you. But don't get cocky.

Already cocky. Stay tuned. I'm just getting started.

> I will say, you're definitely more interesting than the reality show I had on.

High praise. What show?

> The Bachelor Barn. A trash dating show. They make you look stable by comparison.

Ouch!

> No offense.

Honestly, none taken.

The conversation unfolds like improv with a somewhat charming maniac. We trade insults and odd truths. I now know all the Spice Girls' middle names, and we've developed a backstory for Carl the Doll Collector that includes three failed marriages and a surprisingly successful Etsy store.

Unknown is reeling from a breakup. I'm avoiding mine. We're both emotionally unstable and unreasonably witty.

My cheeks ache from grinning. The silence that used to crush me is now filled with unexpected banter and badly timed jokes from someone I don't know.

The text thread goes quiet for a bit, and I'm slightly concerned I offended him. Or maybe he just got bored of me.

Then he resurfaces and we shift. From banter to honesty. From flippant to raw.

Unknown tells me what happened—that he walked in on *Chloe,* when he was going to ask her to move in tonight.

I'm the biggest idiot alive.

Why?

I never saw it coming.

I stare at the screen trying to think of what to say that might make him feel better. But for once, I can't find a joke.

How long were you together?

A year.

Consider it a blessing. Better now than later.

Guess you're right.

I'm absolutely right. People can be selfish assholes. That's not your burden.

Speaking from experience?

Sort of. Different situation.

Different how?

Just... different.

In the hours that we text, we don't say everything. But we say enough. He asks about me, but doesn't push. And I don't explain. My life is mine. Messy, unfinished, and not for tonight.

I failed.

The word slams into me. Not loud. Not dramatic. Just...familiar.

Because yeah, I know that feeling.

Of trying so hard to hold it all together—career, grief, expectations—only to watch it crumble in your hands anyway.

Of chasing wins that never come.

Of being the girl who used to sparkle and now can't even land a pitch.

Of wondering if the people you lost would still be proud of you if they could see you now.

Fail.

That word sticks to everything lately. And seeing it typed out like that—from a stranger who feels just cracked and broken as I do—makes it harder to pretend I'm fine.

> You didn't. She did.

Easier said than felt.

> I get it. But you'll feel better once you take out the trash. Marie Kondo her ass.

Who?

> Never mind. Just declutter your life. Starting with her.

Her? Done. Him? Complicated.

I work with him.

> Oh, plot twist.

Yeah.

> So what's the plan? You gonna murder him? Hide the body?

Depends. You got any tips?

Classified. That's Friend Zone material. Access required.

How do I apply?

Accidental text friendships are uncharted territory. There should be rules.

Such as?

Rule #1: No oversharing, especially about bodily fluids or functions.

Failed. Next?

Rule #2: No deep questions after midnight.

Already failed that one too.

Rule #3: Keep it snarky. No "live, laugh, love" energy.

What about Pinterest quotes?

Immediate termination.

Harsh. But okay.

Rule #4: Texting stops if I'm hungry or sleepy.

Rude. I'm less important than snacks?

Yes.

You're a savage. Rule #5?

Never text "lol" unless you actually laughed.

> Did someone hurt you?

> Yes. And I've never recovered.

> Looking forward to unpacking that more, but I'll "haha" with integrity from now on.

> See. Growth.

> You're oddly good at laying out rules.

> And you're weirdly tolerable for a guy who opened with a genital rant.

> Awe, thank you, I'm touched.

> You should be. It's the nicest thing I've said all day.

> Should I be concerned about how low your bar is?

> Constantly.

> Well, the rules are set. I should probably get some sleep. Thanks for the therapy sesh.

> Next time, I'm charging.

> Worth it. Goodnight, Snarky Stranger.

> Goodnight.

I'm smiling, surprised by how easy that felt.

Before setting the phone down, I slip a hand into my pocket and pull out the compass. The needle wobbles once. Then steadies.

North.

Anchor.

I'm neither tonight. I'm just someone standing still beneath a sky that won't stop spinning. But for now, that's enough.

To be here.

To still look up.

To still believe the stars are worth chasing.

And to find bright ones in the most unexpected places.

# CHAPTER 7
# THE NEPHEW AND THE KNIFE

## NOLAN

SUNLIGHT STABS THROUGH THE BLINDS, nailing me right in the face like a cosmic middle finger. My lower back protests with a dull ache—a not-so-subtle reminder that my couch is not a proper bed. Chloe picked it out. Too stiff. Too white. Too curated.

I should get a new one.

Yeah. I'll do that today.

The coffee table in front of me is a full-blown war zone. Takeout containers teeter like Jenga, an abandoned whiskey tumbler, and a lazy sprawl of laundry that never quite made it to the basket.

Sitting up, I rub the sleep from my eyes, and take in the wreckage.

It feels... lived in. Chloe would've hated this. Her spaces were airbrushed—couch pillows karate-chopped into magazine perfection.

"We should present our best selves," she'd say, smoothing corners that didn't need fixing.

And I let her. Because I loved her.

But now, in the quiet of this imperfect space, I realize how much I missed actually living in it.

My phone buzzes.

A jagged fracture splits across the screen. A memory surfaces—me telling Rorie Adams that cracks meant change. It had been a non-flirtatious line at the time. But now, staring at the spiderweb across the glass, I wonder if the universe was trying to shout through the silence in that moment.

A text from my assistant, Tammy, comes through.

> You working today or what? Your driver said he's been waiting for over an hour and your not answering your phone.

I check the time. "Shit."

I fire off a text to Alan.

> Give me ten.

Launching myself off the couch, I immediately slam my knee into the coffee table. Pain flashes white-hot. I hiss through clenched teeth.

New couch. New coffee table. Noted.

In the bedroom, I tear through my closet, hunting until my fingers land on a charcoal gray suit. Strategic.

I strip off yesterday's t-shirt, catch a glimpse of myself in the mirror. My hair looks is a war crime. My eyes are bloodshot, and dark-ringed. Basically, I look like hell. Feel like it too.

The quickest shower in human history comes next. No steam. Barely warm. Just movement.

Suit on. Tie adjusted. Jacket smoothed.

In the mirror, I look like I've got it together. Inside? I'm a Molotov cocktail with a ticking fuse.

Today, I have to pretend I didn't walk in and find Jackson with my girlfriend. And act like my life didn't splinter into a million shards less than twenty-four hours ago.

I'll play the part.

For my job.

And because there was a shift last night.

One misdial.

One wrong number.

I ended up in a conversation that felt... real.

Texting her—whoever she is—was like finally cracking a window open I didn't realize was painted shut.

She didn't try to fix me. Didn't pity me. She matched my mess with her own. And it felt honest.

A stranger saw more of the real me in one crazy thread than a year of showcased affection ever managed.

I fasten my watch. Grab my cracked phone and swipe it open. My thumb hovers over the thread. Her words still echo, but I pocket it, and head out.

Five minutes later than what I texted Alan, I walk out into the churn of the city.

Alan nods. "Morning, Mr. Rhodes."

"Morning." I slide into the backseat, buttery leather hugging my frame.

The ride is quiet. The city outside blurs—honking cabs, street vendors, sidewalk scuffles. All of it kept at bay by glass and privilege. Everyone and everything is moving. But my mind is stuck on pause, on one image.

Chloe and Jackson fucking.

Her hands. His smirk. The smug ease of betrayal.

No text. No call. No half-assed apology from her. Just absence.

*Fucking bitch.*

The car stops. Big Stream rises above, steel bones wrapped in corporate ambition.

I step out onto the sidewalk, the city humming at my back.

Deep breath in. Deep breath out.

The revolving door spins me into cool marble and quieter air. I cross the lobby, each step louder in the hush of marble stone and corporate calm.

*Ding.* The elevator opens. I step in. The doors close. By the time it lurches to a stop on the twentieth floor, my pulse has leveled, but only just.

I pause, take another breath. *You got this, Rhodes. Fuck that guy!*

The lobby inside Big Stream is sleek glass and chrome. My shoes clap against the tile, echoing loudly.

Tammy, assistant extraordinaire, intercepts me like she's been posted there since dawn, armed with an agenda and God bless her, coffee.

She shoves the cup into my hand. "Morning, sunshine."

This fireball is the heartbeat of my operation. Mid-forties, five feet of fury when needed, and always two steps ahead of me. Her curls are pulled tight, her suit is pressed, and her orange bow glows like a flare. Iconic.

Taking a sip of coffee, I eye her. She's staring. "What?"

"Water cooler says you had quite the night."

I sigh. "Fucking great! Everybody knows?"

"You could've texted me," she says.

"I know."

"I would've liked to be included in the vandalism."

"What are you talking about?"

"Jackson's been screaming about his car all morning. Sunscreen art. Very anatomical. Apparently it etched itself into the paint."

My stomach sinks. Tammy notices the look on my face, that of part guilt, part panic, part should I be lawyering up?

"Relax. I had Imogene wipe the cameras."

I blink. "You what?"

"Boss, you know I keep the felonies contained. You're welcome, by the way. But next time you go full feral and don't invite me—your balls? Earrings." She points to her lobes, where a pair of glittering tiny pink flamingos dangle.

"You think I'm kidding," she adds.

"I do not." *I absolutely do not.*

"Good."

"Please give your amazing white hacker wife a kiss for saving my ass."

"Oh, I'll give her more than that." She winks. "Now. Thatcher. Ten minutes." Tammy turns to leave.

"Oh, Tammy."

She pauses, twists back.

"I need a new phone," I add. "Screen's cracked."

She deadpans. "You want me to replace the whole phone, or just fix the screen? Asking for my sanity."

"Whatever gets it done, Tams."

"Mkay, testy today."

"I'm sorry. It's been a shit twenty-four hours."

She nods. "I get it. Need anything else? Coffee refill? Alibi? Hit Jackson with my car?"

"You're my favorite person."

She winks. "I know."

Then *he* appears.

Jackson leans against my office wall. Pristine suit. Hair annoyingly perfect. He looks fresh. Not like he was up half the night fucking my *ex*-girlfriend.

"Rhodes," he says, like we're old friends.

"Jackson."

"Nice of you to show up for work. Must've had a wild night. I know mine ran late."

Leveling him with a glare, my tone is a jagged blade when I reply, "Funny, didn't realize narcissism required aftercare."

His grin tightens.

"Hey, I heard about your car," I add, feeling dangerous.

"Did you?"

"Yeah. That sucks." I blink. Innocent.

"You wouldn't happen to know anything about that, would you?"

"Nope." I slide one hand into my pocket, the other brings my coffee cup to my lips. I take a sip.

"Hmmm. Well, whoever did it had some *very* strong opinions about male anatomy."

"Yours?" I ask. "I heard it was a micropenis."

"Ha! It's enough to keep Chloe satisfied. Repeatedly."

I walked right into that one.

The air goes razor-sharp. My fists clench before my brain catches up. Blood roars, knuckles twitch, I'm a half-step from launching into him.

"Nope." Tammy slides between us like a human Switzerland. "We are *not* punching nephews before ten a.m., Rhodes."

She turns to Jackson with a smile that could slice the man's throat. "And you? Stop measuring your manhood in other people's bed sheets."

Jackson adjusts his tie. "Touchy."

I exhale through gritted teeth. "Careful."

Tammy nudges Jackson along. "Boys, if this turns into a pissing match, please take it outside. I just had these floors buffed."

Jackson watches me as Tammy pushes him further toward the exit. Even with the added distance, the tension pulses between us.

"Mr. Thatcher," Tammy reminds me over her shoulder.

"Have fun in the meeting," Jackson calls out. "Try not to drag me down, yeah?"

"The only thing dragging you is your own dead weight."

"You've got jokes," he says.

"And you've got insecurities."

I'm hiding my own cracks in my composure, sure. But they're just reminders.

Change is about to happen.

Thatcher's office is an open view of the city—quiet dominance with grey tones, minimalist furniture, and abstract art that's more like a psychological test than décor.

He sits behind his desk, a portfolio open in front of him where he's scribbling notes. His salt and pepper hair is neatly parted, not a strand out of place, and his navy suit looks like it was sewn onto him by a tailor with a god complex. His dark eyes are unblinking. They miss nothing.

"Rhodes," he greets, gesturing for me to sit. "Rough night?"

I wonder, for a split second, if he knows. If he's already heard what his nephew did. If this is his way of testing me—watching for fractures, waiting for me to flinch. But his face gives nothing away. As always.

"Just a late one," I reply, sinking into the seat.

He studies me for a beat before sliding a black envelope across the desk.

"What's this?"

"VIP tickets to the Crossfire event this weekend."

My gut tightens. I hate celebrity events. All flash. An endless parade of fake laughter, and ego disguised as charm. But they matter. Networking is currency, and these parties are where deals start—even if they end in headaches and hangovers.

"Asher Cross is shopping agencies. I want you there."

I nod. "Understood."

"Take Jackson with you."

The silence stretches for a beat as that sinks in, then it screams.

"I know he's your nephew, but... you want him in the room for something that big?"

"He's green. Needs guidance. And you're the man for the job."

I grip the envelope. Jackson accompanied me to a sales pitch a few months in from starting at Big Stream and he managed to single-hand-edly tank the entire meeting. We were in a boardroom with one of the biggest investors we'd ever landed, and Jackson, well, he decided to *improvise*.

Instead of sticking to the script, he went on a twenty-minute tangent about why luxury branding is a scam, complete with a slide he pulled up from some conspiracy subreddit about subliminal messaging, a pyramid scheme theory, and, I kid you not, lizard people running the market.

I wanted to die.

By the time I wrestled control back, the investor was already checking her watch, and Jackson was helping himself to the catered lunch like he hadn't just cost us a multi-million-dollar deal.

So, yeah. Thatcher may love his nephew, but that doesn't mean the rest of us should have to suffer. Especially after what I walked into last night.

"No offense, but I'm not a babysitter."

Thatcher smiles. Not kindly.

He continues, voice sharp as a knife. "This is your proving ground, Rhodes. You guide him, you close the deal, and we talk partnership."

The words burrow deep into my skin.

"You win. You rise. Jackson's new to the game," Thatcher continues, leaning back in his chair like the world bends to him. And most of the time, it does. If we're being honest. "He needs someone to show him how it's done."

"Thatcher—"

"No arguments."

I clamp my mouth shut. I know better than to push. Arguing with

Thatcher is like throwing yourself against a brick wall—pointless, and guaranteed to hurt.

"Understood," I say, but the words are ash on my tongue.

How the fuck did I get here? Jackson doesn't respect the work because he's never had to. Hand him a strategy, and he'll take the scenic route straight into the mountain. Not up it.

And now I'm supposed to wrangle him while courting the biggest client of my career?

*Fan-fucking-tastic.*

He steeples his fingers. "There's more."

*Oh, God!*

"I want you to take Shelby Davidson to happy hour next week."

The name alone makes a noise escape from the back of my throat that sounds suspiciously like a dying fax machine.

Shelby is what happens when too much privilege, too little self-awareness, and an Instagram algorithm collide. She's sunshine captions and designer endorsements. The human version of a sponsored post.

*Double fan-fucking-tastic.*

The last time I interacted with Shelby was last year. I was sitting on a panel where she absolutely humiliated me.

I was the keynote at a convention. *Market strategy in a shifting digital age.*

I was prepared, and devastatingly charming. The usual.

Until Shelby—then an intern with some advertising company, had a front-row seat, and way too much audacity—took the Q&A session hostage and verbally ripped me to shreds.

"That's a really nice way of saying you're resistant to change," she'd said, smiling like a shark in lip gloss.

She wasn't wrong. Which, honestly, made it ten times worse.

There were more layers to that moment—nuance, trauma—but I've spent too much in therapy (and bourbon) compartmentalizing it to go back now.

The clip went viral.

I became the out-of-touch dinosaur.

She walked away a legend.

Cross Media aka Asher Cross scooped her up and crowned her their Creative Director and Asher's right hand gal.

"She's Cross's liaison. Build rapport."

It takes everything not to scream. How Shelby has risen to such a high place is beyond me. But, then again, if there's one thing she excels at—aside from manufactured relatability and obnoxiously perfect hair, it's getting people to buy into her bullshit.

And now I have to pretend I don't *completely* despise her.

"Will do."

"Jackson's going too."

I swallow down the protest. "With all due respect—"

"Make it happen."

Right. So that's it then?

"All good?" he asks, eyes daring me to defy him.

"Mhm," I grit out.

"Great!" He snaps the portfolio shut like he's won something. "I'm counting on you, Rhodes. You're the man."

Rage simmers inside me as I step out. This is more than a deal. It's the fight of my life. If Jackson costs me partner—I won't just put him in his place.

I'll bury him there.

My office is a mix of dark wood, iron fixtures, a chess board in the corner—more war room than workspace. I make it three steps in before his shadow cuts across the doorway.

The devil himself has reappeared. *Why can't I fucking escape this guy today?*

"Teamie," Jackson says, grinning.

I say nothing.

He walks in, casually, and obnoxious, his gaze landing on a photo of Chloe on the table behind me.

He picks it up. Stares too long. His thumb brushes the glass.

"I'll take this now," he says. Like it was his to begin with.

My pulse spikes. I think I'll go ahead and punch him now. Besides, Tammy isn't here to stop me.

But before I can move, he's gone. The door clicks shut. And I'm standing here, breath caught in my throat, staring at the empty space. Like a coward.

I don't care about the picture. Not really. But he didn't ask. He just *took*.

Like he did Chloe.

What's next—my job?

*"You win? You rise. You fail? You vanish."*

Pressure flares white-hot under my ribs, covering the hollow ache Chloe left behind.

I won't let it stand.

Except, by the time I look up, I've already made the decision:

He can have the picture.

But he won't take anything else.

# CHAPTER 8
# GARLIC KNOTS AND RED FLAGS

### RORIE

### GIOVANNI'S IS PACKED

The lunch rush roars around us, a full-blown symphony of clinking plates, shouting servers, and sizzling garlic-scented mayhem.

I'm wedged in a corner booth with Maya and Jeremy where the vinyl is cracked and patched, and the table is sticky despite the waitress's best efforts. I'm picking at a basket of garlic knots that are definitely going to kill my breath. Risky, considering I have a pitch this afternoon. But worth it.

My phone buzzes beside my plate. I swipe it fast.

Spam. Again.

I set it down, screen-up, then turn it face down.

Maya lets out a sigh, equal parts judgment and curiosity. "Okay, Rorie, you've checked that thing more times than a teenage girl waiting on a Snapchat. Spill."

Jeremy perks up, eyes wide. "Ohhh, is this a *boy* thing?"

Maya lifts a perfectly arched brow, tearing a garlic knot in half. "Is it?"

I roll my eyes and push the phone away. "It's nothing."

Jeremy leans in, elbows on the table, as if we're about to unlock national secrets over marinara and mocktails. "Nothing doesn't make your pupils dilate like that, babe."

"It's work stuff."

"Work stuff with cheekbones?" Maya presses. "And maybe a dimple?"

"It's *not* a boy thing," I insist. "Or a Nolan Rhodes thing."

There's a beat of silence. They both stare. Waiting.

Jeremy grins. "So it *is* Nolan Rhodes."

"It's not!"

"Rorie." Jeremy gives me a look that would make a nun confess.

I slump back against the booth. "It's not a big deal. Some guy texted me by mistake last night. Thought I was his ex. I answered. We talked for a few hours. It was dumb."

"Oh. My. God!" Jeremy claps his hands together like a delighted seal. "It's a digital meet-cute!"

Maya's expression tightens, her suspicion immediate. "What's his name?"

I blink. "I...don't know."

She stares at me as though I told her I handed my social security number to a guy in a ski mask. "Let me get this straight. You stayed up texting some random guy for hours, and at no point did you exchange names?"

"It didn't come up," I mutter, peeling at the edge of a napkin.

Maya gingerly sets her garlic knot down. "Rorie."

"Relax, Maya." Jeremy waves her off. "It's a mystery text thread, not a blood pact. You don't exactly get W-2s on *Romance Roulette* either."

"Yeah," she snaps back. "But you *do* get a name."

"Not always a real one. The last guy's username was *ThickRickOfficial*, but he ghosted me the second I asked for proof."

"Why are you still on there?" Maya asks.

He shrugs. "Hope springs eternal. And so do liars with Wi-Fi and a ring light."

"Exactly my point." Maya refocuses on me. "Why'd you keep texting him?"

Because he made me laugh. Because I forgot about Vanguard. About Nolan and Big Stream. About everything I keep failing to outrun. Because it felt like floating after months of trying not to drown.

"I was bored. He was funny. It distracted me."

Maya doesn't buy it. "A distraction is online shopping. Or rewatching crime docs for the hundredth time. This is how Dateline episodes start."

Jeremy sighs. "If I had a dollar for every time Maya accused me of being future true crime content…"

Maya ignores him. "I'm serious, Rorie. You're vulnerable right now. You just lost your parents. You like, *just* broke up with Quinn—" She stops, the name hanging there like a slap. "I don't want to see you get hurt."

"Quinn," I echo. "You mean the guy who vanished the second my life fell apart?"

She doesn't respond.

"I'm not getting hurt," I say, more biting than intended. "It's just texting."

"Texting leads to feelings. Feelings lead to complications. Complications—"

Jeremy throws up his hands. "Oh my God, is this the Jedi path to heartbreak? Let the girl live, Yoda." He turns to me. "This is awesome. You get the fun of flirting without the weird first-date pressure. No bad appetizers, no forced conversation about your childhood dog. Just good vibes."

"Exactly," I say. "It's like a digital-age pen pal."

Jeremy beams. "I would absolutely wear that on a shirt."

Maya mutters, "You two are exhausting."

I laugh.

But then she softens,. "Just don't fall for a fantasy, okay? Because when it crashes, it's all in your head—but the pain is still there."

Her words land with more weight than I expect. I shift in my seat.

Then I smile too brightly. "It's not that deep, Maya."

She exhales, arms crossing. "Fine. But don't come crying to me when your mystery man turns out to be a forty-five-year-old cat dad who types in Comic Sans."

"Hey!" Jeremy raises his glass. "To mystery men and Comic Sans. May they reign forever."

I lift my glass and clink his.

Maya leans forward one last time, her voice quiet but steady. "Promise me you won't get too lost in this."

I nod.

And lie through my teeth.

# CHAPTER 9
# LOVE, LOSS, AND LE CREUSET

## NOLAN

I'M SITTING cross-legged on the living room floor, a half-empty beer bottle hanging from my fingers. The game's on, but I'm not watching. Left work early, told everyone I was going to "do research" on Asher Cross.

Lies.

I just needed out.

And instead of researching anything, I drove to a clinic and got tested. Just to be sure. Just to shut down the voice in my head whispering: *what if Chloe and Jackson gave you more than mental flashbacks to remember them by?*

Now I'm here. Staring at nothing. Letting time crawl by while I wait for it to give me answers, or maybe some clarity, or relief.

Anything really.

What I get is silence.

Chloe's gone.

Jackson's a smug bastard.

And Thatcher just handed me a career-defining opportunity...with Jackson surgically attached like a parasitic intern who snorted a line of corporate buzzwords and called it strategy.

I should walk. I should quit. But I've worked too hard for too long to let them take this from me.

No. If anyone should leave, it's Jackson. He's the problem. Not me.

But while he's out there, thriving. I'm sitting here, mulling over the truth: *I should've seen it coming.*

The warning signs. The pulled-back affection. The headaches. The sex that went from routine to nonexistent.

And now, I'm looking back at the dwindling intimacy with Chloe like an idiot searching for clues in a murder mystery.

The victim? My dignity.

The suspect? Her wandering libido.

The motive? A textbook case of grass-is-greener syndrome, with a dick attached

I've retraced every moment, hunting for the red flags. I've come the conclusion that I didn't miss them. I ignored them because I was scared of what it meant. And deep down, I thought if I stayed steady enough, stayed safe enough, then I would be enough.

Turns out, steady and safe don't mean shit when you're competing with the thrill of someone new.

I've learned that lesson before. Too many times.

First Natalie Stone. My first kiss, first "real" love—went to homecoming with Cash Neilson without even breaking up with me. I showed up to pick her up in my dad's old suit and watched her parents take pictures of them in the rose garden.

Classy.

College? That was Professor McKay. I didn't know she was married. Not until I found her husband waiting in her office.

And then there was Elijah Nichols. The mentor I thought was building me up, only to walk into a boardroom and watch him pitch *my* work—*my* ideas, *my* concepts—as his own.

"That's the game, kid," he said afterward. "If your stuff's good enough to steal, it means you're worth something."

Right.

So I adapted. Hardened. Learned to keep things close to the vest. Because trust is leverage. Vulnerability is legal tender. And once you run out, no one gives a damn about the debt they owe you.

But Chloe? She slipped past all my defenses. Took everything I gave freely and handed it to someone else. Someone who didn't earn it. Who didn't deserve it.

And I'm the idiot holding the receipt for a future that never existed.

My grip tightens around the bottle.

The stupid pine-patchouli candle she loved so much is drifting through the air, the throw blanket folded just so, the bookshelf perfectly symmetrical.

I hate that fucking candle. I want to mess up that fucking blanket. And I want smash that fucking bookshelf to bits.

Then snap a pic off all of it and send it to her.

But that would go against why I deleted her number in the first place.

And besides, her silence is better than any excuse she'd give me.

Still, it guts me.

Because a year should mean something. Apparently, it meant everything to me, and nothing to her.

After draining the rest of the beer, I set the bottle down, rub my eyes. Her self-help book—*Let That Shit Go*—sits on the coffee table, stupid and cheerful in its faux-minimalist font.

I pick it up. Flip it open in my hands.

I can't take this shit anymore.

I rip it in half.

The tearing sound is so satisfying. Pages scatter across the floor like ashes. It's book murder. And I love it.

I keep going until there's nothing left but the hardback cover.

Then I sit in the middle of my new mess, surrounded by pages full of advice she never followed and I never needed.

And I feel… nothing.

Just numb.

I need something else.

My eyes land on the bookshelf.

That photo of us—her windblown, laughing. Me, looking at her instead of the camera. A hiking trip. Her idea. I hate hiking. But I went.

Because she loved it. And I loved her.

The photo is a lie. A frozen moment from a story I didn't know was already ending.

A part of me wants to laugh about all this. But laughter only masks the ache for so long before it breaks, leaving behind a dull, empty sadness. Because the truth is, I wasn't enough for her.

And while she was out having her *vibrant* extracurriculars, I was in the shower convincing myself this was just a rough patch.

My phone buzzes in my pocket.

I don't look at it right away. I know what it is.

Nothing urgent. Nothing I'm ready for.

Still, I swipe it open. No new messages. But a missed call from a number I know by heart.

Dad.

It's been weeks since we spoke. Weeks since the last call ended with raised voices and a hollow click.

But it's the way my chest feels too tight, too raw, that makes me hit call before I think better of it.

It rings.

Once. Twice.

"Nolan?" His voice scrapes across the line, rough, a little too careful. He's trying to place me.

"Hey," I say, clearing my throat. "Sorry it's late."

Silence blooms. Not hostile. Just… blank.

"Something happen?" he asks eventually.

Even though they only met once, I almost tell him about Chloe. About the whole wreckage of it. About how he was right—people leave. People always leave.

But I can't.

Some memories are all he has left. I'm not about to stain them with mine.

"Nothing," I lie. "Had a rough day."

Another pause. My fingers tremble against the phone.

"Don't get soft," he mutters finally, voice fading at the edges. "Rough days make you better."

A dry laugh escapes me.

"You know," he says after a moment, tone softening—an old habit. "Your mother used to say you get your stubbornness from me."

I don't answer. I sit there, breathing him in, this version of him. The one that flickers in and out like old radio.

*"He's just like his mother,"* I remember him saying once.

I was ten. Small. Stupid enough to think love was unconditional.

*"Nolan is young. Cut him a break,"* my uncle had argued.

But even then, there'd been that undertow of doubt.

*"Too much heart,"* my dad had said, like it was a flaw. *"Too much trust. You'll see. One day he'll figure it out. Being the nice guy will get you nowhere."*

I press the heel of my hand into my eye. He was right. I did figure it out. But not soon enough.

"Well," he says a little softer. "I guess it's good to hear your voice."

I close my eyes. "Yeah. You too."

We sit in it for a second. Not a connection. Not a reconciliation. Just a layover in familiar silence.

"Call me when it's a good day," he says, a trace of hope threading the words.

"Yeah," I whisper. "Okay."

The line clicks.

For a long time, I sit there, phone pressed to my ear, listening to the silence.

Leaning back, I rub at the bridge of my nose, thoughts swirling, and like an old habit, I start replaying my mistakes. Self-blame is practically second nature.

I stand, move over to the picture of Chloe and I then grab it and head up to my rooftop terrace. The warm night air rushes in, carrying the scent of sweet florals.

The city vibrates below, oblivious to my heartbreak.

Fixing things with Chloe started small. She'd get quiet after an argument, her frustration radiating in waves until I caved and apologized—sometimes for things I didn't even do. It was easier that way. *Keep the peace, Nolan. Don't rock the boat. Just bottle it and move on.*

Except now, the boat is capsized, and I'm drowning in the wreckage.

And I missed *all* of it.

I've come to realize that the smug fucking smirk engraved in Jackson's face was never just a smirk...

It was a message.

And all those lingering glances at Chloe during company parties.

A warning.

The way he found a reason to stick around whenever she showed up to meet me after work.

A claim.

It's *so* obvious now.

This is what happens when you see the angles no one else does. When you read between the lines, anticipate the move before it happens, only to realize you missed the one right in front of you.

This is what I get for being the closer. For knowing how to seal the deal, secure the outcome. Except when it comes to the people who *actually* matter.

A year. One fucking year, *gone.*

"Well, sweetheart." My voice is edged with something too bitter to be nostalgia. "Thanks for the lesson. Really top-tier betrayal—textbook, even."

My grip tightens.

"Hope he was worth it."

I launch the frame into the night, watching it disappear into the darkness like the future I once thought we had. It smashes against a building. Someone yells. A car alarm bleats once. Then silence.

One more step toward freedom.

A traitorous tear threatens to stray. But *fuck that.* I'm not crying over her. The only tears Chloe's shedding have *Jackson's* name attached.

So fuck her. Fuck *them.*

Back inside, I shut the door behind me like I'm sealing off whatever was left of her in my life. But the emptiness that follows isn't as satisfying as I hoped.

I need a distraction before Chloe's picture isn't the only thing I hurl off that balcony tonight.

My phone catches my eye. The memory of *Unknown* sneaks in. I grab my phone, unlock it then scroll through the messages. Quick-witted. Not unkind.

She didn't judge me. She made me laugh when I felt like my insides were being fed through a shredder.

Should I text again? Probably not. But that sliver of connection was enough to keep my head above water last night. And I'll never forget that.

I should thank her. Even though I already did.

My fingers linger over the keyboard.

**First attempt:** So, do you offer emotional crisis management as a service, or was that a one-time, free trial situation?

Delete. Too needy.

**Second attempt:** Hey, thanks for the chat last night. Also, if you ever need someone to ruin your faith in humanity, I've got a Jackson to loan you.

Delete. Too bitter.

**Third attempt:** Quick question—what's the appropriate waiting period before a guy can make self-deprecating jokes about his ex without looking like a walking red flag?

Delete. Too *accurate.*

**Fourth attempt:** Are you a licensed therapist or just really good at talking people off metaphorical ledges? Because either way, I'm impressed.

**Delete.** Jesus. I sound like a *lot.*

I am a lot. I drop my phone onto the counter, exhaling heavily.

I'm not texting her. I refuse to be *that guy*—the one who overshares, who overstays their welcome, who can't take a fucking hint.

She gave me a moment of clarity when I needed it. That's enough.

I turn off my phone, pour myself a strong drink, and try not to think about Chloe until there's a knock at the door.

Then another.

Then a third—impatient.

"Hold the fuck on," I growl, setting the glass down a little too hard.

Every step toward the front is heavier than the last. My pulse hammers like it's trying to punch through my ribs. I'm already pissed, already tired, and whoever's behind that door is about to catch hell.

I glance through the peephole.

The world tilts.

It's Chloe.

Standing on the other side like she has any fucking right.

My breath locks in my chest, rage spiking a sudden fever. Every ounce of wreckage she left behind crashes into me all at once.

I open the door without a word.

A cold wave of irritation sweeps over me as she breezes past me in that blood-red coat, her entrance a gift-wrapped grenade, lobbed straight into my chest.

"What do you want, Chloe?" I snap, slamming the door shut behind her.

She doesn't answer. Just stares at the apartment like it's a museum she used to curate, inspecting the damage with that familiar, calculating detachment.

Her gaze lands on the coffee table. On the book—*her* book—shredded, split in two, pages scattered like confetti at a funeral.

It hits her.

Good. Let her stand amongst the ruin she left behind.

"What happened to my book?"

Like she doesn't already know.

I step forward, voice thick with sarcasm. "Oh, your book? Turns out cheating doesn't make for great bedtime reading."

Her fingers tense around the handle of the Birkin bag I bought her for Christmas. I keep going.

"So I did what anyone would do when the words in front of them turn to bullshit—I ripped it apart. Kind of cathartic, actually. You should try it. Start with the fairytale you sold me over the past year."

Her jaw tightens. "Don't be so dramatic, Nolan."

"Dramatic?" I bark out a laugh. "You've been radio silent since I walked in on you riding Jackson like a goddamn parade float. No text. No call. Not even a Post-It."

She whirls around, eyes blazing. "I didn't think you'd want to hear from me. You made that clear when you stormed out."

"You think I *wanted* to walk out?" My voice spikes, fists clenched at my sides. "You think I was looking for an excuse to disappear? All I wanted was closure. Accountability. Hell, a note under the door would've been more than what you gave me."

Her lips press into a thin line. "I thought it was better to just... move on."

"Move on?" I repeat, venom curling around every syllable. "No. You didn't move on. You disappeared."

Her arms cross over her chest. "I gave you space."

"No. You gave me nothing."

A beat passes. Her polish is cracking now—her shoulders inching higher, her jaw tensing. What is she holding back?

"I'm here to grab my stuff," she says quietly. "That's it."

I scoff. "You're unbelievable. All that we shared, and now you want your measuring cups and throw pillows like this is a goddamn asset split?"

Her gaze hardens. "Some clothes. A few kitchen things. And the Dutch oven."

"The *Dutch oven?*" I laugh, dry and bitter. "You're seriously here for a cast iron pot?"

"I also need my key back," she adds, brushing hair behind her ear.

"Gladly." I snatch my keys out of the bowl and yank hers off the ring, the metal biting into my palm. But then there's that shift. That pause. Her hand tightens even more around her bag.

And I know.

"Why do you need your key back?" I ask, even though I already feel the answer, cold and rising.

She doesn't even hesitate. "Because I need to turn it into management. I'm moving in with Jackson next weekend."

The words land like a battering ram to the ribs. I don't breathe for a full minute.

"You're *what?*"

She lifts her chin. "I'm moving in with him."

The key cuts deeper into my hand. I didn't think I had anything left to be blindsided by.

Turns out, I was dead fucking wrong.

"It just makes sense," she says softly.

"Sense." The word tastes like blood in my mouth. "Right. Like fucking the guy I work with makes sense."

I pause. Then lower my voice. "Just tell me, Chloe. When did we fall apart? Was it a slow fade, or did I just miss the second you gave up?"

She doesn't answer. Just stares at me with a blank sort of resolve. She's already rewritten this chapter without me in it.

"I thought I knew you." My voice falters despite myself. "I thought we were building a real life. But now I'm wondering if all I ever loved was the version of you I *needed* you to be."

Still, she says nothing.

"Help me understand," I whisper. "When did *we* stop making sense?"

Her posture shifts, but she stays quiet.

"Why won't you fucking talk?"

"Does it matter, Nolan?" she says finally. "It's over. You're making this harder than it needs to be."

I step closer. "It matters to me."

"I don't know what you want me to say," she murmurs. "It just… happened."

"Yeah. That's the thing about betrayal—it always *just happens*, right?"

She flinches. Barely.

But I want her to hurt. I want her to feel what I'm feeling. Chloe made it look easy—replacing me like I was just a placeholder she forgot to erase.

And I stood there, trying to understand a version of us that apparently only existed in my head.

So I meet her gaze. "It wasn't the lie that broke me. It was how fast you pretended I never mattered."

She doesn't reply, just moves into the kitchen, collecting what she came for then heads into the bedroom for a few minutes. Classic Chloe, always running from conflict.

I stay rooted to the spot I'm standing in, waiting, burning in the silence.

Chloe reappears, a bag slung over her shoulder, the damn Dutch oven propped on her hip. She finally says, "You gave me everything. But you never *really* saw me. You saw who you wanted me to be. You made me into your 'forever girl' as though I was some box on your checklist. But I needed more than perfect weekends and predictable plans. I needed real."

"I was real."

"You were safe," she corrects. "Comfortable. *Way* over the top with gestures, if I'm being honest. But you never asked what *I* wanted."

My brow furrows, taking in her words.

Chloe's voice drops to a whisper. "You were going to ask me to move in. But have you ever stopped to ask yourself—if you were so very much in love with me, why didn't you buy a ring instead of a key?"

Those words sink deeper than the silence ever did.

"You loved the idea of me more than you ever really loved *me*."

I'm mute. I don't have an answer. She's right.

She moves to the door. "I'm not apologizing for wanting more."

"Jackson?" His name curdles on my tongue like sour milk. "He's your more?"

She pauses by the doorway, eyes steady. "He doesn't see who I could be. Or who I used to be. He just sees... me."

I stare at her.

"I'll send a service to retrieve the rest of my things."

Then she's gone. No fanfare. No slammed door. Only the sound of heels against hardwood, and then the quietest click I've ever heard as the door shuts behind her.

I stand there, alone, surrounded by shadows and silence and the faint trace of her perfume in the air.

I'm hollow. Someone scooped out everything good and left the shell behind. Even the air feels borrowed.

Because now it's over.

Undeniably over.

The next morning creeps in like a tender bruise I didn't notice yesterday, and it's just starting to hurt.

I haven't really slept. Not since Chloe dropped what was left of us on my living room floor and strutted out like a divorce court contestant carrying a consolation prize. Apparently, the Dutch oven was the hill she chose to die on.

Her words are still rattling around in my skull.

*You loved the version of me you made up in your head.*

*Why didn't you buy a ring instead of a key?*

Each sentence is a new blade, carving through the carefully built narrative I'd wrapped myself in for a year.

So I do the only thing that makes sense.

I leave.

The gym smells like suffering. Sweat, rubber, testosterone, and a hint of rage. The clang of iron, the raw grind of muscle, the way pain is earned here—it's the only thing that makes sense right now.

I throw myself into the bench press. Bad Omens blasts through my headphones, giving my fury a soundtrack. The bar is heavier than it should be. Doesn't matter. I press through it anyway, chasing the pain.

The bar locks into place with a satisfying clang. Chest heaving, I sit up and wipe my face. The sting helps. So does the burn.

But Chloe's voice slices through the noise.

*You were safe.*

*You never really saw me.*

She's not wrong.

I didn't picture kids. Or marriage. Or even us ten years from now. I pictured Sunday night takeout. Matching Netflix queues. A clean, domestic kind of loneliness that didn't ask for anything more than maintenance.

That's the real betrayal.

Not hers.

*Mine.*

I lift, again and again, until my arms shake.

Would I have listened, if Chloe told me she wasn't happy? Would I have changed? Or would I have plastered over the cracks and called it progress?

The question hurts me more than I expect. I drop the bar. And for the first time this week, I breathe without anger.

What I feel instead… is clarity.

This was never just about her cheating. It was about us never really *being.* Just performing.

A compiled slideshow of a relationship. Whatever I thought I was building before—it wasn't a life. It was a well-decorated holding pattern.

And now that it's over, I want the real thing.

Whatever that looks like.

Whenever that happens.

Whoever it's with.

# CHAPTER 10
# THE BOY BAND BLOODBATH

RORIE

THE PLACE SMELLS like cheap beer and impending triumph.

Jeremy promised nachos. What he failed to mention was the pub trivia night, complete with a tragically regrettable team name, and a bar full of overconfident corporate bros who think quoting *The West Wing* makes them intellectuals.

Maya is perched beside us, nursing a drink pink enough to sue Barbie for copyright infringement. She sits back on her barstool, surveying the room as though she's placing bets. Pretty sure her money isn't on us.

Jeremy and I are elbow-to-elbow at a high-top under a large tv screen that reads:

### BOY BAND BLOODBATH:
### TRIVIA NIGHT OF
### TEARS, TUNES & TRAGIC FROSTED TIPS

"Welcome to Thursday Night Trivia," says the bartender-slash-quizmaster, whose Hawaiian shirt is louder than the crowd. "Tonight's winners receive a free round and the honor of hoisting our sacred trophy, handcrafted from broken friendship bracelets and laminated boy band headshots!"

Jeremy registers our team name with the quizmaster.

"You're going with... CTRL+ALT+DEFEAT?"

"Obviously," he says. "It's intimidating."

"It's a cry for help."

He places his phone between us, buzzer ready and waiting. "Use your overachiever energy for good, Adams."

I'm about to snark back when two shadows fall over our table.

"Well, what are the odds." Smooth. Cocky. Rishi.

Jeremy groans. "Seriously?"

I turn. Nolan *"Rate-Cutting Rat Bastard"* Rhodes stands there in a white tee and dark jeans that do unsettling things to my focus. And glasses?

Thin black frames, casually perched on his nose like he doesn't know they could single-handedly collapse a woman's will to fight.

Next to him, Rishi grins. Mischief practically radiates off him.

Nolan's gaze flicks to mine. Brief. Bladed. It doesn't linger, doesn't soften—just slices through the air between us before cutting away like I'm nothing worth looking at twice.

Good.

Let him be cold. Let him be clipped and clinical. I don't need softness from him. He's the enemy.

I square my shoulders. Raise my chin.

I want to be defiant. Untouchable. The woman who doesn't care. But the truth is—his distance stings more than I want to admit. And I don't know why.

So, I wrap myself in pride and push everything else down deep.

Because fuck that guy. Even though I still feel like shit for making that comment.

"Didn't take you Big Stream boys for trivia types," I say, sipping my spiked cider. "Or I mean, types who enjoy public humiliation."

Rishi slides into the seat across from Jeremy. "Humiliation builds character. You should know a little bit about that."

I sneer at him. "Funny."

"We heard the burgers here come with a side of shame," Rishi says.

"Perfect," I say. "You can choke on those right after we mop the floor with your egos."

"Hey," Rishi says brightly, "how about we pretend we're not all enemies for the next thirty minutes and just dominate trivia like the functioning adults we are?"

My brows lift. "Fraternizing with the enemy? No thanks."

He raises his hands in mock surrender. "Fair enough. I offered. But when we murder your game, just know—I tried to play nice."

Jeremy scoffs. "Good luck, that trophy is ours."

Rishi eyes Nolan pointedly. "You in?"

Nolan's jaw ticks once. He drops into the seat across from me, movements efficient, no-nonsense, but when he folds them over the table, the sleeves of his tee stretch taut across biceps that belong in a thirst trap, not a trivia bar.

Not subtle. Not accidental. And definitely not helping my ability to think in complete sentences

"Ro," Jeremy says, dragging out the syllable. "Your brain just short-circuited mid-glance. You want me to get you a napkin for all that drool or...?"

I snap my gaze to him. "I wasn't drooling."

"Sweetheart, your pupils dilated so fast I thought you saw Jesus."

Nolan doesn't say a word, but hides a flash of a smile behind his cupped hand.

I sneer at him. He adjusts his glasses, eyes locking on mine. That infuriatingly cute dimple peeks out. There's a flicker of heat, or challenge, possibly both.

"I'm in," he says, voice rough with amusement. "Wouldn't miss a chance to watch Rorie Adams choke on her own confidence."

My smile is all teeth. "Aw, look at you. Finally finding something you're actually qualified for—trivia and trash talk."

He tilts his head, eyes narrowing just enough to make it a dare. "You sure you're up for another loss against us?"

"Oh, honey." I sip my drink. "*You'll* be the one crying into your craft beer before the second round."

He grins. Slow. Sexy. Irritating. "We'll see."

I roll my eyes.

Jeremy leans in, smirking like he's just spotted a golden opportunity to stir shit up. "Okay, okay—what's the point of all this bark without some actual bite?"

Rishi's eyes light up. "Agreed. Let's make it interesting."

I cross my arms, arching a brow. "Define interesting."

"If the Laurel Group wins…" Jeremy taps his fingers on the table like a game show host building suspense. "Nolan takes a body shot. Off Rorie."

I nearly aspirate my drink. "Excuse me?"

"Wait, wait, wait," Rishi interjects. "If Big Stream wins, then Rorie takes the shot. Off Nolan."

I whip my head between them. "Why us? Why not you two?"

Maya sips her drink, serene as ever. "Because they're not repressing a five-alarm sexual tension fire and pretending they're just rivals."

Jeremy points at her. "Exactly. Plus, you need a rebound. A hot, emotionally reckless, probably-regrettable-but-memorable rebound."

I blink. "Okay, wow. My sex life is officially everyone's business now?"

Rishi sips his drink, unbothered. "You're not the only one who needs one. Nolan does too."

Nolan's head snaps toward him. "Rishi."

Rishi shrugs. "What? It's true. You've been brooding in spreadsheets and bourbon, and it's getting bleak. You need someone to shake that shit loose."

"And nothing shakes shit loose like licking tequila off your sworn enemy." Jeremy signals the bartender. "A round of shots to set the mood, my good sir."

My eyes swing to Nolan. His jaw is tight. His gaze cutting. But beneath the simmering glare is something else entirely—something bracing.

And those glasses?

Unacceptable.

They make him look smarter than he already is, which, frankly, is dangerous. Add the unfair stretch of his shirt across biceps that deserve their own OnlyFans account and I'm two seconds from abandoning every ounce of self-respect I brought to this bar.

This is a bad idea.

A stupid, unprofessional, wildly inappropriate idea.

The tequila shots arrive. I stare down at mine like it's the start of a war and I've just been volunteered as tribute.

Nolan looks straight at me, "Scared you'll like it?"

I don't flinch. Just meet his gaze—blue fire to bronze steel. The space between us vibrates with the kind of tension that unravels good, sound judgment.

My cheeks are already flushed, but I hold his stare. "Nah, scared you will."

His lips twitch. Not a smile. It's darker, more heated.

With maddening control, Nolan drags his tongue along the inside of his wrist, slow and precise. A show. Or a promise.

Then his hand rises, steady, holding the shot like it's sacred. His lips curl around the rim—plush, devastating. He throws it back in one smooth tilt of his throat. I watch the muscles work. Watch his Adam's apple bob. Watch the drop of tequila he misses trail down his jaw.

And then—God help me—he bites into the lime.

Nolan's lips seal around the wedge. His mouth pulls back, teeth dragging along the citrus, and I swear I feel it in my spine.

I almost forget how to breathe.

Because suddenly all I can picture is that mouth curling around my clit. That tongue licking straight up my center. That perfect, punishing bite against my inner thigh.

My thighs clench, involuntarily. My breath hitches. My pulse hammers loud enough to drown out the bar.

By the time the glass hits the table, my knees are loose and my brain is soup.

Nolan wipes his mouth with the back of his hand, eyes still pinned to me.

"I might," he says, voice low. "But I know you won't be able to hate me after this."

His gaze drags down my body, unashamed. Then he leans forward just enough for me to feel the heat of him, his words rough and raspy.

"Not after the way you watched me lick that salt. Not after the way your thighs clenched when I bit that lime. Admit it, Adams. You don't just want me licking your neck."

A smirk. A pause. That fucking dimple.

"You want my mouth a hell of a lot lower."

My jaw drops.

The audacity of him. The arrogance.

The challenge.

I inhale sharply, the tequila burning my throat before I even drink it. Squaring my shoulders, I stare him down like I've got something to prove. Because I absolutely do.

Then I knock the shot back in one smooth motion, eyes on his the entire time.

"Please, that's your move?" Heat blooms up my neck like I can burn him off my body if I try hard enough.

The corner of his mouth lifts, and it's the sexist fucking thing. But I'm *never* going to admit that out loud.

My gaze dips, first to the lips then to the throat. "You're going to have to do a hell of a lot better than that."

I sit back, arms crossed over a ribcage that's vibrating like I touched live wire. My words say no.

Everything else screams yes.

The space between us pulses, thick and charged with electricity. And no one says a word. Maya is stone silent, blinking. Rishi looks like he's watching the best pay-per-view of his life. Even Nolan—cocky bastard—isn't breathing. Not really.

It's Jeremy who breaks the silence and steals the show. "Are y'all about to start hate-fucking on the table?"

Rishi snorts. Maya's still blinking.

"Someone clear the bar tab now, because I think they're about to break a surface and a hip," Jeremy continues. "Seriously, I haven't been this turned on since that fireman calendar signing in SoHo."

I roll my eyes.

Jeremy whoops. "Battle of the agencies here we come. Literally. Trivia death match. Shot collar edition."

"You mean shot *collarbone* edition," Rishi corrects.

I groan. "You're all idiots."

Nolan smirks.

God help me—I want to wipe that smirk off his face.

With my mouth.

Nolan pushes out of his seat to go and register Big Stream.

"What's your team name?" Rishi asks.

Jeremy beams. "CTRL+ALT+DEFEAT."

Rishi nods approvingly. "Classic. Painfully millennial."

Maya pops a peanut in her mouth. "Who knew trivia could be so intense?"

Nolan returns, tapping their name into his phone. I glimpse it: **Born To Win, Forced To Play.**

"Dumb," I say.

"Don't be jealous that our team name is better than yours," he says, grinning.

"Debatable."

The first question pings: "What was the name of NSYNC's debut album released in the U.S.?"

Jeremy and I slam the buzzer. "N Sync—duh."

Behind me, Rishi whispers, "Was that the one with the marionette cover?"

Nolan sighs. "No, that was No Strings Attached."

Rishi: "God, you're ancient."

Nolan: "I'm thirty-four, not ninety-four."

Round Two begins: "Which member of 98 Degrees is related to a former boy band rival's wife?"

Jeremy aggressively taps the buzzer and yells, "Nick Lachey, married to Jessica Simpson, sister to Ashlee Simpson who dated Ryan Cabrera who looked like a poodle in distress."

"You need help." I laugh.

Jeremy celebrates. "I want fanfare, I want confetti, and I want someone licking salt off someone else's collarbone. Let's make memories, people."

More questions fly: "Which boy band member famously left his group to start a solo career in 2005?"

Jeremy: "Zayn Malik?"

Maya: "2005, not 2015."

Me: "It was Robbie Williams. From Take That."

Jeremy: "Nerd."

Rishi: "This is educational trauma."

"In what city did The Backstreet Boys officially form?"

Nolan: "Orlando."

I squint at him. "You answered that suspiciously fast. Did you study?"

He shrugs. "I came prepared to battle. I won the last time we came here and played, so I have a rep to uphold."

"What was the topic? Hogwarts for smug bastards?"

Nolan chuckles under his breath. "Keep talking, Adams. That second-place energy is loud."

That voice could belong in my future regrets folder.

Next: "Which boy band appeared in a 2001 episode of 'Sabrina the Teenage Witch?'"

Jeremy and I high-five. "*NSYNC*. Duh."

Rishi groans. "Rigged. It's always *NSYNC*."

By the final round, we're neck-and-neck. The screen flashes. The final question lights up: "Name the members of O-Town."

Jeremy clutches his chest. "My moment has come."

He slams his hand down on the buzzer and rattles off: "Ashley Parker Angel, Erik-Michael Estrada, Dan Miller, Trevor Penick, and Jacob Underwood."

Nolan grumbles, "We're doomed."

The quizmaster shouts: "And tonight's winners, by one aggressively niche fact... CTRL+ALT+DEFEAT!"

Jeremy shrieks like he's just been knighted. I toss Nolan a slow, smug smile.

"Let's review," I say, sauntering over to him. "I've outwitted you at the rooftop, outscored you at trivia. What's next? Arm wrestling? Strip poker?"

Nolan steps closer, eyes glittering. "Definitely strip poker."

I walked right into that one.

"Fair warning though, my bluffing game's strong. But my shirt removal game? Next level."

I arch a brow. "You assume you'd win." But even as I fire back, part of me is *staring*. Not at his body—though, yes, *hi*—but at *him*.

Something's off. Not in a bad way. In a *what-the-fuck-happened-to-you* way.

This is not the same Nolan Rhodes who was on a rooftop with shadows in his eyes and a chip on his shoulder the size of Big Stream. That version was all storm clouds and clenched jawlines.

This one?

This one's teasing. Lighter. Almost... *playful*?

And I don't know what the hell to do with that.

"Oh, I wouldn't need to win. Just need a reason to play." He grins, all dimple and easy confidence, but the smile doesn't quite reach his eyes. It lands more like charm, feels like armor. And looks cocky until you realize it's covering something heavier.

He doesn't want me to see something that he's pushed down deep. So maybe this new, lighter Nolan isn't a shift. Maybe it's a shield.

And suddenly I don't know if I want to peel it off...or ask why he needed to put it on in the first place.

He flags the bartender. "Two of whatever she's having. And a tequila shot."

Jeremy perks up immediately, practically vibrating with delight. "Oh, this is better than Bravo and wine night. I might climax."

Rishi chokes on his drink. "Jesus. Reel it in."

Jeremy shrugs. "Don't kink shame my joy."

The bartender sets everything down with a smirk of his own. Lime wedge. Salt. One shot of tequila. And suddenly, the noise in the bar fades behind the pounding in my chest.

All eyes land on Nolan.

He hesitates for half a second, enough for me to catch it. A muscle ticks in his jaw. He drags a hand through his hair, rolls his neck like it's going to help him breathe.

Oh, my, Nolan *"Confidence Is My Love Language"* Rhodes is nervous.

"Where?" he asks, voice low and rough.

Okay, now I'm nervous...*as fuck.*

My brow arches. "Dealer's choice."

His gaze sweeps over me, scanning his choices, and lands just beneath my collarbone. "Here," he says, voice husky.

Grateful he picked a conservative body area, I nod once.

Nolan steps closer.

My heart hammers inside my chest when he brushes my hair back with one trembling hand before lowering his head. Salt first.

His mouth hovers near my skin, teasing, then his tongue drags over my collarbone, achingly slow. The heat of it punches me straight in the vagina. *Holy shit.*

I bite back a gasp as his breath fans over the wet spot he leaves behind. He doesn't move. Doesn't speak. Just lets the tension hang heavy between us. And God help me, it's not the only place I'm wet.

Not even close.

Then, the shot.

He brings the glass to his lips and tilts it back in one fluid motion, grimacing as it burns its way down his throat.

And finally—the lime.

Which he takes from my fingers *with* his mouth, teeth grazing the tips just enough to send a current of lightning coursing through me.

When it's done, he leans back, his face is flushed, his breathing is shallow.

And I see it.

A discreet shift. A hand adjusting his fly. Fast, controlled, like he's trying to pretend it didn't happen.

It did.

My brow quirks. "You okay there, Rhodes?"

He clears his throat. "Peachy."

He won't meet my eyes. That might be the hottest part of all.

Nolan excuses himself for the restroom.

The trophy is handed off—a glitter-splattered horror show featuring a decapitated Lance Bass. Jeremy lifts it like he's won Wimbledon.

"We're celebrating at the pool tables," he declares. "Come dominate!"

"Maya, you in?" Rishi asks.

Maya eyes her drink. "Only if domination comes with a lemon drop chaser."

I wave them off. "You all go. I'll hold down the table."

Translation: I need a minute after Nolan Rhodes just licked my neck.

Jeremy winks.

I rotate my cider glass slowly. Sip. Breathe. Sip. Breathe.

"Careful," comes a voice at my elbow. "Sit too long and I'll start thinking you're afraid of me."

I glance up. Nolan's there. Flushed from what I'll generously blame on the tequila, hair tousled, grin weaponized. He looks like trouble with perfect teeth, and he's riding this loss like it's a win.

"Not afraid," I say. "Just uninterested."

He gestures toward the dartboard in the back corner. "Come on, Adams. One game. Unless you're worried I'll beat you this time."

I shake my head. "No thanks."

"I'm annoyingly persistent."

I stare at him.

He smiles. "Pretty please with cherries on top."

I sigh. "Fine. One game. Then I go back to pretending you don't exist."

At the board, he grabs two darts, offers one. I snatch it from his hand. "I could aim for your eyeball."

"Wouldn't be the first time someone's come at me with a pointy object and a grudge."

My lips twitch. His eyes flicker to the movement for a half-second.

The dartboard is faded and crooked, the lighting overhead flickering. The scent of wood polish and spilled IPA strong in the air.

I take the first throw. Bullseye.

"Beginner's luck," Nolan mutters, stepping up.

He throws, hits a three.

"Did you mean to hit the wall, on the opposite side?"

"Just getting warmed up."

We volley. Darts. Banter. Fire. The tension between us is tightening, threading through each quip like embroidery floss. And he watches me like I'm the riddle he's dying to solve. The way I hold the dart, the way I tilt my head before I throw. Like he wants to memorize every movement.

"You always this intense?" I ask after my third bullseye.

He shrugs. "Only when I'm losing. Or when I'm trying to figure out how to impress someone I shouldn't still be thinking about."

My hand slips. The dart veers wide.

Nolan chuckles, the sound low and warm.

I keep my eyes on the board, ignoring the traitorous flutter in my chest. "So, who's the unlucky girl?"

He doesn't miss a beat. Steps in close, his voice a low drawl that slides straight down my spine.

"I think you know."

Lifting my chin, I force my voice steady. "Well, then you definitely shouldn't. I still very much hate you."

He smiles—not cocky, more like he's okay being hated if it means being remembered.

"Good. Hate's something. Means I'm under your skin."

I scoff, turning to face him. "You're more like a rash I can't get rid of."

He leans in, his breath ghosting my cheek. "Then stop scratching and admit you like the itch."

Behind us, Jeremy groans. "For the love of margaritas, will you two just make out already or start throwing chairs? Either will suffice."

Rishi raises his drink. "My money's on chairs."

Nolan's still staring at me. That look in his eyes? It's not a threat. It's a challenge.

And god help me—I want to lose. But I don't fucking like to lose.

Lifting my drink, I take a slow sip, and shrug. "You poached my clients and tried to set fire to my career. I'm not letting that slide just because your mouth got to wander somewhere it didn't belong."

"Poaching is a strong word," he replies. "I prefer strategic acquisition."

"Right," I say, tilting my head. "I prefer *strategic annihilation*. But hey—semantics."

He leans against the wall, suddenly serious. "How do we move on from Vanguard?"

The ember of heat I've been feeling for him flickers out.

"That wasn't just a client to me. It was a year's worth of trust-building, late-night pitch decks, and—hell—hope. And your billion dollar firm blew it up like it was just another line item by cutting your rates thirty percent."

"You're mistaken. I didn't authorize a cut like that."

"Someone at your firm did. And it wasn't just Vanguard. You've done it with several. You're cheating. I think an insider is feeding you intel so you can benefit."

He steps closer. "You're making a lot of excuses for losing."

"Excuse me?"

He leans in. "It's business. And Big Stream doesn't just compete— we set the pace."

"Is that your tagline or your Tinder bio?"

"Depends on the match."

"You're such a cocky bastard," I say.

"And you're even more beautiful when you're pissed." His lips curl. "Tell me, Adams—when's the last time you lost a deal to someone *less* qualified?"

My jaw tightens.

"That's what I thought."

For a second, we just look at each other. Not talking. Not blinking. He's too close. Too full of himself. Too… right there.

I move to walk away. He blocks me.

"Look, the industry is just a game. And if you're not willing to play it…" His eyes dive into mine. "Then you've already lost."

I smile sweetly. "Oh, you want to play then?"

"With you," he says. "Absolutely."

"Okay," I start, looking up at him through my lashes. "Then let's play, asshole."

I push past him, cider forgotten, blood buzzing.

His eyes are still on me. I can feel them—hot, heavy, tracking every step.

And God help me, I kind of want to turn back around.

But fuck that. I'm not trading pride for a pair of perfect hands and a mouth that ruins reason.

I don't care how good his lips felt on my skin or how they made my pussy tingle.

Let him watch me walk away.

Let him *feel* it.

Because if he wants another taste, he's gonna have to *earn it*.

# CHAPTER 11
# STRATEGIC ANNIHILATION

## NOLAN

COFFEE WARMS my palms as I lean against the front window of the café near my loft—one of those places with mismatched chairs and baristas who judge your order on sight.

Outside, the city hums to life in that familiar, bustling tune. The skyline's softened by morning haze, but my head's still hung up on the girl with the cider and the claws.

Rorie Adams.

That woman called me a corporate vulture to my face and made it sound like a goddamn compliment.

She smelled like late nights, and jasmine, the ghost of a flower that only blooms when no one's looking. And her skin tasted like cinnamon set on fire. I'd chase it until my lungs gave out.

I came home that night and took a cold shower, muttering half-formed curses into the tile like a man possessed. It's been so fucking long since I've had someone under my hands, under my mouth, and I almost lost it.

One lick of that pulse point on her neck, and I was ready to rewrite every rule I ever made about keeping personal and professional separate.

I'm drawn to her. To her bite. Her burn. Her fucking righteousness. I love her fire. But Jesus, she's going to have to get over this feud of ours eventually.

Still, she's not wrong.

*You poached my clients.*

*Your billion-dollar firm blew it up like it was just another line item.*

That's what she said. And yeah, we did. We moved fast. We were leaner. Smarter. That's how the game is played.

But that wasn't a game to her. That was months of sleepless nights and preparations. That was pride. That was her reputation.

And my firm turned it into collateral damage.

It's been looping in my head since she said it. So I asked Rishi casually, in the car on the way home.

"Did we cut rates on the Laurel Group pitch?"

He blinked, frowned. "Not on my watch."

I didn't push it further. If Rishi doesn't know about it, it means someone went around us. Undercut without telling the team. And whoever it was, it worked. We landed the account. The firm celebrated.

But something's amiss. I can feel it. Her accusations don't add up. Neither does the silence.

And now, I can't stop thinking about her, standing there with her spine straight, chin lifted, and her voice shaking, not from fear, but from fury.

Rorie was right. We didn't just win.

We took. Stole.

Whether Big Stream meant to or not, we made her collateral.

I rub the back of my neck, jaw clenched so tight it aches. I've been called worse than a vulture or a poacher. But the way she said it—like I wasn't just winning—I was breaking something that mattered, it all lodged under my skin and hasn't let go.

I'm a fixer by nature. I see broken things, and I want to put them back together. But this? Her?

She's not mine to fix.

Still, I want to try.

My phone buzzes on the table.

**Shelby Asher Cross Liaison.**

*Fucking great.* Tammy probably slipped Shelby's contact into my phone herself. Part of her "Preparedness is professional foreplay" philosophy. Love how she saved her name. That Tammy, always so detailed.

I brace myself.

Whatever Shelby's about to say—it won't be half as loud as the voice in my head whispering Rorie's name.

> Heyyyyy Nolan :) Long time, no talk!

> Daddy Thatcher set up happy hour like he's your social secretary. Cute! 🫣

> Are we still on for next Thursday? Should I bring coloring books to keep your attention? ✏️

> Also… no RSVP yet for Crossfire? 😒 It's TOMORROW, my dude. Way to be fashionably late. LOL

> You do know the point is to show up, right?

> Let me know if I need to drop flashcards at your office to help you remember how career-making moments work 🙄

> xxoo Shelby 🩷🩷🩷🩷🩷🩷🩷

I groan and rub my temples. I hate shotgun texts. No structure. Just emojis and threats like she's throwing glitter at a forest fire.

Still. She's the gatekeeper to one of the biggest clients we've ever gone after. And the world doesn't stop just because I got my heart kicked in and my pride lit on fire.

I'm flattered by the sheer volume of your follow-ups. Somewhere between message four and the emoji assault, I nearly RSVP'd out of fear. I'll be there tomorrow. No need for flashcards or crayons—though if you DO bring coloring books, Rishi might actually stay past the first drink. Try not to spontaneously combust before then. -N

Once I step outside into the New York humidity, heat presses against my skin like judgment. People laugh. Horns blare. The city doesn't care if my head's a war zone.

It just keeps moving.

I should, too.

The streets blur as I walk. Asphalt sweat and car horns, scaffolding shadows, someone yelling at Siri across the intersection, another walking and talking while FaceTiming—it's all too loud. Too much. Like the world's at full volume, and I forgot how to turn down the dial.

I walk two more blocks and duck into my building. The doorman nods. I don't wait for the elevator. Fifteenth floor.

Inside my loft, everything's still where it shouldn't be. The space is lopsided without Chloe's things. One side of the closet looks like it's been robbed. I never realized how many clothes she had here until now.

The bookshelf has a blank spot where her picture used to live. The kitchen counter is missing that stupid ceramic utensil holder shaped like a swan. God, I hated that swan.

I grab a protein shake from the fridge, chug half of it, and stare at the cork board by my desk. It's covered in pitch material for a company named Bone Dust, specializing in gourmet coffee. Unique. Grim Reaper meets high-end coffee house. Think death-themed branding with beans dark enough to haunt your ancestors and caffeine strong enough to wake the dead.

And Rorie Adams.

I saw her name on the internal docket. I knew she was competing for this account before we even showed up at trivia. But it hits differently now. More like a collision course.

My phone buzzes again. Tammy.

> You owe me an answer on the Crossfire wardrobe. No, a navy button-down isn't "timeless," it's boring. Do better.

> Shelby wants a reply too. Be charming. But not like, predator charming. I beg you.

> It's handled.

> Handled? That's vague Bond villain energy. Please try to act like a man who hasn't emotionally shut down.

> Can you pull all correspondence related to Vanguard? Emails, texts, budgets—anything with a timestamp and a paper trail. Someone played fast and loose, and I want to know who.

> On it, Boss.

# CHAPTER 12
# BAD BITCH ENERGY: ACTIVATED

## RORIE

I'M SCROLLING through my messages, deleting the ones I don't need anymore when I come across **Unknown.**

It's been few days since my accidental mystery flirt, and I've officially dubbed it a *One Night Send*.

A flurry of clever texts. A deeply unnecessary emotional overshare. A digital vanishing act.

Classic.

No follow-up. No "hey, you were kind of great." No "sorry I rage-texted into the void like a rejected poetry major."

Just radio silence.

And that's fine.

Totally fine.

Absolutely, definitively, irreversibly…

Whatever.

I still catch myself glancing at my phone more often than I should —like I'm waiting for a text that clearly isn't coming from a number that may or may not have belonged to a heartbroken man with excellent punctuation.

But I can't afford to spiral tonight.

Tonight, I have to look like vengeance in heels.

*Asher Cross's party*—the event of the summer according to Jeremy— is not the kind of place you show up emotionally rumpled.

So I armor up.

Black satin dress, sculpted to stun. A neckline that could start rumors and end careers. Sleek silver heels that scream money and menace. Opera-length gloves for *drama*. A diamond bracelet that used to belong to my grandmother—and now belongs to my revenge arc.

Structured waves. Winged liner. Red lipstick with the emotional maturity of a blood oath.

By the time Maya texts that she's outside, I look like I've been summoned, not invited.

I grab my clutch and head down.

Jeremy's already sprawled across the back seat, one arm draped across his forehead "Finally," he says dramatically—then stops. Stares. Blinks. "Okay, wow. I was ready to roast you for being late, but now I'm just trying to remember how the English language works."

"A wise woman once said: if you can't be on time, at least be iconic." I slide in beside him and buckle my seatbelt.

"You're both. I'm terrified," he says, still staring. "You look like the love child of Ava Gardner and high-level vengeance. And I support that for you."

The Uber glides away from the curb, the city lights sliding across the windows like a prelude to something cinematic.

From the front seat, Maya twists and looks back at us like she's already regretting every life choice that led to this moment.

"Okay, but seriously—we need an escape plan if things go sideways. I am *not* getting stuck in a karaoke cult again."

Jeremy sighs. "Escape plan? Please. This isn't a heist. It's an Asher Cross party. If anything, we need a stunt coordinator and a SWAT team."

"I need a taser," Maya mutters. "Last time I got separated from you two at a party like this, I ended up in a makeshift cabana getting my shoulders rubbed by a guy named *Tré* who said we were cosmically aligned because we both bite string cheese instead of pulling it apart. He sent me unsolicited dick pics for months."

"Oh my God, Tré," Jeremy sighs wistfully. "He was fun. You're too judgmental."

"He used his *man bun* to mop up his drink, Jeremy."

"Eco-conscious king," he counters.

I laugh into my clutch. "Okay. Maya's right. We need rules. We can't just Rawdog this party."

"Rule one," Maya says immediately. "Keep Dr. Fiddlestorm the Third in your pants tonight, Jeremy. We don't need a repeat of the limoncello incident."

Jeremy looks personally attacked. "That was art."

"You got banned from an entire conference...for life."

"I *liberated* the vibe."

I snort. "Okay, rule two: No splitting up without texting the group. This is a party, not a horror movie."

Maya adds, straight-faced. "If anyone offers me shoulder rubs and starts a sentence with 'I'm actually an empath,' I'm setting something on fire."

"What's the signal for 'I'm being emotionally kidnapped?'" Jeremy snaps a selfie.

"Three winks," Maya answers.

"What if you just have dust or an eyelash in your eye?"

"Assume the worst first," Maya counters.

"Rule three," I add, "Do *not* drink anything that glows in the dark."

Offended, Jeremy places a hand over his heart. "That's targeting me specifically, and I'm choosing to ignore the shade."

"You went missing for four hours and came back with a feather boa and no eyebrows," Maya says flatly.

"I was reborn."

"In someone's hot tub?"

Jeremy just shrugs. "Fine. Rule four: make an entrance so legendary it gets me a modeling contract and you both a book deal."

Maya sighs. "That rule has *never* worked."

"It will. Tonight's the night," he says, already pulling out a pair of gold-rimmed sunglasses he fully intends to wear *indoors*. "We are the drama, babes."

I shake my head, smiling despite myself.

The butterflies are there—flickering just under my ribs—but they're quiet. Tamed. Because if tonight turns into a complete shit show... at least I'm not walking into it alone.

When we arrive at Asher's penthouse, the party's already in full swing. Music pulses from every angle, a low, seductive beat that vibrates through the soles of my heels and into my chest.

The rooftop patio spills over with people—model-gorgeous types with glowing cocktails in hand, voices pitched to be overheard, like everyone here is starring in their own highlight reel.

A waitress with a tray of bioluminescent drinks floats by. Maya declines the first two with a wrinkle of her nose, then caves on the third because it has "good" lighting.

"I swear," she mutters, eyeing the green liquid like it might start doing tricks. "If this has glitter in it, I'm blaming Jeremy."

"I hope it does," I say, deadpan. "Nothing says class like gastrointestinal sparkle."

Jeremy's already halfway to the bar, promising to return with something "transformative." We'll see.

Maya gets swept away by a guy in a linen shirt who greets her like an old war buddy. And just like that—I'm alone.

I step onto the patio, letting the warm air wrap around me like silk. The scent hits first—chlorine, coconut, maybe rum, definitely citrus.

The pool glows under string lights like it knows it's the main character. And overhead, the skyline of Manhattan glitters just beyond the railing, distant and unreachable.

This is a perfect little snow globe of anarchy. And I'm on the hunt.

I scan the crowd for power, or money, or just a decent set of shoulders to flirt with.

My stomach bottoms out. Nolan *"Fuck Me He Looks Good"* Rhodes, standing by the pool, half in shadow, half bathed in golden light like some tortured noir antihero. His tux is basically molded to his body, a black jacket framing broad shoulders, a crisp white shirt with bowtie. His hair is artfully tousled. And that scowl on his face is unapologetic.

I hate how hot he is.

I hate how much he knows it.

I hate that I can't stop looking at him.

His eyes rake across the party, detached and calculating until they land on me.

My breath stutters. The glass in my hand is suddenly too warm, like I've been holding it for hours.

Our gazes lock. Hold. Fuse.

A jolt of static zips through, low and slow, tightening muscle and breath. Heat coils at the base of my spine, molten and inconvenient. The air between us is tense, charged with that same sharp-edged electricity as the other night.

Nolan doesn't look away. Neither do I.

His lips tilt. Just barely. One side of his mouth curves up in the kind of smirk that should be illegal in several countries. It says everything he doesn't need to say: *I see you, sweetheart. I know exactly what you're thinking. And it's mutual.*

My jaw clenches. Nolan *"Make-Eye-Contact-and-I-Ovulate"* Rhodes doesn't know shit!

Especially not what I'm thinking.

Of all the broody bastards in this city, why did it have to be *him*?

Also… why is my stomach doing aerial stunts while my thighs try to pretend they're not interested?

I tilt my chin higher, force my lips into a neutral, cold, untouchable smile. His eyes flick down, like he's reading the heat beneath the frost.

God, his mouth. Why does it look like it was carved by temptation itself?

That mouth was on me. I lick my lips.

Fuck, he knows. He *knows* what my body's doing to me right now. And by the smug precision of that smile, he's enjoying every second of it.

I came here to make moves. Not mistakes.

I find Jeremy and Maya posted up by the fountain bar, taking synchronized shots.

"Big Stream is here," I say, setting my drink down with a little too much force.

They both swivel in unison then the rooftop erupts into a swell of gasps and camera flashes.

Because Asher Cross does not enter a room. He *arrives*.

A low thump shakes the patio floor then a *hiss* of smoke jets up from either side of the pool like we're in a Mission Impossible reboot. Lights flicker dramatically until a spotlight finds him.

Asher steps through the fog, aviator sunglasses, shirt half-unbuttoned, wind-whipped hair in a devil-may-care way. It's like he just stepped out of a storm and somehow still smells like leather and sexy man, not a strand of hair out of place, even though it looks like all of them are.

He's flanked by two men who I'm pretty sure were 3D printed from a protein shake commercial. One's got a champagne bottle in each hand. The other just ripped his shirt off and is now raging to absolutely no one.

A cheer breaks out. Someone yells, *"We love you, Asher!"*

I swear someone behind us starts crying.

"This isn't a party," Jeremy whispers. "It's a cult with better lighting."

And then, from the crowd's edge—moving like he belongs there, because of course he does—Nolan *"That Snake in the Grass"* Rhodes appears.

He's already at Asher's side, greeting him like they've done this a hundred times. Confident handshake, a lean-in to exchange a few low words. Nolan's expression is easy, controlled.

My stomach drops.

That's when it hits me.

Nolan isn't just here to smirk at me across the rooftop and make my insides curl.

He's here for the same damn reason I am.

To make a play for Asher Cross.

To win the client.

To win *my* client.

A woman with blonde hair, and heels she's going to regret later, floats nearby in a sparkly blazer, visibly glowing with approval. She's grinning manically like she just lit the match that's about to burn the whole place down.

Rishi and another guy who's styled like a Temu version of a Ken doll with a trust fund hover behind Nolan like background dancers waiting for their cue.

Nolan's gaze slithers down my spine before I even look.

That smirk of his is all slow-burn confidence and ruthless precision, saying:

*I warned you. Big Stream sets the pace.*

*Now watch me prove it.*

My fists clench at my sides.

Oh, no you fucking don't.

"Nolan Rhodes is with Asher Cross," I say.

Maya nearly chokes on her cocktail. "Seriously?"

"Yep." I turn to Jeremy, brows raised. "Did you do what I asked?"

A wicked grin blooms. "Girl, who you talking to? It's locked. It's loaded. It's Broadway with a garnish."

Tension in my shoulders loosens just enough to let a smirk slip out. Nolan *"Big Panties"* Rhodes thinks he's got this account in the bag. Cute. But if I've learned anything lately, it's that success doesn't wait for permission. You don't win by waiting your turn. You win by taking it.

And tonight I'm taking *everything.*

"I'm going over there," I announce.

Maya grips my arm. "Wait, Rorie. What's the actual plan here?"

"To make sure Asher Cross remembers *my* name. Not theirs."

Before she can say anything else, I glide toward the bar. The bartender spots me instantly, nodding like we're sharing a secret. Because we are.

"It's time," I say.

He grins. "Want a show?"

"Not just a show. A headline."

And just like that, the bar transforms. Dry ice spills over the counter, mist from a dream. Neon liquids swirl like galaxies. A suspended sugar garnish spins gently above a flickering flame.

Maya appears beside me, eyes wide. "What is happening?"

Jeremy sips his drink with a flourish. "Honey, you're witnessing *artistry.*"

The bartender sets down the tray, now branded with Asher's place-holder logo. A tray of magic and misrule in equal measure.

I pick up the lead glass—the Titan—and smile. It's not just a drink —it's *a revolution*.

Let's see how Nolan Rhodes likes being outplayed.

The moment I step onto the patio, the energy shifts. Nolan's gaze locks, and his spine stiffens.

*I'm coming for you, Rhodes.*

Asher Cross sits at a corner table, his posture loose, but there's a spark of attention in his eyes. He's used to people begging for it, but tonight, I'm not begging. I'm commanding.

He's a movie star and beach rebel in one—buttoned-up in crisp linen, but with perfect hair and that signature golden glow that screams I don't chase, I *choose*.

I carefully set the tray in front of him and sink into the seat across from him like I belong there.

He leans in, voice smooth, with a low husk of authority. "You certainly know how to make an entrance."

I smile. "You have no idea."

Nolan's glare practically burns through the glass, but I don't acknowledge him. Not yet.

Asher's attention dips to the drink. *The Titan* crackles softly, flames dancing across the sugared rim.

"And what exactly am I drinking?" he asks.

I settle back in my seat, crossing my legs and letting the anticipation build. "It's called *The Titan*. A bold blend of aged scotch, honeyed citrus, and a touch of smoked vanilla."

"And the other?"

"Oh, that's the real showstopper." I motion toward the suspended purple and blue sugar garnish above the second drink, still delicately spinning. "*The Mirage*. A cocktail so smooth it'll have you questioning whether it ever existed at all. We took inspiration from your most iconic roles. *Titan's Fall* was raw power. *Mirage at Midnight*...irresistible deception. You weren't just acting—you were branding emotion. And we captured that."

Asher's brow quirks.

"Imagine having the hottest, most iconic beverage brand on the market. Drinks served in every movie theater your blockbusters play in. Release parties. Not to mention households across the nation, bars in every city. You'd make millions. Maybe billions."

Nolan shifts in his seat, clearly about to interrupt, but Asher doesn't break eye contact with me. His interest is locked in place.

Keeping my posture poised, and my expression confident, I continue, "If you're serious about expanding your reach, then you don't need tired ideas. You need flash. You need execution. You need someone who doesn't hesitate to take a risk and make a statement." I gesture lightly toward the elaborate drinks between us. "You need the unexpected. The unforgettable. Something so absolutely *you*."

Asher nods thoughtfully, drumming his fingers against the table with a smile dancing across his full, very perfect, leading man lips. "And *you* can make that happen?"

I meet his smile with one of my own. "I already have. Take a look around. The moment these were placed in front of you, this party followed suit. Now, everyone is crowding the bar, demanding to drink exactly what Asher Cross is drinking."

His laugh is low and genuine. "I love it. What's your name?"

Before I can answer—

"Rorie Adams," Nolan cuts in, voice flat and sharp as a blade. "Brand Strategist at The Laurel Group. Be warned, Cross. She's pitching you a tacky product that comes a side of circus. It lacks class."

I want to yell, *You lack class!* But then that wouldn't be classy of me, would it?

Asher glances between us, clearly entertained. "That so?"

I give Asher a sweet smile. "I don't like to think of it as a pitch. I like to think of it as a *strategic acquisition*."

Nolan leans back, deceptively calm. But the twitch in his jaw, and how his thumb taps once, then stills, is all the tell I need. He's so mad right now. I fucking love it.

Asher lifts *The Titan* and takes a sip. He raises a brow.

Then he slides *The Mirage* toward me. "If I'm drinking, you're drinking. Fair's fair."

*He would give me the stronger one.*

I meet his gaze and raise the glass. It smells like dusk, floral, faintly sweet. The first sip is soft, almost shy. Velvet on the tongue. Lychee, white tea, and a whisper of lavender swirl together.

Then, just when you think you've got it—bam.

A snap of pink peppercorn. A tease of heat at the back of the throat.

Gone just as fast. A memory you're not sure ever really happened.

It's smooth, deceptive, dangerous in the way only beautiful things can be.

Exactly like the roles Asher built his empire on.

Exactly the kind of drink that earns its own cult following.

He leans in, eyes gleaming. "What's your story?"

"Just a girl, with some bad bitch energy, offering the man in front of her the world." I set my glass back on the tray. "Little birdies say you're ready to stretch your brand. I'm here to make sure you do it the right way."

"And why should I hire you?" he asks. "Besides the fact that you can make some very mean cocktails."

"Because I didn't wait for a meeting. I made one."

A beat of silence. Then Asher smiles.

"I do love it when a woman takes charge."

"I bet you do."

The tension is interrupted—again—by Nolan. "Rorie's audacious, I'll give her that."

Asher's gaze doesn't waver. "And what are you, Rhodes? Jealous?"

Nolan stiffens. His response is a shade too slow. And just like that, Asher clues in.

He raises his glass in a mock toast. "To competition. May the best win."

I lift mine. "Oh, I intend to."

Jeremy materializes like a magician, presenting a gold-foiled envelope. "The grand finale," he declares, handing it over.

Asher opens it slowly—inside, numbers, projections, profits. Proof of concept. He flips through the pages, brow lifted in interest.

Then he looks up at me. "Let's talk." He stands, extends a hand.

I rise, placing my hand in his. Nolan watches, silent and simmering. And I swear—just before I turn away—a new emotion flashes behind his eyes.

It isn't anger.

It's fear.

Fear that for once, someone else might win.

And Asher sees it too. His knowing grin deepens as if he's just found his new favorite game.

*Step right up ladies and gentleman. Welcome to my mother fucking circus.*

# CHAPTER 13
# YOU WIN. I WANT YOU.

NOLAN

RISHI WAS ALREADY deep in flirtation mode—schmoozing a band of women by the glass railing as though he's casting the next season of *The Bachelor: Penthouse Edition*.

I'd lost track of how many times he'd tried to loop me in, throwing out introductions. So far, he's attempted to get me hooked up with at least two of them.

But my eyes aren't on any of them.

They're on someone else entirely.

Jackson, ever the smug little shit, had plenty to say before I sent him packing. He paused on his way out just long enough to toss over his shoulder, "So let me get this straight—you let her steal your pitch, and now you're just... standing here, brooding over her?"

I ignored him.

Didn't stop him from doubling down on his way out. "Damn, man. First Chloe, now this. You just gonna keep handing your shit over to people?"

That one nearly earned him a fist to the dick. I let it slide. Barely. Because...public.

And yeah, he's not wrong. Here I am, doing exactly what he accused me of—watching a woman I have absolutely no business watching. Especially after she hijacked my moment with Asher Cross.

Rorie Adams.

She's dancing like the night was built for her, wild, radiant. She's in her element, hair flying, satin midnight-colored dress catching the light like it's being paid to. She twirls under Jeremy's arm, all teeth and laughter. This woman burns too bright and love it.

And I'm not the only one.

They're lining up, buzzards in tuxes. One douchebag in particular swoops in like he invented charm, palm sliding too confidently across her waist, fingers suspended in that narrow space between flirtation and a harassment charge.

Another leans in—*too close*—the guy adjusts his cufflinks more than he listens, whispering words that make her throw her head back in a laugh that lands like a punch to my gut.

She's working the room.

And I'm standing here, watching like a man who forgot how to move.

She laughs again. That laugh is a fucking weapon. Dazzling. Completely unearned by that guy. And a fucking problem. Because it makes my chest twist in ways I don't appreciate.

I should be halfway across the city, licking my wounds and pretending this night never happened.

But instead, I'm still here. Leaning against this balcony. Watching her.

Those glacial blue eyes flick up.

*Right at me.*

It's fast. A glance that barely lasts half a breath. Still hits like a body shot. Direct. Sharp. Right to the cock.

She knows I'm watching. She *likes* it.

Another guy moves in. Slower song. His hands drift to her hips. Rorie doesn't stop him. That gaze of hers darts back to me, quick, and searing, checking if I'm still paying attention.

I am.

I hate that I am.

Draining the last of my drink, ice rattles in the glass as I swirl it once, jaw set hard. I signal the waitress for another.

So, Rorie thinks I'm nothing but a snake in her grass, *strategically annihilating* her client list.

Which, if we're embracing metaphors—

I wouldn't mind slithering through *that* particular terrain.

Still...

The way she looks at me—warily, boldly, like I might bite—makes me feel seen in a way that doesn't come easy.

Yeah, I need to leave. Let her have this win. This stolen celebration.

Call it even. Walk away.

Then again, maybe she needs a reminder that the game isn't over. Hell, it's only getting interesting.

Rorie stumbles out of the crowd, breathless. Flushed cheeks. Kiss-damp lips. Hair a wreck, but gorgeous in its ruin.

Strands cling to her neck. She swipes them aside, scanning the patio.

Eyes lock on the drink in my hand. Not a word spoken. Just *that* look.

I offer it out.

She eyes the glass with suspicion, but there's heat behind it.

"What's that supposed to be?" She eyes me. "A peace offering?"

I shrug, gaze dragging over her. "More of a challenge."

Her brow arches. And then, before I can blink, she plucks the glass from my fingers and tips it back. One smooth, unapologetic swallow.

Her throat works. Her spine stays straight. She doesn't flinch.

Then—because she's a vixen with a vendetta—her tongue darts out, deliberate and slow, catching the stray drop on her bottom lip like it's her job to wreck me in high definition. She doesn't rush it. No. She drags it out, gaze flickering up just enough to confirm what I already know.

She's doing it on purpose.

And it's working.

That's it. That's the moment everything in me locks up. Spine, breath, thoughts. She flipped some internal kill switch.

My dick hardens instantly, aching with so much pressure, it's hard to breathe.

One lick. One look. *Jesus.* She's not even touching me, and I'm already gone for this girl.

"You're going to feel that tomorrow," I warn.

She scoffs. "Please. I've had worse nights and still made it to a breakfast meeting looking like a damn vision."

But I catch the micro-pause, the slight flutter in her lashes. Her hand clamps over her mouth. She's about to lose it.

I lift one brow. Surprisingly, she recovers.

"You were saying?" She tosses her hair and shoves the glass at me like it's beneath her.

I smirk, take a drink. "You are something else, Rorie Adams."

"Fuck yeah, I am. And you're not as clever as you think, Rhodes."

"Sure I am." I push off the railing. "Come with me."

Her arms cross, suspicious. "Where?"

I tilt my head toward the lounge end of the patio. Lanterns glow across cushioned seating, illuminating everything in a haze of soft light and shadows. The air smells like melting citronella, and something sweet like mango juice left out in the heat.

"You trying to get me alone?" she asks, voice low, a little lazy, a little lethal. Like she's sizing up a mark.

I shrug. "Figured I'd tempt fate."

Her gaze traces a calculated path over me—not curious, not impressed, just weighing outcomes. Wonder what kind of worst-case scenarios are playing out in that brilliant brain of hers. Probably best she doesn't know what's playing out in mine.

Rorie's lips curl. "Brave soul, risking going off with someone who fantasizes about your public downfall."

Stepping closer, her perfume reaches me, jasmine and a darker note that's going to haunt me later. "You fantasize about me, Adams?"

Her eyes flash, but I catch that tiny bit of awareness. It gives a man ideas.

"Don't flatter yourself," she says, smooth.

"Too late." I let the words hang, rough around the edges. "Now I'm stuck picturing what that fantasy looks like."

She arches a brow. "It ends with you humiliated in front of a live studio audience."

We're close enough I feel the warmth of her skin. "Am I naked in this humiliating fantasy of yours?"

She snorts, but her mouth twitches.

I don't let up.

"I guarantee, if I'm naked, the only thing getting ruined is your ability to think straight for the next week."

Her breath stutters. Just for a second.

"And that," I murmur, "would be very, very private."

"Cocky son of a bitch." Her tongue flicks out, wetting that pouty bottom lip. Then she turns and heads toward the lounge with a sway in her hips that makes my blood buzz.

And I follow.

Because I don't know if I'm walking into seduction or sabotage.

But I've never wanted both more.

The moment we step away from the noise, the city purrs beneath us. Cars crawl along the avenues, neon signs flicker like heartbeat monitors against high-rise glass. The party still pulses behind us, but here, it's different. Removed. Intimate.

Rorie drifts toward the edge of the terrace, resting her fingers on the wrought-iron railing. The wind lifts her hair in soft waves, tugging loose strands across her cheekbone. She tilts her head back, face tilted to the skyline. She's stealing this view and storing it somewhere only she'll ever go.

I watch her longer than I probably should.

Not just because she's beautiful. There's something deeper with her. She's all long lines and blue, fiery eyes, the kind of pretty that kicks you in the chest if you look too long. But it's more than that.

She's *real*. Untamed in a way Chloe never was. Chloe was a brandished feed. Rorie's the live stream. She's not trying to be watched— she just *is*. And that makes her impossible to look away from.

I track the way she lifts her hair off the back of her neck, exposing the slope of her shoulders, the edge of that black satin dress slipping just slightly lower with the movement. My cock stirs to life like it's got its own set of eyes.

God help me.

It's been days since Chloe detonated my life. Since I realized I was just a footnote in my own relationship. I should be dead inside. But standing here, watching Rorie, my body clearly didn't get the memo.

Don't mistake me.

I don't want a relationship.

I don't want intimacy.

But I want her.

And maybe it's the altitude, or the residual bourbon still moon-walking through my bloodstream, but I need air.

With the soft click of loosening silk, I slide my tie free and slip it into my pocket. My fingers move to the top buttons of my dress shirt, undo two, just enough to breathe. I roll the sleeves up my forearms, one then the other, exposing skin and tendon and just enough muscle to draw attention if someone should perhaps be looking.

She's looking.

Her eyes glance at my throat, down my chest, all the way to my forearms, and back again in that easy way that makes it feel accidental.

But it's not.

I catch it.

And so does she.

Because when our eyes meet, there's nothing accidental about the tension blooming between us.

I lift one brow. Just a fraction.

She doesn't flinch. Doesn't smile. "Okay, Rhodes." Her voice breaks through the fog in my head. "What's the plan? You got me over here. What do you want?"

A loaded question if I've ever heard one.

"Just a drink," I lie. "And a conversation."

The truth:

I want your legs draped over my shoulders while I learn every one of your sounds.

I want your moans stitched into my skin.

I want your thighs trembling, your hands clutching at me like I'm the only thing anchoring you to this fucking earth.

I want to see if you unravel as beautifully as I think you do.

And I want to split you open with my cock while I watch your mind go blank and my name spills from your lips.

But I can't tell her *any* of that.

So, I sip my drink instead, lean back, casual as hell, like my dick isn't straining against my zipper.

She arches a brow. "Well... start conversing."

I wave a server over, order her a water—because someone's got to keep this civil—and a refill of my bourbon. When the server returns, Rorie raises the water to her lips. She sips slow, and I watch her throat work. And this is the first time in my life that hydration looks like foreplay.

"How about a truce." I step a little closer.

She doesn't move. Doesn't flinch. She lets me come to her. Power play. I respect it.

"Just for tonight," I say.

"A truce?" She lifts a brow, skeptical. "You were just shooting the shit with the guy who controls the fate of the biggest branding deal of the year. You're here for the same reason I am. To win."

"Rorie—" Her name tastes good in my mouth.

"We're enemies."

"Not necessarily." I let my voice dip. "We could be something else."

Her eyes narrow, unamused. "Don't flirt your way out of this."

"I'm not." I shrug. "I respect you too much to lie."

She laughs once—dry, almost disbelieving. "Rich coming from the guy who's team took two of my clients and a prospective third."

"We've been over this. That wasn't personal."

"Not for you," she says, voice softer now.

And there it is.

A flash of honesty. Vulnerability wrapped in steel.

I take another slow step forward. There's less than a foot between us now. Enough for the tension to thrum, but not enough to touch.

I look down at her. Her chin is tilted, her expression defiant, but her breathing's changed—slightly faster, shallower.

"You know what I think?" I ask.

Her eyes challenge me. "What?"

"You're terrified you might actually like me."

She scoffs. "You're arrogant enough to believe that."

"Maybe. But I also think you're standing here instead of walking away."

She doesn't deny it.

Silence crackles between us, thick and pulsing. Her gaze moves to my mouth—quick, instinctual—and back.

I want to kiss her.

What would she taste like? Rich, heady, a little spicy, just like her neck.

I move just a breath closer. Her shoulder brushes my chest.

She doesn't back down.

Her voice drops low and sultry. "If you kiss me right now, I'll bite."

"Promise?"

"Yeah. You want soft or one that leaves a mark?"

I smirk. "Oh, definitely a mark."

Her steady eyes hold mine. "Good. I don't do soft."

*Christ.*

I lean in so our mouths hover, heat brushing heat.

A beat passes. Two.

"Am I interrupting?"

*Fuck me sideways.*

Asher Goddamn Cross.

She pulls back. Just an inch. But it might as well be a mile.

"Can I steal you away, Ms. Adams?"

My fists clench. Don't say yes. Don't *fucking* say yes.

"Absolutely." Her lips curve.

"Game's not over, Rhodes," she says, stepping away. "Try not to lose track of what you really want."

"I don't intend to."

She disappears into the darkened edge of the terrace with Asher, hips swaying.

And I just stand there.

Burning.

On my rooftop, I sink into a lounge chair, another bourbon in hand. I'm trying to outrun my own damn thoughts.

The amber in my glass catches the city glow, swirling in slow, lazy loops—like it's got nothing better to do than keep me company.

The city lights glitter—a thousand tiny promises, sirens wail in the distance, tires screech against pavement. It's all background noise, white static against what's inside my head.

I should be focused on damage control. On the account. On the moves I need to make to keep Big Stream ahead. But instead?

I'm thinking about *her*. The woman who walked into my night as a goddamn plot twist.

She didn't just throw off my game, she took the entire board and flipped it over, then poured herself a drink and dared me to keep up.

And I *can't* stop seeing her.

That mouth. That fire. Those fucking eyes—frost cold enough to burn. She looked at me like she already had me by the balls... and she absolutely does.

I tip my glass back and swipe open my phone.

LinkedIn

There she is.

*Rorie Adams. Brand Strategist. The Laurel Group.*

The headshot is businesslike, professional, but the smirk ruins the illusion. Her smile says, *I know something you don't. And I'm not telling you shit unless you impress me.*

Beneath that is a bullet-point warpath of wins. She's not just talented. She's *lethal*.

I flip over to Facebook. Locked tighter than a vault. Figures. But there are a few public photos.

In one, she's mid-laugh at some networking event, fingers curled around a glass of champagne. Another in front of a stack of books, head tilted, mouth curled, eyes lit with mischief. That grin is giving off the vibe: *I will flirt, fight, and emotionally destroy you all before brunch.*

Instagram is where things get personal.

Coffee shops. Skylines. Sunlight slanting through tall windows. There's a softness here, but no softness around *who* she is. Her world is controlled. Gorgeous, but distant.

No family. No holidays. No birthday brunches or sleepy-eyed selfies with a sibling.

Just her.

And one strange photo from three months ago—a weathered compass sitting in an open palm. No caption. No context. But it sticks with me.

The post isn't random. It means something.

What?

Estranged? Grieving? Guarded?

Whatever it is, she's not offering it freely. Which makes me want it even more.

I scrub a hand down my face and shake my head like that'll do a damn thing. I'm spiraling.

And I *like* it.

I flip open my texts. Pull up Tammy.

> I need a full work-up on Rorie Adams from The Laurel Group.

> Like CIA-level deep dive. Work history. Prior deals. Mentor names. If she owned a hamster in the third grade, I want its dental records.

> Also, find everything you can on Jackson. Go all the way back to his Pre-K days if you have to.

Already on it, Jason Bourne.

I toss the phone onto the side table, take another sip of bourbon, and stare out across the rooftops. A man smokes on a nearby balcony. A couple argues on another. Life moves on.

Like Chloe.

She's probably hanging curtains at Jackson's place right now, nesting in her new betrayal.

Me?

I'm here. Stalking a woman because she looked at me like I was both the enemy and the prize.

Is it too soon? Is it just my ego talking? Or is this the first thing that's made me feel *anything* since I caught Chloe cheating?

If it's going to be someone...

It might as well be Rorie Adams.

The bourbon sits heavy on my tongue as I drain the glass and set it aside. My skin itches with restless energy, my mind electric with the weight of those lips, her voice, her fucking eyes.

I shift in my chair, legs stretched out, but tension's coiled low in my gut now—tight, relentless.

I shouldn't.

But I want to.

Fuck, I *need* to.

Because this desire crawling through my veins is not casual. Not fleeting. It's focused.

And every inch of it is hers.

I reach down, palming myself through my joggers just to ease the ache. But the second my hand touches the hard length pressing against the fabric, I'm lost.

Her voice flashes in my head, low and sultry: "Good. I don't do soft."

Neither do I.

Slipping my hand beneath the waistband, I fist my cock, already thick and throbbing. I hiss through my teeth, head falling back against the chair as I stroke once.

The first image that comes to mind is her mouth. That smart, smug, wicked mouth wrapped around the tip, eyes locked on mine, daring me to lose control.

She would tease. She'd hum against me, tongue slick and slow, watching me twitch. Then she'd smirk when I begged.

My grip tightens.

Pumping lazily, I groan low as another image hits me: her legs spread out, her back arched, one hand tangled in my hair while I eat her pussy, deep and thorough.

"Tell me how you want it, Adams," I growl into the dark, half-laughing at myself.

"You want slow and filthy? Or hard and goddamn endless? Say the word. I'll destroy you sweet and oh so good."

My hips lift slightly, chasing the friction as heat floods through me, my body burning for a woman I'm not supposed to want, fantasizing about a mouth I've never kissed and a cunt I've never touched.

This shouldn't feel real.

But it does.

The way she tilted her chin tonight, challenging me. The heat in her eyes.

Fuck, I'm going to come.

I stroke harder now, eyes shut tight, stomach tensing.

*Rorie.* I don't say her name, but it echoes anyway—a curse and a prayer at the same time.

Pleasure tears through me in waves. Hot. Violent. Mind-numbing.

I bite down on the inside of my cheek to keep quiet as I spill over my hand, the aftermath leaving me panting in the chair, chest heaving, head foggy with satisfaction and something somewhat close to regret.

But it's not regret. Not really.

It's want. Need.

Raw, and brutal for a woman who's going to rip me apart.

I wipe my hand on my shirt and go inside to change into a new one. Afterwards, I reach for my phone again. Her profile lights up.

I stare at her smirking headshot for a second. Then I swipe away.

But it's too late.

She's already burrowed herself deep under my skin.

# CHAPTER 14
## DIGITAL WHIPLASH
### RORIE

I'M flat on my back, staring at the ceiling, the soft amber of the city slipping through my window and pooling across the floor. Everything is still.

Except me.

Because tonight…I was *on fire.*

I nailed it. Captivated Asher Cross. Had him hanging on every word. His gaze lit with curiosity. His interest palpable. That kind of spark doesn't happen every day.

I should be high on that win.

I should be basking in it.

But instead?

I'm twisted in sheets and contradictions.

Because Nolan Rhodes happened.

His voice still echoes in my mind, low and teasing, every syllable sliding over me like silk that bites. His dark eyes assessing, amused, they cut through me with precision, leaving sparks in their wake. That man's presence isn't something you brush off. It clings. Like smoke. Like heat. Like trouble you don't want to escape.

He was going to kiss me. I saw it in his eyes.

Worse—I wanted him to.

And I have no idea what the hell to do with that.

I want to blame the drinks. The high of the win. The rush of the night.

But deep down, I know it wasn't the alcohol.

It was him.

Oh, and that look he gave when Asher pulled me away. The barely contained fury, the tick in his jaw. He was holding back words—or something rougher. But it wasn't because he lost Asher's attention. It was because he lost mine.

Except Nolan's reading the wrong script. Asher isn't interested in me. In *that* way.

He's head-over-Hollywood-heels for Maya.

The man who jumps off buildings for a living and has fans screaming his name from balconies is completely, stupidly enamored with my best friend.

But because his entire career is built on the illusion of availability, he's got a team managing a fake relationship with Celeste Monroe—his current costar in the *Black Rhombus* spy thriller franchise and PR-approved girlfriend.

So what does a man like that do when he's too famous to flirt?

He recruits me to do it for him.

Apparently, dodging bullets is easier than facing the possibility of rejection from a pretty girl.

So, I'm his wingwoman. His go-between. His secret weapon in the war for Maya's heart. Or at the very least, a date.

Whose life is this? I'm playing matchmaker to a man whose face is printed on pillowcases. I even had to sign an NDA.

I say all this to say: Nolan, you had the wrong idea.

And that what stings more than it should. Because when he looked at me like he did—as if I was something worth fighting for—it felt good. Addictive.

And that's troubling.

I know what it's like to be wanted... right up until I'm not. Quinn taught me that. He loved me until I became inconvenient. Until my grief became something heavier than he wanted to help me carry.

One day I was his world. And the next, just a girl in his rearview mirror.

So yeah, Nolan's gaze? The slow drag of his eyes across my body, taking in the shape of me? That should've meant nothing. Because he means nothing.

Except it didn't.

Now I'm in my bed, skin flushed, legs restless, and heart hammering like I just ran a marathon barefoot in the rain.

And the image of Nolan *"Please Ruin Me"* Rhodes is burned behind my eyelids—a brand I never asked for.

But God, the way his tux hugged his body. It was custom built to destroy my last nerve. The open collar of his shirt once he took the tie off. He rolled his sleeves up over those toned forearms and I nearly came undone just standing there watching him do it.

His scent. Bourbon and cedar and something spicy. Sin in a bottle.

I press my thighs together, a desperate, useless attempt to ease the ache building inside me.

Damn it.

I hate him.

But I want to know exactly what those hands would do on my skin. I want his mouth on mine—dragging me in, backing me against a wall, pinning me there and consuming me all night.

Would he take his time?

Would he devour me?

Savor me?

A tremble courses through me.

I roll onto my side, but it only makes things worse. The friction of the sheets reminds me of what I don't have—of what I'm craving.

Of what I shouldn't be thinking about.

Nolan would be thorough. Precise. He wouldn't just touch me—he'd claim me.

My fingers trail down my stomach, hesitant, testing the heat that's been building since the second he looked at me like I was already his and said, "Oh, definitely a mark."

I want him.

I want that tension. That edge. That ache that won't quit until someone breaks.

I want to know how Nolan Rhodes takes apart a woman, piece by piece.

My hand dips beneath the hem of my sleep shirt, skin electric at the contact. I close my eyes, letting the fantasy rise to meet me.

Nolan's hands, his breath, his voice a low rasp against my neck.

What would he say to me?

*"Open for me, Rorie. I'm not stopping until I've got you dripping on my tongue and your taste burned into my fucking memory."*

My tongue flicks across my bottom lip, slow and instinctive, as my fingers trail lower, skimming over the slick heat between my thighs. I circle my clit once—twice—barely brushing it, a teasing rhythm that makes my breath catch.

A soft gasp escapes, swallowed by the quiet hush of my bedroom, every nerve strung tight with wanting.

His name flutters in the back of my throat, unspoken but pulsing in time with the ache building inside me. The image of him is carved into my mind—eyes dark with intent, mouth drifting over my skin, whispering filthy fucking things to me.

I drag my fingers through my wet heat, before easing two of them inside, slowly, the way I imagine he would. My hips tilt instinctively, a low moan spills from my lips. I begin to move as lazy, languid strokes make my body clench and my pulse stutter.

I pretend it's him—his hands, his fingers, the confident, hungry way I know he'd touch me. The way he'd look at me while doing it. He would want to ruin me slowly… see how long it took.

And I would love every filthy, perfect second.

Reaching the edge faster than I'd like to admit, a breathy whimper snags in my throat as my body arches, trembling against the wave crashing through me.

But when it's over—when the storm inside me settles—I'm not relieved.

I'm restless.

Because that wasn't enough.

Because it wasn't him.

And as I lie here, chest rising and falling in the hush of the aftermath, I realize the worst part.

I'm already aching for more of *him*.

And I *hate* it.

I sit up, my heart still fluttering, chest tight, the room cloaked in that hush only cities know—quiet but never still.

My phone buzzes. **Unknown Number.**

> You up? Or did I use up all your goodwill the other night?

I should ignore it.

I should.

But not responding feels wrong. Like leaving a story unfinished or quitting a puzzle with one piece missing.

> Didn't expect to hear from you again. No crisis tonight, I hope?

A long pause.

> Not yet. But the night's still young.

> It's 2am. Then again, you are the "drama after midnight" type.

> ☺

> Ugh an emoji. New rule! You only get three before I start judging your taste in memes.

> Only three? Why are you such a killer of fun?

> It's mercy. Trust me—four is a red flag.

> You're really going to keep count?

> Rules are rules. And that's #6.

> You just like bossing me around.

> You have an issue with authority?

I'm terrible at following rules.

> Figures. I bet you eat fries straight out of the
> bag before you even get home.

Who doesn't?

> People with self-control.

Sounds boring. Fun fact, fries are better when
stolen.

> That explains so much about you.

The tension in my chest eases slightly. Somehow, this stranger has a way of lighting up everything. Even when I'm dragging the weight of the world behind me. And the guilt of fantasizing about my sworn enemy.

So now that we're officially on round two, what
should I save you as in my contacts?

> You're assuming I'm into repeats.

What? I pop your accidental texting cherry,
and now you're playing hard to get?

> If that was my first time, I'd expect flowers, a
> parade, and a commemorative plaque.

A plaque, huh? High standards.

> Always. But don't get too cocky—you're not
> THAT memorable.

And yet…here you are, texting me again.

> Temporary lapse in judgment. Don't let it go to
> your head.

Too late. Now I'm officially your first AND second. I'm a trendsetter.

Or just lucky I'm bored. And have snacks.

Hey, whatever gets me the three-peat.

God help me—I'm smiling. This is ridiculous. But it's also... nice.

So, what should I save you as?

Oh, we're actually doing this?

Saving contact names? Uh, yeah.

No, pretending you didn't ghost me.

Ghost has such a negative annotation.

You vanished.

Strategic silence. Can I plead to Rule #4 and say I was sleeping?

Not a chance.

Not fair. You didn't text either. Pot. Kettle.

Touché.

Full confession...

Chloe came by. Took her things. I've been reflecting.

Oof. That's rough. Okay. I'll let it slide. This once.

Your kindness knows no bounds.

Believe me. I know.

So, smartass, let's try again. What's your
contact name?

Let's start with yours. Dashing Stranger?
Clueless Texter? Doll-Loving Carl?

How about Persistent Charmer?

Let's not get ahead of ourselves.

Fine. We'll trade. You name me, I name you.

Dangerous, but I'm in. You shall henceforth be
known as... Carl the Doll Collector. With the
pigtail girl emoji.

Offensive. Change it.

Nope. Actions have consequences. Next time,
don't ghost me, CARL.

You're a menace.

And you're stuck with me.

Lucky me. Also, you've used one emoji. Two
left.

Shaking my head, I type the name *Carl* into my contacts. It's dumb.
It's nothing. But it's also a tiny morsel of control in the storm of everything else.

Fine. But you're not getting off that easy either.

Yeah, yeah. I'm terrified.

What do you want to call me?

A lot of things. Mostly trouble.

Interesting coming from someone who started this mess.

Hey, I'm just trying to keep up with your chaotic energy.

Stop stalling. What's my name?

Textually Frustrated.

Hmmm...okay, fair.

Thought so.

So what's with the dramatic reappearance? One minute you're MIA, next minute you're texting me like nothing happened.

You ever hate someone?

That's random.

Is it?

A little. Most people don't text strangers deep questions at midnight. Also, you broke Rule #2.

Guilty. But I gave you fair warning...I've always had a thing for breaking rules... especially when they come with consequences. Should I be expecting punishment? Do I get to pick it?

Keep talking like that and I'm adding a Rule #7: No flirting with your therapist.

Too late. You should've led with that one.

Back to your question, Carl.

Hate is pretty harsh.

So no enemies? No one's labeled you
something you're not?

My fingers pause over the screen. Yeah. There is. A few.

People see what they want to see.

And what do they see when they look at you?

Depends who you ask.

What if I asked you?

That's a deep, personal question. And you've
already used your one.

Rule #2. No deep questions after midnight.
Got it.

Break it and I block you.

Ruthless.

Don't test me.

So what happens when people do you wrong?

Ignore them. Or make them regret it. I'm
flexible.

Ah, revenge. The professional's therapy.

With better outfits.

Sounds like you've mastered it.

> PhD in proving people wrong.

There's a pause. Longer this time.

> How long should someone wait... before moving on?

Oh. *Oh.*

> You are all over the board tonight, Carl. Are you like...asking me out?

> Carl: 😳

> Emoji two.

> You're skating close to the edge. First, you emotionally manipulate me with fry discourse, now this.

> Just exploring the line between rebounding and rediscovering.

> Completely subjective. Could be a day. A month. A year. Could be the moment you realize your ex is a garbage person and you dodged a flaming dumpster fire.

> A flaming dumpster fire?

> With raccoons.

> Um...okay.

> Just saying. The moment you realize someone's not your person, you're free. You don't owe them a grieving period.

> So, no rules.

> No rules. But there's one guideline.

Let me guess. No rebounds.

Careful rebounds. Nobody wants to be the
emotional stand-in.

But what if she's not a stand-in?

Then you already know the answer.

Another pause.

So, us? Friends?

Sure. But let's keep the mystery.

No real names. No pressure. Just drama,
sarcasm, and borderline emotional blackmail.

I do enjoy emotionally blackmailing you.

And I live for it.

But you're still Carl. 😊

Menace. And, emoji number two. We can skate
that line together.

Anytime.

# CHAPTER 15
# TEXTUALLY ACTIVE

## NOLAN

RISHI TEXTS ME.

> You. Me. Beer. Bad decisions. Let's go.

> You had me at beer. Lost me at bad decisions.

> C'mon. We'll call it "networking with benefits."

> Pretty sure I've already exceeded my weekly limit on both.

I'm sprawled across the couch, one leg over the armrest, the other stretched out, heel anchored to the coffee table like I've got nowhere else to be and nothing else to feel.

TV's on. Some voice narrates deep-sea horrors, creatures with translucent skin and rows of teeth meant to tear through silence. It's white noise. Background hum to an emotional tornado I've dressed up as relaxation.

Earlier today, I attempted to plot my comeback from the Rorie Adams storm, in which she stole the room, and made off with my deal like it was her divine right. And looked damn good doing it too.

What's worse than losing Asher's attention?

Wanting her.

And wanting to undo that zipper on her fire-breathing confidence and see what's underneath.

So, to distract myself from the truth throbbing between my legs, I scroll. Mindless, numbing.

Until karma shows up in the form of Chloe and Jackson, filtered to perfection. Her smile is syrupy, head tipped into his chest. His hand stakes a claim low on her back, thumb resting just shy of skin. Golden hour renders their betrayal beautiful. Marketable.

The caption reads: *Sunshine & Jax: unstoppable together.*

I grit my teeth.

Forgot to block her. Rookie move.

I tap through her stories, not because I care. Because I'm human. Because curiosity's a parasite and I'm the willing host.

Last night—a bar. She's laughing into her glass. Jackson watches her like he's discovered gravity and decided to orbit.

Guess I know where he disappeared to after I threw him out of Asher's penthouse.

Figures. Chloe never did like loose ends. She just cuts them.

She looks happy. Not the brittle, fake kind. Actual joy. That part cuts deeper than the cheating ever did. It's not that I want her back. It's the illusion. The version of Chloe I built in my head. The one who never existed outside of my hopes.

I toss my phone onto the cushion, stare at the ceiling like it might offer a new perspective.

This apartment is too still. The silence here creeps in through the cracks. Dismantles. Unpacks. Reminds me I was stupid enough to love someone who never actually saw me.

I don't miss Chloe.

I miss believing she did.

I press a palm to my face, exhaling slow, then shut off the TV.

See, guys don't melt down to sad indie soundtracks and tubs of ice cream.

We bench press it.

Bury it under bourbon.

Fuck it away.

Or we distract ourselves so hard it nearly becomes religion.

That's the male strategy. Sort it into categories, label the pain, file it, and stack it behind our pride.

Me? I've tried them all.

Yes, I'm counting Rorie Adams. I've mentally fucked her more times than I can count in the last few days.

I don't want to want her.

But I do.

I want her on my lap, my mouth, my hand, everywhere. When she's tearing into me with those sharp-as-hell words and looking like sin in stilettos, I crumble.

And fuck, it's been too long since I've tasted anything that fucking delicious.

But she's not a one-night detour.

Rorie Adams is a woman you memorize in phases. Slow. Intentional. She's not for the careless or the cowards.

Which makes this complicated.

Because I'm still bleeding from Chloe in ways I haven't stitched shut. Still bristling at the idea of letting anyone close enough to bruise me again. And Rorie? She wouldn't bruise. She'd brand.

Her type of fire makes you beg to burn.

I'm not ready for her.

But that hasn't stopped the wanting.

I drag myself off the couch and grab a bottle of water from the fridge, chugging half like it might douse whatever hell is trying to light up inside me again.

It doesn't work.

I'm horny as hell, lonelier than I care to admit, and I miss the weight of a woman against me. Heat and curves and breath that isn't mine. Something solid. Human.

I need a distraction.

The best kind.

I tap my screen.

**Textually Frustrated.**

Thumbing through our texts, a smirk curls up my mouth. I don't know what we are. Friends. Something else. It doesn't matter. It's honest. It's light. And for now, it's enough.

I need a distraction.

Bad day?

It's a woman.

Tell me everything. I've got popcorn and questionable morals.

She's smart. Competitive. Brilliant. And hot in this slow-burn, totally-ruin-your-life way.

Also, I'm fairly certain she wants to bury me alive.

So naturally you're into her.

Of course. But she's deemed us enemies.

Spicy.

She hates me. Like... with her whole soul.

Mmm. A classic. Go on.

She's also sexy as hell.

I can't stop thinking about how she might taste.

Hold up.

Back up.

Did you say taste?

...

Are we talking metaphorically tasted? Or have her thighs on your shoulders and your tongue halfway to heaven taste?

Let's just say she's been on my mind.

Okay wow.

I'm gonna need a minute.

You're supposed to be talking me off the ledge, giving me a reason to NOT knock on her door and make her hate me a little less.

You're the one that opened the gates of horny hell. Give me a second to process.

Tell me I'm an idiot. That she's off-limits. That I need to walk away.

You're an idiot.

She's off-limits.

You need to walk away.

But you won't.

No.

No. I won't.

# CHAPTER 16

# THE BREW BEFORE THE STORM

RORIE

I bring news from the edge of civilization. I have survived. Barely.

JEREMY. WHAT. We've been trying to reach you all weekend. Maya was two hours from hiring a psychic and a sniffer dog.

I apologize for my silence. I've been detained by the Canadian government. Dr. Fiddlestorm III may or may not be listed as a public threat in Ontario.

WHAT DID YOU DO?

Technically? Nothing illegal. Emotionally? Several things I'm not proud of. One involved a karaoke machine, a goose, and a maple syrup martini. Don't ask.

You promised no more international discord.

You promised to stop judging my self-expression. Here we are. Tell Maya I love her and that customs confiscated my dignity.

You're buying lattes and explaining everything.
Also, she's still mad.

Fair. I'll bring emotional support pastries.

THE ESPRESSO MACHINE shrieks like it's dying a violent, overly dramatic death.

I scowl down at it. "If you keep this up, I swear to God, I will replace you with a French press and some emotional resilience."

Maya leans against the counter, arms folded, sipping her latte with the grace of someone who has never known struggle. "You realize if that thing had feelings, it would have already filed a hostile work complaint against you, right?"

I jab the reset button, punishing it. The shrieking stops, replaced by a mocking silence that's somehow worse. "It deserves it. It's sabotaging my entire existence."

She quirks a brow. "You mean your under-caffeinated meltdown, or the one where your bun is auditioning to be a sad houseplant?"

My fingers fiddle with said bun, which is barely clinging to life. "Stop judging me."

Maya gives me a once-over, lips twitching. She's trying not to laugh. Good for her in her effortlessly casual outfit of jeans, super cute fitted blazer, and tousled blonde waves that all belong in a lifestyle blog.

Meanwhile, I'm giving off "unhinged barista" vibes.

She sets her drink down. "Alright. Spill. You're losing it and trying to pass it off as espresso rage. What's really going on?"

I sigh and take a too-long sip of coffee that is both scalding and underwhelming. "Bone Dust is threatening to pull out of the campaign. Apparently, it 'lacks emotional resonance.' Which, as you know, is corporate for 'we have no idea what we want, but we'd like to blame someone.'"

"Oof." She winces. "Want me to draft an email that politely tells them to shove it?"

"As satisfying as that would be, I don't think Laurel would appreciate a lawsuit before lunch."

"Okay, but just say the word. My middle name is Petty. With a capital P," she says, popping the "P."

Before I can answer, my phone buzzes. **Laurel.**

**Meeting. My office.**

I pale.

Maya leans in. "Oh no. Is it...?"

I hold up the screen. "It's about the Asher Cross thing. She's going to skin me alive."

"She'll get over it," Maya says quickly. "You landed the hottest man on earth's attention and impressed half the industry. You should be getting a bonus."

"Yeah? Well, I got a flaming-hot email thread that included the phrases 'reckless,' 'not a PR stunt,' and my personal favorite— 'laughing stock.'"

Maya smirks. "At least you got a *reaction*. That's better than half the firm."

I force a laugh, the nerves still rattling like dice in my chest.

"Hey." Her voice softens. "You've got this. You were a badass. Asher was into it. Laurel will calm down. Just... own it."

Nodding, I slowly exhale. "Yeah. Okay. Enough about my potential public execution. Let's talk about you and your stalker."

Her brows knit. "Stalker?"

"Asher Cross," I say, sing-song sweet. "Six-foot-plus, devastating jawline, and currently asking me more questions about you than TMZ."

Maya groans. "There is no *me* and Asher Cross."

"Yet."

She looks around to make sure we're alone and replies in a low tone. "I'm serious, Rorie. I don't know if I could handle someone like that. The scrutiny. The flashing cameras. I'd end up hiding in a supply closet for the rest of my life."

"Babe," I say, softening, "you *do not* belong in a supply closet. You belong at the center of the room. The center of someone's world."

She scoffs.

"I'm serious." I lean forward. "When was the last time you let something happen? No five-year plan. No exit strategy. Just... mess and magic."

She doesn't answer right away. Just sips her coffee and looks out the window like the answer's buried somewhere in the skyline.

Finally, she says, "It's not that easy."

"Nothing worth doing ever is."

Her eyes cut to mine, unsure.

So I reach into my back pocket and pull out the sleek black metal card. It catches the overhead light as I slide it across the counter, face-down.

Maya blinks at it. "What's that?"

"Asher's personal number. Direct. No handlers. No assistants. No publicists. Just him."

She stares at it as though it might detonate.

"Maya," I say gently. "No pressure. No games. Just... see what happens."

Her hand hovers over the card like it's burning. Her lips part, but she doesn't respond. Instead, she sighs, running a hand through her hair. "You're really pushing this, aren't you?"

"Only because you deserve someone who looks at you like you're the best damn thing in the room."

She huffs out a laugh. "And what about you? When are you going to take your own advice?"

I frown. "What do you mean?"

She rolls her eyes. "Rorie, a guy has never looked at a girl the way *Nolan Rhodes* has looked at you literally every night we've run into him."

I laugh, but there's a tightness in my chest at the mention of Nolan. "Yes they have."

Maya lifts a brow.

I hold her gaze. "Asher Cross looks at *you* like that."

Her mouth opens, then closes. "That's—"

"Unexpected? Yeah, well, you should let yourself be surprised for once."

Maya slides the card off the counter and her lips twitch.

"Good girl."

My grip tightens around the lukewarm coffee as I turn for the door. I've got a meeting to survive.

Laurel doesn't bother with pleasantries.

The moment I step into her office, she gestures to the chair across from her with the kind of pointed efficiency that makes me brace for a verbal beating. I've already prepared three different apology speeches and mentally drafted my resignation—just in case.

But instead of the tight-lipped scowl I expected, she's smiling.

No—beaming.

"Well, if it isn't the woman of the hour," she says, folding her hands over her crossed knee. "Tell me, Rorie... do you always make a habit of rewriting the rules mid-game?"

I blink, caught completely off guard. "Uh... depends. How mad are we talking?"

She lets out a genuine laugh—an actual, from-the-gut laugh—and leans back in her chair like we're not boss and almost-fired strategist, but two old friends catching up over brunch. Which, technically, we sort of are, if you count that she used to steal my mom's hairbrush in college and once taught me how to use a tampon in the back of a Chili's.

"Mad?" she repeats. "Try impressed. Shelby Davidson called me this morning. Personally."

"She called you?" I ask, pulse accelerating.

"Oh, she did," Laurel says, her smile only growing. "And she wasn't just impressed—she was *ecstatic*. Wants you front and center at their Pitchpocalypse for Asher's upcoming brand expansion. We leave in a month."

The words hit me like a freight train.

"A *what*?" I choke out. "Wait—Pitchpocalypse? A month?"

"Yes!" Laurel's hands clap together, her rings flashing. "Asher's hosting an exclusive, invite-only pitch event at his private island. *The White Thorn*. Five firms will compete for his brand. One will win it. And thanks to your little cocktail performance, we're officially invited."

I stare at her, barely processing.

This is big. Like, *career-defining* big. A once-in-a-lifetime, holy-fuck-ing-shit-who-even-gets-these-opportunities kind of big.

And all I can think is:

Nolan. Rhodes.

"Do we know who else was invited?"

"So far?" Laurel shrugs. "Just us. But I'd bet my Bentley Big Stream's on the list."

Of course they are.

"I'll be ready," I say, channeling a confidence I'm not quite sure I possess yet.

Laurel beams again. But this time it's not the polished smile she wears in boardrooms, and meetings like this. It's gentler. Warmer. The one that slips past her armor and actually means something.

"I know you will be," she says. "Now, go do that brainstorming thing you do so well."

I start to turn, but she stops me with a quieter voice.

"And Rorie?"

I pause in the doorway, glancing back.

"Don't make me regret betting on you." She keeps it light, but her eyes settle on me with quiet conviction. Pride, pressure, and something almost protective swims inside them.

I offer a grin, just shy of cocky. "No pressure."

Laurel exhales a short laugh, then adds, almost as an afterthought, but not really, "Your parents would be proud, you know."

She winks and my throat tightens. I don't say anything—just nod once before stepping out, my heartbeat suddenly louder than it was a minute ago.

# CHAPTER 17
# MONDAYS ARE FOR MISTAKES

## NOLAN

MONDAY SHOULDN'T SUCK this much.

But the second I step into the office and spot Jackson already there —arms crossed, legs sprawled, that smug fucking smirk like he spent all morning fine-tuning it in the mirror—I know today's out for blood.

No coffee. No peace. Just his stupid face.

"You're in early," I say as I brush past Jackson, already regretting showing up at all.

"And you look like shit."

I pause mid-stride. Grit my teeth.

Breathe.

Keep walking.

I hit my office and drop into my chair with a groan, raking a hand over my jaw. The weekend is still stuck to me, wrapped around my brain like static. Rorie's voice, Rorie's lips, Rorie's—

Nope. Not going there.

Jackson appears again, of course. The man is a housefly with a trust fund and too much free time. He plants himself in the guest chair across from me because of course he does.

"Is there something you want?" I ask, leveling him with a look. "Besides to be a walking HR complaint?"

He leans back, grinning. "Thatcher wants to see you. About the Cross party."

My stomach dips, just slightly. I can do damage control in my sleep, but Thatcher?

He's not exactly known for handing out grace. And I know that party wasn't a clean win. Rorie hijacked everything with style, sass, and a damn sparkler.

And Asher ate it up.

"I've got drinks with Shelby this week," I say. "I'm not worried."

Jackson raises an eyebrow. "Saturday was bad, Nolan. She sabotaged us."

"No, she one-upped us." I grab my mouse and click through unread emails, trying to ignore the way my jaw tightens.

But I can't, not when I'm already carrying too much tension. And especially not when I'm fairly certain Jackson's the reason for Rorie's anger toward me slash us. Since he's the one dishing out the *strategic flexibility* talk.

"Speaking of sabotage," I say. "Did you undercut another firm's rates by thirty percent just to land a deal?"

Jackson blinks. Shrugs. "What if I did?"

"How'd you know what they were offering?"

His smirk sharpens. "I'm playing the game."

"Yeah, playing fast and loose with predatory pricing and dragging the entire firm into a legal shitstorm." I lean in. "That kind of stunt puts us on the radar. We start violating antitrust laws, and it's not just dirty—it's *dumb*."

He scoffs, all confidence and recklessness. "Relax. It's less than a handful of clients. Besides, that kind of thing barely sticks in court. You know that. And hey, if the other guys wanted to win, they should've been smarter."

*Jesus Christ.*

"And I'm the one getting dragged into Thatcher's office?" I snap. "Unbelievable."

Jackson checks his watch, already bored. "Hey, if it makes you feel better, I'm ready to watch him rip you a new one. Front row seat."

My phone buzzes, screen lighting up with a new message from **Textually Frustrated.**

And because the universe has a sense of humor, Jackson's nosy little eyes catch the notification. His gaze bounces back to me with mock horror.

"Textually Frustrated?" he repeats, like he's just witnessed a crime. "That's got to be the saddest, thirstiest pet name I've ever heard. You sexting your therapist now?"

"Get out before I forward your browser history to IT."

He rises slowly, chuckling. "Love our little chats, buddy."

The door clicks shut behind him.

Finally. Silence.

Did you taste test your nemesis yet?

> Starting strong. No hello, no how's your mental health—just straight for the throat.

Or lower. I figured you'd appreciate the direct approach.

> Unfortunately, no.

> No enemy dessert.

> No sampling.

> I'm on a strict sarcasm and self-loathing diet.

Tragic. You seemed so... enthusiastic last time.

> My enthusiasm has consequences.

> Now I'm nursing a hangover made of guilt, tension, and the ghost of her skin.

The ghost of her skin should be the name of your band.

> Or my memoir.

You're not still texting her though, right?

Nope. No texting. I don't even have her
number.

Just daydreams. Nightmares. Flashbacks.

All very healthy.

Carl, I say this with affection—you're a
disaster.

But I mean that in a good way.

Appreciate it.

Tell me again how you're the emotionally well-
adjusted one in this friendship?

I never claimed that. I'm just less obvious
about spiraling.

So what you're saying is... we're equally crazy,
just aesthetically different?

Exactly. You spiral in drunk rage texts. I spiral
in leggings and retail therapy.

And somehow we meet in the middle. Text
purgatory.

Where all good banter lives. And occasionally
dies when you get too horny to function.

One time.

And here you are, pretending she didn't set
your brain on fire with one look?

She's inconvenient as hell. Especially when
she shows up in a dress that murders logic on
sight.

Oof. Hot?

TOO hot. And she's in my head again. Thanks for that!

Want me to save you from yourself again?

Yes. Desperately.

Hit me with something distracting.

Pick your poison:

A...Ridiculous hypotheticals

B...Unhinged flirting

C...Emotional vulnerability disguised as sarcasm

Dealer's choice.

But let's start with C.

Since you're the reigning queen of unsolicited opinions, I need some serious advice about my dilemma.

Oh, I live for this. Proceed.

BTW is this girl the reason why you asked me if I ever hated anyone?

Perhaps.

How did it all start? Workplace thing? Did you insult her outfit? Park in her spot? Run over her dog?

No dogs were harmed. But yes, work-adjacent. Let's call it... professionally adversarial foreplay.

I'm listening.

I don't know what to do.

Well, start by deciding what your goal is. You trying to win her over or just mess with her until she hits you with a stapler?

That's the issue. I don't know.

Please. You do know. You just don't want to admit it because admitting it scares the fuck out of you.

O Enlightened One!

Answer this...

Do you want to get to know her? Understand her? Or just nail her and call it character development?

If you want to get to know her, and or understand her, then that's dangerous.

Dangerous how?

Because once you understand someone... you can't pretend they don't matter anymore.

...

Hit a nerve, huh?

Possibly.

If you just wanted to bang her, you wouldn't be texting me, asking questions you already know the answer to. You'd be working on your playbook. But you're not. You're hesitating.

Because she's so deep under your skin, she's practically part of your nervous system. And the second you touch her, REALLY touch her, you know damn well she won't be easy to forget.

So yeah. Keep pretending.

Just don't come crying to me when your whole emotional equilibrium goes up in flames.

> Or you're wrong, and I do just want to screw her.

Mkay.

Carl, honey...she's going to get under your armor, and when she does, she won't just mess with you—she'll annihilate you.

And you know it.

> You assume a lot about me.

I haven't been wrong yet.

> You're annoying.

It's my charm. But you're vulnerable right now.

> So what's the play then?

That depends.

Do you want to win AGAINST her?

Or win HER?

Those are very different games, Romeo.

I stare at the screen. Her words hit like a steel-toed boot to the ego. Win against her or win her?

Shit.

> That's a heavy question for a guy who just
> wanted to flirt and vent.

> I don't do half-assed advice. I'm a full-ass
> commitment.

Before I cross the threshold toward Thatcher's office, I double back and jab my head into the bullpen. "Rishi."

He looks up from his monitor, chewing the end of a pen. "What's up?" he asks, already wary.

"Thatcher. Now."

Rishi doesn't ask questions. Just grabs his notebook, mutters something to the intern about covering his meeting, and falls in step beside me.

"On a scale of one to scorched earth, how bad is this?" he asks under his breath as we approach the office.

"Let's just say Jackson's already been in there, and I'd bet half my net worth he poured gasoline on the entire conversation before striking a match."

Rishi sighs. "Fantastic. Love a Monday roast."

Thatcher's door is already cracked open like an invitation to hell when Rishi and I arrive. We pause outside of it.

I adjust my cuffs like and then ask. "Ready?"

"No," he deadpans. "But I did sign that death waiver when I took this job, so…"

"A boutique firm." Thatcher's voice slices through the air before I even step inside. He's standing behind his desk, arms folded, expression carved from stone. "A goddamn boutique firm outplayed us?"

Okay. So *not* in the mood for nuance.

I stay quiet. Let him get it all out. Jumping in now would be like trying to reason with a grizzly mid-mauling.

His eyes volley between me and Rishi like we're joint disappointments, but only one of us deserves the title.

"Do you two have *any* idea how bad this looks?"

Jackson—who's leaning so far back in his chair he might as well be on a beach—answers for us. "Pretty bad?"

My head whips toward him. I narrow my eyes, hoping they could shoot daggers if I squint hard enough.

Thatcher's already moving on. "Cross is hosting a pitch event at his private island in a month. Invite-only. Five firms. Three invites have already gone out. If we don't get one..." He pauses, just long enough to twist the knife. "Don't worry about making partner, Nolan. Worry about finding a new job."

I don't blink. Don't flinch.

Jackson lets out a low whistle like we're discussing fantasy football standings, not my damn livelihood. "High stakes."

The urge to throttle him rises like bile.

"I have a plan," I say, keeping my voice calm.

Thatcher leans in. "Then make it work. Fast."

"I will. But I need to talk to you about—"

He slices a hand through the air. "Don't want to hear it. Just fix it."

"I—"

"No excuses. No explanations. Just. Results." Every word lands like a hammer.

I clamp my jaw shut. Press my tongue to the roof of my mouth before I say something I'll regret. Because I *will* circle back to this conversation. But not with Jackson in the room feeding him lazy smirks and frat-boy shrugs.

Thatcher waves us off like we're crumbs on his desk.

The second we're out the door, Jackson claps me on the back like we just wrapped up a casual lunch. "Well, *that* was fun."

I brush him off. "Shut up."

He grins. "If he'd had a fireplace behind him? Full villain monologue."

"Yeah, and somehow you walked out without a scratch."

"Family perks," Rishi says beside me.

Jackson winks. "Also, unlike you, I don't swing for the fences when the game's already lost."

My glare could melt steel. "You're the one who *sabotaged* the game."

"Relax. It was just a little price adjustment."

"A thirty percent drop is not a 'little' anything."

"Wait, what?" Rishi clues in now. "Who approved that?"

Jackson leans in, eyes gleaming. "I did. And if it helps us win? I guess I'll be the villain."

"You already are."

Tammy appears before I can murder him in cold blood, a flash drive clutched in her hands like it's radioactive. "Rorie Report," she says, tone flat.

Jackson cranes his neck to peek. "Nice. A dossier on your crush. Adorable."

"Go make yourself useful, Jackson," I mutter, snatching the drive. "Rishi I'll brief you on everything later."

He nods, walks back toward his office. Jackson smirks then follows suit.

Once they're gone, I motion Tammy into my office and shut the door.

She folds her arms. "You sure about this?"

I raise a brow. "It's just competitor research."

She studies me for a beat. "If this is just strategy… why does it feel like stalking?"

I don't answer. I can't. Not with her staring straight through the suit and the ego and down to whatever messy, twisted motive is actually driving me.

"I've seen what's in that file, Nolan." Her voice softens. "It's not just LinkedIn summaries and old yearbook photos. There's real shit in there. Her *life*. You open it, you're not just learning about her. You're taking it. Without permission."

I flip the drive around my fingers, contemplating.

She gives me one last look. "You wanna win this? Fine. But don't forget, Rorie Adams isn't a stepping stone. She's a person. Don't treat her like a checkbox."

And then she leaves, the soft *click* of the door landing louder than it should.

I stare at the small stick. Then I slide it into my computer, open the documents, and stop.

*What am I doing?*

I yank the flash drive out and shove it into the front pocket of my briefcase.

Out of sight. Out of mind.

Kind of.

My phone buzzes. A new notification.

**Clinic Results: Confidential**
**View Your Lab Report.**

I click it open before I can overthink it.

Negative.

*Thank fuck.*

Sinking back into my chair, heart racing, I scrub a hand over my face.

One disaster averted.

Now to figure out how to survive the next thirty days—and, somehow, *not* let Rorie Adams get too much further under my skin.

My screen barely dims before a new notification flashes across it.

**Internal Memo**
**Client Pitch Audit: Vanguard**
**Subject: Acquisition Summary**

When I swipe it open, the blood drains from my face.

The attached report outlines the full acquisition history on the Vanguard deal. There it is in black and white:

*Proposal submitted by Jackson Butler.*

*Strategic Rate Drop: Approved*

Approved... by *Thatcher*?

I blink. Re-read it. Then again. My stomach turns.

So that's it?

He knew. He fucking knew.

*Uncle's* blessing. He let Jackson undercut the deal. Let him screw The Laurel Group over. And now they've got me out here defending our brand like some idiot golden retriever while they feed the snake accounts under the table.

My hands tighten into fists, jaw locking so hard it aches.

> Carl, I'm having a MOMENT here. I just landed the opportunity of a lifetime. Like HUGE. And I'm excited. And terrified. Mostly terrified. But also excited. You get it.

> Congrats. That's great.

I stare at the message. Dry. Cold. The emotional equivalent of a wet sock.

> Wow, Mr. Enthusiasm. What's with the buzzkill energy?

> Nothing. Just dealing with something.

> That's vague. Cryptic. Suspicious. Are you in a basement somewhere rearranging your dolls?

> No. Just not in the mood right now.

> Well, aren't you a ray of fucking sunshine today? Since when did you become King of the Cold Shoulder?

> Since five minutes ago. I just need to be in my own head right now.

The words come out more severe than I mean them to. But I don't delete. Don't soften. Not today.

> Look, I get it. I do. If it's about that girl let me do what I'm good at.

> It's not about the fucking girl!

> Fine. Fuck. Okay.

> Congrats on whatever it is. I just don't have time for this right now.

> We'll talk later.

Three seconds. Five. Ten.

> Don't bother. You've made it pretty clear I'm just another thing you don't have time for.

I pinch the bridge of my nose. I'm being a complete dick. But I can't stop the swirling emotions inside me right now.

Not when betrayal's still bleeding at my heels and Jackson's smirk is chewing holes through my composure.

> What do you expect?

> Oh, I don't know... a little less brooding asshole, and a little more human decency?

A dry laugh escapes me. It's not humor—it's habit. I can practically hear the edge in her voice, even through text. The way she's disappointed but covering it with sarcasm.

Because that's what we do. We cover. We dodge. We hide behind clever words.

And right now, I just built a whole damn wall.

And shut her out behind it.

Jeremy and I are going to a 3D printing art class. Tonight. 7PM. Be there or be artistically underdeveloped.

YASSSSS, join us! We're making sculptures that speak to the soul. Mine might have abs. And a tail. TBD.

I don't even want to IMAGINE what Jeremy's soul sculpture looks like.

His will probably something with fangs and commitment issues.

You say that like it's a bad thing. Art is pain. And also a little horny.

I'm staying in tonight. Catch you weirdos on the flip side.

Coward. Respectfully, J

You're missing out. This is how geniuses are born.

Have fun.

MUNCAN FOOD CORP smells like smoked tradition and deli-born pride. Salt and spice drift in the air, clinging to walls, shelves, skin. One breath, and you know exactly where you are: somewhere sacred, savory, and unapologetically cured.

A slicer whirs. A lady hassles a worker over the wrong salami. I breathe it all in. Aromatherapy for the emotionally damaged.

I don't come often, only when I'm in the mood to pretend I'm building a charcuterie board for guests I don't have. Today is one of those days. An edible distraction is the thing that might shut up the mental monologue titled: *Why Carl Suddenly Turned Into a Brooding, Dickhead.*

I grab a wedge of manchego and drop it into my basket with unnecessary force, follow with a sleeve of fig crackers I absolutely do not need. Self-control is not on the menu.

More people enter the store. I ignore them. I'm too busy inspecting a jar of imported mustard I'll never open when I round the corner and stop cold.

Nolan *"Why-the-Fuck-Are-You-in-My-Meat-Market"* Rhodes stands in front of the glass case like it's the Louvre, wearing shorts and a tshirt. The backward baseball cap is just cruel. Built biceps and veined fore-arms flex as he points at a cut of steak. I'm not proud of the sound my throat makes.

My rival looks wildly out of place and unfairly edible. Did he stumble into my quiet Queens meat temple just to mess with my blood pressure?

One hand slides casually in his pocket. The other holds a basket full of stuff. Of course he sees me at the exact moment I try to pivot and pretend I didn't.

Nolan blinks, then grins when he sees me. A slow, toe-curling grin that should come with a smoke alarm and a fire extinguisher.

"Well, well." His gaze prowls over me in a way that's far too appreciative for a deli aisle. "Didn't peg you as a meat market regular."

"Ditto," I deadpan. "Though, on second thought…"

He laughs. "This place is my secret weapon. Been coming here for years."

I glance up at the thick sausages swinging from their hooks above him then on instinct—because my brain is in the gutter—my traitorous eyes drop to the front of his gym shorts.

"So, Adams, this is where you come for all the thick meat?"

My eyes snap back up at him. He smirks.

"I could ask you the same."

His teeth catch on his bottom lip.

"It looks like someone already stole the best cuts." I shoot him a look. "Shocking."

He shrugs, unapologetic. "I got here first. And I've already told you...I prefer strategically acquired."

"Mhm."

He follows me through the narrow aisles, two steps behind. I pretend not to notice. He pretends not to be watching the way my ponytail swings.

We reach the checkout, and while I'm digging in my crossbody purse for my card, he sidesteps me, slides his steak onto the belt like we're grocery shopping together, and pays without breaking stride.

"I don't—why did you do that?"

The cashier hands me the bags. He snatches the heavier one out of my grip before I can argue.

"I'm just being neighborly," he says.

"Please tell me you don't live here." I follow him toward the door.

"I don't. Tribeca. And I'm being a gentleman, Adams."

"Didn't know you knew how to."

"Occasionally." He pushes open the door and steps aside so I can pass. The early evening air wraps around us like a weighted blanket, sun slipping low over Astoria, golden light sprawling across the brick buildings and fire escapes.

"So, you live nearby?" he asks casually, adjusting the bags in his hands as we step onto the sidewalk.

I stop walking. "What are *really* you doing in my neighborhood, Rhodes?"

He smirks. "Meat. I told you."

"That better be all you're here for."

His eyes sparkle with zero innocence. "Can't a guy pick up a few steaks without getting interrogated?"

"We keep running into each other and I'm starting to wonder if you're stalking me."

"Trust me, Adams," he says. "I'm definitely not stalking you. But the universe obviously has a plan."

"Right. A plan."

Nolan lifts a shoulder, biting back a grin, and that damn dimple is cocky as ever. I should be alarmed. Instead, my pulse kicks.

As he carries the bags, I watch his muscles shift beneath that tight tshirt, and several thoughts enter my mind, ones that should be censored. The sun catches on his stubbled jaw, then climbs higher over cheekbones, the slope of his neck, up to that stupid backwards hat barely keeping his hair in check.

Nolan walks up to a man standing by a sleek black car, looking mildly amused as Nolan hands off a few of the groceries and then turns to me.

"Your executive privilege is showing," I say.

"You're not wrong." He smiles. "You need a lift?"

"I can walk."

"You sure? It's hot. And the bag are heavy." He gestures to my groceries.

"They're not heavy. I'm good," I say, raising an arm, but he holds the bags out of reach.

"I'll consider it cardio," he says.

I let out a sigh, dramatic and mostly performative. "Fine."

"I'll text you," he tells the man who nods at his instruction and opens the driver's side door and gets in.

"Lead the way." Nolan grins wider—full-blown satisfaction blooming across his face as he follows me down the block like this is some weird, meat-centric rom-com we accidentally wandered into.

We walk side by side, the hush between us buzzing with tension, like a fuse inching toward a flame.

The disappearing light filters through the leaves above, causing fractured shadows to dance across the pavement. Somewhere nearby, a delivery truck rattles by and a kid shouts from an open apartment window. I could pretend I'm focused on the street ahead, but the truth is—I'm hyper-aware of all things Nolan Rhodes right now.

The way his shoulder brushes mine whenever we drift too close. The way the paper bags crinkle faintly in his hands as he adjusts them. His spicy cedarwood scent cutting through the city air and messing with my resolve.

I sneak a glance as we cross the street. He's relaxed, shoulders loose, no tension in his face, just an easy kind of calm, like he's exactly where he's supposed to be. Each step beside him tightens the thread between us. And I don't know where it's pulling me, only that I'm not fighting it.

We turn the corner near my building, and his gaze flits to me. I keep mine stubbornly forward.

The worn brick facade rises above us like it's judging the bad idea swirling in my mind right now. Like, inviting Nolan Rhodes up for a drink.

"This your spot?" he asks, nodding toward the building.

"Yeah," I say, slowing to a stop at my stoop. "Drop-off zone ends here."

He doesn't hand over the bags. Not immediately. Instead, his eyes trail from my face to the curve of my shoulder, as though he's working something out in his head.

"You want to grab a drink?" he asks suddenly.

Caught off guard, I blink. "What? Why?"

He shrugs, casual as hell. "Figured the least I could do is buy you a drink."

"Why?" I repeat.

"For hogging all the good cuts. And, you know... emotional restitution."

I fold my arms, one brow arching. "Emotional restitution?"

"That steak looked important to you."

"It was. I made eye contact with it."

"And I'm prepared to make amends. Preferably with wine. And professional destruction," he adds. "Don't forget that part."

My mouth opens. Closes. My brain cranks up the wattage on the *bad idea* sign in my head. But my pulse says: *just fucking do it.*

"There's a place around the corner," I hear myself say. "Decent wine. Cozy."

"Cozy huh?"

"Don't get any ideas, Rhodes."

"Well, lead the way, Adams. I'll try to keep the ideas to a minimum." He finally offers the bags. "I'll wait here for you."

I take them, careful not to touch him, though it still feels like we did. "Five minutes."

Nolan's grin kicks up half a notch. "I'll time you."

I roll my eyes and head up the steps, pulse quickening with each one.

Once inside, I dump the bags into the fridge, don't even bother taking the contents out, and release a breath I didn't realize I was holding.

What the hell just happened? Nolan Rhodes—steak thief, account pirate, living, breathing hot as fuck problem—is standing on my block, waiting for me to grab a drink with him.

*Voluntarily.*

I catch my reflection in the hallway mirror as I pass and immediately double back. Yikes. My hair's a windblown mess and there's the faintest sheen of sweat on my collarbone—not the sultry kind either, the drippy, hiked uphill in the heat of summer kind.

After tugging the elastic from my hair, I give it a quick brush until it falls into something closer to intentional waves. A swipe of deodorant. No two. A tiny spritz of perfume. Lip gloss. The bare minimum, I tell myself. Not for him. For me. Because I look like an alley rat who wrestled another for a baguette.

I open the closet. My hand hovers over a black top with a plunging neckline that says *I didn't plan this* but *also, yes I did.* I eye it. I eye my reflection. I eye the clock.

"I'm not changing for a man," I mutter. "Especially not *that* man."

Cut to: me, changing into the black top anyway.

As I'm slipping my lipgloss into my purse, I catch my reflection one more time. "Don't do anything stupid, Adams, like kiss him," I mutter, then leave and lock the door behind me.

And with that, I head back down, pretending I'm not about to meet the human embodiment of temptation for a drink around the corner.

Nolan's still there when I step outside, leaning against the brick like he belongs to it, like Queens is a stage and he's been waiting for his cue. One foot crossed over the other. Thumbs scrolling over his phone screen.

His gaze finds me and slides from my neckline to my heels with no shame and enough reverence to keep it from being a crime.

"Alright." I brush past him, pretending there's zero heat blooming across my chest. "Let's go toast to our mutual talent."

"Ruin and sabotage?" he drawls, falling into step.

"Exactly."

His head tips, that half-smirk catching fire under the glow of the streetlamp. "Can't wait, Adams."

The wine bar is tucked into the corner of an old brownstone, all exposed brick and low lighting. The air is cloaked in warmth and red wine and whispered conversation. A string of Edison bulbs trails overhead like the last remnants of a forgotten constellation. The whole place smells of roasted garlic and candle wax.

I slide into a booth by the window while Nolan heads to the bar, his silhouette cutting clean through the candlelit crowd. His shoulders flex under his t-shirt as he reaches for his wallet, and I try to ignore the way every woman within arms reach turns to look at him.

After a minute or two, he returns with two glasses of deep crimson. "Tempranillo," Nolan says, setting one in front of me like he's unveiling a rare gem. "The bartender said it pairs well with tension and rivals who secretly want to make out."

I blink. Once. Twice. Then I snort. "Wow. Okay. That's a line."

"Is it?" He takes a seat, one brow arched like he's genuinely unsure. "Felt more like a public service announcement."

I pick up my glass, mostly to hide the way my face is doing weird, traitorous things. "I *do not* want to secretly make out with you."

"Mhm." He doesn't even flinch.

"I don't," I insist, sipping to cover the sudden dryness in my throat.

It's good. Bold. A little smoky.

Nolan leans back, all long limbs and easy relaxation. "Sure."

"You're ridiculous."

"And yet, here we are. You. Me. Wine. A guaranteed good time."

I lift an eyebrow. "You really do come with your own PR campaign, don't you?"

"Only when I know the product's worth selling."

His tone is light, but no one's ever looked at me like the way he's looking at me right now. Like I'm not just here, but I'm inevitable.

I sip. Let the taste linger. Let him watch my mouth. I meet his gaze and say, "Careful, Rhodes. Keep looking at me like that and you're going to end up making promises with your eyes you can't take back."

Eyes narrow and voice deep, he replies with a zinger, "I always make good on my promises."

I clear my throat and change the subject. "So, what's your deal? You've got layers. Like a smug onion."

He exhales a dry laugh, eyes glinting in the candlelight. "Smug onion.? That one's new."

"I'm full of creative descriptions."

"You are," he says, then spins his own glass slowly. "So, full tragic origin story or the spark notes version?"

"Tragic," I say immediately. "Always."

"Alright." He leans in, forearms braced against the table. "Grew up in Chicago. My father and uncle were business partners, but we moved here when my uncle passed. I was around nine years old. Dad was a corporate raider. Think Gordon Gekko without the good hair. He taught me how to negotiate over breakfast and to pick profit over people. Every time. I wanted more than that. So, I decided I could do it differently. With ethics."

"With ethics?" I question.

"It's a work in progress," he says, voice even. "But yeah. That's the goal. I've spent years trying to unlearn what he drilled into me. And lately…" He pauses, runs a thumb along the rim of his glass. "Lately, I've been reevaluating things. Especially after what you said about Vanguard."

I stiffen.

His eyes meet mine again. No smirk. No charm. Just clear-eyed intent. "Rest assured, I'm looking into it."

"You should," I say, more steel in my voice than softness. "It's unethical otherwise."

A spark flickers behind his eyes. A subtle shift. Not defensive, really. Just...listening. It throws me, this version of Nolan Rhodes—less swagger, more substance.

He might actually give a damn.

"You're serious?" Although is not quite a question. More like a verbal prod, testing the weight of his words.

His gaze doesn't waver. "I am."

I glance down at my drink then back up at him. "Well, shit. Now I feel bad for calling you a corporate sociopath in my group chat."

A smile ghosts his lips.

Nudging my glass toward his with a clink, I add, "You might be doing the right thing now, but you're still part of the machine."

His eyes warm. "Maybe it's time someone rewired it."

My head tilts, my lips twitch. I need to steer us back to the previous conversation before I crawl across this table and prove I'm a liar about secretly wanting to make out with him.

"So, let me guess," I say, "your dad told you idealism was cute until it cost money."

He takes a sip. "Said I'd either be devoured or delusional. Still waiting to find out which."

There's something in the way he says that—like the sting hasn't dulled, like part of him still wonders if his father was right.

I open my mouth to ask more, but he beats me to it.

"He's retired now," Nolan offers. "Lives in a community upstate."

"Is your mom there too?"

"No, my mom died when I was seven." The words fall clean, practiced—but they land hard.

"Oh—"

"I don't remember her, not really. A few stories. Some secondhand memories. She liked lilacs. Played solitaire. That's all I've got."

I study him for a long moment. "I'm sorry, Nolan."

Eyes glued to his glass, he shrugs. "Don't be. It's a gap. One you don't know is missing until someone else points it out."

It hits something deep in me, and I don't push. I know better than to ask for things someone isn't ready to give.

Still, I find myself softening toward him in a way that isn't strategy or rivalry or lust. It's just human. And I realize Nolan Rhodes and I have more in common than I thought.

"And now you're the guy everyone wants in the room," I say. "So, looks like you figured life out."

"Some days I believe that." His brow furrows. "Others...not so much."

The conversation continues. It flows easily. He asks how I got started in marketing. I tell him about marching into The Laurel Group at twenty-three with more ego than experience.

"Laurel and my mom were roommates in college," I admit. "That opened the door. But I had to kick it down."

"I don't doubt that," he says, voice quiet.

"I had one shot," I continue. "So I handed her a single sheet of paper. No resume. Just six words: Stop chasing trends. Start dictating them."

Nolan huffs out a laugh. "You've got guts, Adams, I'll give you that."

"Damn right, I do."

We sip. We flirt. We edge closer without even realizing it. And then we stop talking about work.

Instead, we drift toward relationships—or the minefield where they used to be.

He asks why I'm single. I lie and say I've been busy.

I ask the same, and he says nothing, lifts his glass and drinks.

We keep going. Stories. Jokes. He tells me about the worst first date of his life. It involved a bearded dragon named Princess and a girl who tried to hand-feed him sushi.

I nearly choke on my wine.

"Okay, that's unhinged," I wheeze. "But I'll raise you. Once, I went on a date with a guy who brought his mom. As in, she sat *with us*. Ordered the steak. Critiqued my posture. Told me I have 'fertile eyes.'"

Nolan coughs, covers his mouth with a hand to keep from spewing his drink. *"Fertile eyes?"*

I nod solemnly. "And then she asked if I'd ever considered natural childbirth. During appetizers."

He stares at me, torn between horror and fascination.

"Still not sure if the date was for me or for her," I add.

And then, when the second bottle is nearly empty, I lean forward, elbows on the table.

"Tell me something real," I say. "Not a headline. Not a stat."

He meets my eyes. "I like your thought process here."

"Nope," I say, wagging a finger. "No marketing answers. No branding. Just Nolan."

He considers that, fingers tapping the table. "I've never had a one-night stand," he says finally.

That earns a blink from me. "Seriously?"

He give me a shameless grin. "Not for lack of opportunity."

I roll my eyes. "Of course not."

"I don't do surface-level. Even when I try to keep it light, I end up going deep. It's annoying as hell."

"You get attached?"

"I get curious. Then invested. Then stuck. And by that point, it's not casual anymore. It's complicated but with better lighting."

I don't know what to say to that. So I look at him. *Really* look at him.

"You know, I've got to admit." I pick at varnish on the table. "I had you pegged as a full-blown fuckboy."

His brow arches, but he stills, subtly. I've brushed a nerve he didn't expect to feel.

"Big firm. Big ego. Bigger charm," I add, flashing a saccharine smile.

He leans in, voice dipping low. "Is that your way of asking if something else might be... proportionate?"

The line hangs in the air—unapologetic, daring me to flinch.

I don't. I refuse to let him see the heat his words ignite. My breathing does stop for half a second too long though.

"Well," I say, biting my lip. "I figured all that confidence was compensation. You know—great suits, chiseled jaw, big dick energy. Classic misdirect."

He smiles, but it doesn't quite reach his eyes this time.

My body falls back against the booth. "You've surprised me, Rhodes. And that's annoying."

"Annoying?" he echoes, amused.

"Yes. Because now I can't decide if I want to kiss you or keep you talking." *Holy shit I said that out lout. But, you know what? Fuck it.*

"Why?" he asks, voice deeper than before.

"To see what other honest, messy, human thing you'll admit next."

That dimple reappears with his lazy smirk. It does things to my nether regions. Tickly things.

"Kiss me." His voice is threaded with heat. "And you won't hear another word. Not one."

My stomach flips.

His dark eyes dark focus on my lips. "But keep me talking, Adams... and I'll make you *want* to kiss me."

Shit.

I grip my glass a little tighter. "That's cocky," I murmur, hoping my voice doesn't betray me.

"It's confidence." His gaze drops to neckline of my shirt. "Which, for the record, is not compensation."

"Is this your idea of foreplay?" I ask.

"No. That would involve a lot more touching."

My pulse stumbles. My knees go warm.

We fall quiet. Not awkward. Not forced. Just still.

The warmth of our booth wraps around us like a bubble—one I'm not ready to pop. The candle has burned down low, the dregs of our wine gone warm, and the air between us shifts again. Less barbed, more magnetic.

Tracing the rim of my glass with a finger, I glance out the window, where the street flows with the pulse of a city winding down.

"I should probably head home," I say finally, though my voice is soft, reluctant.

Nolan doesn't move. He watches me.

"But..." I glance back at him, mouth quirking, "I don't really want to walk alone."

That earns me a spark in his eyes. His spine straightens slightly. "I'll walk you home, Adams."

I nod, wondering about what might happen when we reach my stoop again. Will he try to kiss me? Do I want him to?

Neither of us says anything as he leaves a few bills on the table. I don't miss how his palm brushes the small of my back as we weave through the tables and out into the night.

Outside is quiet, the city mellowing into that late-evening lull where even the taxis seem to glide softer. Summer heat curls between us. The sidewalk glows under the low buzz of amber street lamps, long shadows falling into step beside us.

We don't rush.

We're not in a hurry.

We pause at the crosswalk at the end of the block, where the breeze lifts my hair and the sounds of laughter drift from the patio behind us. For a moment, it's just us.

Nolan glances down at me, one hand slides into the pocket of those sinfully loose shorts. Boxers? Briefs? Or nothing? Like me.

His eyes drop to my mouth, and I swear he's about to say something I might not be ready for when a voice slices through the quiet.

"Rorie?"

I freeze at the sound of my name, turning slowly, already regretting it.

My ex, Quinn, walks toward us, hand intertwined with a woman who looks like she was styled straight off a Pinterest wedding board—beachy waves cascading over her shoulders, glowy skin, and teeth so white they practically have their own sponsorship deal.

And glinting under the streetlamp, bold and bright, a diamond so big it has its own gravitational pull.

The breath leaves my lungs in a stupid little gasp I don't manage to catch in time.

*Three months.*

That's how long it's been since Quinn walked out of my life. Since he told me he couldn't be what I needed anymore. That my grief was too heavy. That loving me felt more like *drowning*.

And now he's here.

Grinning. Glowing. Hand-in-hand with his upgraded life. That's a punch right to the center of my chest.

My mouth goes dry. My pulse skyrockets. I don't move. I don't breathe. I stand there like someone hit *pause* on my nervous system while the rest of the world keeps playing.

Nolan shifts beside me, a subtle, almost imperceptible movement. And when he steps in close without a word, it's not nothing. It's presence. Steady. Quiet. He knows I'm one breath away from falling apart and he chooses to be the breath that holds me together.

Quinn's eyes lock on mine. For a second—a mere second–his smile falters.

Good.

I might look like I'm holding it together, but inside I'm collapsing. Not because I want him back. Because I want to understand how someone who once whispered promises into my ear could move on like I was a chapter he skipped by mistake.

*Three months.*

That's all it took for him to trade in heartbreak for a hashtag engagement shoot.

*Fuck. That.*

My jaw tightens. My chin lifts.

"Hey," I say, and it comes out too light, too airy. Like I've inhaled helium. "Hi, Quinn."

He looks... a bit pompous. That smile curving his lips is a mask, and I know it because I used to watch him rehearse it in the mirror before meetings.

"This is Paisley." He lifts her hand with theatrical flair, and the diamond on her ring finger glints in the light like a blade, ready to be shoved straight through my heart. "My fiancée."

"Oh, wow. Congratulations," I manage, though it tastes like lemon peel and bile. "That's... really great."

Paisley offers me a polite, noncommittal smile—the kind you give someone right before you judge their entire outfit. "We *just* got back from a weekend in Montauk. He proposed on the cliffs at sunset."

Because of course he did.

Next to me, Nolan is a wolf catching the scent of something off. He clocks the entire exchange with terrifying efficiency. A strong arm snakes around my waist in one slow, deliberate motion. I look up at him. He winks, and that dimple I refuse to find charming makes a dangerous appearance.

My heart flips. Nolan somehow felt the ground shift beneath me and he stepped in without a word, and that's unwinding something tight in my chest, tugging at threads I thought I'd knotted down.

I look up at him. He winks.

This infuriating, impossible man, is doing things to my resolve. He's supposed to be the enemy.

But all I can think is—

*God, it would be so easy to fall for you.*

"Amazing," I say to Paisley, because I don't know where else to aim the awkwardness. "Well, we were just heading home."

Quinn's eyes narrow with curiosity as they size up Nolan. "So... you're together?"

Nolan doesn't hesitate. He slides his hand from my waist, extends it toward Quinn like he's closing a deal.

"Nolan Rhodes," he says. Cool. Collected, flat enough to be convincing. "We were grabbing drinks. Celebrating."

"Celebrating?" Quinn repeats, his expression faltering.

Nolan's smile curls, amused. "Her brilliance. My luck. The beginning of her 'no more mediocre men' era."

Paisley blinks.

I cough into my sleeve to hide my laugh. Nolan's hand slips into mine as though it's always belonged there, and I let him.

Quinn shifts. "Well. Glad you found someone who can... handle your life."

That hits harder than I'm ready for. He means it. That passive-aggressive dig cloaked in civility. *Your grief. Your mess. Your weight.* The things he couldn't carry.

Nolan hears it because his fingers tense slightly. His head tilts. He doesn't say anything right away, but there's a shift behind his eyes.

"So, how'd you two meet?" Quinn asks, like he cares. His fiancé's attention bounces between all of us.

"Oh, we um–"

"Work together," Nolan cuts in. "Got paired up on a special project." And then his voice drops an octave, "You ready to go home and... debrief, honey?"

My brows lift.

Nolan's mouth grazes the shell of my ear. "I've got visuals. Charts. Graphs. And a very *thorough* presentation planned. Hands-on demonstration included. You'll want to take notes."

Playing along, I elbow him. "Keep it in your pants...honey."

But I'm smiling.

And I don't pull away.

Quinn stares for a moment longer, looking like he wants to say something, or defend himself. Maybe ask why I'm glowing in a way I never did with him.

But instead, he says, "Well, nice running into you, Rorie."

"You too," I lie with alarming ease. "Congrats, again."

"Bye." Paisley's heels clack against the pavement as they turn away.

When the two love birds disappear into the night, Nolan's hand slips from mine and I swear he's fighting the urge to ask me *exactly* what that was about.

I beat him to it. "Don't."

His mouth quirks. "I wasn't going to say anything."

"Liar."

"You're welcome, by the way." Voice silk and trouble. "And FYI, you now owe me another Cabernet and Confessions night. Strictly professional, of course. So you can explain *who* the hell that guy was."

"Definitely a story for another time," I mutter.

"I'm holding you to it."

We reach the corner and pause beneath the streetlight. Standing. Breathing. The silence between is full of desire. And unsaid things.

"I had fun," he says.

"Honestly, me too." I look down at the ground for a beat then back up at him. "Hey, I want to say I'm sorry. For assuming you were a player. And a flirt. A guy who's only interested in quick and casual. It was wrong of me to label you. And I could tell how much calling you a fuckboy bothered you back at the wine bar."

His hand finds mine, not a grab, not even a move. It's the softest drag of skin across skin.

"Rorie?" he says.

"Yeah?"

His thumb skims the inside of my wrist. Light. Gentle. I meet his gaze, wary, but drawn in.

"Thank you for your apology, but so we're clear..." Honey-colored eyes find mine. "When I touch you..." A rough knuckle grazes the side of my hand, a stroke so slow and sensual it makes my breath hitch. "It won't be casual."

The crosswalk light changes behind him—an unspoken cue to walk away.

I don't.

A flood of reasons break open in my mind.

Like, why should I?

Because Quinn is somewhere, probably giving Paisley a recap of the woman he left mid-breakdown and how thrilled he is she's *thriving*.

Because I just watched the man who swore I was too heavy to love flash a diamond like it was proof he'd been right all along.

Because Nolan Rhodes just looked at me like I'm not baggage but the whole damn destination.

Because I want—no, *need*—to remind myself I'm not the girl Quinn left behind.

I'm Rorie *"The Reckoning"* Adams.

My eyes meet Nolan's, and different kind of energy hangs between us. Not a spark. Not a sizzle.

A crack.

Hairline, but one that means something's about to split wide open, like a door creaking, daring me to walk through.

So I do.

One step.

One breath.

My fingers find the back of Nolan's warm neck, solid, familiar in a way that makes no sense.

He stills. Blinks once. Again. A guarded look in his eyes flutters.

He doesn't think I'll do it.

Let's show him he's wrong.

Rising onto my toes, I press my mouth to his. No fanfare. No hesitation. Only heat and will and the heady rush of crossing a line I can't uncross.

Hands cup my jaw, but Nolan doesn't deepen the kiss. Doesn't take over. He lets me lead. Lets *me* claim *him*.

The moment crackles.

My mouth surges with urgency and Nolan groans against my lips like I've set him on fire. The sound makes me lose my balance. It's a low, deep exhale as though he's been holding his breath for days and I'm the thing that finally lets him breathe.

My fingers fist the front of his shirt, tugging him closer, needing more—needing *him*.

But Nolan stays slow. His lips move like he's memorizing mine, a study in self-control. Every brush is measured, purposeful, a promise, not a possession.

His mouth doesn't demand—it asks.

It listens.

It learns.

His lips map the shape of mine, tracing them with the barest hint of tongue—tentative, teasing, coaxing my mouth open. It's so gentle it guts me. I melt, completely, knees softening as the world around us fades out. No traffic. No city noise. Just us.

And this kiss.

One hand slides to my waist, anchoring me with that impossible steadiness of his, and the proof of how badly he wants more nudges into me. He's holding himself back. And somehow, that restraint makes everything burn hotter.

Tilting my head, I chase him, deepening the kiss in tiny, fragile increments, like we're both afraid to break it. Like if we move too fast, it might shatter.

When I finally do pull back, breathless, and aching, my lips swollen, my chest a riot, Nolan doesn't say a word.

Dark, heavy-lidded eyes watch me. We've undone something in each other.

Heart thundering, I take a shaky breath and step back.

His hand lifts mine again, he presses a second kiss to the knuckles. A little smug. A little reverent. All heat.

"Sleep well, Adams." He turns and walks away.

My mouth is still tingling. Nolan's kiss carved itself into me, like it knew it was meant to stay.

What am I supposed to do with that?

# CHAPTER 19

# PENITENT DICK ERA (™)
## NOLAN

I'M on cloud fucking nine when Rishi's text comes through.

> Yo. How'd the steak turn out? Medium rare perfection or amateur hour?

> Didn't get to it.

> ???

> Ran into Rorie Adams.

> Ran into? As in physically? Or biblically?

> We talked. That's it.

> Uh huh. And by "talked" you mean—

> I mean TALKED, you menace.

> Damn. Wasted steak and sexual tension?

> Tragic.

I took the day off. And now I'm pacing my apartment like a man waiting for a transplant. Which, in a way, I am.

My new couch is due to arrive any minute now, and I keep checking my phone even though the delivery window still says *twenty to forty minutes.* I'm hitting refresh like that will magically make the truck teleport to my doorstep.

The living room looks empty as hell—no couch, no coffee table, no remnants of tastefully displayed furniture. Nothing but a bare floor and wide open space.

It's the best kind of empty. A Chloe-free zone. Like my dick. And my life.

After getting the all-clear on my lab results, I decided it was time for a cleanse. Spiritually, emotionally, sexually. The couch she swore was *"elevated and European"* but felt like it belonged in a dentist's waiting room?

Gone.

Hauled out like the poor choice it was.

The chic, soul-sucking coffee table with the razor-sharp corners that murdered my shins at least once a week?

Also gone.

Hopefully now living its best life in a shelter where no one gives a damn about *"aesthetic."*

The new couch is mine. I picked it. Deep, moody green. Oversized. The kind of couch you could sleep on for eight hours and still wake up thinking *damn, that was cozy.* It's bold. Loud. The visual equivalent of flipping off Chloe's shrine to beige minimalism.

Every time I sit on it, I want to remember this: *I don't have to perform anymore.*

Not in relationships. Not in my own damn living room.

I glance around, imagining how the space will feel once it's fully mine—plants I won't kill, books I've actually read, maybe even a ridiculous espresso machine I'll never learn to use but *need* for the hell of it. I'll start cooking again. Or get a dog. Or become one of those guys who owns throw blankets for reasons other than sex appeal.

The buzzer rings.

I nearly faceplant over my own feet getting to the intercom.

"Come on up." Way too enthusiastic. I sound like I won the lottery instead of bought new furniture.

The delivery guys are fast and unfazed. They maneuver the couch through the tight doorway like it's just another day at the office, which I guess it is. To me, though?

This is Christmas.

No—this is Reclamation Day.

Dropping onto it, I sink into the cushions. I'm being swallowed by the best kind of monster. The kind that feeds you chips and beer and gives you back your personality.

A slow smile creeps across my face, the kind that comes from finally, *finally* doing something for myself.

Freedom feels like velvet. I run a hand over the fabric. And smells faintly of new beginnings.

I want to celebrate. I want to shout it from the rooftop of my building—or at least from the top of this new damn couch.

Because a couch isn't just a couch—not when the last one had Chloe's perfectly manicured fingerprints all over it. Not when every corner of this place used to smell like her shampoo and that overpriced pine and patchouli candle she swore "set the mood."

Now it smells like leather and sawdust and manhood.

*My* life. *My* choice.

And for the first time in a long time, I'm actually myself again.

I want to tell someone.

Rorie, the Silver-Tongued Siren Who Might Be My Professional Undoing, drifts across my brain like a whisper.

She'd laugh at this, make some snarky comment about me choosing furniture that doesn't scream: "CEO of Sad Beige, Inc."

She'd lean back, swirl her wine, and ask something like, "Does this couch pair well with brooding?"

That little minx has invaded my network, my meat market—and somehow still managed to take up permanent residence in my brain.

Especially since last night—

Her eyes, her laugh, the way her breath caught when I told her my touch would be anything but casual.

And that kiss.

Slow and wrecking. Her fists curled in my shirt like she needed more, while I held back, letting every brush of my lips ask instead of take. Her warm mouth opened, answering me in ways words never could.

I'm still unpacking that. Still figuring out if I'm on a slow slide into something I'm afraid to name yet... or if I'm finally waking up.

I smile before I can stop myself.

The one that deserves an apology. **Textually Frustrated.**

She doesn't know me. Not really. But somehow she sees straight through me anyway. And I owe her more than silence.

Pulling out my phone, I open our thread. Her name stares back at me, bright and unbothered, like it hasn't been collecting dust while I ran away, kissed a girl, and bought a new couch.

Let's see if she's still speaking to me.

> So, hypothetically, if someone completely shut you down while you were sharing really exciting news, how badly would you drag them for it?

I stare at it, then unsend it.

Too try-hard.

I type: *What's the penalty for being a total ass? Asking for a friend.*

Delete.

Even worse.

I try again: *Guess who's back from the brooding dead?*

Delete.

God, no. Am I okay?

I exhale, press my thumbs to the keyboard, and finally go with what I should've said days ago:

> Me: Hey. Sorry for being a dick.

Sent.

My chest tightens as I watch the screen, eyes locked on the empty space where her reply should be.

Seconds tick by.

A minute.

Then two.

**Read.**

No reply.

Oof.

Her rejection stings. The weight of it is suddenly unbearable, the phone falls into my lap.

Another connection fractured. Another thing I might've ruined because I couldn't get out of my own damn way.

I lean back on the couch—my couch, my clean slate—and stare up at the ceiling like it holds answers.

It doesn't.

I need to fix this.

A few hours—and one personal meltdown in Hobby Lobby later—my loft looks like a kindergarten art project mated with a disco ball and filed for divorce.

There's glitter in my eyebrows. Glue on my pants. And somewhere under the mess, the sad remains of my pride.

The t-shirt I sacrificed in the name of redemption now lies across my kitchen table like a cotton confession.

I've written a message in neon puff paint and surrounded it with little lightning bolts and rhinestones, because if I'm going down, I'm going down with flair. Rishi told me once there's healing in glitter. So, here goes nothing.

The front reads:

*SORRY FOR BEING A DICK!*
*TEXT ME FOR FURTHER APOLOGIES*
*(555) 977-1529*

Yes, my actual number.

Yes, in all caps.

Yes, I hate myself.

The back is even worse:

> *IM SORRY TEXTUALLY FRUSTRATED!*
> *I AM SEEKING REDEMPTION!*
> *PLEASE DON'T BLOCK ME!*

I stare at the shirt for a full ten seconds before grabbing my phone and snapping a photo. In case I die of shame and someone needs to tell the story at my funeral.

Then I text it to her.

> Exhibit A. I'm calling it my Penitent Dick Era.

My thumb hovers over the screen. No way to undo it now. Not after I branded myself a walking billboard for emotional turbulence.

This is what desperation looks like. This is what *trying* looks like.

I hope to hell she laughs. Or forgives me.

Either way, it's done.

I've officially glitter-glued my sins to a cotton-poly blend and offered them to the gods of forgiveness.

Now all I can do... is wait.

## CHAPTER 20
# GLITTER IS MY LOVE LANGUAGE

### RORIE

I'M EXACTLY three bites into a questionable bodega croissant and halfway through a client call that's circling the drain when my phone pings with a text.

**Carl.**

Annoyed with myself for not deleting him. I sigh, glance at the screen expecting an apology or a meme, but what I get instead—

Holy. Shit.

A photo.

Of a man-sized white t-shirt stretched across what I can only assume is his kitchen table. It's covered in glitter, surprisingly good handwriting, and what appears to be a decent attempt at bedazzling.

In the middle, like some neon-lit declaration of shame, it reads:

*SORRY FOR BEING A DICK!*
*TEXT ME FOR FURTHER APOLOGIES*
*(555) 977-1529*

I choke on a crumb. My client asks if I'm okay. And then I swipe to the next photo.

The back.

## *I'M SORRY TEXTUALLY FRUSTRATED!*
## *I AM SEEKING REDEMPTION!*
## *PLEASE DON'T BLOCK ME!*

I stop breathing.

Not out of horror.

Out of pure, awe-struck disbelief that this man not only created this masterpiece but sent it to *me*. Sober, presumably.

I stare at the phone. Then the wall. Then the phone again.

This cannot be real.

This is either:

A) The dumbest apology I've ever received.

B) The best apology I've ever received.

C) A textbook case of glitter manipulation... and unfortunately, it's working.

My fingers move.

> You made a glitter shirt?

A statement piece, actually.

> Is this... punishment? Or performance art?

Yes.

> And the phone number? Really?

If I must suffer, I want strangers to witness it.

I laugh. Out loud. *Loudly*.

It's too much. It's absolutely too much.

And exactly enough.

> Okay. Fine. You get points for commitment. And rhinestones.

> But I'm still mad at you.

I expect nothing less.

> I might be slightly less mad than I was before
> the glitter.

So... am I forgiven?

> No. You're on parole.

Do I get visitation hours? Possible conjugal
visits?

> Don't push your luck, Picasso.

Understood. But so we're clear—I would have
worn it in Central Park. Alone. With snacks.

> Carl...

Yes?

> If you ever wear that shirt in public... I'm gonna
> need proof.

Challenge accepted.

> You are insufferable. Effective. But insufferable.

I"ll try again. Forgiven?

> Apology accepted. Pending further review.

Tough crowd.

> So what was the reason for your dickness the
> other day?

Something at work. My boss threatened
my job.

I was pissed. Came in hot and took it out on
the wrong person. That's on me.

I stare at the screen for a second too long. The honesty is unexpected. And kind of disarming.

That sucks. But thanks for the truth. And the
apology. I respect it.

Easier to be honest when I can't see you
judging me.

Who says I'm judging? Maybe I'm impressed.

You're flirting.

Don't flatter yourself, Carl. You still owe me for
the emotional whiplash.

I'll add it to the glitter debt. Speaking of which
—What's the big news you were dying to tell
me before I acted like a complete dick?

I chew on my bottom lip, debating how much to share. I don't
know why I care what he thinks. But I do. But I also want to keep our
mystery thing in tact.

Let's just say...

A career-making opportunity landed in my lap.
It's huge. Terrifying. The kind of thing that
either launches you or buries you.

So basically: high stakes. Just how you like it.

How would YOU know how I like it?

A hunch. You've got that edge.

You don't know me.

Don't need to. I know your type. Probably talks
back in meetings.

...accurate.

You like the pressure. You chase the win.

P.S. It's my favorite type

And what type is that exactly?

Girls who scare me a little.

Like the girl who hates you?

Exactly like the girl who hates me.

Any updates on that?

I don't kiss and tell, TF.

# CHAPTER 21
# EGGS OVER EMOTIONAL

NOLAN

SYRUP. Burnt toast. And enough caffeine to revive a dead man.

That's Buzzy's Diner.

Which is perfect, because I'm not dead—I just feel like it.

I slide into the booth across from Tammy, who's already halfway through a stack of pancakes like she's training for a carb-based Olympic event.

She's wearing gold hoop earrings, a denim jacket over her office blouse, and an expression that says she's about to reorganize my entire life with color-coded tabs and a smile that dares me to stop her.

"You're late," she says, spearing a piece of pancake without looking up.

"You ordered without me."

"Because I know you. You'd have rolled in here, moaned about how you're starving, then spent ten minutes fake-scanning the menu like you weren't gonna order the same three things you always do."

"Okay, rude—but also correct."

"Glad I could validate your nonsense."

I flag down the server, order my usual—black coffee, eggs over easy, bacon, whole wheat toast, and I add on a Belgian waffle.

"Ha! I ordered *four* things." I settle back against the red vinyl booth. Tammy watches me for a beat, chewing slowly. Then she swallows, wipes her mouth, and gives me a look.

Shit. Here it comes.

"So." She takes a delicate sip of her orange juice like she's not about to interrogate me. "You gonna tell me what the hell is going on with you, or do I have to keep guessing?"

I blink. "Define 'going on.'"

She points her fork at me. "Don't play cute. You've been off. Not just post-Chloe-off—worse. Broody. Distracted. And now you're making shirts for some girl."

My jaw tightens. "I should've never shown you, or asked for your opinion because you're never gonna let that shit go, are you?"

"Absolutely not." She levels a glare. "Is that what's got you all you twisted? Did you make the shirt for Rorie Adams? The woman you had me investigate."

"Investigate it a tad over the top."

Her glare hardens. I hesitate. Sip my coffee. If we were in a movie, this would be about the time the tumbleweeds breeze between our standoff.

Tammy pounces. "Holy shit. It's Rorie, isn't it?"

"No." I set the mug down. "The shirt was someone else."

Her brows shoot up. "Excuse me?"

I exhale, rub the back of my neck. "Okay. There's this... person. I accidentally texted her by mistake the night of the Chloe Catastrophe. Wrong number. She responded. We kept talking."

Tammy sets down her fork. She's locked in now. "And?"

"And nothing. We text. It's... fun. Easy. She's smart. Keeps me in check."

"And Rorie?"

My silence answers her.

Tammy shakes her head. "Two women. One you're professionally pitted against, and the other you've never met in person?"

I groan. "Perfect. It sounds like a dating app horror story."

"It *sounds* like you're a man in need of therapy and a whiteboard."

"Mystery Texter's just a friend. And Rorie?" I pause. "Well, she's the splinter in my dick I can't tweeze out. Sharp, buried deep, and somehow flares up when I least expect it."

"First off, gross." Tammy squints. "Secondly, is that a metaphor for feelings or a spicy medical condition?"

I groan. "I don't know what it is. All I know is she's under my skin. And in my head."

Tammy's quiet for a beat. She reaches over, grabs my toast, and takes a bite. I give her a look

"You're a disaster," she says, crumbs in her voice.

"You worried about me?"

"I'm always worried about you, you idiot." She waves a hand. "You spent a year trying to be someone you weren't for Chloe. Now you're finally showing your real self—and if that girl sees it too? Let her."

I blink at her. "That was... almost sweet."

She shrugs. "Don't get used to it. I'm still stealing your toast."

"Don't be worried." I stab a piece of egg, but don't eat it yet.

"Don't get murdered," she replies. "Who knows who your mystery texter really is? You know?"

"It's not like that with either of them. I'm not trying to fall in love. I'm just trying to figure out which version of myself I'm supposed to be now. And they both get different pieces of me. But they both make me feel like I'm not completely crumbling."

"I'm here for you. Imogene too." She taps my plate with her fork. "Now eat your eggs. You're gonna need the protein to survive tonight."

I frown. "Tonight?"

"Shelby Davidson. Happy hour." Tammy grins. "You forgot, didn't you?"

"I didn't forget." I smirk. "But thanks for the reminder."

She sips her juice again, smug. "Don't worry. I already blocked it on your calendar and added a thirty-minute pregame slot so you can rehearse your charm."

I chuckle. "You're a menace."

"I'm your assistant."

"Same thing."

She tips her glass toward me. "Remember, Nolan—whoever this mystery girl is, and whatever the hell you think you're doing with

Rorie Adams, don't lie to yourself about what you want."

I nod slowly. And try not to think about how I want both women to be the same person.

"Which is the Asher Cross account."

Oh, right. And that too.

After breakfast, I wandered the city half-heartedly sipping a lukewarm latte and pretending I had errands to run. I didn't.

What I did have, however, was a phone full of unsolicited dick pics. Not of me. No, no.

I wore one joke shirt—ONE—and suddenly every man within a ten-block radius decided I was the chosen one. The Keeper of the Dongs. The digital dick oracle. And now, like the generous bastard I am, I'm about to forward the worst of them to the only person on earth who might actually appreciate the absurdity: **Textually Frustrated.**

> I hope you're somewhere safe because I'm about to send you something deeply disturbing.

Why do I feel like I need to call my lawyer before I open this?

> Too late. Sending.

> [Image attached]

WHAT THE ACTUAL HELL, CARL?!

> Are you impressed?

> Or deeply, profoundly afraid?

I need to dunk my phone in holy water.

Wait! Is this YOU?

I never said it was MY dick. Should I?

You should have prepared me before scarring me for life.

I've received too many of these in my time, TF. My inbox is basically a shrine to unsolicited manhood. Some are artistic, some are distressing, and others...well, I'll admit, some have made me question my own self-worth.

Are you telling me there's a spectrum of dicks in your phone?

A dick-tionary, if you will.

I WILL NOT!

Too late. You're in this now.

I hate that I'm about to say this but... send more.

Are you serious?

Look, if I have to live with what you just burned into my retinas, I might as well see what else is out there. Consider this an educational experience.

I appreciate your scientific curiosity.

[Image attached]

OH MY GOD. THIS ONE HAS PROPS.

Yep. That's "Creative Enthusiasm." He used shadows and everything. True commitment to the craft.

I have so many questions.

> You and me both. But none I actually want answered.

> [Image attached]

...Is that a sock puppet?

> Meet "Whimsical Horror."

> He sent this with the caption: "Let me be your puppet master."

I'm calling the police.

> No, no, no. I have one more. This next one's special.

> [Image attached]

WHY DOES THIS ONE HAVE A BACKGROUND STORY?

> Because some men go the extra mile, TF. This guy titled his "The Lone Wanderer" and wrote an entire paragraph about how his dick is on a quest for love and acceptance.

Please tell me you responded.

> Of course I did. I told him his dick was brave and I wish him well on his journey.

You're a true humanitarian.

> I do what I can. But now I have a serious concern.

What's that?

Are we penis-shaming? Should we be penis-shaming? Is this wrong?

There's a difference between shaming and acknowledging that some men have too much free time and questionable artistic vision.

Fair point.

So, keep sending them?

Oh, absolutely! This is my new favorite segment of our friendship.

I'm honored.

But if you ever send me an unsolicited one of YOURS, I will find you and break your face and your phone.

Let's be honest... you'd be curious.

I will deny that in a court of law.

Oh, this is fun. I'll title this chat "Dick Talks with TF."

I hate you.

No, you don't.

...Send another one.

Already on it.

[Image attached]

# CHAPTER 22
# VAGINA TAKE THE WHEEL

## RORIE

THE CURSOR on my screen blinks with the passive-aggressive energy of someone who thinks they're better than me. My notes for the Pitchpocalypse are a messy doc of half-baked ideas, floating buzz-words, and the desperate scent of burnout.

*Luxury tailored experience. Immersive branding strategies. Elevated consumer pathways.*

Blah, blah, blah.

It all sounds important. Looks strategic. But it's smoke and mirrors. There's no spark. No heartbeat. Only a pile of marketing jargon held together with duct tape and denial.

I spin my pen, hoping the motion will conjure up some amazing idea. Instead of inspiration, my mind, bless its twisted little heart, keeps drifting back to Nolan Rhodes.

Rooftop banter.

Boy Band bar trivia.

Asher's penthouse.

Wine. That kiss.

*"When I touch you, it won't be casual."* He said it like it was both a threat and a prophecy.

How am I supposed to write a strategy deck like that didn't melt my spine?

Dropping my pen, I blink at my screen like it might erase all the dirty thoughts swirling in my head.

Nolan's broad build. How he fills out a pair of jeans. How he carries himself with a level of self-assurance that suggests he has never —*not once*—disappointed a woman in bed.

And if the very solid evidence pressed against my hip during that kiss was any indication…

Let's just say I'm suddenly very curious about the specifics of Nolan *"How Big is His Dick"* Rhodes, and what he might be working with below the belt.

Unfortunately, that curiosity is not helpful. Or healthy.

It's made me into a woman with a vibrator and a vendetta. God, I'm so emotionally unstable and stupidly horny.

This is stupid! I have a pitch to prepare.

I shove back from the desk. I do not have time to lose myself in thoughts about licking, sucking or fucking Nolan *"Please Let Me Do All Three"* Rhodes.

I snatch my coffee and take a long sip like caffeine can somehow course-correct my entire personality. I need to keep things in the lane. The unbothered, definitely-not-horny lane.

*Buzz.* **Carl.**

What's up, Buttercup?

Working

Me too!

What did you say you do for a living?

I thrive in corporate chaos.

That sounds…soul-sucking.

Oh, it is. But I'm elite at it. The chaos bends to me. (Well, most days)

Modest, aren't you?

Honest. Now YOU. What's it like being the
reigning queen of snark?

Exhausting.

Heavy is the head that wears the crown.

Do you ever take breaks from all that royalty?
Or is it a 24/7 gig?

I'll let you know if I ever get a break. So far, it's
been a one-woman show.

Well, consider this your commercial break.
Popcorn optional. Crown stays on.

Ugh, please don't segue into unsolicited life
advice about "letting go" and "living in the
moment."

Tempting... but no. I know better than to poke
royalty with a motivational quote.

I'll just say this—whatever this weird little
texting thing is? It's fun.

Thanks for that, TF.

Totally agree. And weird little texting thing?
Rude.

I prefer exclusive, unhinged, yet supportive
pen pal.

Trademark it immediately.

So, what do YOU do for work?

Professional taste-tester for mac and cheese
brands.

Respect. True hero of the people.

If you weren't royalty or landing career-making opportunities, what would you do…if you could do anything?

Honestly? Something with authors.

Like my mom used to.

A writer?

Not sure. Possibly.

That sounds like something worth discovering.

Maybe.

When you're ready, I'm here for the beta reads.

And the mac and cheese reviews.

I laugh. My heart squeezes. And I think: what if we met?
Would it ruin everything?
What if we already have? And don't know it.
Wouldn't that be crazy?
I FaceTime Maya. She picks up on the second ring, her flawless face filling the screen. Hair is sleek. Blue hoops. Latte in hand. Judgey energy locked and loaded.

"Please tell me this is work-related and not you having another crisis over a man."

I set my phone against a stack of books and sigh. "Okay, one—it's *not* a crisis. And two—how the hell do you always know?"

"Because I'm clairvoyant. Also, you've got that look. Like your brain's hosting a late night special called *Horny and Confused*. Spill."

"What if I met my mystery texter?"

Her latte freezes midair. "*What?*"

I press my lips together.

Maya narrows her eyes so fast her face practically locks into a scowl. "Wait, *wait*. Are you telling me you're actually contemplating moving into a visual phase with a stranger who could absolutely be the villain in a Netflix documentary? Please tell me you are not that girl."

I cross my arms and glare. "It's not like that."

"Oh, it never is."

"He's not some creeper in a basement, Maya."

"Yeah? What do you really know about him that isn't suspiciously charming?"

"He's funny. And weirdly sweet. And his shirt was glittery."

Maya sighs, pinching the bridge of her nose. "Girl, don't you dare let a funny t-shirt distract you from reality."

I open my mouth, then close it.

Because reality?

It's standing outside my apartment wearing a backwards hat, lips tasting like heat and red wine, eyes dark enough to drown in.

Maya catches the shift in my expression like a hawk. "Hold on. What was that face?"

"What face?"

"That was a 'there's something I'm not telling you because I'm still working it out in my head and it involves tongue' face."

I fidget with my sleeve. "It's nothing."

Her brows shoot up. "You kissed him, didn't you?"

I go still. "Don't change the subject. We're talking about Carl."

Maya slams her coffee on the table. "You kissed Nolan Rhodes and you didn't tell me?"

"It wasn't planned!" I hiss. "It just… happened. One minute we were drinking wine and then we ran into Quinn—and he's fucking engaged by the way."

"Engaged?"

"Yeah."

She gapes at me. "Okay, we obviously have some communication issues we need to discuss, but we'll save that for later. Right now…I'm still processing the fact that you made out with Nolan and didn't tell me."

I sigh.

Her eyes narrow. "And why the fuck are you even thinking about meeting Carl when you're kissing Nolan Goddamn Rhodes."

"Because Nolan is real," I snap. "He's flesh and blood and complicated and terrifying and not safe at all. Carl is safe. He's a voice and a vibe. He makes me laugh. He doesn't know how I look when I'm falling apart."

I didn't mean for that last part to slip out. Nolan doesn't know me either. But he's seen my cracks. That day at Stanfield I was split open.

"I need some answers, Rorie."

"You and me both."

Her face softens. "Look, as far as meeting your mystery texter... he's safe...until he's not. The second you start bending your own rules —no oversharing, no flirting—you give him the upper hand. It's a slippery slope to heartbreak or homicide."

"Geez, dramatic much?"

"The last time you gave someone too much access, *he* used it to hurt you and now he's with—excuse me, *engaged*, I guess—to a girl who probably orders extra ranch with everything."

"Exactly." I bury my face in my hands. "But it's not like I'm proposing to the guy. It's *nice*. He makes me feel like I'm not doing life wrong."

Her expression softens, but only a fraction. "Be careful, okay? I swear, if I have to rescue you from a warehouse, I'm gonna be *pissed.*"

I laugh. "That won't happen."

"Mhm." She shoots me a look. "And as far as Nolan goes—"

"It was nothing," I cut her off. "Just hormones, buried emotions and a little misplaced curiosity."

Maya arches a brow. "Yeah? Then why are you blushing like a virgin?"

"Speaking of blushing like a virgin," I say, shifting gears. "Have *you* texted Asher?"

Maya's cheeks go pink like a neon sign.

"Oh my god, you *did*."

Her groan could register on the Richter scale. "I hate you."

"No, you love me. Your turn to spill."

"Fine," she huffs. "We *may* have had drinks after the Four Leaf Hotel."

"At the bar?"

"In his suite."

"*MA'AM.*"

"It was innocent!"

I lean in. "Define innocent."

Maya is looking away, trying to avoid eye contact. After a beat, she mumbles, "He walked me to my car."

"Did he kiss you?"

A pause.

"*Maya.*"

"Yes."

I slap the table. "*Maya Justine Torres.*"

"Shhh!" she whisper-screams.

"Was it good?"

"It was... really good. Like, *insanely* good."

"I knew it. He looks like he'd be a *phenomenal* kisser. Describe it. Slowly."

There's a wicked little grin tugging at her lips. "He smells like whiskey and rain. Tastes like it too."

"Dear God," I say.

"And his hands," she breathes. "Big. Warm. Just rough enough."

I fan myself. "Did he do the thing?"

Her eyes flick to mine, and I know exactly what she's about to say. She nods. "He did the thing."

I squeal.

"His hand. My jaw. Thumb tracing my skin."

"Awe."

"A deep kiss followed by the slow draw back, lingering long enough to make me lose my mind." Maya is swooning as she describes the intimate moment. "Mmmm...it was...perfection."

"What happened after?"

"He sent me home."

I blink. "That's it?"

"I know!" she cries. "What if it was one moment only, and now it's over?"

"Did you text him?"

"No."

"Why not?"

"*Because* he's Asher Cross. He should text me." She laughs, but it fades. "He hasn't said a word, Rorie. Nothing."

I study her. "Then you should reach out."

"I can't."

"Don't sit here doubting yourself. May, he kissed *you*. Not anyone else."

She nods, quiet now.

I frown, not liking where her thoughts are going. "Maybe he's trying to figure out *how* to go there with you without completely damaging his career. Because let's face it, dating you in secret forever isn't exactly an option."

She exhales, nodding but still looking uncertain. "I don't know, Rorie. I... I can't get past the feeling that I don't belong in his world."

I study her. "That's exactly why he's interested in you. Because you're *not* part of that world."

Her eyes narrow. "Okay, back to *you*. What's next with Nolan Rhodes?"

"Nothing."

"Liar."

"I'm serious. We had wine. We talked. We kissed. He left."

"Yeah, and you haven't stopped thinking about him since."

I open my mouth. Nothing comes out.

"Exactly," she says. "Don't lie to yourself, babe. You like him."

"Nolan's a complication. I can't like him."

"There you go...lying to yourself again."

"Which is exactly why we're going out tonight." I wink.

"Where?"

"Does it matter? I need to reset. I need to purge whatever twisted, confusing emotions are battling for space in my head. I need to get laid."

"Um—what?"

"Yes. It's all suddenly so clear," I tell her. "The reason my brain is on overdrive is because I have so much pent up inside. You know? I need one meaningless night. No strings. No complications. Fill my horny bucket and move on. Get the poison out, you know?"

"Rorie, I don't think—"

I send an invite to Jeremy to join the group chat. He pops on immediately.

"We're going out tonight," I say. "Two reasons. One, we need to celebrate landing Pitchpocalypse. Two, I need to be carefree and frisky."

Jeremy taps his chin with exaggerated thoughtfulness, his eyes glinting with anticipation. "And when you say *carefree and frisky*..."

"She means she needs to get laid," Maya deadpans, not even looking up from her phone.

"*All in.*" Jeremy claps once and rubs his hands together like a cartoon villain with a flawless plan. "Let's go make morally questionable, potentially reputation-damaging choices!"

"Exactly," I say, already walking out the door. "Tonight, I'm turning off the part of my brain that overthinks every damn thing and letting my vagina take the wheel."

"Yes!" Jeremy points at the screen.

"No romance," I add, holding up a finger. "No feelings. Just sin without names, numbers, and follow-ups."

Jeremy nods. "Heat, poor judgment, and plausible deniability?"

I grin. "The holy trinity."

Maya groans. "You two are actual demons."

"And proud," we say in unison.

# CHAPTER 23
# THE COCKTAIL WITH TEETH

NOLAN

Serious question, Carl: If you had to fight one animal in hand-to-hand combat, what would you choose?

Goldfish. No hesitation. I like to win.

I'd pick a goose. I want the glory.

I respect that. Goose fights are never one-on-one, though. That's how they get you.

Okay, new question: Do you sleep with socks on?

Absolutely not. I'm not a psychopath.

Correct answer. You may proceed with digital friendship.

What's your weirdest comfort habit?

When I'm stressed, I alphabetize my spice rack.

That is deranged and also extremely hot.
Mine's eating cereal dry, with a spoon, like it's
a meal.

Anarchy. I approve.

THE FIRST SIP of bourbon doesn't do shit.

I swirl it in the glass, watch the amber catch the light, and try not to visibly flinch as Shelby Davidson sips her cotton candy cocktail like she invented brand disruption.

I shouldn't be irritated. This meeting's actually going better than expected. Civil. Efficient. Almost like we're functioning adults.

Which is… progress.

Not that it makes her silence any less distracting.

I take another sip. I hate this. Not only the pageantry of it all, but the knowledge that the fate of Big Stream's invite to the *Cross Island Pitchpocalypse* rests in the hands of a woman who once posed on a yacht with the caption: *brunch is my cardio.*

That's Shelby Davidson for you.

She's one of those young (too young for me), influencer types who builds a brand out of food photos, designer loungewear, and perfect candids.

Tonight is no exception.

She's dressed like a walking Vogue shoot–sheer black silk blouse tucked into impossibly tight ivory trousers, her neckline stacked with layered gold chains and pointy earrings that could probably take out a drone.

Strawberry blonde hair slicked back into a glossy power bun, her phone clutched like it's both a weapon and a lifeline. And she's checking said phone like she's waiting for Taylor Swift to personally summon her to dinner.

God, I hope she does so we can cut this short.

Shelby sets it down so she can stab a straw into the ice floating in her side water with practiced flair. She takes a long sip then moves back to her cocktail.

"I read your email," she says, swirling the cotton candy in her drink. "Your ideas are strong, Nolan. I'll give you that."

Oh, well, thank fuck. Gen Z's crown princess approves. Forget my years of experience—over a decade worth—my track record, or the fact that I've closed deals bigger than her online following. What really matters is that *Shelby Davidson* deems my pitch *strong*.

"I appreciate that." I manage not to grit my teeth. "So, does that mean Big Stream has a slot?"

Shelby tilts her head, amused. Then she pats my arm—light, condescending. "You know, this feels a little one-sided. It's like you're courting me but forgot to bring flowers."

I give her a smooth smile. "Would you settle for a steak dinner?"

"I'm a vegetarian."

Right. Of course.

I check my watch. If I power through this last bit, I can still make it home in time to catch the final five minutes of *Bachelor Barn* and roast it in real-time with TF. Nothing like manufactured heartbreak and badly edited confessions to cap off the night.

"Look." I lower my voice. "I know Asher has a lot of options. But this campaign? Big Stream can build it into something iconic. And if we're at the table—"

"Oh my God, stop." She waves a manicured hand. "You're pitching. Relax. This is happy hour, not Shark Tank."

The server comes by, places a fresh cocktail in front of Shelby.

I lean back in my chair, forcing a chuckle. "Fine. No pitch. Just drinks and awkward small talk."

Shelby's eyes glitter with mischief. "I *do* love awkward small talk with you, Nolan. Full confession, I honestly came for the free drinks. And to see you sweat a little."

She snaps a photo of that free drink and then begins furiously typing what I can only assume is her latest caption.

"This drink has more fluff than my ex's excuses. Ten out of ten would sip again. Hashtag sugar and spite. Hashtag networking but make it fermented. Hashtag she came she saw she sipped. And post."

What a little bitch.

I'm about to ask if we can end this charade when the door opens behind her, and I freeze.

Rorie Adams walks in wearing a skirt that's basically a suggestion, not a garment, and a dark green see-through top that short circuits my brain straight back to our kiss.

And my dick goes instantly, shamelessly, to prayer position.

She looks beautiful. Her skin glows like temptation incarnate, her cleavage catching the low light, and that sinful sliver of side boob should come with a security escort.

That woman is dressed to cause problems on purpose. Like she walked out of a fantasy and into my ruin. Confidence sprayed on, hips carved for chaos. And every single part of me—heart, brain, and dick —is volunteering as tribute.

Honestly? My soul's packing a duffel bag and begging to go with.

She hasn't seen me yet. Which gives me three seconds to get my shit together.

Three...

Two...

One...

She looks up.

Our eyes lock.

Yeah, I'm fucked.

Not because she looks hot. But because my night just went from politely kissing Shelby Davidson's ass to navigating the emotional equivalent of a landmine field in high heels after two cocktails.

Maya and Jeremy flank her again, laughing, carrying on.

Rorie falters. It's barely a second, but it's there, a tiny hesitation, a glitch in her perfect entrance because she's realizing she walked into the middle of something unexpected.

To be fair, she did.

Her chin lifts, a little too high. It's her tell. And it lights up something feral in my chest. I love it when she plays tough.

Shelby perks up beside me. "Oh my God, there's Rorie Adams."

I sip my bourbon like it doesn't matter. Like my pulse didn't just trip all over itself.

"She made those drinks for Asher." Shelby goes on, cheerful and excited. "Have you had one? The Mirage? Or the Titan? Obnoxiously good."

"Nope." My voice stays even. "Haven't had the pleasure."

Shelby, of course, waves her over.

Rorie hesitates, and I watch her weigh the scene with her chin at its most infuriating angle. She glides toward us.

Her blouse is doing things to my blood pressure. And her cleavage is a problem. Her legs? Worse.

"Hey, I've been meaning to text you and set a date for drinks," Shelby says. "I'm Shelby Davidson. Creative Director to Asher Cross." She holds her hand out to shake.

Rorie takes her hand but her eyes are trained on me. "Shelby. Good to *officially* meet you."

"Rorie," I say as evenly as I can manage.

She says nothing back.

Shelby beams. "I *loved* what you did at Crossfire. And those drinks! Titan is a banger, but that Mirage? High-key obsessed."

"Thanks." Rorie's eyes bounce from Shelby to me. Then back again. "So…what are you two doing here? Together?"

The question is light, casual. She's connecting dots.

But her dots are all wrong.

I can literally see the two emotions swirling in Rorie's eyes right now.

Caution.

And jealousy.

Caution, because she's wondering if I'm making a move, charming Shelby to get a leg up in landing the Cross account—making it another win snatched out from under her.

And jealousy, because she kissed me, and now I'm here sipping drinks with a beautiful woman who's three hashtags and a filter away from viral. A girl, really—not a woman by my definition, she's only twenty-three—but Rorie sees it. And she doesn't like it.

Not that she'd ever admit that. Not even under torture.

Sitting back slightly, a lazy smirk tugs at my mouth. "Talking shop."

Which is technically true.

"You should join us for a round," Shelby offers, patting the seat next to her.

Rorie glances at me. Then to her friends. Then back at Shelby. "Sure. Why not." She slides into the seat, which is across from me. Her leg brushes mine under the table.

Not an accident.

She's calm, poised, but there's a current buzzing under her skin, making the tension between us is hot enough to warp metal.

She flips open a menu. She's not reading. "So, is Big Stream's hat officially in the ring? Or are you two..." Her gaze cuts to Shelby, pretending innocence. "Having a different kind of meeting?"

Oh, my little firecracker is fishing.

I stretch my arm along the back of the booth, casual on the outside. But inside, every cell is locked onto her.

Shelby cackles. "*Oh my god!*" she wipes a tear from the corner of her eye. "Me and *him*? Please. That's comedy gold."

Rorie's eyebrows lift. "Is it?"

"He thinks I belong at the kiddie table," she says.

"Because you *brought* snacks to my keynote speech," I reply.

"And you probably needed a nap after it, Boomer," she shoots back. "Should I start calling you 'Corporateasaurus'?"

Rorie chokes on a laugh she doesn't bother hiding. My patience frays.

"So what does that make you, then?" she asks me, casually. "Professionally speaking."

I smirk. "Unlucky."

"Underestimating me," Shelby says, all sing-song and sunshine. "As usual."

"You make it easy."

"Keep going and I'll brand you your own adult diaper line," she says sweetly. "I'll even donate the proceeds to your retirement fund."

Rorie snorts. Her eyes flit to mind and the temperature spikes again.

Shelby turns to Rorie. "Don't you think Big Stream sounds like a frat house beer pong team?"

"Or a plumbing accident," Rorie offers.

Shelby loses it. "Oh my god, *yes*. It gives 'frat bro fell off a float mid-urination' vibes."

Rorie grins. "I saw a guy once at Mardi Gras piss off a balcony like he was auditioning for the Bellagio."

Shelby gasps. *"I was there!"*

I drop my forehead into my hand. Great. They're bonding.

"To Big Stream," Shelby toasts. "May it flow strong and straight."

"To Big Stream," Rorie echoes, clinking her glass. "And may the PR team survive it."

I watch her laugh at my expense, loose, unbothered. She tilts her head back and grins at something Shelby says, and it hits me like a sucker punch. The way her mouth curves, the way the light slides along her cheekbone, it all scrapes against something raw in my chest.

I still want her—badly, stupidly—despite the fact that she's sitting across from me laughing like we're not about to go to war over the biggest pitch of the year.

I should let her go.

But I won't.

I can't.

Not when she looks like that. Not when part of me wants to win her just as much as I want to win this deal.

And that, right there, is the real problem.

Shelby claps her hands. "Okay, no more sparring. You both have invites. Let's drink."

Three color-shifting Mirages land on the table. They shimmer like mood rings and smell like they were brewed in a cauldron.

"I took the liberty of downloading your recipe, and sent it to the bartender," Shelby says. "Market research, obviously."

"Careful, these will mess you up," Rorie warns, eyeing mine like it's a trap. "Make you do things you might regret the next day."

"Is that a threat or an invitation?"

No answer. She eyes me as I take a drink.

It's sweet, and citrusy with a strange little kiss of licorice at the end. A drink that sneaks up on you, sinks its claws in, and refuses to leave.

Like her.

"What's in this?" I ask.

Shelby launches into a breakdown worthy of its own infomercial. Mezcal, dark rum, Velvet Falernum, a whisper of absinthe, lime, butterfly pea flower, champagne float, smoked glass.

I stop listening after "seductive and smoky" because Rorie is watching me like she's daring me.

"Sounds mediocre." I finish off the drink.

Rorie lifts hers, swirls it. "We'll see how mediocre you think it is once it hits your bloodstream?"

And just like that, we slide into another round. Then another. Her knee brushes mine under the table again. And again.

Shelby gets louder. Rorie gets bolder, turning into a storm I want to chase.

And me?

I'm not getting reckless.

I'm getting *sure.*

This is tension with teeth. I'm ready to risk it. Reputation, rivalry, restraint—whatever.

Rorie's circling me, and I'm circling right back—with my eyes open and hands ready.

And then she decides to get feisty. Not the fun kind—the kind that ends with moaning and sweat. No, she brings up the goddamn campaign.

Awesome. Nothing gets me off like professional tension.

It's fine. Totally fine.

"So," Rorie says to me, spinning the ring on her finger, "what's your play gonna be? Hashtag campaigns? Instagram filters? A limited-edition candle that smells like Asher's armpit?"

I take a sip. "You know that'd sell."

"I'm sure it would," Rorie replies. "But Cross doesn't want trending. He wants timeless."

"You really want to talk about this right now?"

She shrugs.

I lean forward slightly. "So what's *your* play gonna be, Adams? A mood board? A viral dance? Maybe you'll create a line of pet wear for him, name it after his childhood dog."

Her lips part, and all I can think about is sliding my cock between them. Gripping her hair, watching her take me deep, those pretty lips stretched around me, wet and eager. Possession with her on her knees and me coming down her throat.

Then her phone lights up on the table with a text from her sidekick friend and co-worker, Jeremy.

I don't mean to look, but I do.

> If you don't sit on that man's face, I swear to God, I'm going to do it for you—I will change his world and I won't feel bad about it.

My grip tightens around my glass so hard I'm surprised it doesn't crack.

I look at Rorie. She doesn't breathe. Doesn't blink. Only stares at that message until eyes flick back to mine.

I don't say a word. Don't need to.

She doesn't smile. Not quite. It's more of a grimace. A you-caught-me slip type expression that she's already trying to bury beneath a glare so cutting it could slice granite. The phone might as well have slapped her across the face.

In a way, it did.

Color floods her cheeks. Her spine straightens. She shifts in her seat, like movement might erase the message. I've got news for her. *Nothing* is going to erase that message. Not from her screen. Not from my memory.

And now I can't stop thinking about her thighs caging my head. Her nails digging in my hair while she rides my face like it was her throne and my mouth demolishes her in the best possible way. I'd die happy serving under her reign.

Yeah.

Good luck pretending *that* didn't happen.

Her cheeks are pink from embarrassment. Her eyes lift again and narrow.

I don't look away. I drink her in. And smile.

# CHAPTER 24

# TEXT. SEEN. DEAD.

RORIE

I CAN'T BREATHE.

Not properly, anyway.

Jeremy's text. Nolan's reaction.

If mortification were a game show, I'd be in the bonus round, sweating under the lights and praying for a commercial break.

He *saw it*, and now he's sitting there, arm draped across the back of the booth, bourbon in hand, eyes on me, watching, waiting for me to make the next move.

My face is hot. My blood is pumping louder than the music.

And my drink?

Long gone.

I sucked that shit down about five seconds after I realized he read Jeremy's words.

I'm not sure what embarrasses me more: the fact that Jeremy sent the text and he saw it, or the fact that Nolan's probably playing the image in his head right now in full Dolby surround sound.

Shoving my phone into my bag, I slide out from the table. "I need to pee," I say, which is the most obvious lie I've ever told in my life.

I don't wait for a response. I grab my purse and head toward the bathroom. The air changes the second I walk away—cooler, a slight reprieve from the war zone I just abandoned.

Pressing through the crowd, I shoulder through strangers, every step echoing with the memory of Nolan's gaze and the not-so-subtle reminder that I haven't been touched by a man–*like that*–in a while.

Hence, the reason I'm here in the first place.

And apparently, my subconscious thinks Nolan Rhodes is the emergency exit from my dry spell, because it's already yanking the lever.

*Help me.*

Reaching the bathroom, I shove the door open with more force than necessary. The soft whoosh of air and silence envelopes me like a reset button I'm too wired to press.

I stare at myself in the mirror. My reflection does not say: *woman in control.*

It says: *woman in spiral.*

Hair slightly wild. Lipstick fading. Chest rising too fast.

Gripping the sink like it might stop me from combusting, I whisper, "Get it together."

But the second I close my eyes, dark eyes, lazy grin, cute ass dimple, and the memory of his mouth on mine, hands on my waist, and that look he gives me, they all assault my mind.

I exhale hard and turn on the faucet. Cold water. A splash to the face. A moment to recalibrate.

That's all I need.

I grab a paper towel, dab my face, press it to my neck. Deep breaths.

This is nothing. I can handle this.

It's just a bar.

Just a drink.

Just a man I definitely, absolutely, should *not* be imagining between my thighs.

But I am.

I close my eyes. Behind me—the door creaks open.

# CHAPTER 25
# PUBLIC INDECENCY PENDING

## NOLAN

I'M BUZZED.

No, scratch that—*I'm Mirage'd*

That stupid drink. All smoke and shimmer and sweet smoothness that sneaks up on you. It's a cocktail dressed like a magic trick, and tastes like candy, but ends in jail time.

Basically, it's contradiction in a glass. And speaking of contradictions...

Rorie's been gone five minutes.

Maybe six.

Maya made her way over to our table after Rorie left and Shelby's now giggling with her about god-knows-what, and I've officially reached the end of my patience, *and* the bottom of my glass.

*Fuck this.*

I slide out of my seat, mumble something half-hearted about needing the restroom, and walk off.

We all know that's not why I'm leaving. I'm looking for Rorie. And for reasons I haven't fully unpacked yet, her absence feels like a missing pulse—subtle, but wrong. Like something vital just went quiet, and I can't make sense of the silence.

Of course she's nowhere in sight. Probably still in the restroom. I head that way, push the door of the men's room open and nearly walk straight into Jeremy.

He stumbles back a step, eyes wide. "Oh—hey. Oopsie. Sorry about that text, man."

One brow arches.

"Yeah, so, Rorie fired off a whole bunch of rage messages to me right after. She's like super pissed, but hey..." He shrugs, shameless. "Not my fault she left her phone where God and your erection could see it."

I exhale through my nose. "Jeremy—"

"I'm *glad* you saw it," he cuts in, holding up a finger. "Now she'll fucking pounce already. I mean, the girl's on a full-blown manhunt and I, for one, would like to see her aim that energy in *your* direction."

My mind turns his words over. I plant my hands on my hips. "Manhunt?"

He winces. "Uh, oh. I've said too much again."

I stare. Apparently silence is a cue for him to keep spilling. Which is fine by me.

"She's in heat, okay?" He says it like a confession. "Came here specifically to find someone to fill her horny bucket. Her words, not mine."

"Horny bucket?" I echo, blinking.

"Yeah. Like an emotional bucket, but for orgasms. Hers is apparently bone dry and on fire." A pause. Then he adds, "She's probably worn her vibrator out since meeting you. Poor thing's out here running on fumes and false hope."

"I—what?"

Jeremy pats my shoulder like I'm the idiot. "Go find her. Think of it as sexual hydration. You're the Gatorade, babe." He winks and then slips out the door as though he didn't just shred every rational thought I had left.

I stand there too long. The image of Rorie, flushed and desperate, whispering about needing someone to fuck the sexual frustration out of her, wrapping around my brain like a noose.

Tight.

Merciless.

So wait, she's here looking for someone?

Someone who *isn't me?*

My blood turns molten, burning a lethal path through my veins. After the way she kissed me like she'd been starving for it, aching for it, and she's out here hunting for *someone?*

No.

No fucking way.

The ground shifts under me. Ugly, bitter jealousy takes root.

I move.

Out the men's room.

Across the hall.

Straight into the women's.

The second I push open the door, her eyes snap to mine in the mirror, stunned. Glacial blue gaze pin me in place like a blade pressed beneath my skin, daring me to move.

"Jeremy tells me you're on a manhunt." Might as well be blunt about it.

Her mouth parts. There's a slight rise of her chest.

"What were his words again...?" I pretend to search for it. "Oh. Right." My fingers snap. "You're looking for someone to fill your horny bucket."

Embarrassment flashes in her eyes but she's stalk-still, caught between fight and flight while music thrums against the walls, muffled by layers of concrete and the weight of whatever is about to happen next.

"Love him." Rorie sneers. "But he needs to stay in his lane and out of my sex life."

The pull between us sizzles, electric, raw, and ready to ignite. Heat coils low in my spine as I close the distance, each step fueled by liquid courage and a mix of burning hot rage and possessive jealousy. Which I know I have no right to feel.

Except...I fucking do.

"True, but let me get this straight." My hands brace either side of the sink, boxing her in. "You kissed me like you were drowning, and I was the only breath left. And now you're on a *hunt?*"

Those pretty eyes of hers flick away. Guilty.

My mouth leans in to her ear. "The idea of *anyone* else putting their hands on you makes me want to commit an actual felony, Rorie."

Her head twists to face me. That twisty jasmine perfume winds its way into my bloodstream. It's a scent I'd follow into war.

"You think just because we kissed I'm yours now?" Her voice is tight and trembling but there's an edge of fear threading through it.

She wants me to say yes.

My tongue darts out over my bottom lip, and my teeth drag across it. "That kiss scared you, didn't it."

"Please, it meant nothing."

I'm staring at her lips. "It meant too much."

"You flatter yourself."

"Kind of like how you bullshit yourself?"

Her chin tips up in that sharp, defiant tilt that drives me fucking insane. My cock goes hard so fast it's painful. Every ounce of stubborn fire in her just begs to be tamed.

I want to grab her by that perfect jaw, shove my dick between those pouty lips, and fuck her mouth until she's choking on it. Until every last shred of that beautiful resistance is broken under my hands and mine to own.

"You don't want *someone* else, Rorie."

"No?"

She's baiting me. Testing how far I'll go. How serious I am.

And right now, I'm pretty fucking serious.

"No," I say, firm.

"You think you're qualified for the position, huh?"

My eyes roam over the mouthwatering curve of her breasts, barely contained by that sinful neckline. Perfect. Full. Designed to ruin a man's sanity.

Mark my words—whether it's tonight or ten nights from now—I'm going to bury my face between her thighs, lick her until she's dripping, bite those tight little nipples until she's squirming, begging, and make her ride my tongue like her life depends on it.

By the time I'm done, she won't just be saying my name—she'll be *crying* it.

I lean in, my voice low and rough. "Oh, I'm more than qualified."

"You'll have to submit an application," she says, still playing her little game. "References. Full background check. Possibly a physical. Competition's brutal these days."

I chuckle.

Her brow furrows. "Why are you laughing?"

"Because, Rorie...I'm done playing."

One hand finds her waist, the other lands at the base of her spine, and I spin her quickly.

Her breath hitches. I kiss her. Hard. Deep. Like it's the last thing I'll ever get to feel.

And just like that, we're no longer circling.

We're colliding.

She tastes like challenge and longing. And one of those is a favorite of mine.

My hands slide into her hair as her fingers clutch my shirt, pulling me closer, securing us together. I hoist her up on the counter. A breathless, needy sound she couldn't hold back if she tried, lights me up inside.

That noise? That's not hesitation.

It's surrender.

My palms roam up her inner thighs before coaxing them apart. She lets me, no protest, just a shivery inhale as I step between her legs and press in. My body slots against hers, every rock hard inch of me syncing perfectly.

I glance down at her spread legs and freeze for half a second because Rorie Adams isn't wearing a damn thing under her skirt.

All logic disappears. Time, space, consequences, none of it exists anymore. Just her. Just us. Just this raw, reckless collision of need and want and *more*.

She must see the question in my eyes because she says, "I don't like panties."

"Ever?"

With a wicked glint in her eyes, she shakes her head slowly. "Nope. Especially when I know I'm going to misbehave."

Her legs open a few more inches. An unspoken invitation. An unholy temptation.

A feral growl involuntarily rumbles in my chest.

"What do you want to do, Rhodes?"

"Loaded question, Adams. But if you must know...I want to drop to my knees, bury my mouth in your pussy and make you forget every name but mine."My hand inches up over her mound.

"Oh, fuck," she huffs out, those blue eyes darkening.

"All in good time..." My cock fights against the barrier of my pants as she arches into me seeking pressure. "Right now, I want you desperate for the kind of friction that makes clothes feel like punishment."

Her eyes flash, wild and bare. Her lips part. All that comes out is a soft little sound that nearly undoes me.

My thumb teases the tender skin above the place she wants me most. I lean in and drag my mouth across the curve of her jaw. She's salt and want, heat built over stolen glances and sharp-tongued banter. And she's finally breaking.

I map every line, every shift, every intake of breath. She's tense beneath my touch, wound tight as wire.

"Tell me to stop." My lips brush the shell of her ear. "Say the word, and I'll walk out that door."

She doesn't.

Instead, she palms the back of my neck, tugs me closer like she's afraid I'll disappear if she lets go, and kisses me again. It's anything but gentle.

My thumb finds her wet, needy cunt and I slide it inside. Eyes fluttering shut, she sighs.

"You're pussy is soaked, Rorie." I replace my thumb with one finger. "You've been sitting there all night in this mess, haven't you?" I ease deeper, letting her feel every inch, every slow push. "Answer me, Rorie."

"Yes." It's barely audible. Her hips roll against my hand with unspoken urgency.

Her body tenses when I add a second finger. And when she gasps, it shoots straight to my cock. She looks so fucking good, grinding against my hand while my fingers explore, and stroke.

I draw back a bit just to torture her, but the look she's giving me detonates in my bloodstream.

She knows it.

I know it.

We're dangling on the edge of something irreversible here—and the next move we make won't just ruin the rules. It'll rewrite the whole damn game.

Rorie moans, lip caught between her teeth, her body moving on its own, rubbing, finding the friction she so desperately wants.

She's scorching hot, and when I curl my fingers just right, I swear her temperature rises with each grind. The way she makes tiny mewl sounds has me clenching my jaw to keep from losing it right there.

With two fingers driving deep, my thumb drags up to her slick and swollen clit. I knead, and tease, and I *really* want to suck on that tiny little nub. It takes every ounce of restraint I have not to make her sweet, hot pussy my next meal.

"Nolan," she cries out, jerking beneath me.

"That's it, Rorie." My voice is dark. "Scream my name. Let everyone hear who's making you feel so good."

Her gaze drops to watch my fingers work inside her. I'm buried to the end, my thumb still circling her clit.

"You love watching me fuck your pussy with my fingers— watching what I do to you, don't you?"

"Yes," she whispers.

Her thighs tremble, and my cock throbs. With my wrist twisting, slow and filthy, I let her ride every inch of pressure I give her. Her slick coats my hand, sticky and warm, and I want to feel her crumble with my fingers so far inside her she'll never forget the shape of my hands, or the way I made her collapse one thrust, one breath, one shudder at a time.

I crash into her with a kiss so punishing it's sure to leave a mark. Her fingers tangle in my hair as my tongue sweeps against hers. She moans again—and Jesus, it's the sexiest thing ever.

My lips brush along the curve of her throat, chasing the wild thrum of her pulse like it's calling me home. She tastes like wildfire and surrender, and when her hips roll again, searching, my spine lights up.

Her breath stutters. And for one suspended moment, she freezes like she's realizing what we've done, what we're doing. But then she exhales a shattered moan, her breaths short and choppy as her pussy clenches around me. And fuck, she's so goddamn tight. Rorie Adams, dripping wet and coming on my fingers, is the most glorious thing I've ever felt.

Once her breathing slows, I ease out carefully, dragging the tips of my fingers over her sensitive area, but she doesn't retreat.

She climbs.

Rorie's legs wrap around my waist, tight and hungry, her pussy pressing into the thick ridge of my cock through my pants. She moves again, chasing her high.

Nothing separates us but thin fabric, and it's soaked through now. Every press, every roll of her hips sends lightning through my system. I'm strung so tight I'm two breaths from losing it completely.

"That's it, Rorie," I growl against her neck, my voice raw and wrecked. "Take what you need. Take all of it."

A whimper from her is barely audible, but it shreds me. She's so responsive, grinding harder now—rougher, desperate—like she can't get close enough.

Her head tips back, exposing more of her neck. I don't hesitate. I bury my face there, licking and sucking at her skin while her body rides mine with frantic rhythm.

"Nolan," she gasps. It's a broken sound. A plea. And my name has never sounded like that before.

Snarling under my breath, I yank her harder against me. "You feel that?" I press up into her so every brutal inch shows her how hard she makes me. "Feel what you're doing to me?"

She nods—frantic.

"Say it."

Her lips falter. And then her eyes lock on mine, wide and brimming with heat. Her voice is a whisper that guts me: "I feel you, Nolan. It's so fucking good."

That's the breaking point. That's the moment.

I'm going to come just like this, her writhing against me, moaning for me, melting into every brutal kiss I press into her jaw.

I want her to spike so high she forgets how to breathe. I want her to come undone just from the friction between us. I want her aching from this tomorrow. And I want her crawling back for more.

I tighten my grip, drag my lips along the shell of her ear, and whisper, "Don't stop, baby. Come again for me. Show me how fucking desperate you are for it."

And god, she does.

She moves harder, faster, hips stuttering as she chases the edge, body unlacing with each desperate grind. Her moans grow more fractured, she's barely holding herself together. Every tremble, every twitch of muscle, every fractured breath vibrates against my skin.

She's so damn close.

"Do it right here, baby. Come on me. Make more of a mess."

She explodes, body locking up tight, then breaking wide open. Rorie's falling over the edge once again and it's the sweetest fucking sound.

As her release rips through her, Rorie's thighs clench around me, and a cry punches from her throat.

I watch every second of it. Her lips parting, her eyes fluttering shut, her body going slack for one beat—only one—before she sucks in a breath. She just fell apart in my hands, and on my cock, and she's realizing there's no putting herself back together the same way.

It's the hottest thing I've ever seen.

She blinks up at me, dazed, chest still heaving.

Reaching up, I drag my thumb reverently across her bottom lip. Her eyes are still heavy-lidded, her body limp from the aftershocks, and god, she's never looked more beautiful.

I press my forehead to hers, letting us breathe in the same stolen, shaky air. "You okay?"

She nods.

I let a crooked smile pull at my lips. "You just dry humped me in the bathroom of a bar."

Her laugh is quiet, raspy. "You started it by finger fucking me."

My grin deepens. "And I'm not even close to being finished with you."

But that's when the bathroom door creaks open behind us.

"What the actual *fuck*," Maya's voice rings out like a grenade.

"Maya." Rorie jolts, nearly knocking back into the sink.

I stiffen, hands still on her hips, body angled like I'm protecting a crime scene, which, honestly, I might be.

Maya stands frozen just inside the door, eyes wide, jaw somewhere near the tile floor.

"Well," she says, stepping inside, "I came in here to tell you we've got to get Jeremy home. He's past his three too many phase, and Dr. Fiddlestorm the Third is about to make an appearance. *However,* this is an *interesting* development."

Rorie squeezes her eyes shut like she's wishing for a trapdoor to open beneath her. "I was just—"

"Fucking in a public bathroom?" Maya helpfully supplies. "Yeah. No shit. But hey—your goal tonight was to get off, so... *Mission. Accomplished.*"

"We weren't fucking," Rorie fires back.

I step back a fraction, my palms reluctantly sliding from her skin. The moment evaporates, replaced by fluorescent lighting and the awkward silence of witnesses.

Maya folds her arms, fixing me with a look. "Really? The *bathroom?*"

I rake a hand down my face, still breathless, still painfully aware of my raging hard on. "It's not what it looks like."

"Oh, come on. It's *exactly* what it looks like." Maya lifts a brow, then gestures between us. "And honestly? Good for you. But this?" She points to the walls, then zeroes in on me. "You can do better. She's worth more."

I nod once, voice rough. "I know."

She jerks her chin toward the door. "Then go. Before you start eyeing the mop closet for round two."

Three, actually.

"Maya," Rorie groans, tugging her dress down with all the grace of someone reentering the atmosphere.

"What?" Maya shrugs. "If you're gonna have hot enemy sex, at least do it somewhere that doesn't smell like bleach and broken dreams."

For the first time, Rorie almost laughs. I glance at her as I adjust my sleeves, something electric passing between us.

"Uh–sorry, I'll see you later," she says, hesitant.

Her voice makes my pulse thrum harder.

I press a kiss to her temple. "Goodnight, Adams." Then I move toward the door, acknowledging Maya on the out.

It takes all of two seconds after the door swings shut before I hear, "*HOLY fucking shit*, Rorie! The whole bar heard you in here."

I smile.

And leave them to it.

# CHAPTER 26
# FIVE-FINGERED
# DISCOUNT

### RORIE

When was the last time you had sex?

😐 ...Wow. Not even a "Hey Carl, how's life?"
No "What's up, bestie?" Just straight to THAT?

Fine. Hey Carl, how's life? When was the last
time you had sex? Also, emoji number one.

😑 Unbelievable.

And, sorry, but THIS convo calls for emojis.

Answer the question, Carl.

Define "sex."

If you say something stupid, I swear to God...

Look, if we're talking me, myself, and my right
hand?

Daily. Sometimes twice.

😊 Oversharing!

You walked into this. But if we're talking actual, shared, mutually participatory sex… three months…ish.

THREE MONTHS?!

You don't have to type it like that. It looks loud.

BECAUSE IT IS LOUD.

It's not like I had a choice.

What do you mean? You had a girlfriend.

Chloe always had an excuse. Too tired. Too busy. A migraine. Tummy issues. Not in the mood. Maybe later.

Oof.

So, yeah. Three months of me and the five-fingered discount.

That is both hilarious and so sad.

Thanks. That really helps.

Now it's your turn.

Nope.

TF.

I decline.

I did my time. Now spill.

...

Oh, this is bad.

It's not that bad.

How long?

Just under a year.

HOW ARE YOU ALIVE??

Shut up.

No, seriously. Do I need to check on you?
Send you a care package?? With you know...
toys?

Or one of those singing telegrams but with a
"happy ending?"

It's not THAT bad!

Almost a year is absolutely THAT bad.

At this point, you're just practicing necromancy
on your sex life.

I'M FINE.

This is tragic. Truly.

Whatever.

If you ever get desperate, let me know.

•••••• Are you... volunteering?

Can I?

GOODBYE CARL.

Call me. 😌

# CHAPTER 27
# COSMIC. CORPORATE. CONNED.

## NOLAN

RORIE ADAMS IS GOING to be the death of me.

And I'll probably thank her for my untimely end while she steps over my corpse in five inch heels.

The office scurries outside my door, phones ringing, emails pinging, someone in accounting laughing too loud at something that definitely isn't funny.

Normally, this rhythm fuels me. Today, the noise presses against my skull. Because I can't stop thinking about Rorie.

Not just her—*us.*

That tight body grinding against mine, needy and breathless. Rorie dragging herself across my cock, so starved for it. The burn of her skin. The broken sounds she gave me, like secrets too hot to hold.

And the way she sank into me as though her body had been waiting for this, for me

I fucked my hand three times last night.

Shower. Kitchen. Living room.

Each time, I was chasing the same high—reaching for echoes of a moment I couldn't recreate, a feeling I couldn't catch no matter how hard I tried.

And somehow, in all that intensity… and with Maya walking in, I forgot to ask for her number.

I mean, *technically,* I could have Tammy get it for me. But I don't want it that way. I want *her* to give it to me. Voluntarily. Directly. I want Rorie to take that next step, beyond the kiss, beyond the bathroom, beyond the night we nearly combusted in a single solitary moment.

I want it to mean something—something she *chose* to give me.

Not something I stole because I could. Like the backstory I pulled on her.

Speaking of stolen things, that flash drive of Rorie's life is still a loaded weapon sitting in my briefcase. Untouched. Burning a hole through the leather. I haven't opened it. I don't want to read about her.

I want her to tell me. *Herself.*

Fresh out of a relationship, deadline breathing down my neck, and my brain's stuck on Rorie riding me like it was her full-time job.

The door swings open. Jackson strolls in. *Fucking hell.*

"You know what Chloe said to me this morning?" he says, flopping into the chair across from me as though I want him there.

"That she regrets moving in with you?" I mutter without looking up.

"She said, and I quote, 'Jackson, if you were a spice, you'd be flour.'"

That makes me glance up. "Flour's not a spice."

"Exactly!" He throws up his hands, completely outraged. "She said I lack flavor! Me!"

I rub my temples. I hate this guy.

Jackson backstabbed me in literally the worst way possible, but there's something almost childlike about him. Like a Labrador who got too big too fast and still thinks he can fit on your lap. None of that changes that he's dumb as shit, and fucking an asshole though.

Good luck with that, Chloe.

That's what she needed all along. Someone she could mold. Control. Keep beneath her heel. With Jackson, *she* gets to be the prize. The pedestal. The adult in the room. She could never have that with me. I was never going to bow to her, beg for attention, play small.

We were equals.

Chloe didn't want an equal—she wanted someone to raise.

And me? I wanted a partner.

Which brings me back to Rorie.

Everything about her flips a switch in me I didn't know was there. Lust, yeah, but not the shallow kind. It's something else. It's bigger. Scarier.

Sure, I want to ravage her in so many creative ways. Pin her against every surface and leave her questioning reality, like the world only makes sense when we're skin to skin.

But I respect her. And I want to protect her.

Also hand her the damn world and watch her light it on fire.

She's not casual. Not even close.

And the terrifying part?

I could see myself dating her.

I didn't plan on thinking that. Ever. But it's there. Itching at the back of my mind like a splinter refusing to be ignored.

Jackson props his feet up on the corner of my desk. "Speaking of spice... who's got you all twisted up like a pretzel? You've been staring at that screen like it killed your dog."

"Get out," I say.

"Can't. Too invested now." He leans back and folds his arms behind his head. "This wouldn't have anything to do with that woman from the other night, would it?"

I don't answer.

He grins. "The one who hijacked your moment?"

My jaw ticks.

Jackson whistles low. "Damn, man. She's got you by the balls?"

Understatement.

Yeah, it's true. I haven't stopped reeling over Rorie Adams.

And I won't. Not until I have her again.

Until she's under me.

Over me.

On me.

Wrapped around me.

Moaning my name like it's a mantra, and the one thing keeping her grounded while I drive her higher.

Because whatever this thing is between us?

It's not cooling off.

And I don't want it to.

Jackson watches me a beat longer, then says quietly, "For what it's worth, I'm happy for you, man. I know what Chloe and I did was messed up. I won't apologize for loving her, but the deception was wrong. You didn't deserve that."

He stands, brushing imaginary lint off his pants. "So yeah. Hope this thing with Rorie works out for you in all the best ways."

And then he walks out.

No smirk. No dig.

Just truth.

Weird.

"Nolan!"

Tammy's voice yanks me out of my head like a hook to the spine. She's standing in the doorway, clutching a binder and wearing her signature sunbeam grin that usually makes the world manageable.

Not today. I have too much in my head to truly appreciate it.

"Meeting room in five." She breezes in and slaps the binder down on my desk. "You and the team. Cross prep."

Fantastic. More pressure. Just what I need.

"You okay? You look like you spent the night trying to decode a woman and lost the will to live halfway through."

"Close." I rub my eyes. "Just need caffeine. A lot of it."

"I'll grab you some."

She turns to go, but I stop her. "Tam?"

She swivels back, eyebrow raised. "Yeah?"

"Send an email to Bone Dust. A polite exit from their campaign. Tell them Rorie Adams from The Laurel Group is better suited."

Tammy eyes me wearily.

I lean back in my chair and exhale hard. "Oh, and I need you to send Rorie something."

Tammy's brows shoot up. "Why, exactly?"

Nodding, I rub the back of my neck.

"Okay, what happened?"

I glance up at her, deadpan. "Nothing."

"Oh, *come on.*" She steps closer. She's about to drag the details out of me by force. "You *never* pull out of campaigns because other firms are better suited, especially not million dollar ones. And you never ask me to send gifts unless it's to thank a client, apologize to a board member, or—holy shit." Her eyes widen. "You slept with her?"

"I didn't." I say it firmly, but not fast enough.

Tammy narrows her eyes. "But something happened."

I sigh. "Define something."

She crosses her arms. "You're giving brooding statue with a side of unresolved tension vibes. So either you didn't sleep, *orrrr* you slept in a tangle of emotional consequences."

I swipe a hand over my face. "You're confusing this early in the morning."

"You deflect too well for someone who's obviously spinning."

"I'm not in the mood for a debrief right now."

She tilts her head, studying me like I'm an alien in a Nolan suit. "I don't care. You have that look."

"What look?"

"The *I-just-got-hit-by-a-truck-and-loved-it* look. You're smitten."

I smirk despite myself. "If a truck wore red lipstick and smelled like orchids and trouble."

"Nolan...this is—"

"Don't worry," I say. "I still have all my faculties. I'm not writing her name in my will. Or tattooing it on my chest."

She huffs. "Yet."

"Just send the gift. And make it good."

"Flowers?"

"No. Not her style." Two fingers clutch my chin. "Something different. Something smart. Something... her."

She smirks. "You want her to swoon?"

"I want her to *feel*." I gesture vaguely, like that explains anything. "Just... make it count."

She taps her pen against her planner, thoughtful. "Something that says I can't stop thinking about you without screaming Hi, I've lost all grip on reality."

An idea strikes. I open the calendar on my phone, lean forward, adrenaline humming. "A framed star map. For this date." I show her my phone. "The night sky as it was when—"

Tammy's head tilts.

"When everything cracked open for us," I finish.

She blinks. "You want to gift her... the *cosmic alignment* for–"

"Tams." My voice drops. "Please. No more questions."

Tammy blinks again, but this time, the teasing fades from her eyes.

"I want it to tell her I remember," I add quietly, "without saying a word."

Her pen stills. The air shifts.

"Nolan..." Her voice softens, and suddenly she's not my assistant —she's my friend. The kind who's been through it with me. The kind who's scared right alongside me. "Are you sure about this?"

"What are you asking?"

She closes her planner slowly, folding her hands over the cover. "I'm asking if this is *you*, or if it's the whiplash from Chloe."

My chest tightens.

She presses gently, "You've barely started to unpack that fallout. And now you're... here. Planning constellations for someone you've known for what? A week? Two?"

I exhale, defensive. "Jesus, Tam. I'm not planning a proposal."

"I didn't say you were," she says evenly. "But you don't give *anyone* pieces of yourself, Nolan. And now you're handing them to a stranger wrapped in velvet and stardust."

"She's not a stranger."

Tammy gives me a long, level look. "She's not Chloe, either. And that's why you're so drawn to her. But don't mistake different for safe."

"I'm not."

"Aren't you?" she says quietly. "Because right now, she looks like a lifeboat."

Her words cut deep. But instead of snapping, I sit with it. Turn it over. Taste the truth in it.

"I don't know what this is," I admit, voice rough. "But in that moment—*she*—happened. And I get you think it's impulsive, or too fast, and maybe a goddamn disaster waiting to explode. But I'm done playing it safe. I'm doing this."

Tammy's eyes review me, like she's searching for holes. Then she exhales, "Okay."

"Yeah?"

"Yeah." She stands. "Cosmic star map it is."

I grin, standing too. "Thanks, Tam."

She hesitates at the door, then glances back at me. "Just... keep your feet on the ground, okay? Stars are beautiful. But they're far. And they burn."

Then she's gone.

I'm alone again, the silence enveloping me .

But I don't care.

Because this is worth the burn.

I'm certain of it.

I grab the binder Tammy brought in and head into the meeting room. Jackson's already there, slouched in his chair like he's waiting for a manicure, phone in hand.

Thatcher's assistant, Hannah flips through a neatly tabbed notebook across from him. Rishi's queuing up the slides at the front of the room.

Thatcher enters last. Calm, collected, and—per the usual—annoyingly unreadable. He takes his seat at the head of the table.

"We're in." I tap the binder. "Shelby Davidson personally confirmed our slot at the Cross Island Pitchpocalypse."

That gets everyone's attention. Even Jackson looks up from his phone.

"We'll be one of five agencies there. Competition will be tight," I add, scanning the room. "We'll need to bring heat. Full firestorm."

Rishi clears his throat. "We were thinking: clean visuals, immersive storytelling, something tactile to represent the brand's legacy meeting the next generation of digital—"

"Good," Thatcher cuts in. "You've got three weeks to perfect it. We'll present our initial direction to Cross's team on Friday."

He glances at Hannah. "Prep a draft agenda and send it out before the end of day."

She nods, already typing.

"Sounds like we have a solid start." I rap my knuckles once against the tabletop. "Jackson. Rishi. Give us the room for a minute."

Rishi doesn't question it. Jackson does.

"What? You trying to corner him for extra credit?"

"Now, Jackson," Thatcher says, his voice carrying enough steel to make even that jackass move.

Once they're out of the room, I lean against the edge of the table and cross my arms. "We need to talk about Jackson."

Thatcher looks up from his phone, his face stony. "Be more specific."

"Five new firms onboarded in the past month," I say. "All with Jackson's name attached. All with drastically slashed service rates."

The thick skin of his forehead creases.

I don't wait. "Our baseline for branding packages starts at sixty. *Thousand*. Just in case you thought I meant sixty dollars and a Chipotle gift card. Jackson landed some of them for thirty, other for twenty. Twenty, Thatcher. That's not a strategic discount. That's a fire sale."

"They're small accounts." He brushes it off with a wave of his hand. "Low visibility. It's not going to affect the brand."

"Not all the accounts were small. And it's already affecting us." My voice is cutting. "The Laurel Group has clued in and they're livid. We're undercutting the entire playing field just to flex. And worse? My team had zero knowledge of it."

"The Laurel Group? Please. They're a low level firm. I'm not worried about them."

"It's reckless," I snap. "He's a wrecking ball in a velvet blazer. The bigger ones on the list were Rishi's, and Jackson undercut the rates after the pitch, usurping Rishi completely."

Thatcher's eyes harden.

"And you let him do it," I continue, stepping closer. "Without telling me. Without telling anyone. You approved those rates behind my back."

He lifts a brow. "I wasn't aware I needed your permission."

"I don't care about permission," I say. "I care that you undermined every principle this firm was built on. We don't win accounts by slashing our value. We win them because we *are* the value."

"Don't get precious, Nolan. It's a handful of companies."

"A handful is more than enough," I grit out. "Other firms are already whispering that Big Stream is pulling desperate stunts to keep market share. They're saying we're no longer premium, just willing to play dirty."

"Fuck them." He scoffs. "It's strategy."

"No, it's shortsighted. It's predatory. We don't need to choke out the competition—we *are* the competition. And I'm not going to allow it to continue."

Thatcher's tone drops, direct and cold. "Careful."

I stare at him. "We've spent a decade crafting a reputation for innovation, for elite service, for integrity. And you want to gamble it away because Jackson needed a confidence boost?"

He stands, adjusting his jacket cuffs, shrugging off the conversation. "It's not a gamble. It's business. And you think I don't see what Jackson is?" Thatcher asks, almost bored. "I see him just fine. He's serving a bigger purpose—one you're not privy to."

That's the moment I clue in. Jackson isn't some overlooked mistake. He's an open flame, someone Thatcher will use to burn down whatever—or whoever—he needs, when the time comes.

And when the smoke clears, Thatcher won't be the one coughing.

I want zero part of whatever he has planned.

"Some fires burn themselves out," Thatcher says, brushing imaginary lint from his sleeve. "You just have to stand far enough back."

"At what cost?" I ask. "Your name is on the door. I've built the rest. You brought me in for that reason, because I gave this firm *weight*. So if you're going to let your nephew tank our legacy in exchange for a few participation trophies, or some bigger purpose, then you should ask yourself what we actually stand for."

The silence snaps taut between us.

"You've got it all wrong, Nolan." Thatcher meets my gaze, keeps his voice low. "If you want partner, you'll keep your mouth shut. Do the pitch. Deliver the win. And stop pretending like your morality makes you untouchable."

A slow, bitter smile pulls at my mouth. "And here I thought the whole point of partnership was having a say."

He doesn't blink. "You want power, Nolan? Steal it."

Then, as he turns to leave, his voice lands like a hammer. "But if you can't, you'll resign. Quietly. We won't make it a thing."

I glare at him.

"And if you decide to go out swinging, take this righteous crusade to the press or the industry at large..." His smile sharpens. "I'll make sure the only job you can get is assistant social media manager for a startup that sells artisanal dog probiotics."

A long pause.

He straightens his cuffs. "Your move."

And just like that, I own a title that suddenly doesn't mean shit, and work for a company that feels a little less like mine than it did yesterday.

# CHAPTER 28
# ASTRONOMICALLY SCREWED

## RORIE

> I did something naughty the other night and I can't believe I actually went through with it.

Define "naughty."

Are we talking "I used someone else's Netflix account?" OR "I'm now legally banned from a zoo in three states?"

> Not giving specifics, Carl. Just know that I blushed the entire time

That tells me nothing and everything

> Good. Sit in the mystery.

Fine. But if you end up on a watchlist, I'm not testifying in your defense.

Unless you bribe me with details. Or visuals.

A demonstration?

> Tempting, but I'm taking this one to the grave.

MY BODY'S launched a full-scale rebellion, addicted to one specific memory: *Nolan Rhodes pinning me against porcelain.*

It's been twenty-four hours since I let that man finger-fuck me in a bar bathroom and rode his clothed cock like it was my patriotic duty.

And I regret nothing.

Except maybe everything.

Honestly, I don't even recognize myself. Who makes a decision like that? Obviously, someone with the blind confidence of a woman who's never met shame.

I was possessed. Rabid. Possibly concussed. Drunk. Tipsy?

Nope. Horny.

No doubt about it. There's nothing else I can blame this on except raging hormones. And maybe that dimple.

*Definitely* that dimple.

Groaning, I slump over the tiny café table outside my office, my forehead thunking against the cold metal. I deserve punishment. If karma had any decency, a sink would fall from the sky and crush me on the spot.

Of all my problematic life choices, this one ranks somewhere between giving myself side bangs in ninth grade and telling my grandma her famous potato salad tasted like feet. I've never actually tasted feet, but I'm confident they would've been less... rubbery

Clutching my latte like it's my emotional support beverage, I sip. It's useless. Caffeine can't compete with lust-fueled psychosis.

I'm sitting here like an over-sexed feral goblin, replaying it all on a loop, dissecting every sound, breath, and whimper like it's the goddamn Zapruder film.

Did I moan too much? Or too little? Was the finger fucking supposed to ruin me like that, or am I over the top fragile with a clit that knows no chill?

Dear God, the dry humping! Was it enthusiastic or just... tragic?

Is there a proper technique I missed in health class? Because if so, I need the syllabus and a certified instructor immediately.

Shit, what if I peaked in that bathroom?

Taking another long, shaming sip of my latte, I close my eyes.

I am never recovering from this.

I should be thinking about high-level meetings that could make or break my career. Or the literal job that pays my bills.

But no. I'm sitting here wondering if Nolan is also experiencing a post-hump existential spiral. Is he sitting in his corner-office throne, staring out the window like a man who's known my thighs? Who's tasted sin and can't go back?

Jesus. I need therapy.

"Get it together," I mutter. "You are a smart, competent woman. You are not going to be undone by one man's hands. Or mouth. Or cock. Or—ugh—those unfairly hot forearms."

I groan again, because I've officially become the problem.

He could ask me to burn my career to the ground in exchange for one more round against that sink, and I'd be asking if he wanted matches or lighter fluid.

My phone buzzes. Laurel.

Come see me.

I toss my latte in the trash like the broken woman I am and stand up.

Time to pretend I'm not absolutely incinerated inside.

The invitation rests on Laurel's desk, printed on thick ivory cardstock with a foiled teal border and embossed rose gold lettering that catches the light like it's been kissed by ambition.

Everything about it screams important right down to the velvety texture of the raised font beneath my fingertips. It feels like success. Like pressure. Like déjà vu.

I should be ecstatic. This is exactly the kind of opportunity I've been chasing. A dream client. A high-stakes pitch. A chance to remind the industry that Rorie Adams still knows how to win.

But instead of excitement, my chest is tight. Because I've stood here before. Dressed up in potential. Full of promise. And I walked away empty-handed.

Thanks to Big Stream.

Thanks to Nolan *"Enemy Number One"* Rhodes.

And now, I'll be standing across from him. Again.

He'll be confident, hungry. He'll be charming and cocky and probably wearing some sinfully fitted suit that makes my bloodstream do gymnastics.

I can still hear his voice, low and smug: *It's not personal, Adams. It's performance.*

That's how he views it. Just another board to play. Another checkmate to land. And God help me, I hate that part of him almost as much as I want to kiss it out of his mouth.

He was right about one thing, though. If you're not willing to play, you've already lost.

But I don't want to play *his* game.

I want to win mine.

My fingers curl tighter around the edge of the armrests. I don't need tricks. I don't need backroom deals or slashed prices. I don't need to sleep with the enemy to get ahead.

...Right?

*Then why can't you stop thinking about him? Or his cock?*

Which felt *really* big.

The door opens. Laurel glides into the room like she always does, poised, a quiet power in heels. She sees the look on my face and doesn't say a word. She crosses to her desk and sits.

I brace myself. Laurel notices everything. And right now, I'm too fragile to hide.

"You look like you were about to eat that invitation," she says softly.

"It deserves it."

Her lips twitch. "Talk to me."

"It's nothing," I exhale. "Really, I swear."

Laurel pauses, making the silence heavy. "I've heard some talk, Rorie. Did something happen between you and Big Stream's Creative Director?" Her ask is gentle.

I hesitate, then shake my head. "Nothing I'm ready to define."

Her gaze reviews me, trying to read pages I haven't written yet. "He's competition, Rorie."

"I know."

She waits a beat. "And competition gets messy when emotions are involved. Especially when they're unresolved."

"I know that too."

"So what are you really afraid of?"

That question splits something open inside me. The part I keep hidden. The grief I don't let breathe. The fear I don't name.

"I'm scared."

"Of?"

"That I won't be taken seriously in this space. Or that I'm too much." My voice is barely above a whisper. "Too emotional. Too impulsive. Too messy. I'm not cut out for this—this pressure, this constant push to prove I belong. And yeah, so there's a tiny something going on with Nolan Rhodes. And now I feel...ashamed, embarrassed...also alive. Very much alive."

Laurel doesn't look away. She smiles at that. "Is that fear you have *your* voice, or your mother's? Because you sound just like her."

The tears come fast, no warning. Laurel rounds the desk, kneeling in front of me.

"I don't know. Things are happening. And I don't know which way is up, or down. And God, I miss her," I choke out. "She'd know which direction to point me. She believed I'd make it. Even when I didn't."

Laurel's voice is steady. Fierce. "She was good at direction. And you, Rorie...you are the storm and the strategist. The fire and the finesse. You belong here because you built your place. With talent. With grace. With heart."

Nodding, I blink hard, but the tears flood out anyway.

"She'd be proud of you," Laurel adds, softer now. "But more than that, she'd want you to be proud of yourself."

Nodding, I yank a few tissues from her desk.

"And I love that you feel alive with whatever this tiny something is with Nolan. You deserve that. Forget about the others."

"It's not professional," I reply. "You said yourself, things get messy when competition is involved."

"It can," she says. "When it isn't handled with care. But you're also two grown ass adults. Be mature. And trust the right things will work themselves out."

I swallow hard. "It's just...everything with Nolan is this... avalanche. Like I was standing on solid ground and then—*boom*—buried."

"Then dig out," Laurel says, like it's simple. Like it's survival, not surrender.

I laugh, watery and small. "I just keep wondering if this—him and me—maybe it's not the best idea. I think we're happening at the wrong time."

Laurel leans back, studying me the way only she can. Measuring. Waiting. "I guess you just need to ask yourself one question?"

I meet her gaze, feeling my chest rise, then fall. "What's that?"

"Is he worth is?"

"I don't know."

"Well, you better figure that out," she says. "Without losing yourself."

Her words sink in. Not like a knife. More like a slow tide—pulling at everything I've been trying to hold in place.

The truth is...I've lost myself before. Bent too far. Bit down on every sharp edge just to make someone else more comfortable. I swore I wouldn't do it again. So maybe the question isn't *just* whether he's worth it. Maybe it's whether I can pursue something with him without leaving pieces of myself behind.

And if I can't—well, that's a problem I'll need to conquer. Alone.

I stand.

Laurel rises too, smoothing invisible wrinkles from her skirt. "One more thing." Her voice is casual, but her eyes make me freeze. "I got an email today. From Bone Dust."

My breath catches. "And?"

She lifts a shoulder, playing it off but her smile gives her away. "It seems Big Stream pulled out of the running." She lets that hang for a beat, then adds, "They're going with us."

It takes me a second to process. Another second to find my voice.

"Why?"

Laurel's smile turns knowing. Soft in a way she doesn't often let anyone see. "Apparently, Nolan Rhodes sent them an email." She meets my eyes and drops the final blow like it costs her nothing. "Stating you were the better choice."

I stare at her.

Rattled.

Winning feels good. Winning because *he* stepped back? Not so much.

Because whatever's between Nolan and me—whatever storm we are—I still have my own thunder. And I don't need a handout. I don't need a man stepping aside like he's doing me a favor. I never have. If Nolan *"White Knight Complex"* Rhodes thought I needed saving, he never really understood me at all.

My chin lifts, that stubborn, wild part of me—the part that never has learned how to back down—burns hotter than ever.

Let them all underestimate me. Let them hand me losses, or pity, or a victory they think I didn't bleed for. I don't want the easy win.

I want the *fight*.

I always have.

And the next time *someone* tries to clear the path for me, they better pray I don't bulldoze right through them anyway.

After my meeting with Laurel, I make my way back to my office to look up Nolan's email and give him a piece of my mind. *I am not a charity chase.*

I cross the threshold of my office ad stop short at the sight of a sleek black box on my desk.

Not large. Not flashy. But it is deliberate.

Perfectly centered. Tied with a midnight-blue satin ribbon. A small, gold metallic card sits on top like the final, knowing touch. The navy-embossed script reads:

*Tell me you're still thinking*
*about that sink.*
*Because I sure as hell am.*

My pulse skyrockets.

Not because I don't know who it's from.

But because I do.

I stare at it for a solid minute, heart hammering. It's about to break through my ribcage.

My palms tingle with anticipation and something close to dread.

Is this a post-hookup gesture?

If so, it's... intentional. A line being drawn in a place I swore I wouldn't let it be.

I drop into my chair and immediately send a text to our group chat.

> Emergency meeting. My office.
>
> Now!

Two minutes later, Jeremy bursts in like he's been launched from a cannon. "What's wrong?"

Maya follows, far more composed, holding her phone. "This better be an actual fire or I swear to God—"

I point to the box.

They both freeze, look down at it.

"Who's it from?" Maya asks slowly.

"Nolan."

"*Girl,*" Jeremy starts. "If he gives *this* for a glorified dry hump, and finger fuck, I *shudder* to imagine what happens after full-on dick penetration."

"There will be no dick penetration."

"Uh-huh," he says, circling the desk as though he's casing the joint for clues. "So, are we opening it? Or are we just gonna admire the sexy packaging?"

Maya perches on the edge of the desk. "You've got that *I'm pretending to be mad but also weirdly giddy and freaking out internally* look. Very on-brand for you."

I cross my arms. "It was a mistake. A lapse. We had too many cocktails and a moment of weakness. I've rebooted. I'm fine."

Jeremy throws his arms out. "Oh dear Lord, open it."

I sigh, untie the ribbon, and lift the lid.

Inside is a delicate glass orb swirling with flecks of indigo, violet, and silver. It's a bottled night sky.

There's a tag attached:

*Our stars will never fade.*

Maya snatches the accompanying card and unfolds it. Her eyes skim it. "Oh. Ohhh."

"What?" Jeremy leans in.

Maya reads the card aloud. "March fifth. Five forty-seven p.m. This was the night sky the moment everything splintered. When the universe cracked open and let light slip through. We were tangled in other lives, but sometimes things fall apart to make space for the unexpected. For someone worth the break."

Silence.

Total, stunned silence. Because that day burns through my veins like acid.

Maya's brows lift. "It's *very* Mr. Darcy meets NASA."

I blink, trying to find words that don't exist.

Jeremy swallows then says, "If that's not emotional terrorism, I don't know what is."

"Yeah but what's the date?" Maya asks.

I open my mouth.

Then close it.

Open it again, heat crawling up my neck. "It's the day my dad died."

Maya's head snaps toward me. "Wait. What?"

They stare at me.

"I had just bombed the Stanfield pitch," I say softly. "I ran into Nolan that day. It was the first time we'd ever seen each other."

Jeremy stares at the print, reverent. "Okay, I take back every slan-derous thing I've ever said about straight men. This is the shit."

Maya clutches her chest.

"So this a *first met* star map?" Jeremy asks. "Not a post-dry-hump star map?"

"Apparently," I mutter.

"Oh no, that's actually *worse*," Maya says.

"*So much worse*," Jeremy agrees, eyes wide. "That's not just roman-tic. That's soul-bond-level."

I can't breathe. They're right. He marked it in the stars. And suddenly the orb isn't just sweet or sentimental. It's staggering. It's terrifying. It's a reminder of every moment I haven't stopped thinking about, but definitely haven't been ready to feel.

Until now.

And maybe not even now.

My hands are trembling as I close the box, like shutting it will somehow muffle the roaring in my chest.

This is more than I bargained for. And way more than I know how to handle.

*Our stars will never fade.*

The phrase drifts through my mind, soft and echoing.

But this time, it's not Nolan I see, it's my dad. His arm wrapped around my shoulders, pointing up at the night sky with that quiet certainty only he carried.

"*Some stars are stubborn, Rorie-girl,*" he used to say. "*They hold on. Even when everything else fades.*"

Swallowing hard, I blink against the sting. Nolan has no idea what kind of connection this gift touches. No idea what those words *mean* to me.

He was only trying to be sweet. Romantic. But this cracked some-thing open. And I don't know if I'm ready for what's on the other side.

I slide the box aside, careful not to look at it, because if I do, I'll start spiraling all over again.

My fingers hover over the small business card tucked beneath the lid. *Nolan Rhodes, Big Stream Marketing.* His number printed beneath in elegant black font.

"You going to text him?" Maya asks.

I shake my head no, and slip the card into my wallet, behind my ID. The place where I keep the things I'm not ready to let go of.

Jeremy watches with interest. "I can't believe this man gave you a galaxy?"

Hands planted firmly on my hips, I level him with a look.

"So like... what does his cock get you? A personalized comet? A minor planet? The deed to the moon?"

Maya still hasn't spoken. Which, frankly, is alarming.

Her eyes track the box. She's still trying to compute what just happened.

So am I.

She shakes her head, disbelieving. "I'm literally a professional at this and even I don't know what to say."

My throat is tight. Because I don't either. Not when part of me wants to rip this connection out by the root before it becomes something more...

...and the other part is already watering it like a lunatic.

Maya tilts her head, studying me. "You've got some soul-searching to do, friend."

Yeah.

No kidding.

And somehow, Nolan Rhodes has become the one thing I didn't plan for—

A complication I want.

And that might be the most terrifying part of all.

# CHAPTER 29
# LOVEBOMB DETONATED
## NOLAN

Client moved the meeting to 3. You still good
to lead?

> Rishi, I was born ready.

> Then raised by wolves.

> Then professionally trained in PowerPoint.

God help us. I'll bring coffee. You bring charm.

> I'll bring sarcasm and a strong jawline. Close
> enough?

Honestly? That's why we keep getting hired.

I'M NOT EVEN sure how I got here.

One second, I'm half-listening to Rishi pitch, nodding like a responsible adult.

The next, I'm staring at my phone, pretending to check emails while very much *not* thinking about Rorie Adams. Or whether she got the gift. Or what she thought when she opened it.

And then—

An article catches my eye:

*"How to Know If You're Being Lovebombed*
*(And Why It's So Dangerous)."*

I pause. Blink. Click.

**Lovebombing,** the article begins, *is the act of overwhelming someone with excessive attention, admiration, and gifts early in a connection—usually to gain control or create false intimacy.*

A cold bead of sweat forms at the base of my neck.

*Common signs: extravagant gestures early on, constant texts and check-ins, compliments that feel too intense for how well you know each other, pressure to escalate the relationship quickly, the desire to "freeze a moment" as if it's already permanent.*

I stare.

The glass galaxy. The stars. The whole *"I'll remember forever"* vibe.

*Oh my god.*

Am I a lovebomber?

Sitting up straighter, I scroll faster, panic licking the edges of my chest.

It wasn't supposed to be like that. I wasn't trying to manipulate her. I wasn't trying to scare her. I just wanted to give her something that felt memorable.

My inbox pings.

**From:** Rorie Adams r.adams@laurelgroup.com
**To:** Nolan Rhodes nolan.rhodes@bigstreammarketing.com
**Subject:** Thank You

Mr. Rhodes,

I received your gift. It was... unexpected.

Thank you!

Always,

*Rorie*

Rorie Adams | Brand Strategist
*The Laurel Group*

📞 (555) 683-1772 | (555) 432-0098

✉ r.adams@laurelgroup.com

**From:** Nolan Rhodes nolan.rhodes@bigstreammarketing.com
**To:** Rorie Adams r.adams@laurelgroup.com
**Subject:** Re: Thank You

Thanks for confirming.

In hindsight, the gift may have been... over the line.
That wasn't my intention.

We got caught up. It happens. But maybe we should both
take a breath and recalibrate before it shifts into something
it was never meant to be.

Let's consider it a blip. A one-time lapse in judgment. No
harm, no foul.

Take care,
N. Rhodes

Chief Creative Officer
Big Stream Marketing
📞 (555) 987-6243
✉ nolan.rhodes@bigstreammarketing.com

# CHAPTER 30
# OUTLOOK SAYS I'M A COWARD

## NOLAN

THE SECOND I hit send on that email, my chest caved. Due to my own cowardice.

I did it.

I pulled the plug on something that didn't feel casual. On something that, for one night, felt like a beginning. I hit pause, trying to protect us both but the truth is, I panicked.

That article about lovebombing? Chloe's voice in my head calling me over the top with gestures? Rorie's cautious-vibe email?

All kindling into this wildfire of doubt, and I let it burn straight through my better judgment.

Now I've iced her out in a professionally worded rejection that reads more like a cease-and-desist than a conversation.

By the time I get home, my body is coiled tight with tension, jaw aching from how long I've been chewing on this regret.

My mind hasn't stopped spinning since the second I hit send. The email was short. Neat. Respectful. The kind of message you write when you're afraid of being seen too clearly. When you'd rather ghost your own vulnerability than admit you might've felt something.

I practically engraved distance into the signature line.

So if Rorie was already pulling away, I just handed her the scissors and told her to cut the cord.

*Fuck!*

I step into my loft and let the door slam shut behind me, the sound ricocheting through the stillness like a verdict. I rip off my tie, drag my jacket from my shoulders, and toss it somewhere I won't see it for a while. My clothes hit the floor in a trail of self-sabotage.

Vinyl crackles in the background, moody, low, some jazz track I usually lose myself in.

But tonight, the silence is louder. And for the first time in a long time...

I don't want to be alone with it.

I collapse onto the bed, arms flung out like I've just survived a war. And in a way, I have. The emotional equivalent, at least. Except this battle? I started it. And now I've got no one to blame but myself.

Staring up at the ceiling, my mind drifts where it wants, which, predictably, is straight to Rorie.

That maddening, beautiful, complicated woman has carved herself into my thoughts, lodged deep beneath the skin. And I hate it.

But I wanted that. I wanted her.

What did I do instead?

I freaked out.

I scroll through the article again, slower this time, looking for a punch to the dick I know is coming.

- **Intense gifts early on.**

*Yep. That's a big fucking check.*

- **Over-the-top flattery and attention.**

*Okay... yeah. I basically told her she made a bathroom sink holy ground. That probably counts.*

- **Creating a sense of "us" too quickly.**

*Christ.*

- **Idealizing the person before really knowing them.**

*Triple check.*

- **Emotional whiplash—hot one moment, cold the next.**

*I literally just hit* pause. *I am the whiplash.*

My thumb stalls on the next line.

- **Frequent "coincidental" run-ins or manufactured meetings that make it feel like fate.**

*Shit.*

Because yeah, we've had a lot of "coincidences" lately, haven't we? The rooftop. Trivia night. Cross's party. Even Muncan's, where I just happen to buy my steaks, even though it's on the other side of the goddamn city.

I toss my phone onto the bed, watching it bounce once before landing face-down like even it's ashamed of me.

Jesus.

I just scrolled through a checklist of romantic manipulation tactics and found my name on every single one.

This isn't who I am. This isn't what I do. I don't get swept up. I don't lose control. I sure as hell don't send women constellations after a week or so of knowing them and then hit them with a corporate-sounding "let's pause" email like an sentimental cyborg.

And yet... here I am. Practically waving a red flag.

There's only one person who can talk me off this ledge.

With a groan, I reach for my phone.

> You up?

> That sounded like a booty text. It's not.

> I might be having a psychological emergency.

I flop onto my back and stare at the ceiling. TF's gonna rip me apart for this.

I deserve it.

> Hey, Stranger. How was your day?

> Long. You?

> I've had better. Ate an obscene amount of takeout and spent an embarrassing amount of time debating whether folding laundry is a capitalist scam.

> Interesting take.

Thank you. I'm starting a movement.
#WrinklePride.

Her messages come in rapid-fire bursts of sarcasm and wit that always manage to disarm me. It's muscle memory at this point, my fingers replying before my brain can analyze every word. And that's why I don't stop myself from typing the next one.

I hooked up with someone.

Three dots appear. Pause. Disappear.
Then—

Oh?

Oh? That's all I get?

I drop a grenade and you send me one syllable like we're not deeply entangled disasters with a flair for theatrics?

Get invested, TF. I need judgment or fanfare or at least a dramatic gasp.

Okay, fine—

GASP.

CLUTCHES PEARLS.

Faints onto a velvet chaise.

Happy now?

Now tell me:

Was it good?

Was it bad?

Was it so amazing it's now your Roman Empire?

I regret it.

That bad?

No. That GOOD!

The typing bubbles start. Stop. Start again.

And that's a bad thing?

It is.

Sounds like someone's overthinking.

Sounds like someone doesn't know the full story.

So tell me.

I stare at that message, thumb poised and ready. I could ghost this entire conversation, pretend I'm busy. But the truth is, I've been carrying this around all damn day. And somehow, she's the only person I feel safe enough to admit it to.

It wasn't just a hook up. It was a revelation. And also a mistake.

I'm confused. I thought you said it was good?

I did. That's the problem.

What's the worst that happens? You see her again? Hook up with her again? Date?

The worst that happens is I lose everything.

There's a longer pause this time.

There's more to this.

Yeah. There is.

Typing bubbles. Stop. Start. Stop.

What's wrong? You don't trust her with your heart?

I don't trust myself.

I rest my head against the headboard, closing my eyes as the confession hits the air.

But you want to be with her?

My jaw clenches. Because, yeah. That's exactly the problem.

It's too soon.

Too soon for what?

For anything. I should be dating. Exploring. Rebounding.

Not falling headfirst into someone who makes my brain glitch every time she looks at me like I'm not a mess.

No reply. Not yet. Then—

So... you want her. But you're pushing her away. Because it's inconvenient?

Because it's a disaster waiting to happen.

> You're just scared.

That one doesn't land soft. It knocks the breath right out of me. She's not wrong. Before Chloe, I wasn't like this. I didn't second-guess every good thing. I didn't weigh every choice like it might be the one that sends the whole thing crashing down.

But now, I don't trust the pull. Not even when it feels... true, or right.

So, why is my first instinct to treat it like a threat?

Oh, I know why!

Because finger fucking someone in a public bathroom weeks after having your heart ripped out doesn't exactly scream stable mental health.

> I'm terrified.

> I don't know if I can tell the difference between something fleeting and something worth persuing.

> And if it is worth pursuing? I'm afraid I'll ruin it.

> That's a heavy thing to carry alone.

I read her message again.

And again.

> For what it's worth, you're being way too hard on yourself.

> But if you ever need someone to talk to... I'm here.

> No pressure. Just—here.

That simple reassurance hits like a balm. She doesn't offer solutions. She just offers herself.

> Thanks, Trouble.

Anytime, Problem.

I smile. It's stupid how much better I feel.

Wait. One last thing.

What?

I'm about to send you something exclusive.

Brace yourself.

I laugh, already curious.
A photo loads.
It's... her elbow?

Behold. My WENIS.

What the actual hell?

Excuse you, that's top-tier content.

I don't think I'll ever be able to look at elbows
the same again.

My wenis is stunning, and you will show it
some respect.

I'm actually uncomfortable.

Now you have a piece of me.

You're welcome.

I'm stunned. And grinning like an idiot.

Alright, I'll match your energy.

Feast your eyes.

I send a photo of my ankle.

> 💀 Sir. That is aggressive.

This is who I am.

Raw.

Vulnerable.

Bare-ankled.

> It's just... so much. I feel...
>
> Exposed.

Be honest. You're swooning.

> I'm deeply moved.
>
> Emotionally shaken.

Good. That's the goal.

Remind me, what was the point of this conversation?

> Just to make you smile, or hopefully laugh.
>
> Did it work?

Yeah. It did.

This whole picture exchange was stupid. Pointless.

And yet—I laughed.

Actually laughed. The kind that sneaks up on you. The kind that makes you forget—for a second—that everything around you is burning.

I stare at the screen long after her last message, heart finally slowing its frantic pace.

For the first time all damn day, the pressure in my chest loosens its grip.

Cross. Thatcher. Jackson. Rorie.

All still there.

Still loud.

But TF's words landed somewhere quieter. Somewhere buried.

She didn't try to fix me. Didn't press. She cracked a joke, tossed me a lifeline, and sat in the dark with me like it wasn't something that cost her anything.

And that was enough.

What kind of person does that for someone they've never met? What kind of friend is she to the people who know her in real life—who get her laughter in person, who get to see her face when she smirks, who get to trace the exact shape of her sarcasm with their own hands?

The question creeps in like fog through a cracked window—quiet and unwelcome.

*What if were her?*

What if the voice behind the screen—the stranger who gives me peace when the rest of the world feels like it's closing in—

*is Rorie?*

No.

No, it's not. It can't be. She wouldn't do this. Wouldn't lie.

Would she?

I scrub a hand over my face, hating that the thought came at all. Hating even more that it stuck. Because if TF *was* Rorie—if this softness, this gentleness, this safe place I keep crawling back to...*was her*—then maybe we'd be okay. Maybe I'd have known her better before I broke her.

# CHAPTER 31

# WE KEEP OUR CROWNS
## RORIE

[sos]

> Maya!
>
> You're back from your trip early?

Yep. Trip imploded. Wine required.

Bring tissues and judgment.

> I'm on my way. Don't move.

THE RESTAURANT IS SMALL, tucked into a quiet SoHo side street, dimly lit and rich with the scent of garlic butter and aged wood. It's a place where secrets melt into candlelight and feelings slip loose between sips of wine.

And judging by the SOS Maya texted me an hour ago, I'm about to find out what secret is bleeding all over the bread basket.

Maya's halfway through a bottle of red when I arrive, one dainty hand curled around her glass, the other attached to her phone. She's not scrolling. Not texting. Just sitting, shoulders stiff, jaw tight, eyes locked on the flickering flame in front of her, distracting her from whatever ache she's feeling.

"So," I say, sitting across from her and forcing lightness into my voice, "what are we drinking to?"

She lifts her wine, but her smile falters. "Clarity. I think."

"I take it your business trip-slash-secret Asher escape didn't end in rose petals and orgasms?"

"Not even close."

"You okay?"

Maya exhales, gaze dropping to the untouched oysters. "Not really."

I go quiet, waiting. She doesn't rush. Maya never does. But when she finally speaks, it's soft. Careful. Like her words might splinter if she says them too fast.

"I'm ending things with Asher."

I blink. "Why? They've only just begun."

Her fingertip swirls around the rim. "Or at least... I'm preparing to."

My heart sinks. I've watched this almost-thing between them unfold for weeks now, felt that intense spark between them from across the damn room. "Maya..."

"I can't do it, Ro." She looks up at me, and her eyes aren't glittering with sarcasm or confidence or even frustration. They're just sad. "I can't be someone's secret."

My heart sinks.

"You know what you got after one impulsive, arguably irresponsible dry hump, complete with a symphonic finger fuck?" she says with a dry laugh. "A galaxy."

Her words don't strike all at once. They seep in, sinking deeper with every heartbeat until I feel them everywhere.

Because she's not wrong.

It was reckless. Ill-advised. Created from heat and hunger and very little forethought.

It was also one of my best.

For once, I didn't overthink it. I didn't run. I let myself *feel* something wild and exciting and messy. And for a moment—just one—I existed outside the boundaries of fear.

My throat tightens. "Maya—"

"No, I'm serious," she interrupts gently. "You got a man who tracked the stars and memorialized the moment you met. Meanwhile, I've got a man who can't even say my name in a crowded room."

Oof. That one hits.

"I don't want to be a hidden thing. I want to be center stage, not buried in the credits." She lifts her chin a little. She's trying to convince herself. "If he can't give me that, then he doesn't get me at all."

The silence aches between us. I know it's not just about Asher. It's about everything Maya's ever fought for—her image, her worth, her place in this industry.

"I'm proud of you," I say quietly.

She smiles, but it's soft around the edges. "It still sucks."

I reach across the table and squeeze her hand. "You're not alone."

Maya squeezes back, then exhales and peels her hand away. "God, I've been talking about Asher non-stop. I completely blanked. How are *you* doing? With... you know." She wiggles her eyebrows like we're in middle school and not grown-ass adults dealing with actual heartbreak and questionable professional etiquette.

I force a smile. One of those tight-lipped ones that says *let's not.*

I haven't talked about the galaxy he sent. Or the email that followed.

Not to her. Not to Jeremy. Not to anyone.

It's been a week since I opened that box and felt the floor drop out from under me.

A week since I read those words—*a one-time lapse in judgment*—and locked that part of me away as though it never existed.

I didn't cry. Didn't rage. Just... closed the door. And turned the key.

Because if I said it out loud, it would be real. And if it's real, then I have to admit how humiliated I am.

Because in a few weeks, I'll have to see him again. Work with him. Compete against him.

Pretend that my mind isn't haunted by the way his fingers made me sing like a goddamn aria behind that bathroom door.

Pretend I don't still feel him in the hollow ache between my thighs when I'm trying to sleep. That I'm not picturing him every time my thoughts drift into dangerous places.

And pretend—worst of all—that it wasn't the best I've ever felt.

Nothing about this is professional.

And now, no matter how hard I try, I can't seem to scrub off the shame. It's lodged in my skin, jagged, stubborn, like a barnacle.

And God help me, I loved every fucked up, unprofessional, dizzying second of it.

But it's done.

"Nolan?" I fill in the blank, already feeling the wave of discomfort roll in.

"Mr. Stars-In-A-Box himself. What the hell kind of maniac move was that?" She leans in, eyes wide. "Did you thank him with a mind-blowing, toe-curling blowjob?"

"Jesus Christ, Maya." I groan and cover my face with my hands. "Well." I grab my water hoping, start gulping it like it might drown the shame. "I haven't seen or heard from him. I sent him a thank you email and about two seconds later, he replied me a rejection."

Her face drops. "A rejection?"

"Yup."

"Okay–but *why* would he do that?"

I shrug, but everything about it feels tight. Coiled. "It was all just... *a lot.* One minute, I was plotting the corporate downfall of Big Stream, and the next I'm orgasming against their top exec in a bar bathroom? What the hell is wrong with me?"

She tries so hard not to laugh, she snorts into her glass. "Rorie, I'm begging you—never change."

"I'm serious." I slump back against the chair. "All I wanted was a one-night stand. With some *random* guy. Some fun-sex to reset the algorithm."

"And instead," Maya finishes, "you got Nolan Rhodes, emotional mindfuck and CEO of Making You Forget Logic Exists."

"I've got a mental highlight reel of his hands in my hair and my thighs around his waist," I groan. "I haven't been able to blink without seeing that adorable dimple of his. It's a mess."

"It's not a *mess,*" she says gently. "It's chemistry. Chaos-flavored, sure. But it's not nothing."

I exhale. "But that gift was from a man trying to fall in love, and the email was from a man trying to walk back a mistake. Two sides to the coin. Guess he got a taste and decided he didn't want seconds."

Maya tilts her head. "That's not true. What did the email say exactly?"

I swallow. "Said we got swept up in something. That it was probably just a moment."

The words sting more out loud than they did on screen.

"Oh, babe," she whispers.

"Yeah." I force a smile. "So much for the highlight reel."

Maya shifts in her seat.

"I scared something off before I even had the chance to hold it," I say quietly, staring down at the table. "That's the pattern, right? I feel too deeply, want or need too much, and the second it shows, I watch them run. It's my specialty. Pushing men to their limit just by existing." I swallow hard. "Nolan ran for the same reason they all do. Wanting me means having to stay, means handling real emotions, real fire, real fucking weight. And that's too much for men like him. Men who've only ever been taught how to win, the easy, not how to fight."

Maya doesn't say anything right away. She reaches across the table and hooks her pinky with mine like we're sixteen and trying to swear away the worst parts of life. "You didn't scare anything off. You did what you always do when the ground feels shaky, you tried to make it solid. That's not wrong. That's you surviving."

I look up, throat tight.

"And sometimes," she adds, her voice stronger now, "survival looks like control. But giving in to your feelings is not weakness, Rorie. That's brave as hell. Especially for someone who's convinced she has to earn love by being invincible."

I laugh, but there's no humor in it. "One bathroom hookup and suddenly I'm fraying at the seams."

"Rorie." Her voice is still firm, anchored. "You are intense. And brilliant. And turbulent in the best way. Anyone who can't handle that doesn't get to keep you."

A breath stutters out of me, brittle and raw. "So I didn't blow it?"

She squeezes my hand. "He's the one that blew it. You showed him who you really are. And if he walks away from that? Then he was never supposed to stay."

My eyes sting. I blink fast, but it doesn't stop the prickle behind them. "Jesus. Why are you right at the worst possible times?"

Maya smiles, gentle and a little smug. "Because I've been exactly where you are. I know when a woman starts to confuse being *real* with being *too much*."

We sit in silence for a while. Me with my heartbreak, her with her clarity. Two women refusing to shrink for anyone, even when it would be easier.

I sniff. Sit up straighter. "Alright. So… what's our game plan?"

Maya leans back, collecting herself. "We show up. We bring fire. We win this Pitchpocalypse. We prove, *once again*, that we don't need a man—or a headline—to dominate a pitch."

I grin. "Words from a true strategist."

Her eyes sparkle again. We clink glasses, a silent agreement passing between us.

Asher can keep his secrets.

Nolan can keep his distance.

We'll keep our crowns.

And tomorrow, we rise.

# CHAPTER 32

# HOT FRIES, COLD FEET
## NOLAN

[image attached]

Thinking of you

A close-up of a greasy, glorious pile of fries!

I'm honored. Truly. Nothing says romance like sodium and fryer grease.

They're hot, salty, and a little emotionally unavailable.

Felt accurate.

Are you flirting with me or describing yourself?

Why not both?

Daring. I like it.

THE POOL CUE clacks against the cue ball, sending it gliding across green felt before it knocks into a stripe and drops it clean into the corner pocket. Still got it. Not that it matters.

*The Brother's* pool hall is buzzing in that late-night New York way—neon-soaked, jukebox howling the Killers, and a tang of beer and fried something sticking to every surface.

I'm here early. Not for the beer. Not even for the game. Just... to think.

I line up another shot, not really trying, and sink a solid this time. Go figure. I chalk the cue again, slower now, stalling. My phone buzzes from the ledge next to my drink.

Dad.

I stare at the screen a beat too long before finally swiping to answer. "Yeah?"

"Still alive, then," comes his voice—dry, clipped, always one notch shy of accusation. The same tone he's used for years. It's a reflex he can't unlearn.

I close my eyes for a beat. "Been busy."

"Too busy for the man who raised you?"

The words are mechanical. He's said them before. He says them every time and can't remember.

"I'm sorry," I say, deciding not to tell him we spoke last week. "I've got a big account I'm working on."

There's a pause, then the familiar click of him settling deeper into the past.

"So tell me," he says, briskly, "what have you got lined up to win it?"

Pacing a straight line behind the table, my fingers trailing the worn edge. "We've got a solid pitch," I say. "Clean campaign. Strategy's tight."

He exhales, unimpressed. "Substance doesn't close. Leverage does."

There it is. The old playbook. The only one he remembers how to open.

"You've got dirt on a few of the firms, don't you?" he presses. "Use it."

"No."

"Then get some. You want power, Nolan? Play smarter. Not fairer."

The old anger rises, bitter and too familiar, but I shove it down and brace a hand against the wall. "That's not how I operate," I say carefully.

A beat. A breath.

"That's why you'll lose." He says it without heat, without even malice. Just cold certainty.

I clench my jaw. "I'd rather lose on integrity than win your way."

Brittle silence hums between us. He doesn't even hear me. He's already slipped somewhere else, into some boardroom battle that ended decades ago.

"Spoken like someone who's never had to choose between principle and survival," he mutters at last.

"Spoken like someone who chose wrong. Over and over."

The line goes quiet. I can hear his breath, faint and unsteady on the other side.

When he speaks again, his voice is cold as ever. "Don't call me when it falls apart."

Click.

The line goes dead.

I set my phone on the edge of the table, let out a breath then sink the cue ball without aiming and step back from the table.

A familiar voice cuts through the static in my chest.

"You planning on hustling strangers or just brooding over billiards like Batman?"

Rishi strolls up and nods at my drink. "You good?"

"Fine," I lie.

He doesn't buy it. Never does. Orders us two beers and drops onto a stool.

"You've been off lately," he says, swiping a fry. I smile at that. "Even before the last team meeting. You're phoning in. You don't phone anything in. Not even your hair."

I drag a hand through it. "I'm mulling over mistakes."

He raises a brow. "What kind?"

"The Rorie Adams kind."

He stills.

"She sent a thank-you email for this gift I got her. Cautious. Polite. I replied with corporate ice—ended before things got complicated."

Rishi winces. "You hit her with a business-class breakup?"

"Yup." I scrub a hand over my jaw. "It was stupid. I panicked. I read some viral post about *lovebombing* and got it in my head that I was doing too much. Being too much."

"And now?"

"Now I'm pretending I don't think about her every damn day. She didn't even reply. And I don't blame her."

He watches me.

"She's smart," I add. "Scary smart. Funny as hell. Talented. Strategic. And she got under my skin so fast I still don't know how she did it."

"So go fix it."

"I'm the one who bailed."

"So un-bail."

I say nothing.

"You tanked something that mattered," he says finally. "But you're not dead yet."

I smirk faintly. "Just haunted."

"You get poetic when you're crumbling. So what now? Gonna write her a sonnet or some shit?"

"Not unless it includes the line 'I'm an heart cautious idiot with access to a company credit card.'"

"Better than flowers."

I shake my head, but there's a twitch of a smile at the edge of my mouth.

Rishi asks, "So that's it? End of the road?"

I hesitate. "...Maybe not."

He raises an eyebrow. "And that's because...?"

"There's someone else," I say, almost to myself. "Sort of."

Rishi blinks. "Wait, what?"

I nod slowly. "Anonymous. Through text. It's... been a thing."

"Like a sexting thing?"

"Not gonna lie, sometimes I wish it was. But no. We've been talking for weeks. No names, no faces. Just thoughts. Observations. Fries."

"Fries?"

"Don't ask." I line my stick up. Crack. Miss. "It's... different. We're friends. She's cool."

He watches me. "You caught feelings."

"Not really. I don't know. We connect. She's this closed-door kind of woman—never gives too much away—but I trust her. More than I probably should."

"How did this even start?"

"I deleted Chloe's number after I caught her, then tried sending her an angry drunk text, messed up the last number, and fired off a message to the wrong person."

He squints. "You have a secret pen pal *and* a fractured love story? Dude, this is some best-seller list shit."

I sigh. "Yeah. And somehow, I'm the villain."

"Self-awareness is step one." Rishi lifts his glass. "You realize that's a whole therapy session waiting to happen."

"Trust me, I know."

"You need to meet her. In person. Stop hiding behind the glow of your phone."

"I don't want to scare her off," I mutter. "She gets cagey anytime we flirt too close. And right now, with the Cross event coming up? I don't have the bandwidth to tank another connection. Not when I'm already spread thin. Plus...she's not Rorie."

Rishi lets out a low laugh. "So you're emotionally in love with one woman and physically obsessed with another."

"I'm not in love with her," I sigh. "I just really like talking to her. I don't want to ruin what we have, which is actual friendship. But Rorie...fuck, I should've never pulled back."

"You still want her?"

I nod once.

"Then figure it out. Before someone else does."

I give him a look, but it's half-hearted. "You think this island trip is gonna kill me?"

"If Rorie's there? Yeah. It's gonna be your own personal hell."

"She'll be there."

The cue ball spins to a stop. And so do I. Because somewhere between the silence, the sparks, and the mistake I can't stop regretting, I already know.

It's her.

It's always been her.

Even when I tried to pretend it wasn't.

# CHAPTER 33

# HOUSTON, WE HAVE A NOLAN

RORIE

Shall I grace you with another exclusive selfie of my elbow?

Oh, thank God. I was worried I'd never see the elusive wenis again.

What's next? A scandalous shot of your kneecap?

I don't know if I'm prepared for this level of intimacy.

You joke, but I've got a whole folder of body part close-ups.

Next stop: my slightly asymmetrical big toe. You've been warned.

It's a shame you're wasting all that talent on mac and cheese taste-testing when your true calling is clearly avant-garde photography.

The world just isn't ready for my abstract elbow era.

Facts.

Side Bar…what's the weirdest thing you've
ordered on the menu just to say you tried it?

> Octopus and foie gras…mainly for the
> aesthetic.

Interesting. That's the opposite of what I
expected.

> I'm full of surprises.

That you are.

Tell me the one meal that could fix your
whole day?

> My God, what is with the weird food
> questions?

I'm curious

> Grilled cheese and tomato soup.

> The real kind. Not that watery canned
> nonsense.

Ahh, you're a classic. Nostalgic.

Let me guess—childhood favorite?

> Maybe.

That's a yes.

> My mom used to make it for me growing up.

That's nice. She sounds like a good mom.

> She was. It was kind of our thing. On cold
> days. Long days. Basically any day, especially
> ones that needed a reset.

I get that. Everyone needs a reset meal. For me it's peanut butter on toast. Judge all you want.

Absolutely judging.

But also... respectable.

I'm adding grilled cheese and tomato soup to my list. For science.

And I expect a full review. With photos.

Deal. No promises on presentation. I'm told my cheese melting skills are subpar.

THE SUITCASE GAPES open on my bed, a colorful swirl of indecision spilling out of it. Bikinis, sarongs, linen pants, dress pants, work dresses, sundresses, heels, flats, even a floppy sun hat I bought years ago but never had the guts to wear.

What does one even wear to a high-stakes pitch event disguised as paradise? Professional yet relaxed? Chic but not overdone?

I'm overthinking it. And being ridiculous. The whole thing has my stomach twisted in knots.

Except... it's not solely the event that's doing the twisting.

The real for my gastric issues is because it's been weeks. Three to be exact. Twenty plus days since Nolan Rhodes sent me a galaxy, then vanished from my life like he was never in it.

And every single day since, I've thought about him.

I've told myself I shouldn't. That it was nothing. A moment. A misstep. A detour I should have never taken.

The truth is, I haven't gone a single day without hoping I'll bump into him at a networking thing, or glance across the room at happy hour and find that infuriating smirk aimed at me.

I've even started frequenting Muncan's a little too often. Now I have enough frozen steaks and seasonal sausage in my freezer to start a carnivore podcast. Pretty sure the butcher knows my cholesterol score better than my doctor.

But I haven't seen him. Haven't run into him. Haven't heard a thing.

Not a word. Not an email. Not a breadcrumb in the digital void.

Just silence.

Which, is what he wanted. Brakes applied. *Hard.* Well, slammed, really.

Fine.

Besides, I should be excited. This trip could change everything for The Laurel Group. *For me.*

An exclusive island event, A-list guest list, the biggest brands in the game, and a chance to prove we deserve to sit at the damn table. To grow our own big, swinging dick. As Jeremy would say.

So why does it feel like something important got left behind?

My phone buzzes. Carl.

> You packed yet, overachiever?
>
> Or are you stress-eating trail mix and panic-rolling pantsuits?

A slow smile tugs at the corners of my mouth. Somehow, after all the emotional whiplash that followed Nolan, Carl stayed.

I never gave him the story. Not the whole thing. Not the heart-hammering truth. I'm better at being his witty, perfectly composed therapist from the safe side of a screen.

It's cowardly. Especially after everything he's shared with me—Chloe, the fallout, even the girl he hooked up.

I trust him. I do. But some part of me didn't want to risk becoming small in his eyes. I didn't want to be another story he carries. Another girl tangled up in a man who made her feel too much too soon.

So I kept it. Guarded it.

Felt easier to stay curated. Safe. Undamaged. Because the truth is raw. And a little ugly.

I don't want to be something less than what I am in his eyes. Which is his beloved Textually Frustrated.

But I did tell him about Quinn. About how he walked away after my dad died. How he didn't just leave me, he left when staying meant the most.

Carl's reply had come back almost immediately: *What's his address? I just want to talk.*

Then: *With my fists.*

And then, a beat later: *Do you think Amazon sells glitter brass knuckles? I want him to suffer, but in a fabulous way.*

I'd laughed harder than I expected to. Carl didn't ask for details. He didn't pry. He just offered blind loyalty and stylish violence.

And weirdly that felt like more comfort than anyone had managed to give me in a long time.

He also knows I have a work trip coming up for that career-changing opportunity I landed. Code for: a tropical hellscape of forced networking and suppressed rage in business casual.

Needless to say, over the last few weeks, our texting has increased. At first, it was the occasional chat. A meme. A joke. A picture of fries.

But then it became *every day*.

We talk about everything. And nothing. A good morning here, a sarcastic gif there. A running bit about how doing dishes is a social construct. A passionate debate about whether or not soup counts as a meal.

Bad days. Big dreams. Fears. Fries.

Since he accidentally texted me, I've learned that his least favorite word is "moist." Mine is "bulbous."

He watches concerts on YouTube for hours on end. And I hate the sound of the bathroom fan. Makes my skin crawl.

He also sends me links to ridiculous gifs and asks about my day before I've even had coffee.

He's a mystery. He's safe. Not truly real. Or isn't supposed to be.
But he is.

And never asks for anything. Never crosses a line. And that's what makes it so easy to talk to him.

We keep the mystery alive, not out of fear, but self-preservation. We exist in this strangely comforting friend zone that feels safe.

It's not flirty. Not really.

But it's not not either. I get a bit weird when it is. But Carl always eases back.

I don't know who he is. But I know how he texts when he's in a bad mood. *Clipped.*

I know what shows he watches to decompress. *Corporate dramas, and anything with subtitles.*

I know the weird way he organizes his grocery list. *Pantry to fridge.*

I know how he deflects when he's hurting—but who doesn't—and how he always, *always* checks in when I'm quiet.

And yeah…

It's been nice.

Having someone to talk to, literally about everything.

I tap out a reply.

> I've packed and repacked three times. My suits are judging me. My shoes are mutinying. And yes, I ate all the trail mix.

> Wherever you're going, whatever you're doing, you're going to kill it. The suits are just jealous of your power.

> I'm putting that on a tote bag.

> I'll buy ten. And matching mugs.

It's dumb. It's small. It's everything.

And it keeps me from drowning in the ache of a man who kissed me like I mattered then walked away like I didn't.

#StoryOfMyLife

I set the phone aside and zip the suitcase closed, sealing in my clothes, my nerves, and every feeling I don't want to carry with me.

My carry on sits half-packed on my bed, mocking me with its disorganization. My brain won't shut up long enough to finish the task. I try to distract myself by checking off to-do lists, mentally rehearsing my pitch, but nothing sticks. I need a break. Something mindless.

So I open my email.

The first few are work junk, the usual requests for files or confirmations or pitch prep reminders. And then–

**Shelby Davidson**

Subject: *Finalized Itinerary – Cross Island Pitchpocalypse.*

I click.

The PDF opens slow, like it knows what's coming. Like it's trying to cushion the blow.

There it is.

A list of every major player attending. Three names I recognize, two I don't.

But one I definitely do.

His name makes my palms sweat. And for some reason, I click Big Stream's company link, launching the firm profile. I'm poking a bruise.

There he is.

Nolan *"Asshole I Somehow Still Want"* Rhodes. Better known as Chief Creative Officer for Big Stream Marketing.

Black suit. Clean lines. Smirk that could melt steel.

And those fucking glasses.

Sleek, black-rimmed, perched on the bridge of his too-perfect nose. They have no idea the damage they're doing to the female population.

I close the laptop with a snap just to get a grip.

This is ridiculous.

I've kissed this man. Felt his fingers inside me. His mouth on my neck. I've ground against him in a public bathroom like some unholy thirst demon.

And now I'm sitting here stalking his company website, pretending I didn't ride that man's thigh into another plane of existence.

I open the laptop again. This is fine. Totally fine. Just… professional research.

That's what I tell myself as I scroll through the blog posts. They're clever, creative, like everything else he touches. Most of them don't have him in them. Just his work. His ideas. His vision.

Until I hit something older. Buried a little deeper. From last year.

A photo captioned: *Nolan Rhodes enjoying the Christmas party with his girlfriend, Chloe Prescott.*

I stop breathing. She's beautiful. Movie star beautiful. With legs for days and expensive hair that probably has its own agent. But the smile is brittle. Posed.

Still—there's a familiarity to that caption. The name clangs around in my brain.

*Chloe Prescott.*

*Chloe.*

*Chloe?*

*Oh, fuck. Chloe!*

I click back to my messages. Scroll. Scroll. Scroll some more.

There.

*Jackson?! His dirty dick is a perfect match for that rank ass pussy of yours, Chloe. Enjoy!*

My stomach flips.

Carl texted her name.

Carl and Chloe.

Carl and Jackson.

It's nothing. Coincidence. There's a million Chloe's in this world. Probably two million.

Back to the Big Stream team page.

Jackson Butler.

*Account Manager.*

Oh my god.

No. Way.

Grabbing my bag, I frantically dig for the sleek black business card from my galaxy gift. The one I couldn't bring myself to throw away.

Fingers trembling, I pull up Carl's number and read left to right. Right to left. Then again.

Well, fuck.

No.

I'm seeing things. That's the only explanation.

To prove this absurd theory wrong, I enter the digits into my phone.

One. Two. Three.

It autofills.

**Carl the Doll Collector.**

My blood goes cold. I stare at the screen.

*No, no, no, no, no, no.*
Carl is Nolan.
Nolan is Carl.
I've been texting Nolan. Every. Day.
The man I confided in at 2AM.
The man I compared sock colors with.
The man I humped like it was my last night on earth.
My heart sprints. My vision blurs. I've been launched out of my body.
Same. Fucking. Man.

> Tell me something crazy that happened today.

How about the fact that my *comfort stranger* is the same person who once made me see stars without ever taking off my clothes?
I start choking on absolutely nothing. My phone nearly blasts itself into the sun.

> ...uh.

*Flawless.*

> That bad, huh?

*You have no idea.*

> You could say that.

> You okay?

*Oh, buddy.* I am the furthest possible thing from okay.

> Gotta go. Emergency.

Before he can respond, I chuck my phone across the bed like it might self-destruct then I faceplant into a pillow and scream into the void.

I've made some bad choices in my life.

But this? This takes the fucking cake.

And I have to get on a plane.

To an island.

*With him.*

There's not enough vodka in the world.

Kill me.

Or better yet, kill *him*.

No. That's not fair. This isn't his fault. Not exactly.

But still.

*Our stars will never fade.*

My ass.

I don't even think. I claw across the bed, snatch my phone up, take a screen shot of Carl's number then video conference the two emergency contacts tied directly to the last functioning part of my brain.

It rings twice before Jeremy's face pops up, mid-yawn, his hair rumpled and one eye half-closed. "You better be dying," he mumbles. "Or actively committing arson. Otherwise, I'm hanging up and haunting your dreams out of spite."

"It is." Voice on the edge of hysteria. "It absolutely is."

Maya joins the call next. Her face is puffy, eyes a little red. Crying. She's been crying.

Her hair is in a messy top knot, and she's wearing a hoodie—in the summer—I know for a fact is Asher's. Before I can even think about saying anything, she straightens, schooling her face into something more neutral.

"Stop analyzing me and tell us why you called." She sneers at the screen.

Jeremy squints. "Wait. You're crying. Oh my God, you're—"

Maya cuts him off. "I'm not crying. My allergies are acting up."

Jeremy narrows his eyes. "What are you allergic to, Maya? The truth?"

Maya flips him off.

"Okay, but for real, Rorie." She waves me on. "What's going on?"

Jeremy leans forward. "Yes, what is the drama? Give it to me. Inject it directly into my veins."

Taking a deep breath, I white-knuckle my phone.

"Carl," I say. "I found out who Carl is."

Jeremy gasps so hard he nearly chokes on air. Maya blinks.

"It's Nolan," I whisper. "Carl is Nolan."

Jeremy releases a scream that could shatter glass. Maya exhales. Long. Steady. Worried.

"Are we sure?" she asks, still eerily calm.

I show them the business card on my screen. "Typed in the number. This popped up." I share the screen shot of Carl's contact.

Jeremy falls over. Just disappears off the screen. His phone goes sideways.

"Jeremy?" I call.

His phone shifts. He's on the floor. Face down. Motionless.

Maya shakes her head. "I think you killed him."

After a beat, Jeremy shoots back up resembling a vampire rising from the dead. "Bitch, I told you once and I'll tell you again. This. Is. A. ROM-COM.

I rub my temples. "Jeremy—"

"No, Rorie. Listen to me." He points a finger at the screen. "You texted a mystery stranger for emotional support. You got all kinds of naughty with a man in a public restroom. He sent you a gift memorializing the fucking stars. Now he turns out to be *the* mystery stranger? This is Hallmark if Hallmark had horny writers."

"This is a nightmare."

Maya crosses her arms. "Or it's a red flag buffet with a side of emotional sabotage."

Jeremy gasps. "Excuse you, I am *manifesting love*. Don't harsh the vibe."

"You're manifesting delusion."

With a groan, I flop backward onto my bed. "I don't know what to do. My brain is a blender and everything hurts."

Maya softens. "Focus on the event. Don't let this derail you. You're too close to lose your grip now."

She's right. I know she is.

Maya continues, voice gentler now. "You can't risk blowing this opportunity by getting caught up in some complicated mess with someone who's already fucked with your head."

Jeremy huffs. "Or she could *win* the Pitchpocalypse *and* the man and become a goddess of legend. Ever think of that?"

Maya levels him with a stare. "Real life, Jeremy."

Jeremy huffs. "Boring. Zero stars."

I cover my face with an arm.

Jeremy is wrong.

Maya is right.

I need to stay focused.

And yet.

I drop my arm and glare into the camera.

"You're both the worst."

Jeremy grins wider. "I know."

Maya sighs. "I'm aware."

I hang up before they can say anything else, because at this point, I'm already too confused.

There's a message from Carl waiting for me.

> Talk to me.

Can't. There's a full-blown bee rave in my stomach. DJ Anxiety is spinning tonight.

Because now I know.

And he doesn't.

I need to walk away. Let it go. I'll ghost him.

Or continue and pretend I never saw his face on that website or connected the dots between Chloe, Jackson, and that old, angry text.

> I'm not sure what just happened. But whenever you're ready, whether it's in five minutes or five years, I'll be here to listen.
>
> No pressure. No expectations. Just... me...if you ever want or NEED to talk about anything.

I mean, I'm practically hosting a therapy podcast over here, and you've been an excellent listener to me. A true pro. But it's mostly been about me. My drama. My ex. My choices.

His words hit hard and fast.

Squeezing my eyes shut, frustration coils around my ribs—barbed wire pulled tight.

The typing bubbles flash for a moment. He's trying to decide if he wants to keep pushing. Then it disappears.

Tension grows between us, stretching across the distance, even through a screen.

For the first time since we started this weird, accidental friendship, I don't know what to say to him.

I wait for another message.

It doesn't come.

And I never reply.

# CHAPTER 34

# ALTITUDE: UNSTABLE

NOLAN

THE DAY HAS ARRIVED, and I'm suffocating in my own private nightmare.

This jet is exactly what you'd expect from Asher Cross—obnoxiously sleek, oppressively expensive, and trying just a little too hard to pretend it's not.

Polished leather that's probably imported from a rare Scandinavian cow. Enough legroom to host a summit. And service so pristine, I wouldn't be surprised if the flight attendant offered to rebalance my portfolio.

I should be reviewing notes. Strategizing. Meditating. Something. Anything.

Instead, I'm white-knuckling the armrest while Chloe fucking Prescott giggles three rows up with Jackson, sipping some artisanal juice as though she's not the living embodiment of all my trust issues. Every shrill little laugh pierces my spine like acupuncture administered by Satan.

Shifting in my seat, I tug at the neckline of my shirt. That's not going to loosen the tightness in my stomach though. The anxiety has been winding around it since sunrise.

And just to round out the comedy of errors, Rishi is sitting directly in front of me, practically halfway into the aisle as he flirts with a woman from Taylor & Blythe. Tammy is updating her planner next to him, trying her best not to lose her shit with him.

"Tell me, and be honest." His voice smooth as butter and twice as greasy. "Do I look more like a strategic brand consultant or a tortured poet with emotional depth?"

The woman—pink lipgloss, high ponytail, dark eyes—smirks. "That depends. Are you the kind of poet who journals in lowercase or the kind who drinks bourbon alone in the rain?"

"Both," Rishi replies, absolutely shameless. "I'm very layered."

She snorts into her champagne.

I text Mr. Lover, Lover.

> If you keep leaning that far into her seat, you're going to end up in her lap.

> That's the dream, Rhodes. Some of us didn't come on this trip to stress-eat our dignity.

I exhale hard. He's not wrong. I am stressing. But eating nothing. Except the envy crawling up my throat every time Chloe tosses her head back and laughs at something Jackson says like she isn't the absolute worst.

I glance down at the tablet on my tray table. Blank screen. Zero notes. The only thing I've written in the past hour is:

*Don't punch Jackson.*

Underlined three times.

This is going to be a long flight.

I check my watch. Twenty minutes until takeoff. Rorie hasn't boarded yet.

Every minute she doesn't walk through that door, my brain spins another worst-case scenario. What if she bailed? Or maybe she decided not to tempt fate by spending a week on an island with me. She could be stuck in traffic. What if she misses the flight?

...No. Rorie Adams doesn't miss flights.

My eyes flick toward the entrance again, trying to make it subtle, like I'm just observing. Not counting the seconds until the woman I haven't stopped thinking about shows up and wreaks havoc on whatever self-control I've managed to scrape together over the past few weeks.

Which is none.

I catch movement near the back of the cabin.

Laurel McKee.

She's angled into a conversation with one of the execs from Halston Inc, laughing at something that probably wasn't funny. Her eyes bounce to the main circle of power players clustered near Thatcher, the section unofficially reserved for those who think God designed the C-Suite as a personality.

Thatcher's right in the middle, lounging like he owns the goddamn plane. He hasn't glanced at Laurel once. Doesn't need to. His silence is as deliberate as anything he could've said aloud.

*You're not one of us.*

Laurel's too classy to show it, but her tight grip on the armrest says it all. Along with the split-second recalibration of her smile. The imperceptible tilt of her chin. She's holding herself upright by sheer will.

She's good.

But Rorie's the reason that firm has fangs.

Laurel might be the name on the door, but Rorie's the one who gave it bite. The one who turned a shaky boutique brand into something worth fearing.

And now Rorie's walking into the lion's den with all eyes on her.

*If* she walks in.

God, please let her walk in.

I look out the window, pretend I'm unbothered. But then there's that shift in the air, a prickle of something electric against my skin.

I turn.

And there she is.

# CHAPTER 35
# CABIN PRESSURE
## RORIE

STEPPING ONTO THE PLANE, I give myself a silent pep talk.

I've done this a hundred times before.

I belong here.

I scan the faces. The power.

My heart hammers against my chest. I'm two seconds away from imploding.

This isn't just a flight. It's sixteen hours of pure, unfiltered hell with business class champagne, gourmet cashews, and a high probability of catastrophic decisions.

The jet is ridiculous, by the way. Cream leather seats. Someone literally handed me a chilled towel when I stepped on board.

However, none of that matters the second I look up, because my heart plummets to my toes.

Nolan *"My-Pussy-Remembers"* Rhodes is lounged in his seat wearing in a navy henley, sleeves tight around his biceps, top few buttons undone. Does he know what that does to people?

To me.

And if he doesn't, then God is playing a cruel, elaborate joke.

Because he looks good.

Unfairly, obscenely good.

He's watching me.

Our eyes lock for half a second. My heart clenches. My breath stutters. And that tight, sharp heat between my ribs—the one I've been trying to starve since he sent that email—ignites as though it's been waiting for this exact moment.

But it's not just Nolan I'm looking at.

It's *Carl*.

He's the man I told things to. The one who made me laugh when everything else felt too heavy. The one who sent me a damn galaxy in a box and then shattered me with a three paragraph email.

That man.

Is this man.

The one who helped me.

The one who hurt me.

Same fucking person.

I don't know where to put *any* of that.

Jeremy's behind me, singing "Danger Zone" while adjusting his aviators he bought special for the occasion.

We're the last to board, and nearly every seat is full.

Except two.

One next to Maya.

The other next to Nolan.

Jeremy speeds up, acting like he's going for the last damn cronut on Earth, throws himself into the open seat by Maya, sprawls like a Roman emperor, and then—

Finger guns.

"Hey!" I whisper-shout, glaring at him.

Unbothered, he grins then tips his head toward the only seat left and says, "May the sexual tension be ever in your favor."

I want to murder him, strangle him with his complimentary blanket.

I want to teleport.

I want to crawl out of my skin.

I don't.

I breathe.

Because that's what you do when your friend double-crosses you and you're about to sit beside the man who fingered you into temporary amnesia.

I glance back at Jeremy. He smirks that smug, sparkling bastard. *Fuck him.*

Maya elbows him but does nothing to help.

Fine.

I can handle this.

I, Rorie Adams, marketing professional and vaguely responsible adult, will hold my head high and spend sixteen hours trapped beside the walking identity crisis that is Carl/Nolan Rhodes, aka, monumental mistake.

Except—God help me—I'm not even sure it was a mistake.

I exhale, slap on the most neutral face I can find in my feelings toolbox, and make my way toward the seat.

Nolan doesn't move.

Doesn't smirk.

Doesn't blink.

Just watches.

"Is this seat taken?" My voice is crisp and civil.

He gestures to the seat beside him like we're strangers instead of two people who share a complicated, semi-anonymous emotional bond and an unfortunately unforgettable bathroom history.

Totally normal.

Totally fine.

Just me.

Him.

And sixteen hours of altitude-fueled tension.

What could possibly go wrong?

# CHAPTER 36
# STUCK BETWEEN A DREAM GIRL AND A HARD PLACE. LITERALLY.

## NOLAN

WE'VE JUST ENTERED hostile airspace.

I look up at Rorie and catch a flash of resignation in her eyes. Or annoyance.

Yeah, probably annoyance.

Though it could be something else entirely. One I can't name, but it knocks me just off-center.

When she slides into the seat beside me, her thigh brushes mine. My body locks up tight.

"So," I say casually, "are you planning to stab me mid-flight?"

She tilts her head, weighing it. "We'll see how the first hour goes."

Christ. Why is that hot?

My gaze snags on her lips, and everything in me goes very, very still.

And then loud.

She's here. Next to me. In the flesh. Flushed and fine and infuriating.

And every ounce of self-control I had? Gone. Blown straight out the emergency exit.

The reasons I told myself to back off? Disintegrated. Burned alive in the pressurized cabin air.

All I want is her.

She's settling in, oblivious to the fact that she's detonated my nervous system. And then my imagination—traitorous as ever—launches straight into a visual.

I don't just think about her mouth. I see it. *Feel it.*

The drag of her tongue. The slow, punishing pace. Her lips wrapped around me as I fist her hair and force her to take more—

Shit! I'm fucking hard.

Dying inside, I adjust in my seat, subtly, discreetly, because my dick is clearly on a different page than my brain. This is bad. I'm wearing gray joggers. *Gray.* The official flag of "Hey, look at my boner."

She smooths out her shirt and clicks her seatbelt. And it's only now I realize she's not in one of her usual man killer outfits and heels.

She's in leggings and a ribbed tank, chambray shirt hanging open as though it was a casual afterthought. Hair in a messy bun that makes her look like sex incarnate. Her scent drifts over—citrusy and soft—and I'm already undone.

And knowing that she might not be wearing anything under those leggings, makes my already inconvenient boner, rock fucking hard.

A few minutes of the worst awkward silence in history go by. My mind keeps drifting to her. Mostly how she made me feel. The way she looked at me like I was the most annoying man alive yet somehow still worth her time.

I miss that. I hate that I miss that.

"Your team ready?" I ask, grasping for neutral.

Rorie doesn't look up right away. She crosses one leg over the other. She's trying to test my soul. Then finally says, "Fifty percent."

"Fifty?" I arch a brow.

She shrugs, all nonchalance and quiet steel. "I don't pitch on anything I haven't experienced. You can't fake connection. You have to feel it first."

There's weight in her voice. Intent. She doesn't pitch products—she pitches emotions. She feels everything. Which is exactly why I'm fucked.

A flight attendant appears with menus. "Can I get you anything to eat or drink?"

Rorie barely glances at the menu before shutting it. "Club sandwich. Fries. And a *really* strong dirty martini. Straight up slutty."

The flight attendant smiles.

"Same," I say, because at this point, I need something solid in my system to counteract the storm swirling through my body. "But bourbon for me, please."

Eventually, our food arrives. Rorie's halfway into her sandwich when I swipe one of her fries.

Her head whips toward me. "Seriously?"

"Mine are meh." I pop it in my mouth. "They're better when stolen."

She exhales, shakes her head slightly and mutters, "So I hear."

It's the way she says it so dryly that knocks something loose in my brain. It's familiar. Exactly how Textually Frustrated would say it.

For one brutal second, I almost wish she were TF. That's not possible though.

To distract myself, I stare out the window, watching dusk bleed into night. Below, the ocean stretches endlessly, its surface a dark mirror reflecting the last traces of sunlight, scattering like embers before they disappear entirely.

This trip is going to kill me. And I still don't know what the hell to do about it. If anything.

My head leans back against the chair. Rorie's nose is buried in a book, her fingers idly tracing the edge of the pages as she reads.

At first, I don't think much of it until I catch a few words on the page. Words that make my brows shoot up and a slow, wicked grin tug at my lips.

Well, well, well.

Leaning over, my smirk curves. "His fingers teased along her wet folds, spreading her open as he—"

Rorie flinches, slaps the book shut. "Jesus, Nolan. Do you mind?"

"Oh, I mind very much." I grin like the menace I am. "I'm very interested in this literary masterpiece. What was the next line? His fingers stroked the desperate ache between her thighs—"

"Stop it." Her cheeks blaze.

"Do you prefer the rough type of book boyfriend? Or the teasing-until-you-beg kind? I can do both."

*Oh my God! Why did I say that?*

Rorie's eyes narrow.

I grin, sheepishly, watching the way her lips part ever so slightly, the way her pulse flutters at her throat. And it's in this exact moment that I know...

I'm going to fix this broken thing between us.

Rorie exhales through her nose, visibly seething. She might actually throw the book at my head. She twists in her seat, meets my gaze, and lets a slow, wicked smile curl her lips. Then she taps her fingers against her spicy read, completely unbothered.

"You really want to know what my *type* is?" Her voice drops so low it makes my pulse stutter. "I prefer a man who knows exactly how to make me come with words alone, how to read my body without needing instructions, how to drag it out until I'm shaking, begging for more, and still doesn't let me have it."

My grin freezes, then fades.

*Well, fuck.*

She lifts a smug brow.

As I open my mouth to fire something back, she tilts her head, eyes glinting with cutting amusement.

"I thought I met a guy like that once," she says. "My mistake."

Her words don't just land—they carve. Right through the armor I thought I still had.

I need to laugh it off. Roll my eyes, make some cocky remark.

Instead, I stare at her, jaw tight. This time I don't have a damn thing to say.

The plane lights dim as the flight drags on, conversations fade and Rorie, for all her lethal confidence and sharp edges, has finally gone still.

She's slumped in her seat, head tilted to the side—*my* side—and the faint glow of her phone screen casts soft shadows across her face. Her earbuds are in, and her breathing has evened out, slow and unguarded. Her scent floats in the air between us.

I could pretend this doesn't mean anything. In fact, I should move. Shift away. Jostle her so she wakes up and spares me the torment of feeling her.

I don't.

My pulse ticks up as her head inches closer, and then, with a barely-there exhale, it happens—she rests against my shoulder.

Something thick settles in my chest.

I don't hate it.

I fucking love it, actually.

The weight of Rorie against me feels good. And when I think I might be able to hold it together, she nuzzles into me.

Jesus Christ.

My fingers ache to touch her, and before I can stop myself, I adjust my position so she's more comfortable. It's a small movement so she doesn't wake up with a crick in her neck.

But it doesn't go unnoticed.

Rorie stirs, whispering incomprehensible babble under her breath then she sighs. And it's that sigh that kills me.

Soft. Content. Like she trusts me despite me already fucking that up.

Glancing down at her, my chest tightens even more. She'd die if she knew she's all curled up next to me, letting her guard down.

Then she moves.

A shift. A tiny one.

But it's enough.

Her arm slides, hand slipping from where it was resting near her lap, gliding downward until—

Oh, *fuck me.*

Contact.

A delicate hand lands right between my legs.

Direct hit.

Kill me now.

My entire body seizes up like a man being held at gunpoint. Every neuron in my brain starts screaming, but there's no escape, no logical plan of action.

Does she realize?

No. No, she doesn't.

She's *asleep*, for Christ's sake, oblivious to the absolute hellstorm she's unleashing on me.

I stare at the ceiling. The overhead compartment. Anywhere but down.

*Do not react. Do not react. Do not —*

I react.

My dick, my *traitorous, good-for-nothing dick*, swells beneath her hand. Of course it did, it just got its own private invitation to paradise.

I flinch.

And you know what she does?

She sighs.

That soft, sweet exhale of contentment, as if my suffering is bringing her peace.

I want to scream. I want to shove her off, shake her awake, demand she take responsibility for the absolute travesty of this situation. But I also cannot, under any circumstances, wake her up to this.

What would I even say?

"Hey, Adams, thought you should know you're currently cupping my junk in front of our entire professional network. No big deal. Hope you're well-rested. Oh, and I liked it. Will you consider doing it again?"

Nope.

Not happening.

Twisting enough to escape, I move her hand off my already tortured situation.

She stirs again.

*Fuck.*

Her hand flexes.

She squeezes.

I black out.

I am deceased.

I have left my body and entered another plane of existence.

This is it. This is how I die.

Death by unintentional hand job.

And then, because as I've mentioned, the universe *hates me*, she shifts again, rolling to the side, pulling her hand away at last.

Relief. Sweet, glorious relief. Until she mutters in her sleep. Soft. Dreamy. Barely there.

"Mmm... *so* big."

My pulse is now rewriting the laws of physics and I'm about five seconds from spontaneous human combustion.

# CHAPTER 37
# VOM-COM
## RORIE

THE TARMAC SHIMMERS under the tropical sun, the horizon a wobbling mirage. Heat punches us in the face the second we step off the stairs. This heat doesn't politely warm your shoulders like a gentle, tropical breeze. No. This heat fucks. Relentless, sweaty, grabs you by the throat, grips around your thighs, slides under your bra, and settles somewhere deep in the hormonal core.

Or that's just sixteen hours sitting next to Nolan *"Sex with a Pulse"* Rhodes. The man made me horny by breathing.

"Jesus," Maya mutters, fanning herself with an oversized hat. "Did we land in someone's armpit?"

"More like ballsack." Jeremy adjusts his oversized sunglasses. "I'd want to formally request a refund." He glances over at me, sees me sneering at him. "You aren't still mad are you?"

"Yes." Traitorous, scheming bastard. My glare could fry electronics. "You set me up."

He raises both brows behind obnoxiously large sunglasses. "Set you up for *success*, thank you very much. Some people call that friendship. I call it horny humanitarianism. I did it because I still believe in you two."

I gape. "You are the *worst*."

"In approximately twenty-four hours, you'll be thanking me. Possibly mid-orgasm. Possibly in interpretive dance."

"Jeremy—"

He holds up a finger. "I don't want details. But if he ruins your posture and rewires your brain, I *do* want a positive review."

I roll my eyes so hard I practically give myself a migraine. "You need professional help."

"I need SPF 500 and a therapist who doesn't flinch when I talk about lube preferences. We all have dreams."

Maya snorts. I turn away to hide my smirk and that's when I see him.

Nolan is standing to the side, talking to Rishi and a few other people. Of course he's already networking. Of course he looks tan and smug and as though the only thing he's ever lost in life was patience.

And of course, he turns.

A hint of collarbone shows, and his sunglasses are hooked onto the neckline like he woke up in a GQ ad and decided to stay there.

My mouth goes dry.

Our eyes connect. Heat flares in my cheeks. Not the sun's fault this time.

Jeremy follows my gaze, then says. "There he is. The reason your vibrator's been working overtime."

I don't respond. I just keep staring. Don't think I didn't consider joining the Mile High Club with the travel-sized rose stashed in my carry-on.

Because the whole trip, Nolan was *too* close. Too big. Too everything.

His thigh touched mine more than once, and neither of us moved, or shifted. We just sat there. Let it happen. Our legs were seemingly on some kind of mutually assured destruction pact and committed to the bit.

Which, fine. Whatever. Airplanes are tight quarters. Appendage grazing happens. *Except this one isn't.* This one has more legroom than my apartment. Which means the only reason Nolan Rhodes's thigh was pressed against mine for half the flight is because he let it be.

And I, in a moment of unparalleled self-control failure, let it stay.

And that scent? Not acceptable. That should've been a federal offense. Cedar and spice, and so unfairly masculine it should be trade-marked. Crotch Siren™

Now available in TSA-unapproved levels of potency.

Honestly, the man violated every rule of basic airplane etiquette:

- No touching.
- No excessive hotness.
- No weaponized pheromones.
- No existing with that jawline at 30,000 feet.
- And sure as hell no reading my spicy scenes out loud like he's auditioning for the audiobook.

Instead of a vibrator, I should've packed a chastity belt and noise-canceling ovaries.

To add insult to injury. I had a sex dream about him. Mid-flight. Somewhere over the Pacific.

One second, I was nodding off to the sound of turbulence and Rishi talking about post-flight oysters to some chick. And the next, I was dreaming about Nolan Rhodes pressed against me in a five-star hotel shower, growling things he has no business knowing how to say.

"Dream" Nolan had his hands everywhere. And they were good hands. Unfairly talented, annoyingly cinematic hands.

The details are fuzzy now—mercifully—but the feeling?

Yeah. A branding iron from the Department of Naughty Thoughts seared that part into my brain.

I woke up breathless, skin flushed, thighs clenched. Sweaty, like I'd just finished a HIIT workout, only the *H* stood for *Horny*, the *I's* for *Involuntary* and *Intense*, and the *T* for *Thighs-never-closed*.

I was wet.

Not metaphorically. Not emotionally.

Literally.

My subconscious had apparently decided to run a full simulation of what it would feel like to straddle Nolan Rhodes as if he was a Soul-Cycle seat. And I didn't even get a warm-up.

Two staffers in bright teal polos and wireless earpieces unload our luggage from the jet. It's a blur of designer suitcases and logo-stamped garment bags, all tagged and whisked away before we can so much as reach for a handle.

Apparently, on White Thorn Island, *you* don't carry *anything* except stress, grudges, and a strategically packed vibrator in your carry on.

After they transfer our luggage, we make our way across the tarmac toward the dockside bar. Laurel already ordered a daiquiri and traipsed off to schmooze with execs from the other firms.

By the time we speed-walk to the nearest shade table, my hair's glued to the back of my neck, my deodorant has officially thrown in the towel, and I'm two degrees away from rage-sweating. The sun is merciless, no warm-up, just raw, blistering dominance. Even the palm trees look offended.

Maya lowers her sunglasses, studies me. "Alright. What's that face?"

Jeremy's leaning halfway across the table, waving down a bartender with the desperation of a man dying for a frozen drink. "She's got Nolan on the brain," he announces.

I shoot him a death glare. "I hope you choke on your stupid tiny umbrella."

"Oh, please. You adore me," he sings. "Sixteen hours of thigh grazing and smoldering tension? Don't act like you didn't enjoy playing sky-high seduction."

"We didn't play anything," I say.

Jeremy leans in, stage whispering, "Right. And your little nappy nap? On. His. Shoulder. Not to mention the blanket situation…"

"Wait," Maya interjects. "Did you give him a handie under a monogrammed throw?"

I groan. "Absolutely not."

Jeremy grins, devilish. "Shame. Would've been a great story. Five stars for turbulence."

The drinks land and we grab them like sinners at communion, parched and desperate, worshipping at the altar of crushed ice and rum.

Maya holds up a finger, suddenly solemn. "Look at me." I do. "Don't let his jawline or your tragic sex drought steer you off course.

We came to win, not to ride the Rhodes." She sips her drink. "Keep your crown, bitch."

My mind stutters back to Maya's monogrammed throw comment.

I blink. "Did Nolan put a blanket on me?"

Jeremy's smirks resembles a cat who just knocked something off the counter on purpose. "Yeah, while you were out cold. Real tender moment. Gave the rest of us heart palpitations."

I replay the scene—me waking up, warm, covered, Nolan pretending to be asleep.

That asshole.

He covered me. Quietly. Gently. Without needing credit.

And now that I know it hits different. Sweet in a way that's lethal. The type that sneaks in when your defenses are down, crawls under your skin, and stays there.

And I *hate* how much it makes my heart squeeze.

But—no. Absolutely not. That is not a narrative I will be subscribing to, thank you.

The frozen margarita glides down my throat, cold, blessedly numbing. I want to crawl inside the glass and live there forever.

Maya's eyes shift toward the dock. I follow her gaze. Nolan is still with Rishi, who's wearing fitted linen pants, designer sunglasses, and a shit ton of confidence. Tall, toned, with that hot professor vibe and the high cheekbones to match.

"Rishi is a walking vacation fantasy." Maya licks her lips. "I might make him my island rebound. I bet he comes with room service and a safe word."

"You said *comes* and my soul left my body via erection."

"You are disturbed," I laugh.

Nolan's eyes are on me. Expression brooding. Glass in hand.

My pulse spikes. I take a long sip of my drink, straighten my spine, and turn back to my friends.

"Okay," I say, voice even. "Here's the plan. We win this thing. We keep it professional."

"Like I said," Maya reminds me.

I nod. "And no matter how good someone smells or how many dreams they accidentally star in, we remember who the hell we are."

"Bad bitches," Jeremy says.

"Bosses," Maya echoes.

I lift my glass. "Let's go sink some empires."

I don't tell them that if Nolan Rhodes so much as breathes in my direction again, I might dissolve into a puddle of lust and career sabotage.

Pretty sure they're already aware anyway.

A sleek white boat pulls up and docks to take us to White Thorn Island. The water stretches endlessly before us, a perfect shade of deep turquoise that would be breathtaking if I weren't currently dealing with a second stomach-turning sight:

Chloe.

Nolan's ex. Jackson's current.

The realization is infuriating.

She steps up to the dock and I recognize her instantly from the online photos. Long auburn hair, perfect glowing skin, the kind of beauty that belongs on display.

I didn't notice her on the plane. She must've been seated too far up, hidden in the plush, early boarding section while I was still huffing my way down the aisle as a woman on a mission—and twenty minutes late thanks to airport security and a very confusing escalator detour.

Now, here she is. Perfectly put together. Perfectly timed. And perfectly ruining Carl's—er—Nolan's trip.

Of course she is.

She's standing way too close to that Temu Ken who was at Asher's party.

I don't know *everything* about Nolan's history with her. Not *all* the details. But I know enough to recognize how much this stings him.

And watching them flaunt their relationship—gross. Chloe's tossing her hair, laughing at whatever nonsense that guy is saying, her hand grazing his arm. She knows exactly what she's doing. It makes my blood boil for my friend.

Who is Nolan.

*Fucking hell.*

I tear my gaze away in an attempt to focus on the boat as we begin boarding. Everyone is enchanted by the scenery, phone in hand, chattering about how pristine and untouched the distant island appears.

I sense Nolan's intense, calculating eyes on me. He's trying to decipher every fracture in my defiant façade. It unsettles me.

So, I refuse to look at him.

Once everyone is on, the boat shudders to life and we slice through the water toward White Thorn Island.

The ride is anything but the smooth, luxurious escape I had anticipated. The choppy waves slam against the hull, tossing the boat unpredictably. Each crest of a particularly large swell sends my stomach lurching as if I'm trapped on a relentless roller coaster.

Maya grips the railing beside me, laughing breathlessly, while Jeremy spreads his arms wide and shouts something about "King of the World."

Bracing myself against another violent dip, I grip the seat tightly when I suddenly hear it—a low, miserable groan.

I glance over, and there's Nolan. But something is off. His posture has collapsed into desperation as he clutches the edge of his seat as if it's his only lifeline.

Nolan's face has turned unnaturally pale, and his jaw is set in a rigid line as his throat fights to hold back the inevitable. His Adam's apple bobs, throat working like he's actively fighting for his life.

"Oh shit," I mutter, recognition slamming into me.

Nolan Rhodes is falling apart. One moment he's that powerful, enigmatic rival, and the next he's lurching over the rail, white-knuckled and in agony, vomiting violently over the side.

My mouth drops open.

Holy. Shit.

Maya stares in horrified fascination. Jeremy lets out a sympathetic whistle.

"Damn," he murmurs. "That's brutal, man."

I don't move. I don't breathe.

Because what the hell am I supposed to do?

Offer him water? A mint? My pity?

Nope. Not happening.

Instead, I do the only thing I can do.

I sit back, watch my nemesis, and the guy who told me to use him in the bathroom of a bar, then inboxed me a rejection email, get absolutely wrecked by Mother Nature.

In that stark moment, the undeniable power surges within me, and yet it is tainted by a deep, gnawing conflict. I'm torn between reveling in his downfall and a reluctant, warring empathy that refuses to let me completely celebrate his humiliation.

What kind of a person does that make me exactly?

Well, it's complicated.

# CHAPTER 38

# THE DOOR BETWEEN US
### NOLAN

I STARE at my reflection in the mirror, gripping the edge of the bronze sink.

Right now, it's the only thing holding me upright. My face is ghostly pale, my hair damp around the edges from the water I've splashed to cool myself down, and there's a faint, humiliating pink flush crawling up my neck that screams: "Hey, remember that time you puked in front of literally everyone?"

I thought I hit rock bottom before this. But apparently, rock bottom has a new name, and it's *Projectile Vomiting Over the Side of a Luxury Boat While Your Ex, and Her New Boyfriend Watch.*

And I saw it. The moment. That fleeting second when Chloe moved forward, as though some residual reflex of caretaking kicked in. Like she cared. But Jackson's hand shot out fast, fingers snapping around her wrist, pulling her back as though I was some charity case he didn't want her pitying.

Which is hilarious, because if she had come over, I probably would've thrown her overboard right after my dignity.

Oh, and let's not forget the pièce de résistance—Rorie, front row to witness my tragic downfall.

She saw me in all my glory, kneeling like a Renaissance painting gone horribly wrong, clutching my stomach, heaving dramatically while everyone else pretended not to notice. Real *damsel in digestive distress* energy.

Except her.

She didn't flinch. Didn't pretend not to notice. She watched.

And now, I have to face her.

Fantastic.

Taking one last deep breath, I wipe my face with a paper towel, square my shoulders, and open the door. *Fuck it.*

The salty island air hits me immediately. It's threaded with tropical blooms I'd appreciate more if my stomach wasn't still threatening a second performance.

The resort is stunning. Smooth lines, whitewashed walls, and open spaces that frame the sparkling ocean making it part of the décor.

Stepping into the lobby, I scan the space, and yep.

There she is.

Rorie stands near the check-in desk with her team. That gorgeous black hair is pulled back in some effortless twist, a pair of sunglasses perched on top of her head, and bag casually slung over one arm.

She's trying not to look at me. But the faintest glance comes my way before she catches herself and then pretends I'm invisible.

But I'm not invisible. Am I, Rorie?

There's that tiny shift in her posture, the way her jaw tightens just a little. She's trying her best to ignore me, but the pity's still there, softening her features, neatly tucked behind her indifference.

I don't want her pity. Although pity means she's got a heart.

And a heart I can work with.

A voice cuts through the room. "Welcome to White Thorn Island!"

We all turn as Asher Cross strides into the lobby with his broad shoulders, perfect hair, his presence filling the space, showing us he was born to own it. Dressed in a linen shirt and pants, he looks like he walked straight out of one of his movies.

Beside him, Shelby Davidson stands sun-kissed and airbrushed down to the molecular level. That silk dress she's wearing probably took three fittings and a brand sponsorship. Every strand of her honey-blonde hair is in its place, her nails are painted an *expensive neutral*, and her expression is a perfect blend of boredom and mild amusement, as though she's watching a reality show where she already knows the winner.

Asher flashes his signature million dollar smile that could sell out an entire theater, one that's both warm and devastating.

"Welcome to paradise." His voice is smooth as the ocean breeze slipping in through the open-air lobby. "We're thrilled to have you here. Our staff will assist you with check-in. Inside your welcome packets, you'll find everything you need, including your room assignments."

His gaze sweeps over the group, lingering on each of us to make it feel personal. But when his eyes land on Maya, they hold a beat too long. Not obvious. Not overt. But enough that I wonder who else notices. Because, isn't he dating Celeste Monroe?

Not that people are monogamous.

Hence, Chloe.

"Dinner is at eight," he continues, voice cracking. "Island casual for dress. We'll go over event details then, but until that, take the day to explore, rest, or just soak it all in. You've earned it."

I glance at Rorie again. She's nodding politely, her arms crossed. I bet she's already running through how to use every spare minute between now and dinner to get an edge.

Squaring my shoulders, I head for the check-in desk, my gaze catching hers for a split second.

I smirk.

Yeah, I puked my guts out. But I'm still coming for you. Because I may have lost my lunch. But I'm not losing this account.

Or you.

The walk to our private cottages is a slow march to purgatory—if purgatory came with handcrafted bamboo railings, lush jungle land-scaping, and ocean views that would bankrupt a poet.

Each cottage is its own secluded, stilted duplex perched off the sand, complete with a shaded porch, swaying hammock, and an outdoor salt water pool designed for sin. Or soaking up the rays. Whichever one prefers.

I prefer sin.

Rorie sticks close to her team, who are flanking her. Personal bodyguards.

Laurel's got the bulldog stride. Maya radiates cool, calm energy—silent assassin chic. And Jeremy is clearly there for comedic flair and dramatic commentary.

They're mid-conversation, and Jeremy's arms are flailing dramatically as though he's giving an infomercial on the perils of airport fashion or the superiority of mini toiletries.

Maya rolls her eyes but doesn't bother hiding her smirk. Rorie cracks a grin before glancing away.

My team hangs back, trailing a few steps behind. They're on full vacation mode, ready for happy hour instead of a corporate blood battle.

Jackson's busy whispering into Chloe's ear, his hand grazing her lower back. Thatcher's scrolling through his phone, already bored with the entire trip. Rishi's flirting with one of the resort staff, teeth and charm. The man has no shame.

Tammy trudges beside him in five-inch wedges and a look that says *I hate sand, people, and this entire damn island.*

The phantom of that boat ride still curdles in the pit of my stomach—a ghost of nausea—but I ignore it. I've got bigger things to focus on.

Such as Rorie's shoulders stiffening every time she knows I'm near. I like that reaction from her. A little tension. A little heat. Tells me I still get under her skin and not in the polite, pass-the-salt way. In the way that makes her breath hitch and heart rate spike. I can feel it. It makes my dick pulse.

I move my carry-on bag in front of me, silently ordering him to stand down as we weave through a series of palm-lined pathways, the island buzzing and the faint sound of waves crashing in the distance. One by one, people start veering off as they find their cottages. Key cards beep. Doors click shut.

But not us.

Rorie and I keep walking.

Eventually, it's just the two of us left, the silence between us thicker than the humidity.

We reach the end of the pathway where the last cottage stands with two doors side by side. Room twelve and Room thirteen.

I stare at the numbers for a beat, then glance over at her.

She's already looking at the door, key card in hand, doing her absolute best to pretend I don't exist.

I can't help myself.

"We're neighbors," I say. "Guess fate's got a sense of humor."

She doesn't respond. Doesn't even flinch. Just slides her key card through the reader, the door beeping as it unlocks. She disappears inside without a word, the door clicking shut behind her like punctuation.

I huff out a laugh, shaking my head. *Cold.*

But somehow, it makes me grin.

I unlock my own door–lucky number thirteen–and step inside, greeted by a rush of cool air-conditioned perfection.

The room is… well, *really* nice.

High vaulted ceilings with exposed wooden beams, modern décor mixed with tropical touches that aren't tacky. Light linen fabrics, rich wooden accents, and a massive king-sized bed that could swallow me whole.

A welcome basket sits on the dresser filled with fresh fruit, champagne, and what I assume are hand-rolled chocolates that probably cost more than my first car.

The bathroom's even better. A rainfall shower with glass walls, stone tiles straight from an architectural magazine, and—because apparently luxury has no limits—a small shelf labeled "Pillow Menu."

But it's the second shower head that catches my attention. Detachable, mounted just right, an indulgence most people wouldn't think twice about.

But I do.

My mind goes straight to Rorie on the other side of that wall, alone in her own suite, probably as restless as I am.

Will she use it?

Would she tilt her head back and let the hot water glide over her clit?

Will she think about that night? About the way she rode my fingers, desperate and wanting, her body completely unguarded for once?

My cock's already halfway to mutiny.

Hell, if she doesn't use that shower head, I might have to.

Equal opportunity, right?

On the counter, is a list of sleep gummies. I'll definitely be taking advantage of those later. I make a mental note to subtly bring all this up during our pitch. People eat this shit up—customizable comfort, personalized experiences. I can weave it into our presentation, sell the idea that Asher isn't just offering stays...he's offering *lifestyles*.

I wander back toward the main room, still taking it all in, when I notice a door.

Not the front door. Not the bathroom door.

A *connecting* door.

I stare at it, tilting my head slightly—

and grin.

Clearly, the universe has decided to throw me a bone. Or the gods are drunk and in a good mood.

Either way, I'm not wasting this blessing.

Stepping closer, I press my palm against it, then lean in until my ear is flat against the cool wood.

I can hear her.

Soft rustling, the faint shuffle of clothes, the muted thud of a suitcase being set down. She's moving around on the other side, completely unaware that I'm eavesdropping like some creep.

*What's she doing?*

Better yet—what will she be doing...tonight? Alone. In that big bed. After her shower. In the shower.

*No, man.* I shake the thought off, and step back before I get blue balls again, or take matters into my own hands.

Needing air, I head toward the sliding glass doors leading out to the private patio. The sun's casting a glow and painting everything in gold-dusted heat. A hot tub bubbles in the corner, steam curling lazily into the thick, tropical air.

Just beyond it, a long, crystal blue saltwater pool reaches to the edge of the deck. The glassy surface reflects the sky, tinted orange and violet by the dying light. It's private. Serene. Too calm for the storm building under my skin.

I slide the door open, stepping out just as—

Rorie does the same.

She freezes for half a second, clearly just as surprised as I am. The layout's design is meant for families who want the option to drift between spaces. A small partition separates the patios, but there's an opening—a shared gate of sorts—that leads between both hot tubs.

"Our patios are connected," I say. I'm an idiot. Of course they are. She can see that. Clearly.

Her eyes meet mine, assessing. She's deciding whether to acknowledge me or pretend she's gone temporarily blind.

I lean casually against the frame of my door.

"Well," I say, my voice smooth and a little too pleased, "Guess fate's got *two* senses of humor."

She doesn't dignify me with a response. Instead, she spins on her heel, storms back inside, and slides the door shut with enough force to rattle the glass.

Can't say I blame her. If our roles were reversed, I'd have slammed the damn thing twice.

Winning her back won't be easy. But she's worth every slammed door. And I'm not going anywhere.

# CHAPTER 39
# SALT IN THE WOUND
## RORIE

"FUCK MY LIFE."

I'm lounging next to a tiki bar overlooking crystal-clear water, a paradise people pay thousands to escape to, and yet, there's this storm brewing in my chest.

The breeze should be refreshing, but it only stokes the fire of my ever-growing stress. Instead of sipping cocktails and soaking up the view, I'm drowning in a mess of my own making.

The bar is coastal indulgence done right—honey-toned wood, hand-blown glass lanterns suspended from knotted rope, and tropical flowers tucked into every corner. It doesn't scream for attention. It lures you in. The island knows exactly what you need before you do.

I take it all in. The textures. The mood. The way the space whispers instead of shouts. Every detail's a seduction, and I'm already filing it away into mental notes, stacking them like cocktail napkins. This is what our pitch needs to be. Confident. Sexy. It belongs here. *We* belong here.

Jeremy's parked on the other side of me, legs stretched out, sunglasses sliding down his nose as he sucks down a colorful drink served in a hollowed-out coconut. There's a tiny umbrella. A pineapple wedge. A pretty tropical flower to be decorative.

"You look disgustingly relaxed."

"You look like you're one mental breakdown away from flipping this entire bar into the ocean," he says as if that's not a perfectly reasonable plan.

And the man responsible for said breakdown? Oh, he's lounging twenty feet away in an island casual wet dream—slouchy tee, smug grin. He shows me forearm porn every time he reaches for his drink and his corded muscles flex.

"Where's Maya?" I ask.

"Suspect claims it's a headache, but I'm pretty sure she's hiding so she doesn't make eye contact with Asher and crumble like a waffle cone under a triple scoop."

My eyes roam back to Nolan, who's laughing at something one of his team members says. She's curly-haired and currently rocking an eccentric neon bathing suit that I'm pretty sure was designed during a sugar rush.

He glances this way. He *feels* me watching.

My pulse flutters. I nibble my bottom lip. And despite the ocean breeze and frozen daiquiri in my hand, I'm sweating under the weight of something I swore I'd never want again.

Jeremy tips his sunglasses down further, gives me the *you're not slick* look. "Alright, who pissed in your daiquiri? Or, more accurately— what six-foot-four, bicep-blessed chaos demon crawled up your ass and started doing laps?"

"We have *connecting rooms*," I hiss, clutching the glass as if it's the last shred of sanity left on this godforsaken island. "Connecting. Rooms. As in, one paper-thin door stands between me and the man who scrambled my brain."

Jeremy doesn't even flinch. His brow lifts as he stirs his drink with the world's most judgmental pineapple wedge. "Rorie, babe. I love you. Truly. But if I have to hear one more tortured diatribe about how the man who emotionally tenderized you had the audacity to push pause, I will personally walk into the ocean and let the crabs take me."

I glare. "Rude."

"Is it?" His head tilts. "Let's recap: He's too rival. Too enemy. Too smug. Too hot. Too into you. And now he's—what? Too gone? Boo-hoo. The trauma."

I scowl. "That's not what I said."

"Oh really?" He leans in, eyes sparkling with challenge. "Because for a month, I've been trapped in a rerun of *Rorie Adams: The Overthinking Years*. You didn't even respond to the man's ice-cold email and now you're mad he respected your silence."

I open my mouth.

"Save it," he cuts in. "You two are clearly still into each other, the universe keeps shipping you harder than TikTok romance edits. And now you're mad it stuck you in a shared cottage? Read the signs, friend."

"Yeah, let's talk about this shared situation," I say, spinning to face him fully. "I was *supposed* to be next to Maya."

He blinks, fake-innocent. "You trusted me to check in for everyone. That's on you."

My jaw drops. "You switched our rooms?"

"Like I did your airplane seats," he says proudly. "You're welcome."

"I *hate* you."

He grins. "And yet, somehow I'm still your voice of reason."

I groan into my hands.

"Ror, be serious," Jeremy says, setting his drink down. "This back-and-forth you're doing? Exhausting. You keep calling him the enemy. But that doesn't make what you two have any less... cosmic."

I blink. "Cosmic?"

He points at me. "Yes. The man literally sent you a galaxy in a box."

Heat rises in my cheeks.

"For the day you met. Not when you first kissed, or when you humped him in a bathroom or had your little emotional fire drill. It was the day you *stepped* into his life. Tell me that's not some next-level shit."

I go quiet.

Jeremy lowers his voice, serious now. "Rorie... you have this glass shard wedged inside you that people leave you when you become too much. And Nolan? He just did it earlier than most. Preemptive exit. But that doesn't make him a monster—it makes him scared. According to Rishi, someone left him too. Don't forget that."

Pain flares up in my chest. I shift in my seat and exhale, trying to joke, trying to rise above the sting. "Okay, now I hate you for being right."

Jeremy just gives a small smile. "Yeah, well. Hate me all you want. But don't ignore it. Stop punishing him for the way *everyone else* handled your heart. You want him? Fight. Forgive. Or, at the very least, fuck him and get it out of your damn system."

I scoff, cross my arms. "The elevated alcohol content in these drinks is getting to you, Jer."

"Not fast enough," he replies, raising his drink in a toast then leaning back against the lounger. "God chose me to be the little match-maker this story needs. Now go. Open that damn door. And either fall in love or ruin his life with some throw-him-off-his-axis, detonate-his-soul, rearrange-his-outlook-on-life high level fucking. Preferably both."

I burst out laughing—part horrified, part hysterical. "You're actually *insane*. That's not happening."

Jeremy's attention snaps back to me. "Then stop bitching about it."

I blink. "Wow. Harsh love today."

He shrugs. "Truth serum comes with the umbrella drink. Did you even hear a word I said?"

My brow furrows.

"Look, I get it. You're playing it safe. Strategizing. Trying to be ten steps ahead. But not everything can be mapped out. Some things you just have to feel your way through."

I go still.

He looks me dead in the eye. "Don't let fear make the call."

A tirade of emotions forms in my brain when my phone buzzes with a new message from Carl. Er, Nolan.

> I know things ended kind of weird between us, and I want to respect your space. Just checking in. Hope you're okay.

The words slam into me. I stare at his message longer than I should, thumb hovering over the screen. Answering would set something dangerous in motion.

And there's this massive, suffocating secret lodged in my chest. It's eating me alive. It's not just the texts anymore. It's him. Nolan. And the guilt has become a constant ache, insistent and impossible to ignore.

My eyes drift across the patio—automatically, stupidly—and land on him.

Nolan's staring down at his phone, brows furrowed, expression grim. He's waiting. He's hoping.

And for a second, I wonder if he knows. If he feels it too, that secret between us, straining with the pressure of a thread pulled too tight, vibrating under every choice I've made since this whole thing started.

Responding would pull the thread loose. Once it unravels it won't just be the secret that comes undone.

It'll be *me*.

There are consequences to texting him back.

Always have been.

That ache in my chest I've been trying to smother with alcohol and avoidance consumes me. My fingers take over.

> I'm fine.

> There she is. I've missed you, you know. You're the one bright spot that showed up when everything else went dark.
>
> I was starting to think I scared you off.

> > Scared me off? Not a chance. I'm way too invested at this point.
> >
> > Besides... you've kind of become my favorite notification and your emotional Jenga tower is way too entertaining to walk away from mid-collapse.

> Good. Because losing you might actually ruin my already questionable faith in the universe.

God, why is it so easy with him?

Why does he have to be like this?

Stupid. Charming. Ridiculously addictive in a way that bypasses logic and scrapes at something much deeper—something I don't want to acknowledge is even there.

And the worst part?

It's not even about sex.

Except... it kind of is.

I know exactly how he kisses. I know the sound I make when he—

Nope. Nope. Nope. Not going there.

I shake the thought loose with the force of someone trying to dislodge a demon.

Here I am, half-tipsy on an island paradise, still texting the man I never should've let inside my ribcage. Still craving the way he listens. The way he *gets* me. Still wondering if he could be real.

*He is real.*

I toss back the rest of my drink in one go.

It burns going down. Rum. And rage.

And regret.

"You should see your face right now," he muses, leaning over his coconut and sucking. *Hard.* His eyebrows bounce. "Who texted you, and how do I make them do it again?"

My fingers stop over the screen mid-response. "What?"

He gestures lazily at me with finger. "That."

"That?"

Jeremy rolls his eyes. "The way you're staring at your phone like it just solved world hunger and promised you a lifetime supply of orgasms."

I scoff. "I am *not*—"

"You *so* are," he interrupts, smirking. "I don't think I've ever seen you look *genuinely* happy while texting someone before. Not even me, and I'm a delight."

I throw a piece of pineapple at him. He catches it, takes a dramatic bite, and continues as if I didn't just try to pelt him with fruit.

"Rorie, just be honest with yourself for once. You're into him. And I don't mean just the sexual kind."

"I don't even *know* him."

Jeremy points at me. He's caught me in a trap. "And *that* is the stupidest excuse I've ever heard. Because you do. You talk to him every single day. He knows more about you than half the people in your life. So tell me why you don't cut all the bullshit?"

I open my mouth to argue. Shut it. Try again. Nothing.

Jeremy smirks knowingly. "Yeah, that's what I thought."

"It's complicated," I grumble, avoiding looking at him.

"It's only complicated because you're making it that way," he counters. "You deserve to be happy, Rorie. And whatever *this* is, it's clearly doing something good for you. So put all the stupid complications aside, stop playing games, and just tell him the truth."

My heart twists at his words, at how damn *simple* he makes it sound.

But it's not simple. It's not *just* a crush. It's not *just* some flirty texting game. It's a secret. A betrayal. A tangled mess of something that never should've started, yet I don't want to stop.

And Nolan has had enough of those in his life.

Secrets. Lies. People playing games with him like he's a piece on their board.

"Look, Nolan has been through some things," I tell Jeremy. "I don't know the full extent of what he's been through, but I know enough to realize that if he ever found out who I really am, if he ever figured out that the person he's been confiding in—the one he calls *Textually Frustrated*—is the same woman he's been trying so damn hard to resist in real life…and I didn't tell him outright…He'd never forgive me."

That should be my wake-up call. That should be the reason to make me shut this down, to stop this before it blows up in my face.

"And I don't want to lose the way he makes me feel when we text —with him I'm more than my work, more than my ambition, more than the competitor standing in his way. With *Carl*, I'm just… Rorie. And I don't know how to walk away from that."

"Soooo, tell him outright."

I stare back at Jeremy. So young yet so wise. "You know, for someone who claims to have no romantic bone in his body, you sure sound like you're made entirely of them."

"Sweetheart, I've got enough *bone* to share with the whole island." He winks. "Now, are you gonna text him back, or do I need to pry that phone out of your emotionally repressed little hands and do it myself?"

"Dinner is served!"

Saved by the bell. Or more accurately, saved by Shelby Davidson.

The evening air is brimming with salt and spice, the scent of grilled seafood mixing with the slow burn of rum in my glass. The long banquet table is set beneath a canopy of string lights, their glow reflecting off the dark water beyond the cliffs. It's elegantly rustic with white linen runners, scattered tropical flowers, and candles flickering in glass lanterns.

Servers weave through the crowd, balancing trays of bright cocktails and plates of food so artfully arranged it feels wrong to eat them.

I slide into a chair between Jeremy and Laurel, trying *very* hard not to glance at Nolan *"Your Real Name Is Carl"* Rhodes, who's chatting with Rishi and Thatcher. He's been mentally terrorizing me all day.

*His laugh carries down the table, low and easy.*

*Don't look. Don't look.*

*…I look.*

*Damn it.*

Jeremy elbows me under the table, grinning. "Subtle."

"I wasn't looking."

Jeremy snorts into his drink. ""Rorie, babe, you just stared at Nolan so hard, I thought your eyeballs were gonna roll right out of your head and land in his lap then suck him off."

Laurel, who's been quietly sipping her wine and pretending not to eavesdrop, lifts a brow. "Should I be concerned that we're talking about sucking off our direct competition in such… vivid detail?"

Jeremy leans in. "You should be concerned that Rorie already came close."

I whack him in the arm.

Her eyes narrow at me. "So, I take it you haven't figured things out yet since our last conversation?"

I suck down an oyster while Laurel stares at me.

"Allow me to fully brief you on *The Rorie Adams Saga*," Jeremy says in a deep voice. "Heartbreaks, mystery texters, work nemeses, and the very obvious unresolved sexual tension."

I groan.

Laurel folds her hands under her chin. "It's nothing to be ashamed of. I've had a Nolan Rhodes before. Several of them actually."

Jeremy perks up. "Ohhh, do tell."

She gives him a pointed look. "One of them was Thatcher."

I nearly choke on my drink. "Wait—Thatcher? As in *that* Thatcher?"

"One and the same."

Jeremy gasps. "I have whiplash. Continue."

I gape at her. "You *dated* Thatcher?"

Laurel smirks. "Dated is a strong word. Let's just say we had a... *complicated* arrangement. Back in my thirties. When I was a whole lot less concerned about the long-term consequences of mixing business with pleasure. Long story short? Office flings can get messy. No matter how fun, no matter how inevitable they feel in the moment, they come with risks. Risks that, if you're not careful, can cost you a hell of a lot more than you bargained for."

"So what do I do?" I ask.

Laurel takes another sip before answering. "Decide what you want."

I nod slowly, letting that settle in my chest.

Jeremy glances between us, then grins. "So, just to clarify—your advice is *don't do* Nolan Rhodes? Or do?"

Laurel hums. "I'm saying... if you *do do*...Nolan Rhodes—"

"You said do do." Jeremy laughs. Clearly the alcohol has taken effect.

Laurel's eyes snap to him. He shuts up immediately.

"Be very sure about what you're willing to lose," she finishes. "If anything."

I've downed four oysters, and am now chewing on a cracker, refusing to glance in Nolan's direction again.

But feel his presence. The cutting edges of my attraction. The pull I keep trying to block out.

Jeremy nudges me. "So, what's the plan, boss?"

I exhale. "To get through this trip without making a mistake."

Laurel raises a brow, takes a sip of her wine. "Good luck with that. Mistakes are part of the job description, babe. You just have to be brave enough to correct them when you can and smart enough to learn from the ones you can't."

My shoulders slump, head falls.

She watches me for a long moment, then sighs, setting her glass down with a soft clink. "Rorie, I don't have all the answers. But I do know this, you don't get anywhere worth going by running your head in circles."

I blink. "That's very wise-mentor of you. Unfortunately, I have no idea what it means."

"It means you're stuck. Circling Nolan, the pitch, the past, the future, waiting for the perfect moment. The right sign. Like it's going to hit you over the head with clarity."

"I'm just being careful," I say, quieter now. "I've worked too hard to screw this up."

"I get that." Laurel's voice softens too. "You're scared. But if there's something there, don't run away from it."

I shake my head. "I can't deal with this right now. Winning Asher is the only thing that matters right now."

"You sure about that?" she asks, not unkindly.

I hesitate. "Yeah. Very."

She shrugs. "Okay."

"What are you saying?"

"I'm saying... you're not moving. So, it's time to pick a direction and start. I hear North is nice this time of year." Laurel glances over at Nolan's table which just happens to be facing north and then winks.

I swallow, something tight and tangled lodging itself in my chest.

*North & Anchor.* The phrase my parents lived by. The compass that pointed forward when they were lost. The mantra I'd been raised on.

"I don't know which way North is."

Laurel leans in and looks me dead in the eyes. "North will find you. Maybe it already has."

This time, I throw my restraint aside, and my gaze finds Nolan.

He's looking back at me—soft and unguarded, a man staring back at the one person he can't stop thinking about either.

And for a second, it's not tension or lust or the remnants of what we were trying to be.

It's longing.

It's everything we're not saying.

And it rips my heart open.

Is Laurel's right?

Has North already found me? Was I too scared to fight for it?

"Just make sure you're the one steering, Rorie," Laurel says. "Not the past. Not the pressure. *Not friends.*" Her eyes swivel over to Jeremy. He shrugs innocently. "And definitely not a man who looks genetically engineered in a lab for the purpose of making women lose all common sense."

Jeremy snickers into his drink. "I mean, if he *was* lab-made, they did a damn fine job."

Groaning, I pinch the bridge of my nose. "Can we please stay focused?"

"That's exactly what I'm saying, Rorie. *Focus.* But focus on what *you* actually want, not just what you think you're supposed to do based on what other people want."

*What I want?* That's the problem. What I *want* is messy. Complicated. Something that rewrites your insides and never asks permission first.

I've spent so long chasing what's safe—what looks good on paper —that I don't even know if I'd recognize what *I* want anymore if it was standing right in front of me.

Which, unfortunately, it is.

With forearms. His signature smirk. And deliciously sweet dimple.

*Clink. Clink. Clink.*

Shelby stands at the head of the table, poised, her sundress catching the light as she lifts her glass.

Next to her, Asher watches with that ever-present amusement, one hand draped lazily over the back of his chair, the other wrapped around a tumbler of something dark. He doesn't speak, but he doesn't have to—this is his show. His island. His game.

But I wonder if it's all just for show. If somewhere beneath that tailored charm and half-smile, he's thinking about Maya. If he feels that hollow ache in his chest the way she does when she talks about him and tries to act like it doesn't matter.

Is he sitting there, pretending to be untouched by it all, while she's in her room, choosing not to come out at all?

And if he is—God, what a coward.

And if he isn't—what a shame.

"We're thrilled to have you all here for what promises to be an unforgettable week," Shelby begins, her voice carrying authority that draws attention from everyone in the room.

As she speaks, I catalogue everything. The atmosphere, the ambiance, the careful compilation of exclusivity. This is all part of the game. A test wrapped in five-star hospitality.

And Asher is watching.

"Each day," Shelby continues, "you'll take part in challenges designed to immerse you in the experience of White Thorn. Some will be with your own teams. Others won't."

Murmurs roll down the table.

"We believe in collaboration," she adds, her smile practiced, professional. "But true innovation happens when you step outside your comfort zone. We want to watch how you adapt, how you thrive, even when paired with unexpected variables."

Translation: They want to see who caves under pressure.

"At the end of the week, you'll pitch your vision for White Thorn. But you're not just here as competitors, you're here as guests. Let this island inspire you."

She lets that settle before flashing a grin. "May the best team win. The rest of you? Well, at least you got a free vacation."

Laughter ripples through the group. I take another drink, letting the ice clink against the glass as I flick a glance down the table, right as Nolan does the same.

Our eyes meet. It does something to me.

The candlelight catches in his whiskey-brown gaze, something shifts there before he lifts his glass in a silent toast.

I should look away first. I should break whatever the hell this is before it gets any worse. But I don't. Of course I don't.

Not until Shelby's voice cuts back through.

"Tomorrow's challenge starts at ten a.m. sharp on the beach," she announces. "Wear something you don't mind getting dirty."

Jeremy straightens. "Ooh, I love dirty."

Shelby's grin lifts higher. "We'll be having ourselves a good old-fashioned sand castle building contest."

The table buzzes with energy.

Tomorrow, the real competition begins.

# CHAPTER 40
# THE COMPASS AND THE COLLAPSE

### RORIE

THE WATER HUGS my body beneath the glittering canopy of stars as I float in the center of the plunge pool. With my arms outstretched, head tilted back, my ears half-submerged in silence, I reflect on everything Laurel said to me.

*North and Anchor.*

I trace the phrase in my mind like a fingertip over worn embroidery—familiar, comforting, frayed at the edges. I used to think I knew what it meant. Find your purpose. Dig in. Don't let anything shake it loose.

But tonight, it feels more complicated than that.

What if North isn't a direction?

What if it's a person?

The sound of soft footsteps on stone breaks the spell. I don't move.

A second later, Nolan's voice carries over the divider, cautious, yet annoyingly smooth.

"Is this a ceasefire zone," he asks, "or am I about to get taken out by a pool float and unresolved anger?"

I sigh. "What do you want?"

"I was walking on the beach. Thinking. Avoiding one of my coworker's voices, which I'm convinced is a direct trigger for high blood pressure." A pause. "Saw the lights. Took a chance."

He steps into the edge of the glow from the patio lamp, shirtless.

And yeah. So much for blood pressure. Mine spikes to a dangerous level.

His chest is composed of lean lines and muscle, like he was hand-crafted by a very horny sculptor. Defined shoulders, abs that could deflect bullets, and a faint trail of hair leading below the waistband of swim trunks that are hanging on for dear life.

My brain cells scatter like pigeons at a firework show.

But what really undoes me—what fucks me up in ways I'm not ready for—is the tattoo over his heart.

A small constellation. Five fine-lined stars, etched in quiet permanence. It's subtle. Intimate. A map only meant to be read up close.

I can't stop staring because he's not just marked by the stars—he carries their gravity. Their pull. And I'm already drifting toward him, terrified of what it means to follow someone that's already burned me, when I wish he'd just lead me home.

"Can I join you?" he asks. "I promise to stay on my side of the truce line."

My arms make circles in the water. "Not a good idea."

He gives me a slow, lazy grin, that irresistible dimple popping out. "Pretty please…"

Why does he have to be adorable?

"…with sugar on top."

"Fine," I huff, shifting to one side of the water. "But if you cannon-ball, I'm calling security."

Nolan steps in gently, his body moving with grace as he sinks down beside me. Water laps at the edges of the pool as we settle into silence.

For a while, all I hear is the distant song of cicadas, the occasional splash of water, and my own heartbeat ticking louder in my ears.

I steal another glance at him and at the ink over his heart. Before I can second-guess it, the words slip out, low and rough,"What's your tattoo mean?"

He glances down at his chest, like he almost forgot it was there. When he looks back at me, his smile is small, shy. A rare thing, for him.

"It's not from the sky." His fingers trail lightly across the surface of the water, breaking the reflection.

"I made it up. A long time ago."

I tip my head, waiting. Not pushing. Not breathing, really.

He shrugs a little, the motion loose. "When I was younger, I used to think... if you couldn't find yourself in the stars that already existed, you could just make new ones. A map nobody else had. A way to get home that only you would recognize."

My chest tightens. Hard. That's honestly one of the most beautiful and endearing things I've ever heard.

Nolan keeps going, voice so soft that the cicadas almost steal it away. "So I put five stars where I wanted them. One for who I was. One for who I thought I had to be. One for the people I lost. One for the people I hadn't met yet. And one..." He pauses, the ghost of a smile curving his mouth. "One for the things I didn't even know I was looking for."

The words land harder than I expect. Like a current, dragging me under. It's not just a tattoo. It's a wish. And a map. A promise to find his way back, no matter the odds.

I don't say anything. I can't. The only sound is the water between us.

The summer night breathes around our bodies. There's a thundering reminder in my chest that some stars aren't meant to be constellations you trace with your eyes, or your fingertips.

Some stars are people, pulling you in, no matter how far you drift.

Even if it terrifies you.

Even if it burns.

"I've been thinking a lot about anchors lately," Nolan says, randomly.

My attention snaps to him.

He doesn't know.

He *can't* know.

Yet somehow he's standing on the edge of a thought I've been circling around for hours.

*North and Anchor.*

And which direction I'm supposed to be going.

"Why?" I ask.

He shrugs. "Don't know. Just popped into my head. It's weird.

What keeps us steady? What makes us stay in one place? I guess I've always thought of anchors as these heavy objects that keep you stuck. But now I've realized that it doesn't weigh you down, it makes you stop drifting."

I glance over, caught once again between fight and flight with him.

That's what he does to me.

Every. Damn. Time.

*I* know what keeps me steady. Or at least... I used to.

It was my mom's laugh in the kitchen. My dad's voice reading constellations off the hood of a Jeep. It was knowing exactly who I was and what I wanted.

But then loss came for me and took all of it, pulled into waters I couldn't chart, with no map, no anchor, and no idea if I'd ever touch steady ground again. It left me drifting. Grasping. Building stability out of ambition and iced coffee and a calendar full of color-coded deadlines.

And then Nolan Rhodes barreled into my life as a hurricane with a dimple, and suddenly, oddly, I felt steady again.

If he's an anchor, he's one that drags you under just as easily as he keeps you tethered. I can't decide if I want to cut the rope or let him hold me in place.

My eyes stay pinned on his profile. The scruff on his jaw. The casual way he says these things that hit deep within my beating heart.

"You ever hear the phrase North and Anchor?"

He shakes his head slowly, eyes fixed on the stars. "No. What's it mean?"

"My parents used to say it. It was their thing. Their compass. Find your North, and anchor yourself to it."

He's quiet for a moment, letting it sink in. "I like that."

"Yeah," I say, voice low. "Me too. I wish my compass would start pointing though. It's been stuck for quite a while."

He looks over at me then—*really* looks. No smirk. No smugness.

Just him.

"It already has," he says, voice a little breathy, still looking at me. "You're scared to follow it. I don't blame you."

The words drop into me like a stone, sinking straight to the center of my chest, then rippling outward until I can't tell where the emotion ends and the impact begins.

I look away first.

Because the truth?

He might be right.

But fear is a fault line, quiet until it isn't. And when it shifts, it cracks through everything you thought was stable. He's the one who made it quake. The one who pulled back. The one who left me staring at my phone, heart wide open and humiliated.

I stare up at the stars again, hoping they'll offer answers.

They don't.

Nolan's voice breaks the quiet. "Your parents sound wise."

I swallow. "They *were* wise."

His face shifts instantly. "Rorie—"

"It's okay," I cut in, not unkindly. "You didn't know."

Another beat of silence passes between us—heavier now. Sadder.

"They would've liked you," I add, before I can stop myself. "My mom especially. She had a thing for people who looked arrogant until they opened their mouths and turned out to be gentle and charming."

That earns me a faint smile. "Sounds like a woman of taste."

"She also threw a sandal at a pesticide solicitor once, so, you know. Balanced."

Nolan chuckles under his breath. "I don't know what I'm more intimidated by, your standards or your fiery family legacy."

I glance at him, my heart doing that awful twist again.

Because I'm still mad.

Still bruised.

But not enough to pretend this isn't something. Not enough to lie to myself anymore.

We fall into that silence again. Not awkward. Not tense. Just filled with everything we've said, and everything we haven't.

Then, at the same time:

"Rorie—"

"Nolan—"

Our names land between us, overlapping in perfect sync. We both blink, then almost laugh.

I shake my head, barely. "You first."

He hesitates for a breath. He's building courage. Then he exhales, shakily, and looks me dead in the eye.

"I'm sorry," he says. "God, Rorie, I'm *so* sorry. For the email. For the way I pulled back. For everything."

My chest tightens, but I stay quiet. Let him talk. He needs this.

So do I.

More than anything.

"I panicked," he admits. "That gift... it felt right at the time and then it felt fast. I saw this article about lovebombing, and I lost it. It hit every single nerve." His voice gets quieter. "I haven't said the thing I need to say. The thing that's been chewing at the back of my throat since I sent that stupid email like a goddamn coward."

I listen, and the silence makes it worse, makes the words rush out of him in a torrent.

"My girlfriend cheated on me," he confesses, voice low, like it hurts to say it out loud. "With one of my coworkers. Jackson. He's here. With her. Laughing like the past year meant nothing."

He pauses, his jaw tightens, not from anger, but shame. "I lost myself in that fallout. Started questioning everything. My instincts. My judgment. What I was worth. I stopped trusting the part of me that feels things too deeply and started playing by rules I didn't write. Pretending I was fine. Pretending I didn't care."

His gaze lifts to mine, steady, raw. "Then I met you. And suddenly I could breathe again."

And suddenly I can't.

"You were a spark in a blackout. At first, I convinced myself it was nothing, just heat, proximity, a fluke I could file away as a rebound before it got deep."

A bitter smile feathers across his lips.

"But it was never just heat. You got under my skin immediately and in ways I didn't think were possible, especially after Chloe. And instead of leaning into it, I tried to contain it. Label it. Push it away, so I wouldn't have to risk heartbreak again."

He leans forward, eyes dark with an emotion deeper than lust. "I should've said screw the rules. Screw the timing. Screw what anyone else thinks. Because my heart was screaming your name. And I didn't listen."

The night wraps around us as those simple words rip holes through my defenses.

Nolan looks down for a second, thumb trailing small circles on the water's surface. "But I should've. Way more than I wanted to admit. And when I started feeling things for you, so quickly, so deeply—" His breath hitches like it hurts him. "I thought I was going to mess it up. Or scare you off. Or make you regret ever letting me in."

My heart thuds against my ribs. It's trying to escape the truth he's pouring into the air between us. I want to look away. I want to hide behind a joke or a jab or literally anything that doesn't require me to face this tidal wave of honesty.

But I can't.

Because it's hitting me now. All of it.

I did the same thing at first. Refused my feelings, pushed him away. It was easier to do that than accept that he might be the one person who sees me—*all of me.*

Then I gave into those feelings. That want. That need. And it's stayed with me ever since. And since we're leaning into metaphors, every moment with him became an anchor in the storm. Not the kind that saves you. The kind that drags. Heavy with what could've been. Sharp with what wasn't.

But even so, it held me still, reminded me what it felt like to want something in the middle of all that loss.

And this man stepped into my shambled life without asking for a map. He offered me steadiness without strings. He pulled away, yes— but not because he didn't care.

Maybe because he *did.*

And now here he is, standing in the aftermath of our storm with his heart in his hands, giving me the choice.

"I hate that I hurt you," he says softly. "But I'm also done pretending I don't feel what I feel."

He smiles, softly. Wounded.

My throat is tight. My heart's an unmade bed of feelings I'm still figuring out how to climb into.

"I don't know what all of this means. I don't have a perfect answer. But I know I've missed you. I haven't stopped thinking about you. About us. About what we could've been if I hadn't let fear win."

Something different ignites between us.

Possibility. Hope.

I inhale. Hold it. Release it.

There's so much I could say. So much I *should* say.

Instead, I gaze at the man who showed up tonight shirtless and guarded and stupidly beautiful, with his heart cracked wide open.

I open my mouth. *I'm Textually Frustrated.*

That's what I almost say. But the name lodges behind my teeth, thick and burning and terrifying.

What if he sees it as a lie? A game? Another secret stacked on the ones he's still bleeding from?

So instead, I choose the piece of truth I *can* give him right now. The one that's safest and still entirely real.

"I've missed you too," I say quietly.

His shoulders relax, a breath escapes him.

"I was mad," I admit. "Still kind of am."

"Fair."

"But mostly I was… disappointed."

He nods, like he understands exactly what I mean.

We've quieted now. No posturing, no plans. Only two souls suspended in water, the night sky sparkling above us, vast and silent, withholding its answers, waiting to see what we'll choose without its permission.

He's watching me.

Not with hunger.

Not with strategy.

With softness.

And then he moves.

Slowly. Carefully.

A hand comes to rest on the edge of the pool near mine, not touching, but close.

When his eyes find mine, they hold both a question and a promise in one.

Nolan leans in. I don't stop him.

For all the ways I've tried to convince myself this is wrong or reckless or doomed, I shove them away. This moment doesn't feel like a mistake.

It feels like gravity.

His mouth brushes mine, not demanding. Reverent. A whisper of lips. A breath shared.

My eyes flutter closed, and then I'm kissing him back, fully, fiercely, like I've been holding my breath since the first time we fought across a rooftop and in this moment, I finally remembered how to inhale.

His other hand rises from the water, threads through my damp hair, and tugs me closer.

I shift in the pool until we're chest to chest, his body heat soaking into mine like sunlight breaking through the dark clouds.

Our kiss goes from tentative to desperate in a heartbeat. It's all consuming and he kisses me like I'm not just another chapter in his story but a turning point.

I give myself to it. To the taste of him. The feel of him. The quiet groan that slips from his throat when my hand brushes down his chest, halting over the small constellation marked on his heart.

And when we finally break apart, we're breathless.

Ruined.

Remade.

"You make me see stars," he breathes, forehead resting against mine. "Ours will never fade. No matter how hard we've tried to make them."

The words echo between us before his mouth finds mine again. Our bodies shift in the water, slick skin brushing slick skin, the world narrowing to heat and breath and the sound of need rising within.

Nolan grips my hips and lifts me with little effort, setting me on the pool's edge, wet, breathless, and completely at his mercy.

His body slots between my thighs. Strong hands claim hips he's already memorized. One swift pull and I'm flush against him. The need isn't subtle. It's carved into the way he touches me. And then he's lowering his lips to my neck, then my chest, moving with such careful intention it makes my whole body ache with need.

"Nolan," I whisper.

"Trust me?"

I nod. I do. God help me—I *do*. Even though I probably shouldn't.

"Lie back."

Tiny kisses over my collarbone, hands coaxing my legs further apart as his mouth goes lower, trailing fire over my ribs, across my stomach, his stubble grazing my skin, soft and rough all at once. I can't tell if the goosebumps are from him or the anticipation.

Nolan's hands drag my bathing suit bottoms down my legs so slowly it borders on cruelty, exposing me inch by aching inch. The night air licks across my heat, but his mouth follows fast. The first flick of his tongue is gentle. Testing. Almost shy.

It's a lie.

His tongue is hungry, and ruinously skilled.

I gasp, hands flying to the pool's edge, gripping tight, as though it's the only thing keeping me from floating away entirely.

Nolan glances up at me, a sinful smirk tugging at his mouth. That devilish dimple is doing nothing but making me wetter. "You taste like moonlight on my fucking tongue."

No one's ever said things like that to me before. And somehow, those naughty words mean more to me than the orgasm.

Grinning, he hooks one leg over his shoulder. His voice is dirty, and lethal when he rasps, "I'd crawl across galaxies to eat this sweet pussy."

My cheeks flush.

Our eyes connect.

One beat.

Two.

He dives in.

Warm lips wrap around my clit with filthy intent. I yelp at the sharp burst of pleasure that tears through me. He licks. He sucks. He *devours* until I'm whimpering, hips jerking, thighs trembling, almost completely undone.

Groaning against me, his mouth burrows deeper, a possessive tongue sliding through my center, savoring every response, every breathless sound then one finger slips inside, curling just right, his mouth never leaving me.

My hips jolt, fingers clawing at the edge as he coaxes pleasure from every trembling inch.

He owns this moment.

He owns me.

My head falls back, eyes fixed on the stars above, every flick of his tongue sketching new ones behind my eyelids when they close.

But then—

He stops.

Air punches from my lungs. My hips buck uselessly, searching for the friction he stole.

Dazed, I blink down at him, seconds from begging.

He grins. Dark. Not devilish.

Demonic.

"Do you want to come, Rorie?" he asks, voice wicked. He knows the answer. He wants to hear me say it.

The tension inside me is unbearable, tight and hot and needy in a way that makes pride feel like a luxury I can't afford.

I try to hold out. Just a second longer. To keep a shred of control. But then he licks his lips, tasting me and I snap.

"Please," I whisper.

His brows lift. "Say it again. Mean it."

Goddamn this man.

"Please, Nolan. I need it. I need *you*."

That's all it takes.

A deep, primal growl erupts from his chest and then his mouth is on me again, tongue stroking and devastating, and his fingers—God, his fingers—slide back inside me, smooth and sure.

There's no hesitation. No mercy.

He fucks me with his mouth and his hand like it's his sole purpose in life to pull these sounds out of me, to find every edge and push me over it.

"Fuck," I gasp, throwing my head back, eyes opening and closing as he works me open with his mouth, his tongue, that fucking *talent*.

My hips rock against him, helpless, frantic, desperate. And when I come it's not quiet. It's not sweet.

It's a fucking collapse.

My legs shake. My lungs forget how to breathe. My voice breaks on his name.

And as the pleasure crashes through me as a tidal wave, I swear—for one stupid, terrifying, beautiful second—I feel something deeper pull tight in my chest.

With deliberate ease, he crawls out of the pool, water trailing down every inch of him. His hands plant on either side of me, his body following until he settles between my legs, dripping wet and devastatingly handsome. His eyes are lit with mischief, and shadowed with heat as he looks down at me like I'm the night sky itself. Like I'm something holy.

But what I give him is nothing short of sinful.

I cup his erection and he groans—loud, *feral*—before his lips latch onto me. He doesn't ease in. He consumes. Tongue hammering, lips sucking.

"Nolan," I whisper, voice barely mine. "I want you."

Eyes wild, chest heaving, he says, "You have me."

"No." I tighten my grip, dragging my thumb along the ridge that makes my pulse skip. "I mean I want you. Inside me."

His jaw clenches. For a second, I think he's going to end all of this right here and now. But instead, he hisses a curse through his teeth and drops his forehead to my shoulder.

"Rorie," he says, voice rough, reverent. "I don't have any protection."

I blink, breathless, aching. "Are you seriously telling me you're the kind of guy who shows up to a tropical resort unprepared?"

"I didn't exactly plan on fucking my rival in paradise."

I laugh—half annoyed, half turned on—and run my fingers through his hair. "Liar."

He looks up, smirking. "Give me ten minutes and a very fast golf cart."

"I'm clean. And on birth control. Sooo, if you're okay with it..."

My fingers tease the edge of his swim trunks before diving inside them. And, oh my.

Licking my lips, I stroke his very large, very girthy cock.

"Don't threaten me with a good time," he says rolling us over so I'm straddling him.

It takes me all of two seconds to yank his shorts down. When his cock springs free, my mouth waters with anticipation. It's glorious.

And he's so beautiful.

As I drink him in slowly, my tongue darts out over my bottom lip. I can't take the wait any longer and lick up his veiny shaft once. Nolan's response pulses through me.

"Baby, get on me before you make me lose it. I want to feel you."

My pussy throbs as I climb onto him. Our eyes latch onto each other for a beat then I line up the head of his cock with my entrance. I'm so ready for him.

Nolan's hands grip my hips, waiting and then I lower myself onto his rock hard length. His chest rises and he lifts a hand to slide my bikini top up, giving him access to my breasts, his thumb teasing my pebbled nipples.

I roll my hips against him, gentle at first, then faster, riding him with purpose. With power. With a desperation I don't bother hiding.

He *loves* watching me fall apart, and I swear it shoots straight through me like lightning.

I grind harder, chasing it. Needing it. Needing *him*.

And Nolan takes it. All of it. Mouth parted, eyes locked on me. I'm both the storm and the surrender.

Every roll of my hips against him sends another jolt of pleasure spiraling through me. His cock is greedy, *perfect*, pounding inside me in ways that make my legs quake and my breath stutter.

His hands grip my ass, holding me in place as I work him harder, deeper. Heat coils in my belly, tight and bright and *relentless*.

My pace falters.

My thighs begin to shake.

He groans. That sound—that deep, vibration—shoots straight to my core, and I whimper, hips jerking. My fingers claw at his chest, gripping just enough to ground myself as the pleasure crests, rising, rising—

My mouth falls open, a gasp catching in my throat.

"Nolan—" It's barely a word.

He lifts my hips and takes over so that I can shatter.

The orgasm tears through me. A cry rips from my throat, my thighs clamp, and the stars above blur with every tremor of his warm release inside me.

He doesn't stop. He rises, kisses me through it, slows only when my thighs twitch and my breath comes in jagged bursts. His hands are gentler now. Soothing. Steady. Worshipful.

When I finally collapse, breathless and limp, my entire body buzzing, he lifts my chin and looks at me with the filthiest, most satisfied grin I've ever seen.

And somehow, the most reverent.

I slide off him, legs jelly, heart pounding. He shifts beside me, gleaming with smug delight.

"This," he says, voice low and wicked, "was significantly better than a public bathroom."

My laugh bursts out, ragged and real. "You think?"

"Oh, I know." He props himself up on one elbow, trailing a finger along my thigh. "I think the whole resort heard you though."

I cover my face with both hands, groaning. "I genuinely hate you."

"Say that again." His lips graze my shoulder. "And I'll make you scream it the next time those words leave your lips."

Well, that makes me want to say over and over, to see if he'll make good on that promise.

I glare at him from between my fingers. "You are absolutely insufferable."

"And you're absolutely ruined." His voice drops, darker now. "So…shall I prepare for round two?"

# CHAPTER 41
# ENEMIES TO ARCHITECTS

## NOLAN

WE SPENT THE NIGHT TANGLED—LIMBS locked, skin slick, mouths greedy. Sleep came in waves, interrupted only by hands searching in the dark and soft, broken sounds whispered against my throat.

Rorie Adams is a goddamn force. Insatiable. Relentless. And I'll never say it out loud, but she wore me the hell out.

Thanks to all of the above, I slept like a fucking rock.

When I finally stirred, the sheets were warm beside me, her scent smothering the pillow. But she was gone.

Left only a note.

*See you on the beach, Rival.*

I've got a feeling she's about to act like nothing happened.

Too bad for her I remember *everything*.

Every sound she made. Every way her body moved. Every time she begged and every time I gave in just to hear her again.

And I'll be sure to remind her…

Slowly.

Torturously.

Endlessly.

My cock stirs at the memories and the possibilities. How she clawed at me. Bit my shoulder. Shoved her hand over my mouth like it would muffle the sounds I made when she slid down on me like sin in silk.

I've tasted the queen.

And now I want the whole kingdom.

The sun is already a smug bastard by the time I join the others on the beach. The sand is hot underfoot. Everything about this place is too bright, too loud.

Adjusting my sunglasses, I pretend to size up the competition. My goal is to look strategic, thoughtful, even intimidating. You know—like a man focused on winning.

But truthfully, I'm mostly thinking about what I want to do to Rorie later tonight. In the hot tub. Or with that detachable shower head in her villa bathroom.

I find her standing next to her team, and God help me because she's wearing a pink bikini today. Thin straps. Tied at the hips. It's killing me.

Absolutely killing me.

My cock is now in a state of emergency. Her sarong sits low, hips bare, and when she laughs, throws her head back and shines like summer itself, it's a punch to the chest. In the best possible way.

She looks at me. Smirks, even. We have a secret we've burned into each other and now we're just waiting for nightfall to burn again. Or maybe lunch.

Brunch?

Now?

So yeah, I'm not exactly focused on sandcastle strategy right now.

Shelby strides onto the beach with her signature confidence, sundress billowing, sunglasses perched on her head, and not a single bead of sweat betraying her despite the heat.

"Good morning, everyone!" she calls out, her voice somehow carrying over the sound of waves and the occasional squawk of a seagull probably plotting to steal someone's snack.

The crowd quiets, all eyes on her.

"Today's challenge," she continues, "is simple: build the best sandcastle. But—and this is important—you won't be working with your teams. You'll be paired with people from other firms. As I stated last night, we believe the true test of teamwork is adaptability. You'll be judged on creativity, structure, and, of course, how well you work in a group."

She starts reading off the team assignments. Names blur together as I focus on not staring at Rorie's ass like it's the eighth wonder of the world.

"...and for our final team: Nolan Rhodes from Big Stream, Jeremy Brooks from the Laurel Group, Sierra Lin from Taylor & Blythe, and Marcus Dean from Halston, Inc."

The sun beats down, baking not only us but the sand beneath our feet as we gather around our designated patch of beach. Sierra and Marcus start debating structural integrity and sand-to-water ratios like this is the Olympics of sandcastle building.

I'm not really listening. Rorie Adams is on all fours in the sand, skin kissed golden by the sun, that thin bikini top doing everything but hiding temptation. Her back arches slightly as she shifts, and her legs stretch out behind her, gleaming and sun-drenched. The sarong slips again, baring more of her thigh. It takes every ounce of restraint I have not to get behind her and bury myself to the hilt.

Jeremy doesn't look at me right away, but when he does, his expression is deeply judgy.

Rorie crouches, molding a wet cylinder of sand, lips parted slightly in concentration, and I am seconds from losing it.

All I picture is her giving me a hand job, those same fingers wrapped around me instead of wet sand. It doesn't help that she smooths the sides slowly, purposefully, like she's got nowhere else to be and all the time in the world to ruin me.

I clear my throat, trying to snap out of it. "We should build a moat. You know, for structural... defense."

"A moat?" Jeremy deadpans. "What are we defending it from? Your fragile ego?"

Marcus snorts. Sierra doesn't even look up.

I force my attention back to our team. Marcus squats down and sketches a rough outline of a castle in the sand, while Sierra tilts her head, evaluating.

"We should elevate the foundation a little," Sierra suggests. "The higher the base, the less likely the structure is to collapse when the tide comes in."

"Good call," Marcus agrees. "What about towers? We could go for something grand, like a medieval fortress."

Jeremy nods, tapping a finger against his chin. "That could work, but we need to think about stability too. Wet sand holds better. If we reinforce the walls with a mix of damp and dry sand, it'll keep things from caving in too easily."

I glance at Jeremy, impressed. "Didn't take you for an expert in sandcastle physics."

He shrugs. "Was in a physics club in high school. Won a few contests."

Marcus grins. "Guess we know who the real mastermind is."

Jeremy follows my gaze and finally smirks. The kind that says, *You're not as subtle as you think you are, bro.*

His smirk fades. "We need to talk," he says, quieter now.

The team disperses to grab supplies, and before I can come up with an excuse, Jeremy yanks me aside behind one of the display boards.

"I'm just gonna shoot it straight," Jeremy says. "You and Rorie? There's something there. Cosmic-level shit. Like fate and fanfic had a baby."

I blink. "That's—."

He holds up a finger. "But, if you're not serious? If you're even *thinking* about ghosting her or playing some casual office-rivalry hookup game. *Again*. I will personally remove your balls with a souvenir spork from this event. Capish?"

I blink again. "Yeah."

"Good." He nods, adjusting his sunglasses like some mafia beach dad. "She's been through enough. Her ex did a number on her. And before that? Life did a number on her. She doesn't need a third round with a guy who doesn't know what he wants."

I open my mouth, but Jeremy's not finished.

"Now, don't get me wrong—part of me ships it. Like, hard. You two have that tensiony enemies-to-lovers, workplace rivalry thing going on. Makes for great drama. But I care more about Rorie's heart than I do your cheekbones, and trust me, that's saying something."

I laugh. I can't help it.

He smirks. "That's right. I'm funny and emotionally evolved. Try to keep up."

I shake my head, a reluctant smile tugging at my mouth. "You done?"

"For now. Just know I'm watching you like a hawk." Jeremy points two fingers at his eyes, then at me. "A hawk with killer intuition and excellent taste in prey."

"I understand."

He claps me on the shoulder. "Excellent. Now, giddy up, mother-fucker. We're about to build the kind of sandcastle that makes grown men weep."

I smile. This guy is actually freaking hilarious.

"I've been training for this since my kindergarten sandbox days. Don't slow me down."

He rejoins the team and immediately makes a wildly unhelpful suggestion about decorating the castle with seaweed hair.

We get to work, and the beach becomes anarchy in the best way.

Some groups go full *Game of Thrones*, others sculpt mermaid thrones or giant octopi. One team is building a nearly ten-foot replica of Poseidon complete with abs and a trident made out of driftwood. Another creates what looks like a sand coliseum with actual bleachers.

And then there's one poor team near the shoreline who've clearly given up. Their castle is a single lumpy dome with a sad stick flag poking out the top like it's begging to be put out of its misery.

Jeremy stares at it. "Tragic."

"Mercy kill?" I offer.

"Nah. Let it suffer. Builds character."

We all laugh.

We're hot. We're sweaty. We're covered in sand. But weirdly? I'm feeling good. Better than good.

Because Rorie looks up at me now. And when she smiles, bashfully, it feels like something real is finally taking shape.

# CHAPTER 42
# EVERYTHING, ALL AT ONCE

RORIE

THE SUN MELTS into the horizon, rich shades of amber, peach, and blood-orange streak across the sky. The light makes everything feel cinematic, like the world hit pause just for us, just for this moment.

Our bare feet press into the damp sand, the tide flirting with our ankles, warm and teasing. The only sounds are the hush of the waves and the occasional gull overhead.

Nolan walks beside me. He captures my hands, interlaces our fingers. I can smell the sun on his skin. He's been mostly quiet, letting the rhythm of the sea fill in the space between us.

I can't stop glancing sideways at him. I try to keep my attention forward, but he's so beautiful, it's hard.

I should feel calm. This should be a moment of peace. But my chest is tight with a truth clawing up my throat, and the longer I keep it in, the more it feels like a betrayal.

Nolan lifts his phone and stops. "Sunset's too good not to capture."

He's right. The sky's gone all apocalyptic in the prettiest way with gold bleeding into coral, and violets and indigos dancing across the water.

His phone angles it toward me. *Click.*

"Did you just—?"

"Had to." He smirks, that dimple peeking out. "You look like magic."

I laugh, but it comes out shaky. He's staring at his screen, admiring the photo and butterflies in my stomach erupt.

"I'm using this as your profile photo," he says casually, opening up his contacts. "I need proof you're real."

And just like that, the butterflies nosedive straight into a meat grinder. Dread slithers in, winding itself around my insides, waiting for its cue.

Now it's center stage.

I know what's coming.

And I'm the reason everything's about to potentially fall apart.

"Nolan..."

The light hits his eyes just right, softening that impossible shade of golden brown—half storm, half salvation. I wish I could swim in that look. I wish I deserved to.

"What's your number?" A thumb hovers over his screen like it's just another casual request. Just a normal guy on a normal beach, asking for a normal girl's number.

Only this isn't normal. None of it is.

My heart's punching at my ribs. A deep, aching rhythm that feels like the truth begging to be let out.

"There's something I have to tell you," I whisper.

When he sees my expression, and the worry in my eyes, his whole body stills. It's a subtle shift. But it's there.

Nolan's weight balances. His shoulders lock, but his eyes stay on mine. Steady. Open.

"Okay..." His expression tells me he thinks I'm about to drop something that might change us, and what we have right now, in this moment.

And that breaks me a little.

I've been keeping this secret wound so tight it's cut into me. Saying it out loud could unravel everything.

Carl is the one who made me laugh on my worst days.

The one who never saw my face but somehow *saw me*.

The one who made the silence feel less empty.

And I'm terrified that if I pull the thread, I'll lose the one part of my day I looked forward to.

The messages. The banter. The person on the other end of the unknown.

The version of me that felt *safe* behind a screen.

Not too much.

Not too little.

Just... enough.

But Nolan is Carl. And it's time to let him share this secret with me.

"I'm not *just* Rorie Adams. I mean, I am. But I'm also..." My throat goes tight.

Nolan's head tilts, a teasing smile tugging at the corner of his mouth. He doesn't look nervous. He looks *giddy*. He's convinced I'm about to say something adorable, not earth-shattering.

"Well, I mean—who else are you?" He takes a step closer. His fingers graze mine. "Like... are you also Rorie Adams, *my* girlfriend? Is that where this is going? Because if this is your version of asking me to hit the next level with you, ten out of ten. I'm swooning."

My chest caves in. And his smile, God, it's *so* sweet. So happy. He doesn't see the wrecking ball coming. Part of me wants to freeze it here, capture this perfect second before the storm breaks.

My fingers tremble as I dig my phone out of the back pocket of my shorts.

Nolan blinks. "Why do I feel worried?"

"Get close to me." I lift the phone, snap a picture of the two of us with the sun dipping low behind us, painting the sky in wild strokes of fiery colors.

*Click.*

I open my message thread for Carl.

> [image attached]

> So, this is me.

His phone buzzes in his hand.

I see it hit him like a slap. That familiar ping. His brows furrow as he opens the message. His giddy grin slips. The sunset behind us may as well disappear too.

Confusion crashes in first... then realization.

Silence.

Loud, terrible, crushing silence.

All those texts.

All the banter.

The comfort. The confessions.

His jaw tightens. Is he angry?

"You?" His voice is hoarse. "You're—*you're* TF?"

Nodding, I quickly say, "I didn't mean for it to happen like this."

His attention snaps to me. The sky's burning around us, like even the sun can't look away.

"How long have you known?"

"I put it together the day before we flew out. I didn't know how to tell you—"

"You didn't know how to tell me?" His voice is quieter now. "You've known this whole time. The jokes. The confessions. The *texts*. You *knew* when we—" He stops short, swallows. "Jesus, Rorie."

He starts walking.

Not fast.

Not storming off.

Just walking.

His shoulders are tight, hands curled at his sides.

"Nolan," I call, following. "Wait—please, let me explain."

"I'm not running," he says, without looking back. "I just... I need a minute to process this."

I stop walking. Chasing him would be selfish. He deserves that minute.

My chest hurts. I want to scream that none of it was a game to me. That I was scared. That I'm *still* me.

But he's gone, swallowed by the curve of the shoreline, the dying sun catching the back of his neck.

And all I can do is stand there, sand in my toes, heartbreak in my heart, wondering if I just lost the one person who made the ground feel steady again right when I'd finally stopped gripping the walls.

# CHAPTER 43
# TEXTUALLY, FRACTURED
## NOLAN

THE SKY IS ablaze with fire and gold, and for once, it mirrors the way my insides burn, not with anger, but with the sick heat of realization. Like I've walked into a room where everyone else already knows the secret, and I'm the last to figure it out. The last to understand what she's afraid of. The last to see her. And the last person she'll ever trust to hold it all.

Standing barefoot on the beach, the tide pulls at my ankles, warm and constant. The wind lashes salt against my skin, but it's not what stings.

That award goes to Textually Frustrated, i.e. Rorie Adams.

Digging my phone out of my pocket, I pull up the contact.

No photo. Fake name. Just two words that somehow carried a whole damn world.

For a long moment, I just stare at it, remembering the first message. The sarcasm. The wit.

My mind fast-forwards to the way she slipped into my nights like she belonged there. Her words filled the silence and made it bearable. She knew exactly what to say. And she was always, always her.

And I was me.

I swipe through our old texts, thumb dragging slow. It's all so glaringly obvious now—the humor, the stubbornness, how she cared too much even when she pretended not to.

Every word.

Every joke.

Every late-night confession…

On instinct, I back out of the messages and switch over to my inbox.

Rorie's last email is sitting there—sharp, professional, signed with her full name. I click into it. And there, embedded in the contact block at the bottom, is her number.

I blink. My chest tightens. It's the same number I've been texting for months. The same one I never saved because I'd sent her that goddamn pause email and walked away like a coward. Never even thought to program it in. Never looked closely.

*It was her.*

Rorie.

*Rorie.*

The tornado in heels I kept walking into, even when I swore I shouldn't. Every jagged word between us, every stolen glance, every brush of skin, charged the air like lightning waiting for a place to strike.

And damn, did she strike.

I wanted her the first second I saw her.

Before Textually Frustrated gave me late-night texts and whispered secrets. Before Rorie's lips touched mine and rewrote my idea of desire.

The chemistry between us was never subtle, it burned in silences, sparked in every argument, pulsed with every breath. Even when I tried to bury it under professionalism and pride.

She was the one I wanted with a hunger I didn't know how to tame.

Not just for her body. For her *mind*. Her chaos. Her heart.

The part of her that laughed at my arrogance and still saw through it.

And now?

She's the same woman I went to for everything. My friend. Without realizing it or even knowing it was her.

And I just left her.

She called after me, voice cracking open the night, and I fucking kept walking. Just like that jackass from her past. The one who made her believe that needing someone when you're at your worst is asking too much. That leaning on someone means watching them walk away.

Shit.

I'm no better than him.

I did the very thing she was terrified of. Proved her fears right. Made her feel like she was *too much* just for telling me the truth.

First the email. Then the silence. Now this.

I'm fucking this up.

Left and right.

My jaw clenches as I stare out at the darkening horizon, the last of the sun bleeding into the sea like a wound. I should be beside her. I should've stayed.

I have to fix this. Not for me. For the girl who made me laugh when I was shattered. For the woman who kissed me like she *meant* it. For the person who trusted me—until I gave her every reason not to.

I turn back toward the lights of the resort, the sand biting at my feet.

Time to prove I'm not like the one who ran.

Time to be the man who stays.

# CHAPTER 44

# CHOSEN

RORIE

MY PHONE BUZZES on the nightstand.

> I messed up.

> I said I needed time, but what I needed was you.

> The real you.

> The one who made me laugh when I couldn't breathe.

> The one who saw past every defense and stayed anyway.

> I see you now, Rorie. All of you.

> And I'm sorry it took me this long to realize.

Another buzz.

> I'm outside your door. Not to argue. Not to demand. Just to show up. For real this time.

My chest caves in on itself.

I rush to the door. He's there, same gray shirt, same dark eyes, but everything else is different. Softer. Clearer.

He holds up his phone. The photo I sent him earlier—us, standing by the ocean, sun melting into the sky—is now his contact picture. *Textually Frustrated.*

No longer anonymous. No longer a secret.

He puts the phone away and says, "I want to remember the moment before I knew. Before the guilt. Before the noise. Just... us."

I'm not breathing. I don't think I know how to anymore.

"I thought you hated me," I whisper.

He steps forward, slow, and intentional. "I hate that I hurt you. I hate that I didn't make you feel safe enough to tell me. That's on me. Not you."

My eyes sting. "No—"

"I just—" He stops himself, the space between his brows pinching. "You didn't just get under my skin, Rorie. You became the reason it felt like I had any at all. Everything felt numb until you started texting me. And then I couldn't stop needing more of you."

My heart cracks open. The light inside seeps through.

"Rorie, you made me feel...everything." Slowly, reverently—he closes the distance.

His hands cup my face, thumbs brush my cheekbones, and his eyes are on me like I'm the only star in the entire sky.

No heat. No rage. No roughness.

"Let me make this right," he breathes, so close I can taste the confession in his voice.

"I should've told you." My voice shakes.

"Shhh..." He leans in, forehead pressing to mine. He doesn't kiss me yet. Instead, he lets his hands slide down, featherlight, across my shoulders, down my arms, until they settle at my waist.

"Adams," he says softly. "I don't want fast, or frantic, or furious. I want to learn you. I want to commit every shiver and sigh to memory until I can rewrite the definition of love for you."

His lips brush mine, a breath of a kiss. I lean into it, but he doesn't deepen. He pulls back with a wicked smirk.

"Still mad at me?" he asks, voice like velvet.

"Yes," I manage.

"Good," he whispers against my neck, lips skating lower. "Because making-up is my favorite part. And now I'm going to show you exactly what happens when you keep secrets from me."

The air narrows, folds in on us like the secret we've kept too long. He's in my space, my breath, my bloodstream. Every inch of him is just shy of contact, but I feel him everywhere. In the thrum beneath my skin. In the anticipation coiling low in my belly. In the silence that begs to be broken by us.

"You and me," he breathes. "We're a goddamn mess."

His hands find my waist.

"But maybe," he whispers, "we make beautiful wreckage."

He kisses me. And it's not sweet. It's not slow.

It's a goddamn implosion.

A kiss that carves, that bruises, that bears the weight of everything we've said and everything we couldn't. It's need without apology, desperation without shame. His hands slide beneath my shirt, starving for skin.

My fingers are in his hair, tugging him closer, anchoring myself to the one thing that's never felt like a mistake.

Because this isn't a mistake.

This is inevitable.

Clothes become obstacles. Buttons snap, zippers hiss, fabric is discarded. He spins me, presses me to the wall, one hand gripping my hip like it belongs to him, the other burying into my hair with a control that trembles at the edge.

I moan as his mouth trails down my throat, his teeth scraping enough to cause a delicious hurt, enough to make me arch. He soothes it with his tongue, then does it again—marking me, claiming me, giving me the apology we never put into words.

His hand slides higher, wrapping gently around the base of my throat—not to squeeze. Just to hold. To remind me I'm his. I've always been his.

My pulse pounds beneath his palm.

He feels it. Tracks it. Feeds off it.

"That mouth of yours has lit me on fire for weeks," he growls, "and now I'm gonna make you feel every fucking word."

I can't breathe. I don't want to.

Spinning back, I yank Nolan into me, our mouths crashing, tongues tangling in a kiss that doesn't ask for permission—it seizes it, conquers it.

We stumble toward the bed together in the same breath. His urgent hands are everywhere. And when he speaks, it isn't pure, unfiltered heat.

"I'm not just going to fuck you, Rorie."

Pressing me into the mattress, he settles above me, gaze burning into mine. His eyes are molten, roaming over every inch of me like I'm a puzzle he's waited his whole life to solve.

His hair's wild.

His breathing's ragged.

His soul is naked.

"I'm going to show you what it means to be wanted. Worshipped. *Chosen*."

And right then—

I choose him too.

"Promise?"

His mouth crushes mine. Every kiss is a possession. Every bite, a confession. It's pure euphoria running in my veins.

Nolan draws back, looks at me. "Spread your legs, Rorie." His voice slides into my chest, and slithers down my core, heat rolling through me like thunder.

Breath shuddering, I hesitate, a little dazed by how badly I want to obey him. How easily he could make me come with nothing but that voice and the weight of that look.

Slowly, I open for him.

He smiles.

Not cocky. Not cruel.

Just confident.

Like he already knows how this ends. And it's with me, beneath him, whispering his name into the dark, begging for me.

Licking his lips, he slides down my body with reverence and hunger—like the only place he's ever belonged is between my thighs.

And then he's there.

And holy God.

It's not sweet.

It's not careful.

It's filthy. It's fevered. It's feral.

Quick, devastating licks against my clit punch the air from my lungs. Again. Again. No mercy. No hesitation. Only relentless devotion to every moan, every tremor, every gasp he drags from me as proof I'm his.

My hand fists his hair, holding him there. The other claws the sheets, desperate for something solid as my body starts to shake.

I'm undone.

Unmade.

This man is a storm. I've never wanted to drown so badly.

He tugs my clit with his teeth. Cruelty and devotion are wrapped together.

I gasp, hips arching, desperate for more, begging for anything.

But he doesn't give it.

He doesn't move.

Doesn't touch.

He watches me, lips wet, eyes darkening, chest heaving with the restraint it's taking to hold himself back.

"You said you wanted a man who could make you come with words alone," he says voice lethal, sin dipped in silk.

Oh, damn he remembers.

I was being a brat in that moment on the plane. And now I'm about to pay for it.

My pulse hammers, body tightens.

"I've thought about that, Rorie." His gaze drops to my thighs, still parted for him, still aching, my wetness smeared across them, ready for him. "Thought about how wild your mind must be. How filthy. How greedy."

His words graze over my skin.

"Bet you pictured it, too. Me whispering in your ear... telling you how soaked you'd be for me. How your thighs would start to shake before I ever even touched you."

He leans in close, but not touching, his mouth hovering beside my ear.

"And you're close, aren't you, baby?" he whispers. "Your clit's still throbbing from my mouth. You're so fucking wet, you can feel it dripping, can't you?"

A whimper breaks free from my throat.

His smile is all devil. "You want to come, Rorie? I want you to. I want you to fall apart from the sound of my voice alone. From the things I'd do to you."

My legs tremble, pussy tightens.

Nolan shoves his shorts down. I watch his swollen cock twitch under my gaze. I want to straddle him, slip his fat mushroom head inside me, and torture myself endlessly with just the head of his glorious dick.

He fists his cock, slides his hand slowly over the silky skin of it. "Jealous of my hand, Rorie?"

I don't hesitate with my answer. "Yes."

I want to touch him. I reach for him, but he stops me.

"No, baby. But if you're good, and you come for me by words alone, I'll let you have as much as you want." His voice threads into the most intimate part of me.

His hand keeps moving, stroking himself. "Imagine this cock sliding inside you achingly slow. Deep. Feel every inch. I'd let you claw at my shoulders. Let you swear, and sob, and lose every thought except one."

He pauses, then says, "Mine."

A gasp rips out of me, involuntary.

"Visualize me fucking you until your legs forget how to stand. Until your voice cracked on my name. Until you begged me to stop and keep going in the same breath."

My eyes flutter shut. *Fuck.*

"Do it," he murmurs, pumping himself harder. "Let go. No hands. No help. Just me."

My hips buck. Desperate. Empty.

"Nolan," I gasp, one hand darting toward the throbbing ache between my legs.

But he catches my wrist midair.

"Don't," he growls. "I already told you, naughty girl, you don't get to touch. Not until you do what I ask."

I whimper, trembling as he pins my arm gently to the mattress. My thighs are quaking, my skin is buzzing with every unsatisfied nerve.

"Beg me with that filthy mouth."

I squirm under him, another broken sound leaving my throat. "Please—"

His body presses down over mine, but he still doesn't give me what I crave. His voice is the only thing he allows.

"You're already so close, baby. Think about my mouth on your clit. You want to know what you feel like under my tongue?"

Frantic, I nod.

"Sweet. Addictive. A taste I'd chase through every lifetime."

I arch. "Oh, God…"

"That's it. Say it again."

"Oh God," I cry out, hips rolling into the air, but there's nothing there. No friction. No contact. Only his words and the hot press of his breath.

"You're dripping, Rorie," he says, a groan rumbling from his chest. "I can see it. Bet you'd soak my fingers the second I slid them in."

I reach for him again—wild, untethered—but he pushes my hand away with maddening ease.

"Still no," he says. "Not until you come. My voice. Your mind. That's all you get."

I'm shaking now, legs trembling, moaning with every breath. "Please…"

"Come," he demands, lips brushing the shell of my ear. "Picture me inside you. Deep. Bare. Pushing you open. Whispering every filthy thing I want to do to you."

"Oh fuck," I gasp.

"I want to fuck you slow, Rorie. Until you scrape my back and tell me you can't take it anymore. I want to keep going. Hold you still, make you feel every inch, every vein, every throb."

"Nolan—" My voice breaks.

"Come, baby."

"Yes—"

"Come. Right now." He pumps himself. I know he's just as close as me. "Let me hear it. Let me *feel* it."

And I do.

Without touch. Without pressure.

With only his voice in my ear and his words crawling under my skin.

My body crashes, spasms, heat rushing through me so fast I cry out, back bowing, hands fisting the sheets. I scream his name into the room like it's the only word I've ever known.

And through it all, he holds me still. Kissing my throat. Whispering, "That's my girl."

His hands are on me, steady and sure, commanding without demand. There's a power in the way he touches me, like I'm both wildfire and worship. And then he's there, lowering himself between my thighs.

The broad heat of his body presses into mine, his chest flush against my breasts, his mouth brushing the hinge of my jaw. His cock nudges at my entrance, the blunt head dragging over my clit with a slow, devastating precision that rips a gasp from my throat.

My hips jerk instinctively, desperate for more. He holds still, savoring it, savoring me.

His voice is a whisper against my skin. "Ready for me, baby?"

I nod, breath caught in my throat, and he slides in.

Not fast.

Not gentle.

*Deep.*

So deep it rewrites your anatomy, carves out space and fills it all in one movement.

As he sinks into me, I cry out, raw and undone. One hand glides up the curve of my side, fingers trailing fire across my skin. He holds me like every inch of contact is necessary to keep him grounded. His other hand braces beside my head, muscle flexed, keeping him steady as he begins to move.

Every thrust is a claim, a promise, a breaking point, splintering logic and rebuilding it in his rhythm.

And I match him, move for move, gasp for gasp, offering my entire self for the taking.

He groans, low and a little broken. "Fuck, you feel so fucking good."

His hips roll forward again, a punishing grind setting every nerve ending ablaze. His cock drags against every sensitive inch, stroking a place so deep I see stars. My walls flutter around him, greedy and desperate, and the sound it makes is filthy, wet, obscene. Sexy.

This is everything.

His thrusts build, measured, anchored, and devastating.

"You feel that?" he murmurs, voice frayed. "That's what it's like when someone's made for you."

And god help me, I believe him. Because I've never been filled like this. Never felt *seen* like this. Never wanted more of someone I already had completely.

And still—it's not enough. I want *everything*.

I want *him*.

His mouth is hot against my ear. "It's not just sex with us, Rorie."

My pulse kicks under his touch, every beat echoing where his fingers splay over my ribs. My nails rake across his chest, chasing the slick heat of his skin.

He thrusts deeper, and my gasp tears through the room, timed perfectly with his next words.

"It's ruinous."

Lips brush across the curve of my neck. He presses a kiss there. Then another. Then another.

"It rewires you," he breathes, hips rolling into me in a rhythm that feels older than logic, deeper than language. "It burns through every thought... every breath... until the only thing that exists is this. Us."

Another thrust. Another kiss. Each one slower. More deliberate. His hand teases over my breast, fingers tightening around my nipple with increasing intensity until I'm arching into him, shameless and starving.

"You crave it," he whispers, his voice feathering kisses across my collarbone. "Just like I do."

A pause. A heartbeat.

"It's going to undo you, baby," he says, a vow etched in gravel and heat. "I'm going to make damn sure of that. I will be the only man you ever want again."

I feel him grow harder inside me.

"This—" he growls, pushing deeper, his breath ragged, "—this is what you do to me. You burn under my skin. You fucking incinerate me."

And then—

We fall.

Together. Breathless. Boneless. A tangle of limbs and sweat and trembling sighs.

It's not gentle.

It's not quiet.

It's not just sex.

It's surrender, wildfire and homecoming—an unmaking wrapped in the beauty of being seen, known, wanted.

Chosen.

For a long, quiet moment, we just exist, our bodies still humming from the storm, our breath a shared rhythm struggling to find calm. The room is thick with heat. My fingers stay tangled in his hair. His hands stay curled around my hips like letting go means rewinding the world.

For a long, quiet moment, we just exist.

Twined limbs. Tangled breaths. No secrets. No distance. Just skin and truth and the kind of stillness that only follows after the rain finally stops.

My fingers stay curled in his hair. His hands don't leave my hips— not even a fraction. He doesn't let go. And this time, I know he won't.

The silence between us isn't fragile now, it's full, heavy with everything we already know.

His forehead presses to mine, our skin slick and warm, our hearts thudding out the same, steady rhythm. My palm finds the tattoo on his chest, feeling it beat under my hand like a vow.

He pulls back to look at me. His thumb strokes along my jaw, and when he speaks, it's a whisper.

"I just need you to know—" His voice cracks, and it shatters something soft inside me. "You freed me."

I smile, but it wobbles, because now the truth doesn't feel like a burden.

It feels like home.

"I'm not sorry," I say. "For any of it. For the texts. For the fight. For falling."

He exhales like he's been holding that breath for months. "You could've told me."

"I was scared," I admit. "But I'm not anymore."

A beat.

His hand moves to the back of my neck, fingers threading through my hair. His mouth finds mine again. This time with a sweetness that aches. A love that feels like staying. Like choosing.

Like it's final.

When we break apart, his eyes are bright.

"I don't want temporary," he says. "Not with you."

"Good," I breathe. "Because you're stuck with me."

He laughs, quiet and beautiful, pressing a kiss to my cheek, then my temple, then the spot just above my heart like he's sealing it.

And when he pulls me fully into his arms, holding me like he's never letting go—

I believe him.

# CHAPTER 45
# STEAM ME UP, SCOTTY

## RORIE

IF SOMEONE HAD TOLD me a week ago that I'd be willingly participating in a competitive game of drunk flamingo yoga on a paddleboard—I'd have laughed, possibly cried, and definitely asked for an early ticket back to New York.

But here I am. Three days in, sun-kissed and sore in muscles I didn't know existed, surviving what has officially become the most unique and also unhinged team-building resort experience known to all humans.

There was the salsa dance-off that spun wildly off course when Jeremy tried to dip Laurel and accidentally flung his shoe into the air... where it smacked the CEO from Taylor and Blythe in the head and launched his toupee into a server's champagne tray.

Then there was the mixology competition, where Nolan decided he absolutely *had* to outshine my Mirage and Titan by flirting his way behind the bar. Five minutes and an unnecessarily cocky wink later, he debuted a drink called *Rhodes Rage*—a concoction of tequila, bitters, sin, and a vengeance shot so potent it may have burned through the stomach lining of at least two fellow guests.

The whole night turned into a disaster. One guy kept crying, another proposed to a potted plant, and Rishi tried to legally adopt the bartender, who was clearly twenty plus years older than him. Shelby led a conga line through the cigar lounge wearing someone's yacht club blazer, chanting, "Shots before strategy!" like it was a corporate mantra.

And Laurel was caught doing the walk of shame from Thatcher's suite at sunrise, barefoot, bed-headed, and clutching her heels like they'd personally betrayed her.

Oh, it doesn't end there.

They have an escape room built into an old cabana, where I discovered that Nolan is terrifyingly good at solving riddles under pressure… and also prone to gloating. Loudly. Complete with a celebratory moonwalk and a grin that nearly cracked a mirror.

Yesterday, we had an underwater scavenger hunt. I may or may not have screamed into my snorkel when a fish kissed my mask, only to realize later, it was actually a shark.

And, of course, the burlesque night.

Oh, burlesque night.

I don't know who allowed Jeremy in the prop room, but let's just say I've seen enough feather boas and rhinestone nipple tassels to last a lifetime.

He managed to "accidentally" sign us up as the opening act for the talent portion of the evening. I played the "classy distraction" with a fan. Jeremy wore leather pants and lip-synced *Lady Marmalade* with more conviction than any performer ever. I'm eighty-seven percent sure someone from another firm invited him to perform at their upcoming wedding.

And through every ridiculous, wild, beautiful moment, there's been him.

Nolan.

The connecting door between our rooms has stayed open since our confession night and I wake up to the sound of his voice when he's dreaming, uttering nonsense about spreadsheets and coffee. We drift to sleep with our limbs tangled together, like our bodies forgot they ever existed separately.

He devours me in so many delicious ways.

And God, does he take his time.

Nolan's mouth is…

Well.

I'm convinced that whatever God built into my pleasure centers, Nolan Rhodes has discovered the cheat code

He kisses me like he's trying to etch me into his bones. Tastes me like I'm his favorite flavor. His mouth is a slow build and focused worship—tongue teasing, fingers pumping, rooting me in place as he draws out every stuttering gasp and broken plea as though he wants to own them.

And he never rushes.

He'll whisper filthy promises against my thigh one minute, then make good on every single one the next.

Every time he brings me to the edge, he looks up at me like I'm the answer to a question he's been asking his whole damn life.

It's... addicting.

Because somewhere between burlesque boas, stolen glances, and whispered laughs under moonlight, we've blurred the line between rival and lover.

And we're okay with that.

Right now, Nolan's in a final prep meeting for their pitch. I'd offered to head back to my room, give him space, but he just smirked, kissed my forehead, and said, *"Absolutely not."*

So now I'm here, lounging on his bed, wearing one of his soft T-shirts that smells like cedar and heat and that warm spice that is so Nolan Rhodes, half-listening to the ocean outside.

Eventually, I pad toward his bathroom, bare feet silent on the hardwood. The air is still tinged with the last traces of his body wash. I twist the shower knob, steam filling the glass enclosure in seconds.

The hot water cascades down my back, easing the tension in my shoulders. I grab his body wash and lather it into my skin, slow and indulgent. The scent is rich, woodsy, masculine, and it only makes the ache between my thighs more persistent.

Eyes closed, I lean into the spray, hand drifting lower as a naughty idea strikes and I yank the other shower head out of its resting position, turn it on, and switch the setting.

The pressure sharpens. And when I move it between my legs, a gasp escapes my lips as my head falls back against the tile.

My hips roll gently, breath catching as sensation pulses through me. It's not enough, but it's something to take the edge off.

I hear the door creak.

Footsteps.

Suddenly the steam shifts behind me.

"What is my naughty girl doing without me?" Nolan's voice is laced with desire.

He steps into the shower, still dressed, t-shirt soaked, eyes dark, and wolfish. "I've been fantasizing about that shower head since we got here."

"I'm sure you have." My gaze slides down his dripping body. He's so beautiful, some days I can barely stand it.

Nolan undoes his pants, hooks his thumbs into the waistband, eyes locked on mine, daring me to blink.

I don't. I lick my lips, hungry with anticipation.

He shoves his pants down, and his thick cock springs free, flushed deep with need. The sight of it makes my mouth water.

God, he's huge.

I drag my eyes back up to his, smirking as heat coils low and tight in my belly.

"Get over here," I whisper. "I want you in my mouth."

The look in his eyes shifts from amused to absolutely animalistic. He yanks his shirt over his head, baring inch after inch of slick, warm muscle. He discards the soaked garment in the corner.

Steam wraps around us, water cascading off his chest as I run my hands up his thighs.

"Don't move," I warn, tone soaked in intent.

He doesn't. Not even a little bit.

I press a kiss to the base of his abdomen, then another, my lips trailing along the taut line of his abs as he stands there, barely breathing.

Nolan stares down at me like I might be the one thing he'll never recover from. And I fucking love that.

My hands glide up the backs of his thighs before clamping myself there as I look up at him—dripping wet, waiting.

The spray pounds at my back, steam cocooning us in something hot and intimate.

"You were saying something about wanting me in your mouth." His lips quirk.

Snarky bastard.

Wrapping a hand around his slick, firm length, he's hot and pulsing, straining with need. My thumb circles the tip, teasing, testing.

"Fuck," a groan rumbles through him, echoing off the tile. One hand flies to the wall for balance, the other fists in my wet hair.

Lowering my mouth, I kiss the head gently, then drag my tongue along the underside deliberately slow.

He swears under his breath. It's killing him. Another thing I fucking love.

Water trails down his toned stomach. I take him deeper, letting the weight of him fill my mouth. The steam blurs everything but the feel of him, the taste of him, the raw heat pulsing between us.

His fingers tighten in my hair. He's breathing hard, hips twitching like he's seconds from losing it.

I circle my tongue around him while he's inside me, and he lets out a strangled sound, part moan, part prayer.

My head bobs as I suck him hard. He's holding back. But I don't want him restrained.

I want him undone.

My mouth moves faster, rhythm measured, tongue swirling, lips slick and greedy. Every sound he makes punches straight through me, and I am so wet.

His legs tremble. His stomach clenches. I don't let up. This moment is mine.

He is mine.

Glancing up, my lips curve. "Will you fuck my mouth?"

One side of his lips quirk back. "Rorie, I'd let you ruin my credit score if you asked me."

I smirk.

"Now open." His tone drops when he makes the order.

I do. A little too eagerly.

His hand comes to the back of my head, not rough, but firm—guiding, reverent. His cock slides between my lips, thick on my tongue, and for a second, neither of us moves until his hips roll forward with a controlled thrust.

Then another.

And another.

He watches every movement, loving how my mouth stretches around him, the way my throat flexes as I take him deeper.

"Fuck," he breathes, the word torn from his chest.

His free hand joins his other and fingers clutch my head, holding me steady.

Nolan starts pounding, racing, giving himself to me. One deep, devastating thrust at a time.

And I take it.

All of him.

With greedy, aching want.

I choke on him and it's the most delicious thing. I want more.

Nolan grunts, low and desperate. "Fuck, Rorie—I'm—"

I don't let him pull out. I hold him tighter and take him deeper, allowing him to pump hard between my lips, until he spills into my mouth with a full-body shudder, a groan so guttural it echoes to my soul.

I swallow every last drop. And when I look up through my lashes, he's staring down at me.

"You are so beautiful." His chest heaves. His hands fall to his sides.

Rising, I kiss up his torso, tasting water and him. He catches my waist as I reach his face, and when I kiss the corner of his mouth, he exhales as though it's the only breath he has left.

Dazed and grinning, he leans back against the tile. I brush my thumb across his lower lip, cocky and content.

"Here I was thinking we were just going to have a little fun. Not get spiritually baptized in my own shower."

"You're welcome."

# CHAPTER 46
# FULL THROTTLE
## NOLAN

IT'S the kind of morning that smells like sunscreen, ego, and imminent humiliation. Welcome to the ATV relay challenge—White Thorn's idea of team building, corporate bonding, and bloodsport all in one.

The stakes?

Bragging rights, a luxurious dinner, and a strategic advantage in the pitch competition.

The real prize?

Watching your rival eat your dust. Literally. Because in five minutes, we're all about to launch down the sand in souped-up death carts while pretending this is just "fun."

It's not fun though.

It's war.

With helmets. And eye protection.

I should be focusing. Strategy. Speed. Securing an early lead in the challenges.

But my mind is firmly stuck on last night. On the way Rorie's eyes found mine across the candlelit table at dinner. How she kept catching me looking. And the fact that she never looks away.

And later, when the night had gone quiet and everyone retreated to their cottages, we lay in bed with only one thought pulsing behind my eyes: is she falling for me as hard as I'm falling for her.

God, I hope the answer's yes.

Rorie's stretching by her ATV now, completely unaware she's single handedly sabotaging my mental stability. Lavender workout shorts. Fitted tank top. High ponytail bouncing with every move. She's temptation wrapped in sunshine and sass.

My traitorous brain wanders straight to grabbing that ponytail. Fisting it. Tilting her head back. Letting my mouth trail down her slender neck before I slide my cock into her pussy.

*Jesus. Get it together, Rhodes.*

I tear my eyes away, forcing myself to focus before I end up pitching a tent in my race gear. When I glance back, she's laughing at something Jeremy said, shaking her head, biting her lip, and that laugh? That's the real problem. It hits me right square in the chest.

Yeah. I'm fucked.

But I love it.

Shelby steps up to the mic, and the crowd gathers. Rorie's behind me now. I don't need to look, I feel her. Like static in the air before a storm.

"Alright, competitors," Shelby says. "Relay format—one rider per round. You'll tag in your teammate at each checkpoint. The course is marked, but don't let that fool you. We've added some... spice."

Laughter ripples through the crowd.

"First leg: Maya for The Laurel Group versus Rishi from Big Stream. Then Jeremy and Nolan. Final stretch? Rorie against Jackson."

She keeps going, rattling off the rest of the brackets, but my focus flatlines the second I hear that last matchup.

My head snaps toward Rorie. She's already looking at me. And not with fear. Not with nerves.

With fire.

Which should settle me. But it doesn't. Because Jackson's not just fast, he's cutthroat. The guy plays dirty and smiles through it. And Rorie's pride in a power ponytail, but I've seen how Jackson gets under people's skin.

And if he so much as tries that with her...

My jaw tightens. I don't like this matchup. Not one damn bit.

"Try to keep up, Rhodes."

One brow arches like a blade. "Or what?"

"Winner gets fucked?" She winks.

"So, basically, a win-win?"

She smirks. Oh, that smirk. I want to wipe it off her face. With my mouth. Or my cock. Yeah, definitely the latter.

The engines roar to life.

Game on.

Shelby raises the flag and yanks it down. Maya and Rishi take off. Sand sprays in every direction, the crowd erupting with cheers. Jeremy screams something about "JUSTICE FOR MY PEOPLE" at a pitch that could shatter glass.

I don't ask. I never ask.

Maya handles the terrain like it's personal. Rishi's hot on her heels. When she nearly wipes out in a patch of deep sand, Rishi closes the gap. But she holds strong, skidding just ahead of him.

"Come on, Maya!" Rorie shouts, bouncing up and down, which, in turn, makes her tits bounce up and down.

Fuck. Me.

Rishi gains on Maya just as they hit another checkpoint. Maya barely manages to edge him out, before leaping off the ATV and sprinting toward Jeremy, who's already mounting his ride.

Maya and Jeremy tag.

*Come on, Rishi.*

Before he takes off, Jeremy turns his head toward me, narrows his eyes, and declares in a voice that could summon a legion, "THIS IS FOR THE FALLEN."

Who are the fallen?

Again. Not asking.

I crack my knuckles and shake out my shoulders. My turn is coming fast.

Rishi, never one to back down, burns rubber to the final checkpoint. He overshoots it and eats dust. But he recovers quickly and rushes toward me.

"GO!" he shouts, smacking my back with enough force to knock out a lung.

I'm off like a shot. ATV humming, sand exploding behind me. My blood thrums with speed and instinct.

I'm in control here. This—I understand.

Every turn is precision. Every bump, every curve, I read it like a map. I catch Jeremy in the corner of my eye and gun it, pushing harder. The ramp looms, and I hit it clean, landing smoother than I expected.

Jeremy, on the other hand?

He hits the ramp like it personally insulted his mother.

Airborne, he flails one arm like he's lassoing invisible cattle, the other clutching the handlebars for dear life. "YEEHAW, BITCHES!"

He lands with a bounce that sends his helmet askew and one of his flip-flops flying into oblivion.

"Did you just lose a shoe?!" I shout.

"Sacrifices must be made!" he calls back, wildly unbothered. "Besides, I race better asymmetrical!"

I inch ahead, every second earned. I push hard, taking turns fast, catching sight of my opponent up ahead. I lean into the curves, controlling the throttle with precision, every instinct locked in on closing the distance.

The next obstacle looms. It's a small ramp leading over a patch of rocky terrain. I brace myself and hit the jump, the ATV catching just enough air to make the landing smooth.

I'm gaining. Fast.

By the time we hit the checkpoint, I've pulled ahead. I glance to the side, locking eyes with Jeremy for a brief second before digging in, forcing my ATV ahead by a fraction.

My tires hit the mark first, and I'm already leaping off as I hand the turn off to Jackson.

"Go!" I shout as I tag in Jackson.

He tears off. Rorie's not far behind, yelling something about destiny or dominance. I'm not sure, I'm too busy trying to catch my breath and not think about how good she looks mid-battle cry.

Jeremy slaps my back. "If she doesn't win, I challenge you all to a duel. Pool noodles. At dawn."

"Do you even hear yourself?"

"Loud and clear, baby."

Shaking my head, I turn and watch Rorie ride. She was built for the aggressive, the fearless, and the controlled.

She gains ground. Jackson tries to move ahead, but she cuts inside on a tight turn, stealing his momentum.

And then—he veers. The back of his ATV clips hers. It's subtle. But on purpose.

Rorie adjusts, but the hesitation lets him recover.

Obstacle after obstacle, they battle it out. But Jackson keeps playing dirty. A bump here. A spray of water there.

The final stretch—dunes.

She's gaining again. Until he hits her. This time, it's not subtle. His ATV swings, clips her at an angle, and she hits a patch of soft sand.

Her tires skid.

She goes down.

The sound of her hitting the ground is a punch to my chest. My legs move before I think.

Eyes wide with pain, she's on her side, blood seeping from a long gash on her leg.

Jackson brakes and spins around, all faux concern. "Shit! You okay?"

He's *smirking*.

That son of a bitch is smirking.

I lunge toward him, but before I can say a word, a hand clamps my shoulder. Hard.

Thatcher.

His voice is cold. "Don't. Not here."

Fury bubbling up, I stare him down, but he doesn't flinch.

"Play the game, Nolan," he warns. "Remember what's at stake."

I swallow back what I want to say. My fists are balled up at my sides. I don't trust them right now.

Shelby's calling for a medic.

"No time," I say. "I'll take her."

Shelby nods, barking directions to the infirmary. Rorie's shaking, blood running in a thin line down her thigh. Maya and Jeremy rush over, worried chatter buzzing around us.

"I'm fine," Rorie insists, but her voice wobbles.

Crouching, I lift her gently from the ground. She hisses through her teeth but doesn't protest. I place her on the ATV and hop on in front of her. Her hands tighten around my middle, no sass, no bite. Her fingers tremble when she fists the hem of my shirt, attaching herself to me.

"Ready?" I ask, glancing back.

She doesn't answer. But she holds on.

And I drive—faster than I should, one hand on the throttle, the other brushing her knee: I've got you.

# CHAPTER 47

# I BRUISE, YOU BURN
### RORIE

PAIN PULSES in my leg with every heartbeat. The infirmary is minimalist and pristine, white lacquer surfaces, glass accents, and lush, green plants.

The air smells faintly of antiseptic and high-end linen spray. It's cold enough to raise goosebumps. I shift on the exam table—no crinkly paper here, just smooth leather stitched with care—and wince as the motion sends another throb through my thigh.

A beach towel Nolan snatched off a sun lounger in the mad rush over is still wrapped around my thigh, now streaked with blood and sand. The edges are bunched where he tied it in a knot, hands shaking slightly.

Across the room, he paces a few steps one way, then back again. His fingers twitch at his sides, brushing over the hem of his shirt, then raking through his hair. Every few seconds, his eyes dart toward me, then away, like he's debating if now is the right moment to speak. The silence between us crackles with tension, raw, unsettled, jittery.

I watch him. Watch the way his fingers twitch like he wants to punch something. Watch the way his chest rises and falls in controlled breaths, like he's trying not to break.

There's something lurking beneath the surface, coiled, and unsaid —a secret lodged in his throat that he hasn't worked up the nerve to spit out yet. He thinks if he stays quiet long enough, I won't notice. But I do. I did. Silence doesn't erase what Thatcher said. Or what he didn't.

I give it a second. Let him stew in it. Then, finally—

"So," I say, breaking the silence. "You shut up real quick back there."

Nolan's head snaps up, eyes narrowing. "What?"

I cock a brow. "When Thatcher put his hand on your shoulder, you didn't say a word."

"It wasn't the time or place to argue," he says, voice clipped.

I let out a short, humorless laugh. "Right. Just like it wasn't the time or place to question how you win your accounts?"

His nostrils flare. Still no bite.

"This again?" he grinds out. "I told you, that's not how we win."

I tilt my head. "It's how your teammate does."

He drags a hand down his face, then drops it, fingers flexing like they want to curl into fists.

"You want the truth?" he says quietly, like it costs him something. "Jackson's the one undercutting everyone. He's Thatcher's nephew. The day after I caught him and Chloe, Thatcher called me in, said he needed someone to 'groom him for leadership.'"

I blink. "So he made you—"

"Take him under my wing. Smile through it. Pretend it never happened."

Jesus.

Nolan swallows hard. "You were right, Rorie. About the pricing. About the market. I brought it to Thatcher. Told him we were cutting corners. And you know what he said?"

I wait.

"He said if I wanted to keep my job—and every future opportunity —I'd shut up. Told me if I so much as whispered about Jackson's bull-shit, I'd be blacklisted."

Silence folds around us again, but it's different now. He's not hiding. He's exposed. Bleeding.

And I feel for him. I really do. But that's not enough.

I level my gaze. "When are you going to speak up for yourself?"

He blinks, startled. "What?"

"When are you going to stop swallowing your tongue to protect people who don't give a damn about you? When are you going to fight back? Not for me. Not for Chloe. For you."

He doesn't answer. Doesn't move. Just stands there like the floor might split open under his feet.

I lean in. "Have you bled for your job? For Thatcher?"

"Yes."

"Well, why not for something that fucking matters? Like integrity. Or morals."

His jaw ticks.

I let out a short laugh. "Yeah, that's what I thought?"

Nolan's expression hardens. Before either of us can say anything else, the door swings open, and the doctor finally strolls in, holding a clipboard and looking vaguely unimpressed.

He slaps on a pair of latex gloves. "Alright, let's see what we've got."

The doctor starts to slowly unwrap the towel from around my knee, but the fabric sticks to the wound, pulling at the raw skin. I don't cry out, but it hurts like hell. A strangled groan escapes me, and before I can even wrap my head around it, tears are leaking from the corners of my eyes.

In mere seconds, Nolan is by my side, his hand slipping into mine. I squeeze the absolute shit out of it, gripping like a lifeline, and to my surprise, he doesn't pull away. He just lets me hold on, his thumb brushing over my knuckles helping me work through the pain.

The next ten minutes are a blur of prodding, poking, and instructions I only half-hear. Something about swelling, rest, and pain management. Then, he picks up a suture kit, pulling on fresh gloves.

"You're going to need about twelve stitches," the doctor says, matter-of-fact.

My stomach tightens, but I nod. The doctor retrieves a syringe and injects a numbing agent around the wound, the sting fierce but quick.

"Give it a minute to kick in," he says, his voice clinical. I breathe through it, feeling the burn fade into a dull pressure.

When he starts stitching, I still feel the tug, the pull of the thread through my skin, but the sharp pain is mostly gone.

My fingers tighten around Nolan's hand with each pull, my grip relentless. He doesn't flinch. He keeps his grip steady, his other hand resting lightly on my arm. The numbing agent dulls the worst of it, but I still feel every knot tied off, the sensation foreign but bearable.

And then, the final humiliation.

"She needs to stay off the leg as much as possible for the next twenty-four hours," the doctor says, scribbling something onto my chart then gesturing to a wheelchair. "Which means—"

"No," I say immediately.

"Yes," he counters, already waving Nolan forward. "You're getting a ride."

I gape at him. "I can walk."

Nolan, to his credit, tries to smother the smile twitching at the corner of his lips. "Doctor's orders, Rorie."

I shoot him a look that could fry him where he stands. "Don't."

He doesn't listen. Of course he doesn't. With one annoyingly smooth motion, he wheels the chair in front of me and—because this day can always get worse—he lifts me from the table and settles me into it as though I weigh nothing.

I hate the warmth of his arms around me, the way his scent curls into my lungs and I feel like I'll never be able to exhale. I hate that, even now—with my pride scraped raw and my body stitched together by adrenaline and gauze—I lean into him, drawn to his steadiness.

Because the truth is, I don't hate him. Not even close.

I love him.

Fiercely. Stupidly. With every broken, terrified piece of me that still believes in something as dangerous as hope.

But I can't tell him that. Not yet.

Not when everything between us is sparking with contention.

Nolan doesn't say anything as he pushes me out of the infirmary, but his eyes are on me. And for once since landing on this damn island, I don't meet his gaze.

I don't know if I want to see whatever's in his eyes right now.

We roll past cottage after cottage, and before I know it, we're back at my room. Nolan pushes me inside, then moves toward the bed, his hands slipping under my legs again.

I open my mouth to protest, but I don't get the chance. In one fluid motion, he lifts me again and gently places me onto the bed.

He adjusts the pillows behind me, propping up my injured leg and that's irritatingly thoughtful.

"I can do it myself."

He shrugs. "Probably. But it wouldn't have been as fun for me."

I scowl, but he ignores me, grabbing a bottle of water from the table along with a couple of pills.

"Take these." His voice is softer than I expect.

I hesitate, but the throbbing in my leg convinces me otherwise. I swallow them down, chasing them with a water, while he sinks onto the edge of the bed.

The air shifts. Suddenly, we're not bickering. We're just... here.

His elbows rest on his knees, hands clasped together, and when he looks at me, it's different. Raw.

"You're right," he says, his voice quiet.

"About what?"

His fingers tap against his knee before he exhales. "Everything." He looks away for a second, then back at me. "I'll take care of it."

I raise a brow. "Take care of it how?"

His jaw tightens. He meets my gaze. "The right way."

Nolan means it. But I can't let it stop there.

"Then do it, Rhodes." My voice is sharp at the edges. "Not for me. Not for the pitch. For yourself. You don't owe that man your silence. You don't owe him your loyalty."

His brows pull together.

"You're not his puppet," I say, softer now. "And you're sure as hell not his shadow. So stop acting like one."

A beat of silence swells between us, weighted and full of emotion.

I lean back against the bed, lips twitching. "Besides," I add, "it's about time you made a little noise."

And for the first time since I met Nolan Rhodes, I see it.

A flicker of rebellion.

A fissure in the armor.

The spark of a man ready to set fire to the strings that once held him still.

# CHAPTER 48

# THE RECKONING
## NOLAN

MY KNUCKLES STRIKE the door in three sharp raps.

I stand outside Jackson's suite, jaw clenched, breath seething through my nose, each exhale a barely contained inferno.

The door swings open. Chloe stands before me in a barely-there bikini. I don't spare her a glance.

Her voice is strained when she starts in, "Nolan—"

"Where's Jackson?" I plant my hands on my hips, securing them so I don't rip the door off its hinges.

"In the shower," she answers, brow furrowed.

I shoulder past her, ignoring the startled gasp she makes and beeline it for the living area. Rage simmers below the surface as I take in the space.

Seconds later, the bathroom door opens. Jackson strolls out completely naked, water dripping from his smug, unbothered frame.

"Jesus Christ," I groan, throwing up a hand. "Jackson, I've seen your dick more than my own reflection. Put it away."

"Nolan," he drawls, rubbing a towel through his hair. "Didn't expect a house call."

"I bet," I snap, voice hard. "That stunt you pulled today...the reckless, arrogant, idiotic move you thought was clever? That shit stops now."

Thankfully, he wraps the towel around his waist with infuriating nonchalance, tilts his head, that same stupid smirk still carved into his face.

"Oh, come on. Don't be so dramatic."

I'm in his face before he finishes the sentence. "You don't get to play goddamn bumper cars on an ATV course, Jackson. You hurt Rorie. She needed stitches. You could've ended her if she'd landed wrong. Do you even give a damn?"

He blinks. Shrugs. "It's a competition. Shit happens."

I punch him. My fist connects with his jaw so fast it stuns us both. He stumbles backward, crashing into the minibar with a grunt, ice clattering from the bucket.

Chloe yelps behind me.

"You son of a bitch," Jackson snarls, clutching his nose. Blood gushes between his fingers. "You're done. I'm telling Thatcher—"

"Go ahead," I bite out, stepping forward, crowding his space. My voice venom-laced. "Tell him how you sent Rorie flying off that ATV. How you nearly got someone *hospitalized* because your ego couldn't handle losing to a woman."

Jackson opens his mouth—I don't let him speak.

"And while you're at it?" I snap, eyes blazing, "Ask him how many NDAs it takes to cover up the trail of women you've fucked while on the clock."

That lands.

Jackson stops short for a beat then his gaze cuts to Chloe. Guilty.

Yeah. That's what I thought.

"What's the matter?" I ask, turning toward her now. "You didn't know? No, of course not." I set my attention back on Jackson, who's turned ghostly white. "I've got everything. Every email. Every message. Every late-night 'conference call' you never knew he had. Pulled from his company phone. Time-stamped. Cross-checked. Explicit."

Her face goes pale.

"And before you ask—yes. Some of them overlapped with you. More than some, actually." I tilt my head, smile cold. "Pretty sure Jackson's dick made it around more departments than the holiday memo."

"Fuck you," Jackson growls, stepping forward again.

"No thanks," I snarl, stepping right back. "You don't get to touch this narrative anymore."

I turn to Chloe again, letting the truth hang heavy in the air between us. "Still think he's worth it?"

She doesn't answer.

She can't.

"You both did me a favor, you know that? You broke something that needed breaking. And because of you..." I exhale once, lips curling. "I found a woman who accepts me. Who challenges me. Who *terrifies* me in all the best ways. Someone with power in her step, and fire in her spine."

I lean in, right into Chloe's space. "So thank you. For cheating. For lying. For showing your true colors. Because I never would've found her if you hadn't fucked up so royally."

Then I straighten, glance at Jackson one last time, and walk out without looking back.

Because this time?

*I win.*

My phone is already in my hand before the door closes behind me.

I text Tammy.

> You need to start working your CYA magic. Not for Big Stream—for us. Me, Rorie, and anyone else who's not a raging liability.

Three dots appear. Disappear. Reappear.

> Define scope of "magic."

> Get Imogene to pull every second of security footage from today. Especially the ATV relay. Is that possible?

> Please. She could hack into the Pentagon with a smartwatch and decent WiFi. Consider it done.

Another message comes in a beat later.

Who do I need to bury and how deep?

I stare at the screen, the corners of my mouth twitching.

> I just shoved Jackson into his own grave. Tell Imogene thanks for the last info she pulled. It was gold. Now it's Thatcher's turn.

As I wait for Tammy's next message, a memory flickers to life.

My dad, standing over our kitchen table with the Sunday paper in one hand and a glass of scotch in the other, muttering, *"The smart ones don't get mad. They get strategic."*

He taught me how to read a room before I could drive. How to keep my voice level even when the world was on fire. How to play the long game so well no one even realized they were playing until they'd already lost.

And now here I am, using every trick he ever hammered into me.

Leverage. Timing. Precision.

Those were the words he used in nearly every speech, every lesson.

And I'm going to incorporate each one. Only this time, it's not to get ahead. It's to protect someone who actually matters. Someone who didn't ask for a war and still got dragged into mine.

Guess I'm more like him than I thought.

Just not the version he was.

Better.

Tammy's message comes through with a link.

I click it.

And there it is—buried in the fine print. Something I never saw coming. But something I can *absolutely* use.

## CHAPTER 49
# RESET
### RORIE

I POP my next round of pain meds, chasing it with lukewarm water and a grimace. Not because I need the full dose right this second, but because my thigh is throbbing and my pride is in shreds and I'm tired of pretending that I'm not bothered by that.

Four hours. Like clockwork.

The dull ache says: still human. Still healing.

The sharp one says: *he's still out there.*

And then, Nolan is there, standing in the open space that connects our rooms.

No storm in his expression. Only soft eyes, a twitch in his jaw, and a thin hoodie stretched across his built chest because the universe is really leaning into the whole *torture Rorie* theme tonight.

"You okay?" His voice is rough around the edges like maybe he's not.

My mouth opens, but I hesitate. I want to tell him I'm fine. That I'm great. That I'm not actively reliving every second of that ATV crash and the way he didn't say a word when Thatcher shut him up like a puppet on strings. And how he doesn't stand up for himself, or for what's right when it matters.

I nod. "I'm fine."

His eyes narrow. He doesn't buy it. But he doesn't push it either.

Instead, he steps into my room.

And for the first time in hours, I feel my breathing level out. Maybe this painkiller won't have to do all the heavy lifting tonight.

"I brought dinner. Thought we could eat outside? I figured the view might be a decent distraction from today."

The air between us fills with tension-laced silence. His gaze drops to my leg for the briefest second before snapping back up.

I shift on the bed. "Uh, yeah–sure."

He steps back, revealing a cart covered in silver covered dishes, entrees, desserts, a mini fondue pot situation. And a waffle maker?

I stare at it, then at him.

"I wasn't sure what you liked," he says, suddenly sheepish. "So I got everything."

"This is..." I fight the lump in my throat. "...a lot."

He gives a small smile. "You can't say I don't commit."

A laugh slips out, surprising even me. "On a ridiculous level."

He glances toward the glass doors leading to the patio. "But the weather's perfect. And I figured we could use a reset."

*Reset.* The word sends a flurry of emotions surging through me, every single one of them nostalgic.

He wheels the cart out to the veranda and I follow, careful not to wince when my leg twinges. Two oversized lounge chairs face the ocean, draped in shadows and the twinkle of string lights.

The breeze carries a blend of sea salt and rosemary, probably from whatever dish he ordered that looks far too pretty to eat.

Without a word, Nolan moves to adjust one of the chairs. He reaches for a cushion, plumps it with surprising care, then turns back to me.

"Sit," he orders gently. "Let me help."

Before I can protest, his hands are already at my side, steady and sure, guiding me down like I'm something fragile. Like he *knows* I hate being fragile but won't let that stop him.

Once I'm seated, he crouches beside me, checking the angle of my leg, adjusting the throw blanket he grabbed from inside. It's too hot outside for that right now, but I don't tell him that.

"You didn't have to—"

His honey-glazed gaze finds mine. "I want to, Rorie."

And when I'm settled, leg propped up just right, blanket tucked around me, starts lifting lids and revealing a feast of foods.

When he lifts another lid off of a serving bowl, he hands me a memory.

*Tomato soup. Grilled cheese. My mother humming in the kitchen, the press of her palm against my hair.*

Days when I couldn't say what was wrong, and she didn't ask, she just fed me this.

He sees me eyeing the soup and says, "Someone really special to me told me it's really good for comfort."

Blinking back the tears, I swallow the ache in my chest. "This," I say softly, "is perfect."

Nolan doesn't gloat. He smiles, nods his head. "Good."

After he's filled our plates with Mac n' Cheese, fries, and some other delectable foods, he drops into the chair beside mine with a sigh. He stares out at the waves like he's been waiting all night to get here.

Neither of us speaks.

But somehow, it says everything.

We settle in. He pours himself a glass of wine. But when he starts to pour me one, I stop him with a hand on his wrist.

"Painkillers."

He nods, no questions, no judgment. Just sets the bottle down. For a few minutes, we eat, letting the silence do the talking.

"So, are you going to make me one of those famous waffles of yours?"I ask, dipping my grilled cheese into my soup.

"Maybe for dessert."

Nolan has a handful of fries sitting on his plate. Without thinking, I snatch one, popping it into my mouth before he can protest.

He winks. "Tastes better, am I right?"

The corners of my mouth twitch as I shrug, playing it cool even as heat builds between us.

"Okay, so what now?" I ask, nudging my plate aside.

Nolan leans back in his chair, studying me like he's mapping out some private strategy. "Now I ask you intrusive questions, and you pretend not to be scared."

A breeze stirs the napkins on the table, carrying the scent of sea salt and all the things fried and sweet.

I glance at him, caught somewhere between amusement and nerves. "Define 'intrusive.'"

"Relax." His grin is all easy trouble. "It'll be a mildly invasive but well-intentioned interrogation."

I arch a brow. "Is this the kind of interrogation that makes me *over-share*? Because, friendly reminder, we do have rules."

He chuckles. "Pretty sure we shattered half of those by Day Two."

A laugh slips out before I can stop it. "*You* shattered them."

He flashes a crooked smile. "I warned you."

"You did."

He lifts his foot onto my lounge chair and it brushes against mine, sending a spark up my leg.

"So?" Nolan's voice drops a little, a dare threaded through the word. "You in?"

The air between us thickens with things we aren't saying.

I match his grin. "Fine. Hit me."

"Okay, he says," "what's something you never tell anyone?"

I surprise myself with how fast I answer. "I dream about running away sometimes. Not in a dramatic, torch-everything kind of way. Just... disappearing. Starting over."

His eyes don't flinch. "Why haven't you?"

"Because I'd still be me wherever I went. And the thing I'm trying to escape isn't a place—it's me."

Nolan doesn't say anything for a beat, but his eyes never leave mine. He nods, accepting my response. "Okay. That was a big one. You're brave."

I scoff, but it means something that he said it. And I can tell he wants to dig into the previous question more, but instead he goes on to the next.

"Next," he says. "Pizza or music—you can only keep one."

I gasp. "Monster."

"Answer the question," he deadpans. "This could make or break everything between us."

"Music. Obviously."

His mouth falls open in exaggerated shock. "Blasphemy."

"I can't live without music," I say, shrugging. "I'd be soulless."

"Fair point," he concedes. "Okay, next one. If you could be famous for something dumb, what would it be?"

I take a bite, chewing thoughtfully. "I want to invent the perfect way to reheat fries." I swipe another one from his plate. "Still crisp, no sogginess."

"Queen behavior. I respect it."

"And you?"

"I'd be the guy who finally proves Bigfoot's real."

"You don't believe in Bigfoot."

He grins. "No, but I like a challenge."

And just like that, we're Textually Frustrated and Carl again, laughing. Easy. Warm. Our plates empty, the night curling around us like a warm blanket.

Then he goes quiet.

"I hit Jackson."

The words are quiet. He doesn't look at me right away.

"I lost it," Nolan says. "He tried to laugh off what happened today. Like it didn't matter—like nearly getting you killed was just... part of the game."

He pauses. Not for effect, but because the words stick.

"I couldn't stand it. So I punched him."

I say nothing. I wait. Let him fill the silence with the truth.

Nolan scrubs a hand down his face. "He threatened to tell Thatcher. Said I'd be finished. And I told him to go ahead. Told him I was *done* with him, with all of it."

My pulse ticks up. He just punched his CEO's nephew. Risked everything he's worked for—blood, sweat, and ruthless ambition... because of me.

I don't want him to do this for me.

I want him to do it because he finally understands he deserves better. Being someone's puppet isn't the legacy he was meant to leave behind. Fighting for himself shouldn't require a reason outside of him.

He looks over at me, eyes steady. "I had my assistant pull everything. Emails, security footage, texts from his company phone. Turns out the golden boy's been spreading more than sales pitches around the office. He's enough to keep HR busy for a decade."

"And Thatcher?"

"I haven't told him yet." Nolan leans forward, forearms braced on his thighs, eyes fixed on the ground. I can tell the words are heavier than he expected. "But I will. All of it. I don't know what he'll do— maybe he follows through on the blacklisting threat. If he does, I lose everything I've built." He looks up, gaze steady now. "But at least I'll walk out knowing I didn't sell my soul for a title. That I said what needed to be said. And did the damn thing right."

My shoulders slump. This version of Nolan—fierce, vulnerable, decisive—isn't just trying to protect me, he's *choosing* to step out of the shadows. To stand for something. To fight for himself.

And for me too.

"I'm sorry, Rorie. For everything. For the accounts, for not realizing it sooner. For being so wrapped up in the climb I didn't see how high the cost was."

I reach over, my fingers brushing his.

"I get it," I say. And I do. More than he knows.

His neck turns so he can look at me. "You do?"

I nod. "Yeah. I really do."

He doesn't move. Neither do I. But the air between us shifts.

It's soft. Open.

His eyes narrow. I clear my throat and when I shift, a sharp pull of pain tears through my leg and I hiss.

Nolan's expression falls instantly. "You're hurting. And by the blood seeping through, you need to redress that wound."

I wave him off. "It's fine. I'll take care of it."

It's what I always say. What I've always done.

Take care of it myself.

No one's ever really stepped in, not for real. Past boyfriends claimed they cared, but when it came down to it, they let me carry everything. Fight the fights. Bandage the wounds. Be the strong one. And I invited that. I wore independence like armor and dared anyone to challenge it.

But Nolan doesn't flinch. Doesn't back off.

And it's doing things to me.

"Rorie," he says. Just my name. Firm. Commanding.

Something in me wavers.

He understands me. Not just the part I show the world, but the part I keep buried. The tired part. The part that secretly wishes someone would step in without being asked.

"You've held up the world long enough," he says. "Let someone hold you now."

The words are quiet. Gentle. And they settle in places I didn't know were hollow.

I don't argue.

He goes inside, grabs the med kit from the bathroom, and then kneels beside me on the lounge chair like it's the most natural thing in the world. His hands move with slow precision, carefully peeling back the bandage. His warm fingertips graze my skin, and there's an unfamiliar, soft flutter in my chest.

"This might sting."

But it doesn't. Not really. His touch is careful, loving. He cleans the wound with a sort of personal focus. And it hits me that I'm not some temporary person in his life.

God, I want him too.

His brows are drawn, his attention completely on me. It's not just about the injury, it's about how much he cares that I'm hurt.

When he presses the new bandage into place, our eyes meet. And for a breathless second, we stay there, frozen in the glow of the string lights, hearts exposed and racing.

He slips in beside me on the lounge chair, pulls another blanket from off the back, and drapes it over both of us.

My body curls toward him on instinct, as if it always knew where it belonged. His arm snakes around me without hesitation, it's like sunlight after a storm, solid ground after a freefall.

We sit, wrapped in silence. Not empty, but full—of breath, of meaning, of everything we've said and everything we don't need to.

# CHAPTER 50
# OUR STARS WILL NEVER FADE

NOLAN

RORIE'S HAND LIFTS, gentle, sure, and she points.

"Look," she murmurs. "Orion."

I follow the arc of her arm, the way her fingertip moves through the night air like she's sketching stars into existence.

"His belt. Right there, those three in a row. I used to look for it every night when I couldn't sleep," she says. "Something about it made me feel... stable. Like the universe knew what it was doing. Even if I didn't."

She lowers her hand, but her eyes stay skybound. I watch her instead. She's more breathtaking than any constellation.

"Is there another one?" I ask, just to keep her talking.

"Cassiopeia." Her lips curve. She points again. "Looks like a 'W' when it's upright. My mom used to say it was a queen's crown."

"Your mom was into astronomy?"

"She was into everything." Her smile softens. "She was a writer."

A breeze lifts a strand of her hair, brushing it across her cheek. I reach out, tuck it behind her ear, feel her skin. I want to hold this exact second like it's sacred. Like it's breakable.

"Tell me more about your parents," I say, voice quieter than I meant it.

The way her eyes soften, the way her mouth trembles, I know she's trying to hold the tears in. It hits me low. No one's asked her that in a long time. Or maybe... ever.

And now that I've asked, I'm terrified of the answer.

But I want it anyway. I want all of it. All of her.

"My mom believed the stars were ancient messages, waiting to be heard. She'd take me outside when I couldn't sleep, wrap me in a blanket, and we'd just... sit. She said magic wasn't something you had to chase. It was already there."

I don't speak. I won't break this.

"My dad was the opposite," she adds, a small laugh slipping through. "He liked things grounded. A guy who balanced the checkbook for fun. Who measured the grass before mowing it."

She's laughing, but my chest aches.

"They balanced each other," she mutters. "She made everything feel infinite. He made sure we didn't float away."

Rorie pauses. The quiet settles again.

"My dad always said, 'If you ever get lost, look for the North Star. You need a North and an Anchor. A guide and a tether. Something to follow. Something to hold onto.' Like I told you the other night."

I interlace our fingers as she continues, her voice barely a breath. Her eyes shimmer. Does she knows how much they sparkle when she talks about them?

"Their love didn't make sense on paper. Total opposites. He was buying a gift for his boss at a bookstore he never went to, and she was hiding from a blind date. They ran into each other. Like literally. And to top it off, it happened in the romance section." Another laugh escapes. "She made chaos beautiful. He made spreadsheets for fun."

She twists toward me then, and the stars replace that shimmer in her eyes. "But the universe kept putting them in each other's way, like it refused to let them miss."

God.

She smiles like she's telling me a fairytale, but I feel the weight beneath every word. She's trusting me with the most fragile parts of her. And I'm truly honored.

"Now they're both stars," she whispers. "That's how I like to think of it. They were kind of... cosmic."

She doesn't cry. Doesn't break.

But I see the pain, carved into her. The way she blinks is a little slower.

I cup her face. No words. Just touch. Just truth.

"I used to think they were the only real thing I'd ever get to witness. Now I try to not forget what it felt like to be loved like that."

My throat goes tight. I want to give her that. Desperately.

A single tear slips down her cheek. I catch it with my thumb, gently sweep it away then lean in and kiss the place where it fell. Soft. Careful. A vow I haven't spoken yet.

We fall into easy stories after that. I tell her about the lake house summers. The cousin who tried to flirt with a lifeguard using a drone. She tells me about getting stuck in an elevator with a German art critic and a tray of chicken tikka masala. We laugh until our stomachs hurt, until the night swells quiet around us.

The stars blink overhead and her body shifts toward mine, snuggling closer. Her leg tangle with mine. Her head rests against my chest. My arm curves around her. She was made to fit there.

She lets out a sleepy sigh. "I don't want this to end."

I press a kiss to the crown of her head. "It won't."

The tide hushes in the distance. Our hands stay intertwined beneath the blanket, and we fall asleep just like that—

entwined in silence,

wrapped in warmth,

finally

falling.

Together.

Exactly where we're meant to be.

Then we both enter sleep under a blanket of nighttime sky, full stars that will never fade.

# CHAPTER 51

# SLUMBER PARTY CONFESSIONS

## RORIE

JEREMY IS FLOATING on a pool lounger in the shape of a giant martini glass, complete with an inflatable olive bobbing next to his head. He's sipping something out of the requisite island coconut vessel, sunglasses perched crookedly on his nose, looking like the poster child for spring break regrets.

I'm draped on the edge of the pool, one leg dangling in the water, nursing a drink with a little umbrella in it because apparently, I've become that person. The one who has sex basically everywhere on a private island and suddenly thinks she's in a Bacardi commercial.

Jeremy tips his shades down, eyes me over the rim of his drink. "Sooo, how's the Rhodes glow-up treating you?"

I shake my head at him. "Jeremy."

"What?" He grins. "Don't act like you aren't walking different. You've got the gait of a woman who's been rearranged."

"Maybe it has something to do with my leg injury, *Jeremy*."

He shrugs and adjusts his float. "Doubtful. You've got this peaceful, freshly fucked energy."

I splash him. "We are literally pitching to millionaires tomorrow. Can you not?"

"We've had five prep meetings and at least three rounds of team mock pitches," he says. "We're good. The deck is tighter than your abs after a week of hot-girl pilates."

I roll my eyes, but the tension in my chest starts to ease. For once, he's not wrong.

Jeremy grins. "Also, your man, Nolan has the quiet determination of someone who's memorized your orgasm blueprint and is ready to file for a patent."

"I hate you."

"You don't." He lifts his glass. "To growth. Emotional, sexual, and professional."

Maya approaches then, beach bag slung over one shoulder, her bob tucked behind her ears and a slight sheen on her cheeks. She's still gorgeous—even frazzled.

Jeremy perks up. "Ah, the goddess returns. And just in time. I was about to start manifesting you through interpretive float dancing."

"Tempting," she says, slipping off her sandals and sinking onto the lounger next to me. "But I don't think my anxiety could survive a performance piece."

"You mean the one where Jeremy floats backward off the deep end of capitalism?" I offer, earning a soft laugh.

Maya leans back, closing her eyes. "God, I needed this."

She barely gets the words out when Jeremy goes still.

His head tilts, smile fading.

And then I see it too.

Asher Cross, in loose linen pants and sunglasses worth more than my apartment deposit, is strolling toward the pool bar.

And clinging to his arm like a decorative scarf?

Celeste Monroe.

Jeremy reacts first. "Don't panic."

Maya's smile drops. "What?"

I don't even have to follow his gaze. I already feel it.

Celeste's gauzy dress floats behind her as though she summoned it from a perfume commercial. Her laugh is perfectly modulated. Her manicured hand rests on Asher's arm like she paid extra for a good grip.

Maya goes silent.

"Fuck," I whisper.

Jeremy mutters, "This island isn't big enough for her ego and my rage."

Maya stands. "I need air."

"Maya—" I grab her hand, but she's already moving, teeth clenched. "I'm not doing this."

She bolts.

Jeremy is already waving me on. "Go. I'll babysit Prince Privilege and his Instagram filter. No promises I won't hex her, though."

I mouth thank you and follow.

Maya's pacing near the outdoor showers, arms folded tight.

Her jaw trembles. Her voice doesn't. "It's not even that he brought her. Or that he has to. It's how smug he looked doing it."

"You mattered," I say. "She's noise. You were the real thing."

She finally looks at me. Her walls are cracked. It breaks my heart. But this time, I'm not letting her patch them up alone.

"Come with me," I whisper. "To my cottage. For tonight. No drama. No pretending. Just... air."

After a moment, she nods. And we walk back, shoulder to shoulder, both of us secretly loving that Jeremy is at the pool bar, dramatically miming a middle finger salute in Celeste's direction with his cocktail straw.

The cottage smells like buttered popcorn, cheap champagne, and the faint chemical bite of a face mask that definitely wasn't dermatologist-approved.

Maya's stretched out on the bed with wet nails and a chilled wine glass balanced between her thighs. Jeremy is lounging on a floor pillow, robe open, one slipper missing, holding a joint like it's a mic. I'm cross-legged on the floor, attempting to paint my toes but smudging three for every one I get right.

"You know what she did?" Maya huffs, waving her hand. "She called me *thirsty* in the comments. Thirsty. Like I wasn't the one who *taught* Asher how to unbutton my shirt with his teeth."

Jeremy lets out a strangled sound somewhere between a laugh and a gasp. "Please hold while I recover from the image of Hollywood's million dollar man going down on you like a gentleman."

"Ugh, he was so good at that too," Maya whines.

I snort. "Girl, you want more wine or a bat? I've got both."

"Both," she mutters into her glass.

Jeremy perks up. "You know what we should do? TP her cottage. Classic. And disrespectful."

"Jeremy—" I warn.

"No, hear me out." He raises a hand. "We sneak over before dawn. Toilet paper her porch swing, the bushes, the tress, leave a few passive-aggressive notes. Maya signs it 'Your favorite follower.' Boom. Mic drop."

"Or we could put Icy Hot in her shampoo," Maya offers dryly.

"See?" Jeremy says. "This is healing."

I bite my lip to keep from laughing. "We're all under an NDA, remember? There's a clause about retaliation. Plus, this place is packed with security cameras."

Jeremy waves her off. "Pfft. What's a legally binding agreement good for anyway?"

"Seriously?" Maya's brows lift. "You were so excited about signing it. You're the one who made us use codenames in the GroupMe."

"Out of respect," Jeremy says with a sniff. "Also, I didn't want Nolan's boring ass to find out we called him Big Dimple Energy behind his back."

"Like he'd ever know," Maya argues.

Right then, the front door creaks open.

And there he is.

Nolan *"Big Dimple Energy"* Rhodes, standing in the doorway, a container of Thai food in one hand and a thoroughly confused expression on his face.

"...Did I interrupt a séance?" he asks.

Jeremy pops to his feet. "You brought food? You're forgiven. Come. Sit. Let us beautify you."

"What?" Nolan looks absolutely horrified. As he should.

Thirty minutes later, Maya and I return from soaking in the hot tub to find Nolan shirtless, sprawled across an armchair like he's given up on dignity altogether, charcoal-grey sheet mask plastered to his face, and fuzzy slippers that were very much *not* his when the night started. His toenails are drying in a dangerously glittery coral, while Jeremy dabs concealer under his eyes.

"This stays between us," Nolan mutters, voice muffled by the mask. "I'm only doing this because you're Rorie's best friend. And because you threatened me." He pauses then adds, flatly. "Multiple times. In writing."

Jeremy, mid-sip of his possibly-illegal seltzer, watches Nolan as he carefully teases up the front of his hair with my wide-tooth comb. "You rolled your eyes at my serum lineup. This is the natural consequence."

Nolan's shift to look at Jeremy.

"You think this is bad?" Jeremy asks. "I'm *this close* to contouring your abs with bronzer. Not that you need it."

"Only I get to touch his abs, Jer," I warn.

"Then I suggest you start moisturizing them. We're a team now."

Nolan rolls his eyes. "I'm in hell."

"Careful, future husband," Jeremy says, smirking. "Don't run your mouth again, or next time I start with your eyebrows. And I don't ask."

Nolan lifts a brow. "Don't worry. I won't be running my mouth like *you* did. Some of us know how to keep our private footage... private."

Jeremy freezes. Maya and I both go still.

"What do you mean by that?" I ask Nolan.

He says nothing.

"What does he mean by that?" I ask Jeremy.

Nolan doesn't even blink. "So, that little nugget about Asher wasn't exactly news you meant to share, was it?"

Jeremy's face contorts. "Shit."

Eyes wide, Maya slowly turns to look at him. "*Jeremy.*"

"I thought we agreed it was a safe space!" Jeremy yelps, then points a freshly exfoliated finger at Nolan. "And you! You were supposed to be distracted by your *eyebrow crisis!*"

"I was," Nolan says coolly. "Until you casually mentioned something about a spa suite and the 'uncut director's cut' of Asher Cross."

Maya covers her face with both hands. "I'm going to die."

Jeremy groans. "It slipped out!"

"Oh no," I say, snorting into my wine glass. "This is a full-blown slip-and-slide of betrayal."

"I didn't *name* names!" Jeremy insists. "I used code words! And I just said someone might have filmed a sex tape with a certain A-list actor in a certain private spa suite. That was all."

Maya peeks between her fingers. "The words were 'spa' and 'sex tape.' You're the worst codebreaker in history."

"I'm sorry!" Jeremy pleads. "He was shampooing! His hair is so beautiful. I got nervous and panicked!"

Nolan lifts both hands. "Hey—no judgment. Your secret's safe with me and my sheet mask." He taps the glittering gold currently dripping off his cheekbone.

Maya sighs, then levels a look at Nolan. "You're really not going to say anything?"

Nolan shakes his head, serious now. "Not a word. Not to anyone. Especially not to someone who'd use it against you."

"Thank you, Nolan, seriously. I owe you."

He shakes his head. "No, you don't. We've all done reckless shit with people we shouldn't have trusted. Doesn't mean it defines you. Just means you survived it."

The room goes quiet. Even Jeremy, who was halfway through applying gold under-eye patches looks up.

"And for what it's worth," Nolan says. "Asher made a huge mistake letting you go." His gaze flits to me.

Maya's eye water then the tears fall. She shoves a handful of M&M's into her mouth and chews between sniffles.

I rub her back.

Jeremy huffs, "I hate him. He's out there parading Celeste around like you're a deleted scene in his blooper reel."

Nolan's voice lowers. "He's out there trying to prove something. That doesn't make it real. Or true. Maya, don't shrink yourself just because someone else couldn't handle the size of your light."

Jeremy clutches his heart like he's about to faint. "Okay, Shakespeare. Rorie, you *better* keep him."

I roll my eyes, trying to hide the stupid smile tugging at my lips.

Nolan leans forward, elbows on his knees, and looks at Maya again. "Whatever you do, don't let his choices rewrite your story. He's not the final chapter. You are."

Maya swallows hard and nods, but her chin quivers slightly. "God, why does that make me want to cry even harder?"

"Because it's true," I say softly, reaching for her hand.

Jeremy, of course, breaks the tension. "Okay, but also because you're high on those pumpkin enzyme fumes and that mask is probably harvesting your deepest traumas."

Maya bursts out laughing and wipes under her eyes with the sleeve of the giant sweatshirt she stole from me earlier. "You're both disasters."

"Disasters with flawless skin," Jeremy corrects. "And a developing plan for revenge."

"Oh no," I groan, flopping back against the pillows.

"Yes," Jeremy hisses with glee. "We have glitter, crepe paper, a Bluetooth speaker, and access to the playlist I used to seduce my ex-boyfriend. Operation: Emotional Sabotage is a go."

Nolan blinks. "Should I be concerned?"

I shrug. "Probably."

Nolan raises a brow. "Please tell me this doesn't involve glitter again."

"Oh, sweet Rhodes," Jeremy says, grinning as he picks up a notebook filled with hand-drawn maps and sticky notes. "It involves *so much* glitter."

Nolan just leans back, towel turban slipping slightly, and says, "If anyone asks—I was never here."

Maya lets out a long, slow breath. "Thank you. All of you. This was... what I needed."

Jeremy raises his can of questionable seltzer. "To healing. And to not punching A-list actors. No matter how punchable their faces are."

Nolan lifts his, too. "And to future sex tapes with people who deserve us." He winks at me.

We all laugh, and for a moment, the heaviness lifts.

Later, Maya curls up in my bed, face wiped clean, breathing finally steady. Jeremy stumbles out the door muttering something about peeing in Asher's exfoliant.

There's a calm now, the kind that only comes after a storm of truth, carbs, and group confessionals under face masks that smelled faintly of menthol.

I turn and find Nolan still in my living room, standing barefoot near the window, hands in the pockets of his joggers, a soft navy tee stretched across his chest. The string lights from the patio cast golden specks across his face, and when he looks at me, there's something in his expression that's so open—so unguarded—it makes my throat tighten.

"Hey," I whisper.

"Hey," he murmurs, just as soft.

The silence is no longer thick. It's not fragile. It's full of the kind of pull that brings you closer without a word.

I take a step toward him.

He meets me halfway.

Nolan reaches for my hand, threads his fingers through mine, and leads me through the connected door quietly, like it's the most natural thing in the world.

And it is.

We pause just inside his suite, the soft hush of the ocean still audible beyond the windows. He turns to face me, his thumb brushing over the back of my hand.

"I have something for you," he says, voice almost shy. "Picked it up at the island market earlier today."

My head tilts. "You got me a souvenir?"

His lips twitch into a crooked smile as he reaches into the drawer of the nightstand and pulls out a small, soft pouch. He presses it into my hand with no ceremony, only quiet intention.

Inside lies a modest bracelet, made of twine and wooden beads polished smooth by time. At its center, a small anchor charm sways gently when I lift it.

"I saw it and thought... yeah. That's her." His eyes meet mine, nervous and searching. "Stubborn. Strong. You make other people feel safe, even when your in the middle of your own storm."

My throat tightens. "Nolan…"

"It's nothing fancy," he says, like he's more nervous now. "But it reminded me of you."

I stare at the bracelet in my palm, simple and honest and so utterly *him*, it makes my heart ache.

Then I look up at him, and I know.

I'll wear this until the cord frays and the wood fades and the air wears it down to nothing. And even then, I'll still feel the weight of it on my wrist.

Of him.

Of us.

"Put it on me," I whisper.

He does.

And when his fingers brush my wrist, I swear I've never felt more claimed.

"You're something else, you know that?" His other hand brushes a stray hair from my cheek, tucks it behind my ear.

"Is that your way of saying I looked hot in my avocado mask?" I tease, voice wobbling a little.

His smile is slow. "You looked like the woman I'm falling for."

My breath catches.

"I didn't mean for it to happen," he continues, voice low, reverent. "But it did. Every version of you—Textually Frustrated, fierce strategist, absolute menace with a razor sharp tongue… you undid me. Completely."

I wrap my arms around his neck. "Then let me put you back together."

He kisses me like we've got forever. It's soft at first. Sweet. But soul deep. This kiss says thank you. It says I'm here. And it's going to stay.

He lifts me gently, carries me to the edge of the bed where the world narrows to the sound of our breathing and the hush of linen.

Our clothes fall away like whispers, one by one, until there's nothing between us but skin and truth.

His touch is slow. Devoted. Like he's trying to touch every freckle, hear every gasp, feel every heartbeat.

Nolan's fingers slip through my slick heat, teasing and stroking until I'm trembling with need then he pushes two fingers inside, filling me with a slow thrust that steals my breath. "So ready for me, aren't you baby?"

A soft moan escapes my lips, encouraging him further as he skillfully twists his fingers, each movement deliberate and tender, creating a sweet symphony of pleasure within me.

The tension mounts, each pump amplifying the quickening pulse that beats persistently at my core. My eyes lock onto his, silently pleading for the exchange of his fingers for the hard, urgent presence of his cock.

When he kisses me, his tongue pushes past my lips, invades my mouth, delving with relentless force, exploring every corner with deep, fervent thrusts that leave me breathless.

"Please, Nolan, I need your cock inside me."

Withdrawing his fingers, he palms one of my breasts, leans down to take my pebbled nipple into his mouth and I hiss at the delicious contact.

Nolan moves to settle between my legs, finally pushing into me after a beat. We move together in a rhythm, soft moans blending with murmured promises. Hands explore. Eyes lock. He kisses my temple. My throat. My nipples. The spot just below my ear that makes me shiver.

My legs wrap around him, pulling him closer, deeper.

"I've got you," he whispers. "I'm not going anywhere."

And I believe him.

I *feel* him.

Inside and around me. *Anchoring* me.

When I come, it's with his name on my lips and his hands in mine.

And when he follows, it's with a groan that sounds like surrender.

We lie tangled in the aftermath, skin damp, breath slowing, hearts loud.

His arm wraps around my waist. My fingers trace lazy circles over his chest.

"Still falling?" I ask, voice sleepy.

He kisses the top of my head. "Every second."

"Tomorrow, we have to go back to being mortal enemies."

The thought creeps in, cold, even as Nolan's hands keep me warm.

"I don't care if we win or lose," he whispers into the curve of my neck. "Your firm deserves it more."

"You're still gonna bring your A-game though, right?" I tease, nudging him gently.

The corner of his mouth curves up, slow and sure. "Nothing less."

# CHAPTER 52
# PITCHPOCALYPSE

## NOLAN

THE AIR inside the conference hall is a cocktail of nerves, ambition, and way too much perfume.

Every firm is locked and loaded, their top players flanking their team leads like knights guarding royalty. Except ours. Thatcher left the island abruptly. Said he had important business to tend to. Like this isn't. No problem, he wasn't contributing to anything anyway.

CrossMedia execs lounge in white chairs up front. Asher Cross is in the center, Shelby Davidson at his side, Celeste Monroe draped over a different chair, scrolling through her phone.

The energy shifts.

This is it.

The final day. The last chance. The moment everything we worked for either catches fire...or burns to worthless ash.

Across the aisle, Jeremy leans back in his seat, watching the stage with theatrical boredom, but his foot taps out a silent, jittery rhythm that gives him away.

Next to him, Maya sits stiffly, looking poised, polished, but even from here, I catch the slight tremble in her hand when she tucks her hair behind her ear.

I follow her gaze and find Asher flicking glances at her when he thinks she isn't looking.

She's doing everything she can to pretend he doesn't exist. She's poised. And fierce. Go her.

I turn my attention to my center of gravity. Rorie.

The second she moves into position at the podium, the whole world tilts a few degrees closer to her. She doesn't strut or swagger. She doesn't need to.

She stands there, clutching her notes, adjusting the mic with fingers that quiver so faintly only someone who knows her like I do would see it.

My heart punches my ribs. Not with nerves. With pride. She's about to own this room—and she doesn't even realize it yet.

I'm leaning forward, my elbows on my knees, not bothering to hide the stupid smile pulling at my mouth.

She's going to be unforgettable.

She already is.

Rorie breathes in deep, and I see the tiny shift when the nerves bleed out and the steel kicks in.

The woman who made me fall so fast and hard I still haven't hit the ground.

The woman who made me believe again.

"Good morning," she starts, her voice clear and calm now. "You've seen some incredible pitches today. Bold ideas. Big visions. We could've given you another version of that. But we're not here to blend in."

She pauses, lets it breathe, lets the words hang, owning the silence. And then she presses the button.

The first image blazes onto the screen behind her: a glittering coastline, the kind of scene you see in movie trailers right before the plot twists your heart in two.

"This is about something bigger," she continues. "Something timeless. Something unforgettable. Something *CrossMedia*."

Her eyes flick to Asher. To Shelby. And—God help me—to me. For half a second, she smiles a tiny, private smile that's ours.

She's not scared.

She's *home*.

The presentation unfolds like a movie script. Golden beaches, poker tables tucked into shadowy corners, speedboats carving through sapphire water. It's not just scenic. It's cinematic.

It's *not* a pitch.

It's a seduction.

"Cross Media and White Thorn Resort will never be just another luxury chain. You are the memory people hold dear—the place they think about long after they've returned home. And what's more unforgettable than stepping into a world that feels straight out of the most iconic moments in history?"

Images change. Old film stills. Monte Carlo. James Bond. She's not pitching a brand. She's pitching a world.

I glance toward Shelby Davidson. She's leaning in now.

"This," Rorie continues, "is The Cross Affair."

My pulse spikes. Around me, people are leaning forward. Whispering. Hooked.

Shelby looks like she's already mentally packing her vintage luggage for the first reservation.

And me? I sit, watching the love of my life turn a room full of sharks into believers.

Watching her shine.

Watching her win.

Not because she needs me. But because she never needed anyone's permission to be *extraordinary*.

She paints the entire experience like a scene from a high-stakes movie. Cocktail lounges, hidden messages, mystery adventures. She hits every note like she's known them all along.

Her voice softens at the end. "We're not just selling a destination. We're selling an era. A fantasy they'll never stop talking about. And will continue to crave more of, hopefully…forever."

Another glance at me before she finishes. There's a heartbeat of silence and then the applause hits, loud and rolling like thunder.

She steps back from the podium, her shoulders lifting, then falling with a visible exhale. She catches my eye across the room. Her fingers brush the bracelet at her wrist.

The anchor.

Our anchor.

And I swear to God, if there's one thing I know in this moment, it's this:

I didn't lose her.

I found her.

The only thing that ever mattered.

And this time?

I'm not letting her go.

The air tastes like salt and nerves. Rishi adjusts the mic on the podium while I run through the checklist in my head—presentation, lighting, video snippets cued up.

Big Stream's final pitch is supposed to begin in less than five minutes. The room is buzzing, execs stretching, murmuring, drinks being refilled.

Asher Cross leans casually against a side table, chatting with Shelby. Maya's nowhere to be seen.

Rorie's sitting near the back, laughing at something Jeremy said, her bracelet flashing under the lights. And even though we're rivals right now, even though we're supposed to be enemies—I still feel it. That anchor line that never snapped.

"Flash drive," Rishi mutters beside me. "You got it?"

"Jackson," I bark. "Grab the drive. It's in my briefcase."

He grunts, already moving, the cocky little shit with too much gel in his hair and too much entitlement in his veins.

I turn back to double-check the speaker settings.

Behind me—

A click. Soft, like a heartbeat skipping.

A screen lights up.

Not our pitch.

Not the title screen we prepped.

Not the luxury resort logo.

The Rorie Report.

Her name—*Rorie Adams*—sprawls across the center of the massive projection screen in a bold font.

Silence slams down over the room like a dropped anvil. I whip around. My blood goes ice cold.

On the screen:

A scanned page.

Typed evaluations.

Annotations.

Private. Confidential. Personal.

And everyone is reading it.

The first slide sucks the breath from my lungs.

*Subject displays high-functioning performance tendencies masking emotional instability. Possible flight risk. Unresolved grief patterns noted.*

Her mother's medical records. All the years spent in and out of hospitals.

Hospice bills.

Father's obituary.

The next page—

Screenshots of her high school transcripts. Red marks. Failures.

A disciplinary report about a noise complaint from college. Her financial aid almost getting revoked. An eviction notice because her boyfriend ghosted and she couldn't make rent.

Photos.

Notes about Rorie's writing samples, complete with editorial comments picked apart line-by-line.

Her elementary school evaluations.

*Bright but easily distracted. Perfectionist tendencies. Struggles to ask for help.*

It's every mistake she's ever made. Every crack she's ever tried to plaster over. Every vulnerable, hidden piece she *never* gave permission to share.

Projected.

Exposed.

*Ripped open.*

A wounded gasp brushes my eardrums. My eyes snap to the sound.

Rorie.

She's standing now, one hand over her mouth, her face drained of color. Tears welling, wobbling, falling. Her body sways like she's been hit by a bullet.

The room—*this fucking room*—stays silent, stunned into horror.

My heart stops.

*No. No, no, no, no.*

This was never supposed to see the light of day. I surge toward the tech table, rip the cord out of the laptop like it might fix it.

The screen goes black. But the damage is done.

Everyone saw.

I turn and Rorie is already walking. No—*running*.

Pushing past chairs, past startled execs, past Maya and Jeremy shouting after her.

Gone.

Jackson stumbles forward, trying to sputter something about a mistake. I don't hear him. I can only hear the static in my skull—the roar of my own pulse breaking apart as I realize:

I did this.

*Me.*

I let it happen.

I didn't protect her.

She trusted me.

And I gutted her.

Publicly.

Viscerally.

I don't know how my legs move, but they do. Shoving through the stunned crowd. Ignoring the voices calling after me.

I have to find her. I have to fix this.

I have to tell her that none of this matters. That she's *more* than her past. More than her wounds. More than every scar that stupid report dragged into the light. That she's everything.

Everything I want.

Everything I need.

The conference doors slam behind me as I hit the hallway, my breath scraping raw in my throat.

"Rorie!" I call out, but my voice feels swallowed by the cavernous, echoing halls. She's nowhere. Just flickers of retreating footsteps and the distant creak of an exit door swinging shut.

I sprint, not thinking, not breathing, just *moving*.

Down the hall. Past a stunned staff member. Shoving open the glass door to the terrace.

Outside, the mid-morning heat slams into me. The ocean churns in the distance, mocking my frantic heartbeat with its slow, calming rhythm.

There—

A flash of dark hair. A sway of a yellow blouse disappearing toward the private paths that thread toward the cottages.

"Rorie!"

She doesn't stop. Doesn't even glance back.

Chasing her down the winding trail, gravel crunches beneath my shoes. Every step driving the guilt deeper into my chest like a nail.

When I finally catch up, she's standing at the edge of the path, her back to me, her shoulders shaking in silent, furious sobs.

I don't touch her. I don't deserve to.

I stand there, pulse pounding in my ears, trying to find words when *nothing* could possibly be enough.

"Rorie," I rasp, voice broken. "I'm so fucking sorry."

She turns—cautiously, as though even *that* costs her something— and when her eyes meet mine, it's like being carved open with a blade I handed her myself.

"You were supposed to be different," she says, her voice shredded and raw. "You were supposed to be *safe*. You've hurt me too many times."

I shake my head, throat tightening painfully. "I was. I *am*. I didn't... I never meant for any of this—"

"You stole my life," she cuts in, voice rising. "You *knew* things about me I never *wanted* anyone to know. You knew about my mom. My dad. About *me*."

Each word lands like a slap.

Deserved.

"I didn't read it," I choke out. "I swear to you, Rorie. I never opened it. I didn't even remember it was in my bag. That's not who you are to me. You're not... some profile. You're not bullet points. You're—"

I break off, raking a shaking hand through my hair. "You're the best thing that's ever happened to me."

She flinches like the words physically hit her.

"And I ruined it," I whisper. "I hurt you. And now..." I trail off because the ending feels too final. I can feel her pulling away even as she stands there, just feet from me.

Her arms cross in front of her protectively.

"I don't care about a fucking pitch." I step closer. "I don't care about this fucking job. About anything except you. *You* are what matters."

Silence.

The breeze tugs at her hair, sending it whipping across her tear-streaked face.

"I didn't just fall for you," I say hoarsely. "I crashed. Full speed. No brakes. No plan. And I would do it again. Every time. Even if it ends like this."

I step closer. Hands at my sides. Begging without words. *Pleading* for something I don't deserve.

She stares at me for a long, long moment.

I hold my breath until her voice breaks.

"I don't trust you," she whispers.

The ache in my chest splinters, painful and merciless. But I nod. She's not wrong. Trust has to be rebuilt. Earned.

"I understand," I tell her, voice shaking. "But I'll rebuild that. For as long as it takes. I'm not walking away. Not from you."

Another gust of wind whips between us but I barely feel it. All I can feel is her.

Standing there.

Not running to me.

Not forgiving.

Just standing.

And breaking.

She looks at me like I'm the end of something she didn't stopped believing in.

And it kills me.

Because it's true.

"You know," she says, her voice cracking like it's trying to survive her own heart, "I started thinking the universe kept crashing us together because we were meant to find each other."

My chest caves in.

"But now..." She shakes her head—small, devastating. "Now I think the universe kept giving us chances to realize we weren't ready. That some people meet at the wrong time... and keep breaking each other trying to pretend otherwise."

The words hit harder than any punch I've ever taken.

Harder than Thatcher's threats.

Harder than Chloe's betrayal.

Because this? This is *my fault.*

I open my mouth. No words come out. How do you apologize for tearing apart the only person who ever made you believe you could be whole?

She steps back, and I instantly lose my footing. The ground slips out from under me and leaves nothing but sky and regret.

"You taught me something,: she says, and there's no anger now. No venom. Only the brutal, bleeding truth. "You showed me that loving someone isn't enough if you're too broken to hold them right."

I want to fall to my knees.

I want to take it back.

I want to erase every second of pain I've caused her.

But the universe doesn't hand out do-overs.

Another step back.

Further.

Colder.

Her hand drifts to her wrist—

the bracelet.

*Our* anchor.

I shake my head, desperate, silently begging her not to—

She crosses the space between us, not like a lover, not like a friend —like someone delivering the final blow.

Rorie presses the bracelet into my palm. My fingers close around it on instinct, feeling the tiny, cruel weight of what I just lost. She meets my eyes one last time, and it's like she sees everything in me—

every broken piece,

every selfish choice,

every way I failed her—

and still somehow manages to look at me like I was *almost* enough.

"I hope you find your north someday," she whispers, soft as a prayer. "And I hope it feels like home."

She turns, doesn't look back.

The bracelet digs into my hand, a brutal reminder of what I've done.

I stay there, rooted to the spot like a fucking ghost, watching the only person who ever truly understood me walk away.

And she's never coming back.

At some point after Rorie left, I made my way to the beach and have been sitting here for hours.

Her room has emptied, the whispers have faded into walls. The bracelet is still in my hand, still heavy with everything I didn't say.

I run my thumb over the tiny wooden anchor that now feels like a fucking gravestone, staring out over the endless curve of the ocean.

But it doesn't give a damn.

The sky bleeds gold and red, the sun drowning itself without cere- mony. The only thing that stays is the echo of her voice.

I didn't just lose her trust.

I didn't just lose the chance.

I proved her right.

I became every worst-case scenario she ever dared believe in.

But she was never the prize. She was the point.

And I let her think she was just another move on the chess board.

Another tactical advantage. When the truth—the brutal, aching, marrow-deep truth—is I was the one who was outmatched the second those bright blue eyes find mine.

There's no strategy that prepares you for meeting the person who finally makes you want to stay. No blueprint for someone who rebuilds the whole goddamn architecture of your soul.

I press the anchor to my lips.

And for the first time in a long, long time—

I pray.

Not for forgiveness.

Not for another chance.

I pray that someday, somehow, when she's standing on her own again—stronger, fiercer—she'll know I loved her.

That even if I never deserved her, I saw her.

All of her.

And I fell.

Willingly.

Hopelessly.

Irrevocably.

I sit there on the beach, the warm sand swallowing my feet, the tide creeping closer with every passing minute like it's trying to pull me under too.

The sun gives up slow, bleeding gold into bruised purple, then slipping into nothing at all.

The breeze sharpens, carrying the faint scent of salt and firepit smoke, stinging my eyes even though I know better than to blame it.

Above me, the first stars blink awake, cold and dispassionate, watching me fall apart from a distance.

My grip tightens on the bracelet until the edges of the anchor carve little half-moon indents into my hand. Tiny reminders that even now—even when I have nothing left—I'm still holding on.

I don't move.

Not when the tide kisses my ankles.

Not when the last light dies.

Not even when the world forgets we were ever here.

The stars coming out one by one, cold and unbothered overhead.

And I make myself a promise.

Next time, if the universe is kind enough to put her in my path again...

I will not hesitate.

I will not fold.

I will not lose her.

Not even if it costs me everything else.

# CHAPTER 53
# THE COURAGE TO LET GO
## RORIE

THE SMELL of roasted coffee and city rain fills the morning air as I weave through the tables at our favorite café in SoHo. It's early, but the place is buzzing with business suits nursing triple espressos, artists sketching in worn leather notebooks, tourists wide-eyed and overwhelmed.

Outside, the August rain slicks the streets in silver, puddles catching fragments of neon signs and taxi lights like scattered memories. New York beats with its usual pulse. Alive. Relentless.

It's been a month since the Pitchpocalypse. A month since everything changed.

The Laurel Group walked away with the win, headlines celebrated, offers flooded in—and me? Well, I'm about to walk a different path.

I spot Laurel seated near the window, a perfect storm of poise and power in a coral blazer, her phone in one hand, a coffee in the other. She looks up the second I approach, studying me. She already knows what's coming.

"You look like hell," she says bluntly, setting her phone down. "Sit."

I do, the chair scraping softly against the worn floorboards. I press my palms against the chipped wood of the table hoping it might secure me.

"I'm finishing the campaign closeouts this week," I say quietly. "But after that... I'm resigning."

A flicker of understanding crosses Laurel's face. She leans back in her chair, folding her arms. "Why?"

"Because I can't stay somewhere that only asks for the best parts of me without caring about the cracks. I'm tired of polishing a brand when I don't even recognize my own reflection anymore." I pause. "Because it's time"

She smiles at that.

"I spent years fighting for every inch in this industry. Every win. Every scrap of approval," I say carefully. "But somewhere along the way, I stopped fighting for myself. I don't know who I'm trying to impress anymore. I just know it's not me."

Laurel's finger taps against her coffee cup. "Is this about Nolan?"

It is. And it isn't.

"It's about wanting more than survival," I say. "It's about not mistaking ambition for home."

She watches me in a way she rarely does with her quiet, assessing, almost...proud expression.

"You're good at this, Rorie," she says after a long pause. "Better than most. Better than me, sometimes."

"I don't want to be good at this anymore," I whisper.

And for the first time in a long time, the thought doesn't terrify me. It feels like breathing again after being underwater too long.

Laurel nods once, decisive, like she respects the hell out of my decision even if she hates losing me.

"So," she says, "what's the plan?"

I laugh under my breath, raw but real. "Honestly? I don't have one. Move maybe. Open a bookstore somewhere coastal. Or spend a year getting lost in Europe, bartending, living out of a backpack. Find a small town where nobody cares about résumés or LinkedIn connections. Somewhere I can just be."

Laurel's mouth quirks. "North?"

I shake my head. "West, actually."

Toward something wilder. Uncharted. Toward a version of myself I haven't met yet.

"Doesn't scare you?" she asks, her voice lighter now.

"No," I say, smiling for real this time. "It's the first thing that doesnt."

She lifts her coffee cup in a silent toast. "Then go find your way, Rorie Adams. Whatever that looks like."

Emotion wells in my throat, thick and bittersweet.

Before we part, she reaches out, covering my hand with hers. "They don't need to be here for me to say this. Your parents are proud of the woman you've become. I hope you are, too."

The words hit harder than anything else could have. I blink once. Twice. Then the tears slip free, tracing silent trails down my cheeks.

Laurel squeezes my hand. No rush. No awkwardness. Just letting me have the moment.

When I rise, one hand slides into my jacket pocket, fingers finding the compass tucked there. The brass is worn, edges smoothed by time and memory. I lift it, the needle still swings true, steady as ever.

And I think that's the lesson. Even the things we think are broken can still find their way home.

And so can I.

# CHAPTER 54
# THE PIECES WE SALVAGE

## NOLAN

THE SMELL HITS FIRST. Faint bleach, fresh-baked bread, and florals. The lavender air freshener doesn't quite cover the underlying weight of time passing too fast.

I push through the double doors into the lobby of Ridge Hollow Senior Living, my steps automatically slowing like the place itself demands it. Muted lighting. Soft colors. A hushed quiet meant to soothe frayed edges.

It doesn't. It never has.

A woman approaches, a warm, practiced smile smoothing over her face. "Mr. Rhodes?"

Nodding once, I slide my hands into my jacket pockets.

"I'm Margaret. I oversee care planning here." She gestures toward a small glass-walled office tucked just off the main sitting area. "Thank you for coming in."

Inside, the office is neat, a little too staged. Plush chairs, a plate of untouched cookies on the side table. I don't sit until she does, stretching my legs out and folding my arms across my chest like a shield.

Margaret pulls a manila file from the stack in front of her, smoothing it flat with careful fingers. "I know these meetings aren't easy."

I grunt in response. Meetings don't scare me. It's what they're about that ties a fucking knot in my throat.

She clears hers softly. "Your father's cognitive assessments show notable decline over the past few months. More confusion. Some sundowning behaviors. Increased wandering risk."

I stare past her, at the framed photo on her desk. It's a team of elderly residents playing cards, laughing. My mind is stuck on three specific words:

Wandering. Confusion. Risk.

None of this is new. But hearing it laid out like a quarterly loss report still cuts deep.

"We're recommending a transition to the Memory Care unit," Margaret says gently. "It's a more secure environment, structured daily routines, higher staff-to-resident ratio. He'll still have access to activities, therapy, everything he enjoys, just...with more support."

Support. Right.

Another word for slowly losing the person you used to know.

Another word for watching a man who once ran multimillion-dollar acquisitions get lost between breakfast and lunch.

I drag a hand through my hair, letting the silence hang heavy between us.

"He talks to me about deals," I say out of the blue. My voice sounds rough, like it's fighting its way out. "Mergers. Hostile takeovers. It's all bullshit now, but... I let him."

Margaret's smile softens. "That's common. The strongest memories —the ones tied to identity—tend to hold on the longest."

Identity.

My father isn't the man who called every shot in the boardroom anymore. But it's the only version of him left that feels remotely familiar.

Margaret flips another page. "I know it's a lot to process, but Memory Care is really about quality of life. Preserving dignity. Giving him a space where he's not overwhelmed or afraid."

I nod, jaw tight.

I get it.

I fucking hate it.

But I get it.

She slides a form across the table—authorization paperwork. I pick up the pen and hover it over the line, heart hammering, the realization that I'm signing something bigger than just a transfer kicking in. I'm signing off on the last remnants of the man who raised me.

Or tried to.

When he wasn't chasing deals. When he wasn't drowning in ambition so loud it drowned everything else out.

Including me.

The pen scratches against the paper, sealing the decision neither of us ever wanted to make.

Margaret stands, smoothing her skirt. "Take your time. He's in the garden if you want to see him. He's been asking for you."

I look up.

And for a second, I'm not the man I've built myself into.

I'm the kid standing at the door of his father's office, waiting for permission to step inside.

"Yeah," I rasp. "I'll go find him."

When I step back into the hallway, the scent of rain drifts in through the open door leading out to the garden. I need to remind myself that some things don't stop just because I'm not ready. Like people getting older. Life moves on.

I follow the signs toward the garden, bracing for impact.

The rain starts up again as I make my way across the manicured path to the garden courtyard.

It's soft at first, barely there, a whisper brushing over the hedges and benches.

Dad's sitting under the awning, his wheelchair turned toward the little koi pond they have set up, even though most of the fish are probably hiding from the storm.

He's got a navy sweater on over his button-down. The collar's crooked. The sweater's inside out.

Nobody noticed. Or he didn't let them fix it.

Dad was never easy. But he was always *him*.

Today, he looks smaller. Shrunk inside the frame of the strong man I used to know. The man who commanded a boardroom with a glance. Who once taught me how to throw a curveball using a grapefruit and an empty laundry basket because *"real baseballs are for kids with more trust funds than brains."*

He looks up when he hears me, and for a second—one tiny second—I see it.

Recognition.

"Nolan," he says, voice rough like gravel, but there.

A punch to the gut and a miracle in the same breath.

"Hey, Dad," I say, dropping into the chair beside him. The metal's slick with rain, but I don't care.

We sit there for a while, listening to the rain hit the awning. He watches it like it's a ticker tape parade just for him.

"You make the deal?" he asks after a long moment, tapping two fingers against the armrest.

His tell. His old nervous tic from mergers.

I swallow the knot in my throat. Play along. Because it's what I do.

"Yeah," I say. "Closed it yesterday."

He nods once, satisfied. "Knew you would. You've got the Rhodes blood. We don't lose."

I almost laugh. God, if only he knew how much losing I've done lately. How much walking away has started to feel more like surviving than losing.

"You taught me well," I say instead.

He grunts, the way he used to when he didn't want to admit he was proud.

"You keep the sharks off your ankles?"

"Most days," I murmur.

Another long pause.

"You still got the lake house?" he asks suddenly, turning his head toward me.

The lake house. We sold it three years ago. But the memory is still burrowed deep, tied to the marrow of who we were.

The dock that creaked in the summer heat.

The tire swing.

Me, my uncle, my cousin, Dad, and my Grandfather all fishing off the end, pretending we didn't care if we caught anything.

"Yeah," I lie softly. "Still ours."

He smiles, and it's so pure, so *young*, that I have to look away for a second.

We sit like that.

Side by side.

In the rain.

Between the truth and the lies we tell to hold onto the pieces of each other we can still salvage.

Eventually, he reaches out, groping blindly, and finds my hand. His grip is weaker than I remember. But it's still *him*.

"You did good, kid." He squeezes once before letting go.

And I'm ten years old again. Catching my first pop fly. Grinning like an idiot because Dad called me kid and meant it like a badge of honor.

I clear my throat, the lump nearly choking me.

"I'm proud of you, too," I whisper.

He doesn't respond. Just closes his eyes, lets the rain sing the rest of the conversation between us.

I sit there, hands empty, heart breaking open, loving a man who's already half-vanished into another life.

And hoping to God that somewhere deep down...he knows.

By the time the rain slows to a mist and the sky bruises into twilight, he's half-asleep in his chair, and I know it's time to go.

"I forgive you." I press a kiss to the top of his head, a rare, clumsy thing I can't remember the last time I gave him, and leave him there, dreaming whatever pieces of the past still feel safe.

The walk back to my car feels longer than it should, each step tugging at the part of me I tried to armor against him. Against this.

Forgiveness isn't some clean, triumphant thing. It's a choice you keep making, even when it still hurts.

Even when no one says the words.

Even when it comes too late.

Especially then.

The rain starts up again. I sit behind the wheel for a long time, the the drops tapping the windshield like a second heartbeat.

And when I finally pull out of the lot, I don't look back.

Some things, some people, you carry forward, whether they can follow you or not.

# CHAPTER 55

# NORTH & ANCHOR
RORIE

THE BRINY SCENT of the sea drifts through the open doors as I run my fingers over the leather-bound journal in front of me.

Outside, the waves roll lazily against the shore, the winter light stretching gold and pale pink across the water as a quiet promise.

Somewhere nearby, the town's Christmas lights blink against the gathering mist, their colors blurred at the edges.

Inside, the café is alive. Laughter blends with the soft crackle of an old Nat King Cole record spinning on the antique player behind the counter. Pine and cinnamon hang in the air, threaded through with the bite of roasted coffee and the buttery crumble of fresh scones.

I glance up at the sign above the counter with deep green lettering carved into weathered wood.

*North & Anchor.*

Every time I look at it, pieces of glass loosens in my chest. I'm now tethered to something real. Something *mine.*

I never thought much about the names of things growing up, but this one... this one was waiting for me to understand it.

My parents were two halves of the same coin—adventure and home.

Mom was the dreamer, the woman who could unfold a map and spin a whole world out of the creases. She made the future feel wide and shimmering, like the universe itself was a dare.

*"No matter where you go, baby,"* she'd say, her voice soft but sure, *"just follow your North. Your heart will know the way."*

And for the longest time, I believed her. I thought *North* meant movement. That to follow it meant chasing something—success, love, something bigger than myself.

Dad was different. He was the anchor—steady, unwavering, the kind of person who made a house feel like home just by being in it. He believed in staying, in building, in holding onto what mattered.

*"A life well-lived needs both,"* he used to tell me. *"Something to chase and something to come back to."*

And they had both.

Smiling to myself, I remember the small, weathered boat they took to the lake on summer weekends. North & Anchor.

It wasn't much—some cracked paint, rusted metal, and an engine that needed more convincing than it should have—but it was theirs. It was where Dad taught me to navigate by the stars, where Mom showed me that some things—some *people*—are worth holding onto.

At the time, I never thought about what it meant. It was just a boat. Just a name.

But now? Now, it's *everything*.

I left New York thinking I was running away. Escaping, so to speak. But it wasn't about leaving at all.

It was about *finding*.

Because when I landed in Port Townsend, where my Aunt Jane lives, with its salt-heavy air and cobblestone streets, it didn't feel like running. It felt like breathing again.

I was no longer drifting.

I was building.

So I bought a bookstore, in honor of how my parents met. And when it came time to name this place, there was only ever one choice. Because that's what my parents gave me—the freedom to explore and the reminder that I'd have a place to come home to. And I've finally found it. Still, some days, it doesn't feel real.

Six months ago, I walked away from everything I thought I wanted —New York, my career, the constant chase for the next big deal. I packed my bags, bought a car, and just *drove*. I didn't know where I was going, only that I needed out. To breathe. To find myself in a way I never truly had before.

I landed here. Port Townsend, Washington.

Aunt Jane was waiting for me in town straight out of a postcard, with its historic waterfront, cozy stores, and a rhythm that moves just slow enough to make you stop and take it all in.

Here, people know each other's names. They dawdle over coffee, watch the ships pull into the harbor, and talk about the tides like they're old friends.

And now, I know them too.

I glance around the shop half-expecting to wake up and find this is just another impulsive idea that never quite made it past the dream stage. But it's *real*.

*North & Anchor* is part bookstore, part coffeehouse, part writer's retreat for anyone who needs it. Shelves line the walls, filled with handpicked novels, travel journals, and books about the sea. And of course, a romance section housing everything from cozy to downright filthy.

The tables are mismatched, collected from antique stores and refurbished with love. Every corner holds something meaningful—faded maps, compasses, a vintage anchor I found at a local maritime shop.

The space feels like *me* in a way nothing else ever has. And for the first time in a long time, I'm settled.

Almost.

Because not a day goes by that I don't think about *him*.

Taking a sip of my coffee, I stare out at the water, my thoughts drifting before I can stop them.

Nolan.

After all this time, he still takes up residence in the back of my mind, and in my heart. He's a presence I can't quite run away from.

I've tried.

Sometimes, late at night, I catch myself typing his name into Google, hoping for anything that will tell me where he is, what he's doing. But his social media is practically nonexistent. No updates. No new posts. Nothing but old corporate features that mean nothing to me now.

Maya and Jeremy toss me breadcrumbs from time to time.

I know he left Big Stream after the pitch event. I know he started his own consulting business—Rhodes & Co. (because of course he named it something cool and perfect).

Who the & Co. is, though? I have no idea.

And that's it.

I don't know if he's happy. I don't know if he ever thinks about me the way I think about him. If he ever wonders what would've happened if we hadn't both walked away.

I *hate* that I still wonder.

Nolan once told me the best pitches come from something real—something that leaves a mark. And when we sat under the stars that night, wrapped in nothing but silence and story, I gave him mine. North and Anchor. My parents. My heart. He didn't say much, probably because he already knew about them, but he listened. God, he listened.

So when he left me that bracelet, tucked in a linen bag like some kind of quiet vow, I knew. He wasn't just trying to win a pitch. He was trying to give me something back. Something to hold onto.

At the time, I thought it was some cosmic connection, something bigger than the both of us. I still do.

Even though our story ended, I still think he came into my life—accidentally, *cosmically*—for a reason.

And I cherish that.

I run my fingers over the anchor, feeling the smooth wood against my skin. My other hand drifts to the compass I keep on the counter, the small gold thing that's been with me since I was a child. It's a little tarnished, but still points north, steady as ever.

Just like me.

Just like this place.

The bell above the door jingles, and I glance up as a familiar face steps inside—Emily Lawson, one of my regulars. She's in her late twenties, like me. She's a genius. The youngest literature professor at Seattle Pacific University, who spends her holidays and summers here, sipping black coffee and working on the novel she's been writing for years. She gives me a knowing look as she heads to the counter.

"You're in that head of yours again," she says, her voice warm and amused.

I laugh softly, rubbing a hand over my forehead. "That obvious?"

She just smiles. "You're a thinker, Rorie. That's a good thing. Just don't let it consume you. It'll stop you from *living*."

A small chuckle escapes me at the word. *Living.*

That's what I'm trying to do here. To be fully present. To stop chasing after things I can't define.

This life—this town, this shop, these people—they're exactly what I was meant to find.

For once, I'm exactly where I'm supposed to be.

I take a deep breath, smile bigger, and turn back to the café, ready to start the day.

# CHAPTER 56
# WHERE THE COMPASS POINTS

NOLAN

THE THING ABOUT BRIDGES—

Sometimes you cross them.

Sometimes you burn them.

And sometimes you stand there and watch the whole damn thing collapse under the weight of its own lies.

That's what happened to Big Stream Marketing.

No bombshell, no scandal. Only the slow, inevitable rot catching up.

Turns out Laurel had been playing a longer game than any of us realized. Apparently her and Thatcher had a little something back in the day. Which he fucked up.

Guess it's true what they say: *Hell hath no fury like a woman scorned.*

And Laurel went full scorched earth.

At the mixology mishap on the island, friendly drinks led to a little harmless flirting, which led to some late night fuckery in his cottage. Add in a conveniently placed laptop. And phone. Throw in a dash of the perfect timing, and Laurel didn't just blow the whistle—she derailed the train then blew up the station, handing the Feds everything they needed.

Stolen client lists. Cooked reports. Shady contracts buried under mountains of NDAs.

Thatcher didn't see it coming. Arrogance rarely does.

By the time the smoke started rising, Big Stream was already on fire.

Internal audits.

Missing funds.

Clients fleeing like rats off a sinking ship.

Jackson tried to play dumb. He acted like he didn't know the paperwork he was smoothing over had teeth.

And maybe he didn't.

It's possible he was just a fool happy to cash a check and look the other way.

But I doubt it.

Regardless, the fall didn't spare him.

Big Stream's golden nephew is currently neck-deep in depositions, clawing for a life raft that doesn't exist.

And if I'm being completely transparent, I thought Tammy and Imogene were behind it all. Not Laurel. I was sure those reports they pulled for me had something that helped the whistleblowing along.

I asked Tammy about it once, a few months back.

She just smiled innocently and said, "I don't know a thing about what you're talking about, Boss."

Mhm. Sure.

I asked her to pull shit on Thatcher while we were still on the island. I'm pretty sure she did, but kept me far away from it. She's always been so protective of me. Love her.

Even with the satisfaction of hearing Thatcher's about to get what's coming to him, the thought of Big Stream crumbling still stings.

I built that company like it was mine—fighting for every client, every deal, every inch of respect.

And even though Big Stream's fire died out, we forged something stronger. Rhodes and Co.—born from the burn.

As for Chloe?

When Thatcher's empire crumbled, she pulled her golden parachute.

Last I heard, she's trying her luck as a *lifestyle coach*, selling self-worth one Instagram post at a time.

Poetic, in a way.

And me?

I don't regret walking away. I don't miss the politics. The fake smiles. The way loyalty there was just another currency waiting to be spent.

Rhodes & Co. is thriving. Tammy's amazing, as always. Rishi starts next month. And I don't answer to anyone but myself anymore.

Maybe that's the best kind of win.

The quiet kind. One you don't have to shout about.

And now, here I am—in a tiny restaurant tucked into the rainy edges of Seattle, poking half-heartedly at my plate with the tip of my fork, shaking my head like I still can't believe it. Because I can't.

"I can't believe we're working with a mac and cheese company."

Across from me, Tammy snorts, stirring sugar into her tea likes she's mad at it. "Mac and cheese is a billion-dollar industry, Nolan." She lifts her pinky dramatically. "We're not sellouts. We're visionaries."

I chuckle under my breath. "Visionaries, huh?"

"Absolutely. You think you've reached the pinnacle of your career, and then—*bam*—you're branding cheese powder dreams." She leans forward, eyes glittering. "Admit it. It's hilarious."

I laugh, because it is.

A year ago, I was grinding my life away in glass conference rooms that smelled like the desperation of men and women who thought $300 cologne could cover up rotting ambition.

Now I'm consulting for Big Marty's Mac Shack, sitting across from my best business partner, who is currently giving a passionate speech about the emotional impact of elbow pasta.

This is my life now.

And honestly?

I love it.

Mostly.

By every metric that used to matter, I'm winning.

And yet...

There's still this hollowed-out space inside me. A room left half-furnished. I'm waiting for something—or someone—to walk back in and fill it.

Some ghosts don't leave easy.

I reach for a fry on my plate, but before I can even get it to my mouth, Tammy swipes it right out of my hand like a damn savage.

"Seriously?"

She shrugs, completely unapologetic, crunching into it like it was hers all along.

"Proven fact," she says around a mouthful of stolen goods. "Fries taste better when they're stolen."

The words hit me harder than they should. Suddenly, I'm back in that anonymous text thread. Back in the early days when stolen fries were a joke, and a I was part of a slow, beautiful unraveling. Back on that plane, stealing them off Rorie's tray and catching her smile like it was mine to keep.

Rorie.

Her name claws through my chest.

It's been nine months. Nine goddamn months.

And still, she's everywhere.

Everywhere and nowhere.

I push my plate toward Tammy without a word and sit back, scrubbing a hand down my face like that might erase the ache rising up in my throat.

Watching me, she chews thoughtfully. "You okay?"

"Yeah." I reach for my napkin, pretending to wipe my mouth instead of pulling myself together. "Just thinking."

"About?" she presses, casual but not really.

I shake my head once. "Nothing."

She doesn't buy it, not even a little, but she lets it go. For now.

Instead, she leans forward, her mischievous grin slipping back into place. "So. Ready for our big adventure?"

I sigh. Long and suffering. "Tammy, we came to Seattle for work. Not to go sightseeing."

"Well, I'm forcing you to do both. So get your ass in the car, Boss."

I tip my head back against the booth with a groan. "What the hell are we driving three hours for?"

Slinging her bag over her shoulder, she winks, like she's Indiana Jones about to uncover a national treasure.

"A very important piece of Washington history."

I roll my eyes but shove out of the booth after her anyway.

One time. I'll humor her *one* time.

Because honestly, I could use a distraction. Even if some part of me knows, no matter how far we drive, there are some things you can't outrun.

*Three hours later...*

I'll give her this—Port Townsend's a hell of a lot prettier than I expected.

It looks like the setting of an old novel: cobblestone streets, faded brick storefronts, salt-stained windows, and a harbor lined with boats rocking lazily in the gray, misty afternoon. This place doesn't just move slower, it dares you to slow down too. To breathe. To feel.

Tammy parks the car and waves her hand toward the windshield. "Ta-da! Welcome to Port Townsend! Population: Charming as hell."

I'm glancing around, pretending to be unimpressed. "Great. You've kidnapped me. Can we go now?"

She groans, thwacking the back of her hand against my chest. "For the love of overpriced coffee, will you just *relax*? Enjoy life for once?"

I cross my arms, still skeptical. "Tammy. We have work to do."

"No," she says, grinning. "*You* have work to do. I, on the other hand, am on a very important mission."

She flashes me a Cheshire cat smile. "Now humor me. Or I'll start unionizing."

Knowing Tammy she means it.

I exhale heavily. "One hour. That's it."

She beams, victorious. "Perfect. Now walk, Mr. Grinch."

We stroll through the town, and despite myself, I don't hate it. The air's brisk and clean, carrying the briny bite of the sea. Strings of lights crisscross above the street, glowing faintly against the low-hanging spring sky clouds. People meander with paper bags from the local bakery, sloshing around in rain boots, their laughter bleeding into the mist.

It's... nice. Sickeningly nice.

Tammy stops in front of a shop window called *Love & Smells*, peering inside at a display of candles stacked like trophies.

"You ever think about it?" she asks, almost casually.

I stuff my hands deeper into my jacket pockets. "Think about what?"

She shrugs. "You know. Love. Life. Maybe living somewhere like this. Slower. Happier."

I snort. "Nah."

She tilts her head. "Because you're *so* thrilled selling cheese powder?"

Despite myself, I chuckle. "I'm thrilled not answering to assholes, if that counts."

"Counts for something," she says. "But don't act like you're not missing something, Rhodes."

I glance down at the wet cobblestones. Missing something isn't the problem. Missing *someone* is.

She elbows me. "You sucked at lying when we were corporate rats. You still suck at it."

I shake my head. "Let it go, Tammy."

But she doesn't. Not really. Because she knows. And she proves it by nudging my arm and jerking her chin toward a store across the street.

I follow her gaze. And my heart stops.

There. Standing behind the glass door of a small bookstore with dark green lettering carved into weathered wood—*North & Anchor*—is Rorie Adams.

She doesn't see me. She's cleaning the window, her hair swept up in a messy knot. She's wearing a thick sweater that looks like it could smother every bad day I've ever had.

She looks... beautiful as always. More so.

Settled.

Happy.

Like she *belongs* here.

Tammy shifts beside me, but I barely register her. The part of me that's been hollowed out for months, the part I thought time would heal, just split wide open again.

She opens for a few customers, and follows behind them, deeper into the store, out of view.

And somehow, that tiny empty space hurts more than anything else.

Tammy tugs a slip of paper out of her coat pocket and hands it to me without a word.

A phone number. An address.

"She changed her number when she left New York," she says, gentle. "I though fate might need a little nudge."

I stare down at the paper. It's heavy as a stone in my palm.

I look back at the store. Through the display window, Rorie's laughing with a customer, brushing stray hairs from her face.

Life didn't stop for her. She *built* something. Without me.

And that's okay.

She was never supposed to be mine in the first place. But fuck if I can stand here one second longer and pretend it doesn't matter.

I shove the paper into my pocket, turn on my heel, and walk back toward the car without a word.

Sometimes you don't need a plan. You just need a shot. A prayer. And a little glitter.

"Where are you going?" Tammy calls after me.

"I need to make good on a promise I made to myself," I say, looking back over my shoulder at her. "I'm going to need your help. It involves sparkles. And fries."

Tammy whoops, and rushes after me. "Now *that's* the Nolan Rhodes I know."

I smile. After nine long months, I almost feel like myself again.

# CHAPTER 57
# GLITTER, FRIES, AND FOREVER

## RORIE

THE SCENT OF CINNAMON, coffee and old books wraps around me as my second skin. It's a slow afternoon, sun slanting through the windows, a lazy day where time feels thick and syrupy.

Once I finish wiping down the front counter, I move to the display of journals near the front window and start adjusting those.

Basically, I'm trying to keep myself busy. My mind is on overdrive today and there's this uneasiness swirling inside me for some reason.

I can't put my finger on why.

My phone buzzes against the counter. I snatch it up.

A wrong number? The memory of the last one hits hard at first, then slow, like something sacred slipping in through the cracks.

Because that one turned into the most unexpected, electric, heartwrecking connection of my life. An accident that felt like fate. And I still don't know if I survived it...or if part of me is still waiting on the next message.

I swipe it open.

> What's the worst life choice you've ever made?
>
> Asking for a friend.

The memory sneaks in—uninvited but stubborn—the way *Carl*

once said that same latter phrase to me is eerily similar. Back when he was still a faceless number, a mistake I thought I could laugh about.

Nostalgia is a dangerous drug so I reply, because why not?

> Letting a stranger drag me into a text war before coffee. Bold move.

Bold? Or fate?

> Mmm. Sounds like the opening line of a bad rom com movie.

The bell above the door jingles.

"Welcome to North and Anchor!" I call out automatically, eyes still glued to my phone. "Let me know if you need anything."

A beat of silence.

> What about you?

What's the worst life choice you've ever made?

"Stealing your story before you even knew it was gone," that familiar, maddening voice slides down my spine.

My head slowly, *slowly* looks up. And I promptly lose all capacity for logical thought.

Standing in my shop, wearing the most ridiculous shirt, and holding a basket of fries, is Nolan *"What the Fuck"* Rhodes, dimple and all.

I blink. Once. Twice. Because surely I'm hallucinating.

But no. He's real.

The shirt reads, in bold, sparkling letters:

*If Lost, Return to the*
*Nearest Book Babe*

There are actual flecks of glitter clinging to the fabric, catching the light like tiny weapons of mass distraction.

My body wants to bolt, my heart wants to collapse, and my soul is clawing its way to the surface screaming *go to him*.

But my feet are rooted to the ground.

Nolan stays where he is, respectful. Careful. Letting *me* make the first move.

Finally, somehow, I find my voice. "Subtle entrance," I say hoarsely.

His smile tugs wider. "Had to live up to my reputation."

"And what reputation is that exactly?"

He takes a slow, tentative step closer. "Persistent dumbass. Professional fry thief. Guy who once said the wrong thing, did the wrong thing, but never—*not once*—stopped wishing he could make it right."

The whole world fades out.

It's just him. And me. And the invisible earthquake under my skin, shaking loose every piece I tried so hard to glue together after I left.

"You broke me," I whisper. It rips out, sharp and unfiltered, before I can stop it.

Nolan's throat works as he swallows. He doesn't look away. Doesn't pretend. He *takes* the weight of it.

"I know," he rasps, the words tearing out of him. "And there hasn't been a single day since that I haven't felt it—knowing that when you were handing me your heart, I was holding a loaded gun behind my back."

Tears prick my eyes, but I blink them away. I'm so tired of crying over him.

"Rorie," he steps forward and continues, "I know what was up on that screen."

"No, you don't. That was *my* life." I point to my chest.

"Yes, it was. Every grief you've survived, every dream you've buried, every piece you should've been allowed to guard, and I ripped it from you without a second thought. I didn't just break your trust. I broke the version of you that believed you could ever trust someone like me."

Swiping the tears away, I cross my arms over my chest, protectively.

Nolan takes another step closer but I step back.

He halts, exhales then sets the basket of fries carefully on the counter. His arms drop to his sides.

"North is your heart." His voice roughens even more. "You are my North. And my anchor. And I lost you because at one point, I treated you like a finish line instead of a fucking miracle."

My hands shake. God, I want to believe him. I want to tear the walls down, and run straight into him, but the part of me that remembers that day—the betrayal, the humiliation—bites back hard.

"You should've been safe with me, you should've been sacred. And I lost you—the one thing in this life worth fighting for. But I will *fight*, Rorie. For every secret I should have protected. For every piece of you that still thinks love means betrayal. I'll rip down every wall you build, and if you let me, I'll build something better from the wreckage I left behind. However long it takes."

"You can't just show up with glitter and fries and expect everything to be fine," I say, my voice trembling.

Suddenly, he drops to his knees, pleading. Right there. In the middle of my damn bookstore, wearing a shirt that looks like it was bedazzled by a drunk cupid. He's there, with nothing to offer except *him*—raw, imperfect, *real*.

"I don't want fine," his tone is steady even as emotion thickens it. "I want messy. And complicated. And *honest*. I want late-night texts and stolen fries and grilled cheese with tomato soup. And stars." Shaky now. "And you. I want *you*."

My heart shatters and remakes itself all at once.

One deep breath. Then another.

Crossing the space between us, I crouch too. We're eye to eye, chests heaving. His hand shakes when it lifts to tuck a strand of hair behind my ear.

I grab his wrist. Hold it there.

"You really think glitter and carbs are enough to fix this?" I whisper, a smile trembling at the edge of my mouth.

Nolan's lips curve—hopeful, wild, *his*. "No. But it's a start."

His grin is devastating. The kind that once made me want to punch him and kiss him in the same breath.

He points to the fries and says, "Truce?"

A beat of silence.

And then—*fuck it all*—I pull him into a kiss so fierce, so desperate, that the whole universe tilts sideways.

The bell above the door rings again as the wind rushes in.

But we stay right there.

Home.

Exactly where we were always meant to be.

# CHAPTER 58
# ANCHOR ME
## NOLAN

OUTSIDE THE CAR WINDOW, snow dusts the dunes like powdered sugar, the ocean a silver stretch in the distance. The town is strung up in twinkle lights, wreaths on every lamp post, windows glowing gold and warm.

Everything is perfect. Or at least, as close to perfect as it can be when the person planning it is me, someone who definitely doesn't do things the traditional way.

I pull down my mirror, check my reflection.

It's funny. I've done this before. Stood in front of a mirror, adjusting my collar, rehearsing what I was going to say, planning a future I thought I wanted.

But this is different. *Way* different.

This is her.

I'm about to do the single most stupid, ridiculous, perfectly *us* thing I have ever done.

I check my pocket. Still there.

I almost laugh, because of course this is what I'm using. A ring box would be too easy, too expected. But a compass? That's my Rorie.

Letting out a breath, I roll my shoulders back.

*Game time, Rhodes.*

I step through the front door of our house, the coastal air crisp against my skin before it seals shut behind me. Smoothing my hands down the front of my sweater, I exhale.

Our cute coastal house smells like cloves and apples, and the faint sweetness of the cookies she just pulled from the oven. The fire crackles in the stone hearth. The tree glows in the corner, ornaments glinting in the soft light.

There she is, standing by the kitchen island, barefoot, in leggings and an oversized sweater, humming to herself. Just like how her mom used to, so she's told me

She's completely unaware that her entire life is about to change.

Hopefully.

I cross the room with my hands shoved in my pockets. "Hey, Adams."

Her head pops up, her face breaking into a smile, like she's just happy I'm here.

God, I'm a goner.

"What are you doing home?" Brushing a stray hair from her face, the wooden anchor dangles from the bracelet I gave her. "I thought you had that meeting with your Mac and Cheese company."

"I did. It's over."

"How'd it go?"

"Fine."

Her eyes narrow suspiciously. "You're acting weird."

"Am I?"

She nods. "Yeah, babe. What's going on?"

Before she can interrogate me further, I slide the gift box onto the counter, setting it right beside the old compass her father gave her.

"I thought..." I start, but the words jam up in my throat. Clearing it, I shift awkwardly. "I thought you needed a new one."

Her brows pull together, confused. "A new what?"

She's flushed from the heat of the fire. Barefoot and beautiful and stronger than anyone I've ever known. And somehow, still looking at me like *I'm* the miracle.

She blinks, glancing down at the box, then back at me. "It's not another galaxy is it?"

My heart actually *stops* beating for a second.

Nodding toward it, I tap the lid lightly with one finger. "Open it."

She hesitates, and for a second, panic grips my spine. But her fingers untie the ribbon and lift the black lid, and it hits her.

Her shoulders curl inward like she does when she's trying to hold herself together.

"Something to follow… something to hold onto."

She stares down at the new compass like it's glowing. Mine isn't flashy or expensive. But it's got weight. Story. Meaning.

Fighting the crack in my voice, I say, "You shouldn't have to look for those two things alone anymore."

Her fingertips brush the edge of the compass like it's fragile, and precious. She doesn't say anything for a long moment.

Doesn't need to. Her silence says it all.

Finally, she whispers, "You're ridiculously sweet."

I smile, not the cocky kind I used to hide behind. Now it's soft. Real.

"Yeah," I say. "You do that to me." And that's the truest thing I've ever said.

Slowly, she lifts the compass out of the box and opens it. Her jaw drops. My pulse spikes.

Inside, where the needle should be, nestled in the center—is the ring.

The gold band catches the firelight, delicate but strong, etched with tiny waves along the sides, subtle as a secret.

At the center, a vintage-style bezel holds a stunning emerald, deep green with flecks of gold that glow when she tilts it toward the tree lights.

*North and Anchor.* The sea and the sky. Earth and compass.

Tiny diamonds flank it like distant stars. Not about the carats. Not about the cost.

It's about *her.*

About the way she once sat by the ocean, grief threading her voice, and told me you always need a North and an Anchor. How she's spent her life carrying heartbreak like it was stitched into her skin, and still found ways to stay soft. And the fact that I fell for her without even trying.

That I *see* her. Still. Always.

And tucked just beneath the stone, engraved in the curve of the setting—

## *Anchor Me.*

Not "Marry Me."

Because even when she drifts, even when the world tilts sideways, she'll never be alone again.

She'll always have me.

Her hand flies to her mouth the moment it registers.

I take a breath. Not nervous. Not scared.

Sure.

Picking up the compass, I cradle it between us and drop to one knee.

"You once told me," I begin, voice low, "that North isn't just a direction. It's a feeling. It's the thing that keeps pulling you forward, no matter how lost you get."

Her eyes shine, tears brimming at the edges, her hand still pressed to her lips.

"I've been lost before. Then I met you. And suddenly... I wasn't."

A shaky laugh slips from her lips, but she doesn't interrupt.

I take her hand, thumb brushing slow circles across her knuckles. "This is your fault," I tease, smiling against the tightness in my chest. "You made me believe in things I never thought I could. You made me believe in *us*."

Her fingers squeeze mine, her breath hitching.

"So here's the deal, Adams," I say, letting the smile bloom, soft and confident.

"You and me. Always. That's what I want. That's what I've *always* wanted." My grip tightens, voice dropping lower. "I can't promise I'll always say the right thing. Or that I won't steal your fries. Or that I won't drive you completely insane at least twice a week. Maybe more."

She laughs, broken and beautiful, a tear slipping free.

"But I can promise this—I'll love you. Every single day. For the rest of our lives." I nod toward the compass, my heartbeat steady now, sure in every cell of my body. "So what do you say, baby? You wanna follow North with me?"

She lets out a laugh that cracks and melts into a sob, shaking her head like she can't believe this is real—can't believe *me*.

And then—

She launches herself at me, arms wrapping tight around my neck, burying her face against me like she never plans to let go.

"Yes," she whispers against my ear, voice breaking with joy.

"Yes. Yes. Always yes."

I catch her, hold her, bury my face in her hair and breathe her in.

Because this—

This is home.

Her arms are tight around my neck, her body pressed against mine like she's never letting go, and I never want her to.

I rise from my knee, carrying her with me, my hand cradling the back of her head as I hold her close.

She laughs against my throat, a soft, broken sound, and the world tilts under my feet, spinning around this woman, this moment.

Above the mantle, the galaxy globe I sent her spins slowly with tiny constellations drifting in glass, glowing softly in the firelight. It catches her reflection, mirrors the stars outside, and for a second, it's like the whole universe bent just to bring us here.

The fire crackles behind us, the scent of pine and cinnamon weaving through the air. Snow drifts against the windows, the first stars pricking the sky, faint, but burning bright.

I back her toward the tree, its lights casting soft halos across the wooden floor, until we sink together onto the thick rug in front of the hearth.

The warmth of the fire kisses our skin, the glow painting her in golden shadows, and for a long, breathless moment, all I can do is look at her.

She's so beautiful. And so mine.

Rorie's hair spills across the rug, her sweater slipping off one bare shoulder, chest rising and falling in uneven, elegant breaths as her eyes —God, her glacial blue eyes—burn into me, fierce and unguarded.

I touch her as a man who knows he's holding something sacred. Slow, aching strokes of my fingers down her arms, her ribs, the delicate dip of her waist. Every inch I uncover is a gift.

She helps me pull her sweater the rest of the way off, tossing it aside. The firelight illuminates her flushed skin.

She tugs at my shirt next, impatient now, a hungry sound catching in her throat when my bare chest brushes hers.

The first kiss is sweet. Gentle.

But the second is heat and desperation and want stitched into a single breath.

I settle between her thighs, the thin barrier of her leggings sliding against my jeans, friction sparking everywhere we touch.

Her hands roam my back, nails scratching lightly, sending a shudder down my spine.

"God, Rorie," I whisper against her mouth, my voice wrecked. "You are everything."

Her legs tighten around my hips, anchoring me to her, pulling me closer until there's no space left to hide.

The lights from the tree twinkle around us, tiny galaxies spinning wildly as we find each other, piece by piece.

Clothes fall away in a trail of heat and fumbling hands, neither of us able to move fast enough now. Not when the need is this sharp.

This deep.

I press her down into the rug, the fire casting us in molten light, every brush of skin a brand.

Her body arches to meet me, wild and wordless, and when I finally sink into her, we crack open.

Every seam, every scar, every hidden place giving way not to break us, but to make room for everything we're about to become.

Shattered sighs, whispered names, raw urgency. She fits around me so perfectly it feels like the earth could tilt on its axis and I'd still find my way back to her.

Our rhythm is slow at first, reverent, savoring every grind of skin on skin, each breathless hitch, and the soft, pleading sounds that fall from her lips.

But it builds, inevitable, and unstoppable, just like us, until we're moving in a messy, almost hungry rhythm that makes the whole world fall away.

I cup her face in my hands, our foreheads pressed together, sweat slick between us, our mouths brushing, breathing each other in.

"I love you so much," I groan against her lips.

Her nails dig into my back, pulling me deeper, closer, until there's no telling where she ends and I begin.

And when she comes, it's silent and violent, her walls clenching tight around me, her body trembling from her release and her head is thrown back, hair tumbling.

I follow her over the edge a moment later, falling with her, for her, because of her—

Because there's no other choice.

We stay tangled together on the floor, breathless and spent, the fire crackling beside us. Her head rests against my chest, her hand curled over my heart, tracing the constellation there.

I kiss her hair, her forehead, the damp skin of her shoulder, every kiss a silent promise:

*I'm here. I'm yours. I'm home.*

"It was always you," she whispers.

I hold her tighter, like I can imprint the feel of her against me, until there's no separating us.

Until there never will be.

The Christmas tree lights paint the room in quiet wonder. The snow thickens beyond the windows, wrapping the world in white.

But here, by the fire, in her arms, there's only warmth.

Only forever.

Only us.

# EPILOGUE

JEREMY

LOOK, in my defense, nobody *explicitly* said:

"No getting your dick sucked by the hot server in the linen closet before the ceremony."

Especially not by a server named Jamie, who smells like gin and dry cypress, and had arms that could bench press a small horse.

Not a pony. A full-ass horse. Let's be accurate here.

Mistakes were made.

Regrets?

Not a single goddamn one. Because, let's be real, his cock gave those biceps a serious run for their money.

And Mr. Fiddlestorm wants what he wants, when he wants it.

Straightening my tie in the mirror, I swipe a thumb over the suspiciously smudged lipgloss in the corner of my mouth and grin.

Not lip gloss, technically.

Lip balm. Don't be gross.

Flavored. Peach. You're welcome for that visual and no, I will not apologize.

And listen, I'm a gentleman. I reciprocate. Because manners. They're important. And so rare these days.

After adjusting my boutonnière, I shoot myself a wink in the mirror for surviving that whole extremely life-affirming experience, and slip out the door like the very picture of innocence.

I even give Jamie a wink on my way out. He salutes me with a tray of champagne flutes like the god he is.

Outside, the music's picking up, the salty breeze kicking through the open doors and scattering flower petals down the aisle like confetti.

The sun's slanting low over the ocean, setting everything on fire in that golden, holy-hour kind of way, and honestly it's almost disgustingly beautiful.

Nolan and Rorie's setup should be a freaking magazine spread. Driftwood altar wrapped in eucalyptus and white roses, fairy lights strung between the dunes, rows of chairs tucked neatly into the sand.

It's not just gorgeous.

It's *them.*

The wedding party is lined up and mostly behaving.

Mostly.

Maya is stiffly linked arm-in-arm with Asher, and the tension between them could power a small city. It's like watching two beautiful magnets desperately trying not to touch. I give it twenty minutes before one of them throws the first insult disguised as a compliment.

Fifteen if the champagne hits early.

Asher keeps sneaking glances at her like he's torn between kissing her and pushing her over the side of this cliff. Maya's jaw is so tight you could probably cut glass on it. It's going to be *delicious* later. I'm already pre-writing the group chat jokes in my head.

They'll probably fuck tonight.

Oh, let's hope so.

Tammy's muttering about how eloping is "99% more time-efficient" while her wife, Imogene, taps her pen against a clipboard, trying her best to keep everyone in line.

Good luck with that.

Some chick named Emily—who, according to Maya, is some genius professor who has befriended our Rorie—is stress-devouring mints from the favor baskets.

And me?

I'm trying not to get misty-eyed before the damn thing even starts.

It's a whole beautiful disaster out here.

Today isn't just another coastal wedding with top notch seafood and an open bar. It's the day two of the most gloriously broken, stubborn, perfect-for-each-other idiots I know make it official.

Imogene says it's time and we make our way down the aisle, taking our places on our respective sides.

Laurel is seated at the front, next to Nolan's father and his caretaker.

For a second, I catch a glimpse of Rorie's parents's photograph tucked into the flowers at the end of the front row, right by a picture of Nolan's mom.

His dad sits stiffly, his hands folded tight in his lap, but he's here. He showed up. And somehow, even with all the cracks, all the history, it feels like both of them are finally getting the kind of beginning they always deserved.

With family behind them.

With love all around them.

Right where it matters most.

The music shifts.

The crowd turns.

And there she is.

Rorie—barefoot, radiant, with that same "I dare you to survive me" energy she's always carried—floating down the aisle as though the entire ocean decided to part just to let her pass.

Nolan looks like he just forgot how breathing works. He's locked on her like gravity stopped existing and she's the only thing holding him to the earth.

I feel something tighten in my chest, sharp and stupid and full of far too many feelings.

Damn them.

Damn this day.

Damn how *right* they look.

They meet at the altar, laughter catching in their throats, hands fumbling together like they can't stand the space between them for even a second longer. And suddenly it's not a wedding anymore.

It's a homecoming.

A battle won.

A lighthouse found in the middle of a storm.

The officiant talks about love being messy. About how real love isn't the absence of cracks. It's the hands that hold you steady anyway.

Nolan pulls out the compass—the one he gave her when he proposed—and presses it into her palm. I almost lose my shit right there.

An anchor.

A vow.

And when they kiss, wild and soft and a little desperate, survivors finally, *finally* reaching the shore, the whole beach erupts.

Maya whoops. Asher mutters something under his breath like "about damn time"'" and Tammy elbows him so hard he stumbles.

Emily dabs at her eyes and Rishi launches into a victory dance so aggressive he nearly takes out the front row.

But I just stand there, hands jammed in my pockets, grinning like a fool. Because somehow, after all their wreckage, all the wrong turns, all the scars—these two found their way back to each other.

Not perfect.

Not polished.

Real.

And real is better anyway.

The reception is everything you'd expect:

Laughter spilling over wine glasses. Feet bare in the sand. Fairy lights blinking, same as the lazy stars overhead. The ocean humming in the background like an old, familiar song.

It's wedding magic at its peak with a side of clusterfuck, just the way Rorie and Nolan would want it.

Deciding to raid the food, I catch Rishi flirting with Emily near the raw oyster bar. Like, full court press. Hand on the table, leaning in, giving her the kind of smile that probably got him voted "Most Likely to Be a Problem" in high school.

Emily, for her part, looks approximately one wink away from snapping a butter knife in half. Poor girl's been mainlining mints all day and now she's got Rishi tossing pickup lines like he's training for the *Bachelor Barn*.

Honestly, it's excellent entertainment. I make a mental note to check in later. Purely for documentation purposes, of course.

And then—because this day *cannot* just behave—I realize Maya and Asher are... MIA.

Gone.

Vaporized.

Not at their assigned table, not at the bar, not even heckling each other near the dance floor.

*Hmmmmm.*

Suspicious.

Very suspicious.

I take a long, slow sip of my drink and grin. If those two don't, at the very least, make out in the dunes tonight, I'll eat my boutonnière.

Jamie finds me again, slipping a fresh whiskey sour into my hand with a wicked grin that promises a lot and apologizes for nothing.

I'll be finding a way to thank him properly later. But right now, I set my attention off him and toward the head table, where Nolan's gazing at Rorie as she talks, the look in his eyes so stupidly in love it almost hurts to watch.

She catches him staring, blushes, and kisses him so tenderly it's practically an art form. When they separate, he kisses her knuckles like she handed him the stars.

God, these two.

I raise my glass in a silent toast—to good timing, and the absolute shitshow of love when it's strong enough to survive it all.

And with that,

To love that cracks you open.

To second chances.

To surviving bar bathrooms, boardrooms and broken hearts.

To choosing each other—again and again and again.

Some people spend their whole lives looking for it.

Some people crash into it when they least expect it.

Some people—the best people—choose it anyway.

And hell, if Nolan and Rorie can do it, there's hope for the rest of us.

Especially if Jamie's working the afterparty.

# ACKNOWLEDGMENTS

Writing this book was a dream I tucked away for a long time. Finishing it feels like magic. And this magical dream was made possible by the people in my life who believed in me, pushed me, and occasionally bribed me with caffeine and compliments to keep going. You reminded me that stories are worth fighting for—and so am I.

*To my husband, Ben.* You are the reason Nolan exists. Your wit, your stubborn charm, your hidden softness, your big heart—you're in every page. Thank you for letting me steal your one-liners, for *always* supporting my ramblings, and for being the love story that makes writing them worth it.

*To my parents.* Thank you for giving me a childhood filled with stories, creativity, and unconditional love. For every Saturday at Enid library, every book you placed in my hands, every dream you encouraged, and every moment you reminded me that I could do *hard things* —this is because of you.

You taught me how to work with heart, to speak with courage, and to never stop chasing the things that set my soul on fire.

I am who I am because of you. And I carry your love with me in every chapter.

*To Emily. My Sweets.* This book wouldn't exist without you. While your dad might have inspired the book boyfriend, *you* are the heart of this story. Our rom-com nights—filled with laughter, and the occasional debate over the best on-screen couple—are some of my most treasured memories. You bring so much joy, wit, and warmth into my life, and I'm endlessly grateful for the moments we share.

Thank you for being my movie buddy, my sounding board, and whether you realize it or not—the spark behind this book. I hope it brings you even a fraction of the joy you bring to me. With all my love, Suga.

*To my incredible kids.* You make life louder, messier, funnier, and infinitely better. Thank you for the hugs, the patience, and the constant supply of craziness that somehow keeps me inspired. Never give up on your dreams. Ever. Period.

To my *Pitch Perfects* (Amanda, Christina, Shanna, Sierra, Lisa, Samee, Heather, Tina, Lara, Sarah, Jenn, Cynthia), my hype squad, my alpha and beta readers, and every friend who asked, *"How's the book coming?"* even when I was hiding from it. Thank You. Your encouragement meant the world. And I will hold it in my heart forever.

*To every teacher, librarian, and author* who taught me that stories are more than words—they're lifelines—thank you for showing me the power of the page. Thank you to my second grade teacher, especially. My author journey started with her.

*To my sister, Shanna.* Thank you for being my built-in best friend, my sounding board, and the person who's always believed in me, even when I wasn't sure I believed in myself. Your support means more than I can ever put into words (and I literally write books). Your insight, encouragement, and editorial eye helped turn this draft into a real story. Thank you for polishing me, and cheering me on through the rewrite. Hopefully Dad will never read this.

*To Sara.* Twenty years this month. You've been there since the very beginning—back when we dog-eared pages in vampire romances and dreamed out loud about what *could* be. You've carried this dream with me longer than anyone, through every high, every heartache, every rewrite, and every wild, wonderful plot twist.

Thank you for the laughter, the nighttime rants online, the endless support, and the way you never once let me forget why I started.

It's been a ride and I wouldn't have made it here without you. Here's to what's next, whatever shape it takes. I'm just glad you're in it.

*To my book club*—Sharon, Nichole (my Boo), Maria, Me'Lisa, and Trish—

Thank you for being my safe space, my hype team, and the loudest voices in the back yelling *"JUST PUBLISH IT ALREADY."*

You've laughed with me, cried with me, and read all the spicy stuff without even flinching (okay, maybe flinching *a little*). Your support, love, and deep, always fun group chats have meant the world to me.

I wrote this book—but you helped me believe people would want to read it. I love you more than all the books in the world.

*To Renata.* You were my rock when the words felt like quicksand. You read *every* version, even the messy middle drafts I wanted to throw into the sun, and somehow, you still showed up with love, insight, and the kind of encouragement that made me believe this story needed to be told.

You gave me life when I felt drained, laughter when I wanted to cry, and the best kind of accountability—fierce, funny, and full of heart.

This book carries your fingerprints. Thank you for never letting me quit. I'll never stop being grateful that you stayed with me through every sentence, every spiral, every single page.

*To Kate.* You showed me there was another way.

When I thought the only path to holding my book in my hands was paved with gatekeepers and closed doors, *you* opened a window.

You inspired me to believe that telling my story on my own terms wasn't just possible, it was powerful.

Your words lit the fire.

Your journey gave me the map.

And your faith in me gave me the courage to follow through.

You are the reason I didn't give up.

You are the reason this book exists.

I will never forget that.

*And to the readers* who picked up this book and fell for Rorie and Nolan. Thank you for trusting a debut, for texting your friends about it (you *did*, right?), and for loving messy, complicated, laugh-out-loud love as much as I do. This story was for me. But now it's yours, too.

# ABOUT THE AUTHOR

 CEDAR JAMES writes swoony, slightly unhinged romance for readers who love their banter sharp and their slow burns deliciously drawn out. An Oklahoma native now living in Houston, Texas, she juggles life with four kids and a brain full of fictional stories. When she's not writing, Cedar's spending time with family, falling in love with her next set of characters, or plotting spicy comebacks she'll never say out loud. She believes every love story needs a little heat, a little heart, and a whole lot of trouble.

**Let's Get Social**
Website: authorcedarjames.com
Social Media: @authorcedarjames
Facebook Group: CJ's Swoon Room